THE
ISLAND
of
WORTHY
BOYS

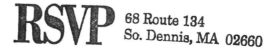

68 Route 134
So. Dennis, MA 02660

THE
ISLAND
of
WORTHY
BOYS

A Novel

CONNIE HERTZBERG MAYO

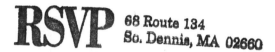

RSVP 68 Route 134
So. Dennis, MA 02660

SHE WRITES PRESS

Copyright © 2015 by Connie Hertzberg Mayo

All rights reserved. No part of this publication may be reproduced, distributed, or transmitted in any form or by any means, including photocopying, recording, digital scanning, or other electronic or mechanical methods, without the prior written permission of the publisher, except in the case of brief quotations embodied in critical reviews and certain other noncommercial uses permitted by copyright law. For permission requests, please address She Writes Press.

Published 2015

ISBN: 978-1-63152-001-3
Library of Congress Control Number: 2015936026

For information, address:
She Writes Press
1563 Solano Ave #546
Berkeley, CA 94707

She Writes Press is a division of Spark Point Studio, LLC.

"What is the Best Method for the Care of Poor and Vicious Children?" by Charles Loring Brace by was originally published in Journal of Social Science, G.P. Putnam's Sons, New York, New York, 1880.

In memory of Charles H. Bradley,
Superintendent of the Boston Farm School,
Thompson Island, from 1888–1922

I wish I had known you.

AUTHOR'S NOTE

WHILE THIS IS A WORK OF FICTION, THE BOSTON FARM SCHOOL did exist on Thompson Island, under a variety of names, from 1833 until 1975. Superintendent Charles Bradley, his wife Mary Bradley, and their son Henry were real people (and they did have a St. Bernard, although his actual name is lost to history). By all accounts I could find, Bradley was a particularly enlightened and kind superintendent. Evidence of his dedication is abundant, including the fact that he died on the island at the age of sixty-three after being superintendent for thirty-four years.

I have tried, unsuccessfully, to locate any living relatives of the Bradleys.

All other characters in this book are fictitious; any resemblance to real persons, living or dead, is coincidental.

"*In great establishments for children, there are half-grown boys and girls who exercise a perverse and depraved ingenuity in corrupting those younger than themselves. This is one of the many insidious perils of large reformatories. They spread a physical and moral contagion; the morality in large establishments is commonly greater than elsewhere, and the standard of morality is low. Routine and indifference prevail, and the minds of children become enfeebled and corrupted.*"

—**Charles Loring Brace**
"What Is the Best Method for the
Care of Poor and Vicious Children?"
Journal of Social Science II (1880)

PROLOGUE

September 1889 • Boston Harbor

THE STEAMBOAT PUFFED AND CHUGGED THROUGH THE HARBOR, cleaving the gunmetal water in front and churning it white like boiling laundry in the back. The boat was at the halfway point in its ten-minute trip, with its bow pointing toward the leafy island and its stern saying good-bye to the gray buildings of Boston.

Built to hold twenty, the *Pilgrim* had only three passengers this morning: one man piloting the boat, and two boys who were an age somewhere between knee pants and shaving razors. The pilot and the blond boy were squinting in the sun, looking for the island to come into view, but the other boy saw only the damp bottom of the boat as he gripped the seat, white-knuckled, face ashen.

Bored with a trip he had made a hundred times, the pilot thought about his charges. The Weston brothers, the superintendent had said. That didn't happen often, two accepted at once. Funny, how the pair of them looked as different as chalk and cheese. That one Charles—quite a scrapper with that upturned nose, leaning over the edge of the boat into the breeze, grinning and catching the salt spray on his face. Was he actually tasting the spray? Happy fellow. Too bad the brother wasn't like-minded. Back at City Point, that one, Arthur, had looked around in a panic with huge brown eyes, lashes long as a girl's, and that was the last he'd shown his face. The boy had planted his chin on his chest the minute he sat down in the

1

boat, and hadn't moved since. *Hope he's not ill,* the pilot thought. *Might they quarantine him? Won't do to be getting the other boys sick.*

"Charles, how fares your little brother there?" the pilot called out.

Charles looked over to the pilot while putting an arm around Arthur. "Nothin' a little dry land won't fix. He's a mite nervous 'bout the water."

Arthur shrugged his brother's arm off his shoulder and hung his head even lower. *Odd. Why wouldn't he take comfort from the only kin he's got left?* But the pilot only had time to puzzle over this for a few moments before they arrived. *Ah, well,* he thought as the boat bumped against the wharf and he wrapped a hairy rope around the pier post. *Who can fathom what goes on inside a family?*

Charles and the pilot helped Arthur out of the boat and walked him well away from the water. Right away the color began to return to his face. The pilot went back to the boat and retrieved the two sacks that held all of the boys' worldly possessions, and when he plunked them down, little clouds of dust puffed and then settled on their boots.

Their eyes all raked up the hill to the imposing brick building at the top. "Welcome," the pilot said, hands on hips, "to the Boston Asylum and Farm School for Indigent Boys."

PART I

Mainland

Washington Street, Boston

CHAPTER 1

April 1889 • Boston

CHARLES WHEELER WAS VERY, VERY HUNGRY.

This wasn't the mosquito buzz of hunger that he felt in most of his waking hours, familiar as his one pair of dirty trousers. It wasn't the hunger that hit him like a boxing glove when he woke up in the morning after dreaming of roasts with gravy and tarts with fruit fillings that ran between his fingers. No, this was the grinding hunger of a missed meal. Or what passed for a meal.

A year ago, when he first started living on the streets, Charles went for hours without thinking about food. He could swipe a few apples off a cart, duck into an alley to eat them, core and all, and feel so full that if another apple had rolled into the alley, he would have stuffed it in his pocket for later. But now his twelve-year-old body was hungry all the time. It had grudgingly come to accept a schedule of small but regular deliveries of food, but today, with the routine disrupted, his hunger blotted out everything else.

If he had anything at all in his stomach, he would be down by the waterfront, relaxing and watching the boats unload their cod and haddock as he leaned up against a greenish pier post. But for thieving at this time of day, there was only one place to be: Washington Street. The sidewalks here were so crowded that foot traffic spilled out onto the cobblestone street, slowing the progress of carts and carriages, and you had to yell to be heard over the thrum of the crowd and the occasional neighing of horses. Awnings reached out from building fronts, signs shouted from every flat piece of facade, gaslights stood in defiance of the mass of humanity flowing around them. This was where Boston was most alive, and with all these distractions abounding, there was no better place to steal and get away with it. So Charles's lack of success today was driving him a bit mad.

When he was this hungry, his eye fell on boys his age—with shoes, with shirts that had no holes at the elbows and pants clean enough to tell their color—and he imagined with bitterness how they would head home at the end of the day. How their mothers would have supper waiting, curls of steam rising from the serving platter, and how those boys didn't even mutter a thank-you before they bolted from the table, didn't appreciate food appearing when they wanted it. Charles knew this because several years ago, this had described him as well, though he didn't see himself in these other boys. He just felt resentment smoldering in the pit of his stomach. He hated these boys, spoiling their appetite at the penny candy store in the late afternoon, climbing into their beds every night with a full belly.

Early this morning, he had gnawed around the blackened parts of two raw potatoes he'd found behind a grocer's shop, but since then, he'd eaten nothing. Not for lack of trying, of course. But every pushcart vendor seemed to read his intentions from twenty paces, and every trash barrel behind a restaurant had already been picked clean by some guttersnipe.

Around midday he'd changed strategies and turned his attention to the acquisition of money, but that approach was proving equally fruitless. Twice this afternoon he'd seen a promising situation while scanning for unguarded funds, but in both cases, it required stealing from a woman, and he had yet to cross that line. In the winter, this was a particularly hard rule to follow, since he often saw ladies with their reticules resting just inside their fur muffs, practically begging to slip out. But still he'd stuck to targeting men, and now as the sun slid down behind the buildings, he saw the mark he'd been looking for.

The man carried several cloth sacks and was negotiating the price of flowers with a street vendor. His red hair and fair complexion suggested a recent boat trip from Ireland, which made him an appealing victim, since Charles was of the firm opinion that the city was lousy with Micks. Until the day she died, Charles's mother had complained bitterly about how all the dirty bogtrotters took the washerwoman jobs away from decent Americans such as herself, and Charles had never thought to question this judgment. Now that petty crime was his means of survival, he reasoned that stealing from the Irish was ideal—in a way, it was returning what ought to have been American money into his American pocket. And maybe if enough Micks got their pockets picked here, they'd go back to Ireland where they belonged.

When the man pretended to walk away from the cart until the vendor called him back for a better price, it brought a smile to Charles's face. If he wasn't mistaken, the man had a clubfoot. *Perfect*, Charles thought. *Won't even try to chase me.*

Hands in pockets, Charles casually zigzagged his way over to the man, scanning for the police as he strolled. Seeing none, he pretended to look in a window at the sign for "Painless Dentistry" as he kept tabs on the conversation behind him. While the men argued on about the fair market price for roses, he became distracted by the advertisement, as he had a tooth on his right side that was aching more every day, and he knew from experience that the pain would only stop once the tooth was out. Maybe he could acquire enough cash to see what this new Painless Dentistry was all about. With a jolt, he remembered what he was supposed to be doing, just in time to hear the man say to the vendor, "All right, all right, 'tis a hard bargain you drive, but I haven't time for this." Charles counted two breaths to give the man time to bring out the cash, and then he slowly turned around.

Like a beautiful dream, there the man struggled: trying to balance his sacks on the vendor's cart, pulling some bills off a small roll, bowler hat slipping down his brow. The vendor blew air through his teeth in impatience and looked over his shoulder. Daylight had faded, but the lamplighter had not yet made it to this street. The timing was perfect. Charles moved in quickly and yanked the roll of money out of the man's hands.

He ran for only a few joyful strides before a horrible feeling swept over him like a wave of cold water. Half a block ahead, a policeman stared him down with a menacing glare. For a heartbeat, it was just the two of them alone on the busy thoroughfare, neither of them moving, the policeman getting a good look at the filthy street Arab that had just grabbed an innocent man's earnings, Charles unable to move his legs or even hide the stolen bills behind his back.

When the policeman took a step toward Charles, the spell was broken. Charles bolted across the street with the policeman in pursuit. From his constant scouring of this part of the city, Charles knew the layout of all the streets—better, he hoped, than the copper chasing him. He could hear the slap of the policeman's leather shoes on the pavement behind him, but Charles's bare feet didn't make a sound as his toes hugged the rounded cobblestones for traction. When he thought there were enough pedestrians behind him to obscure the copper's view, he dashed into an alley and stopped short before he ran into a pile of broken furniture and barrels. Quickly, he crawled behind a busted-up ash barrel toward the back of the pile and tried to slow his breathing, striving for silence and a limit to the amount of ash he was inhaling. In the near pitch dark, he tried to count off how many bills were in the stolen roll.

As his breath began to come more slowly, the only other sound in the alley the squeak and rustle of rodents, Charles grinned. There were six bills, so a minimum of six dollars, perhaps more if they weren't all ones. A fortune! He could eat for weeks, perhaps even get his tooth taken care of. On a rainy night, he could pay for a spot in a flophouse. And shoes, he could get shoes! Five minutes from now, he would walk out of this alley as rich as he'd been in recent memory.

Charles had spent his take several times over in his mind when he heard someone run into the alley. The furniture around him started to move, and a figure wormed its way into the pile, ending up in front of Charles's barrel. He could just barely make out the shape of this person, who looked to be a boy around his size. The boy was balanced on his haunches, breathing hard, and clearly had no idea that Charles was there.

Now Charles had to noodle this new development. It was a safe bet that this boy was running from the police, which meant that any minute now the law could come charging into this alley. He quickly began to hate this intruder. After Charles had gotten away free and clear, ready to stride out onto the street to enjoy the fruits of his labor, this arsehole was about to ruin it all! What policeman would believe that two boys hiding in the same pile of trash were not in on the same crime? But much as he wanted to give the boy a rude shove and a few choice words, any noise could give them both away. His best hope was that the boy would eventually leave without ever knowing he shared his hiding space with another. So Charles would wait. It would be hard, pushing all that anger down, but it was worth it. Five minutes, maybe less. The boy would leave, and Charles would never see him again.

After a minute, the boy relaxed his tense posture a bit and covered his eyes with his trembling hands.

"Jaysus," he whispered.

And of course he's a goddamned Mick, Charles thought, and his rage boiled over. Forgetting his resolve, he gave the boy an enormous push, causing him to tumble out of the pile of trash and skid onto a patch of decaying produce.

CHAPTER 2

Aidan Sullivan slid on the patch of decaying produce but was able to stop himself before his head hit the brick wall.

He stood up slowly, trembling, not sure what had just propelled him out of the pile of furniture. Out of the exit hole that Aidan's body had made emerged a figure, fists clenched. Aidan almost laughed in relief. Even in the dim light he could see it was just a boy that had shoved him, maybe not even as tall as he was.

"What the hell are you lookin' at, you stupid eedjit!" shouted his assailant. "You nearly got us both hauled off to jail!"

"I had no idea anyone was in my pile of furniture."

"YOUR pile of furniture! I was there first, obviously!"

"Well, *obviously* I didn't know that, or I would have chose another pile of furniture."

Even in the dim light of the alley, Aidan could see that the boy was poorer than Aidan, which was saying something. At least Aidan had shoes and a spare shirt drying on the line behind his West End tenement—that is, if his mother was well enough and sober enough to get out of bed today and wash their few pieces of clothing. Still, as bad as things were at home, as much as he'd lately had to resort to some money-earning activities that he couldn't tell his mother about, it unnerved him a bit to see up close, in this boy, how much worse things could get.

Just then, the lamplighter lit the gas lamp at the mouth of the alley. "Hey," said Aidan, now that he could see more in the light, "I know you. You're Charles. Charles . . . Wheeler. We were in school together a couple of years ago. Aidan Sullivan, remember me?"

"Well, ain't this a lovely reunion. Now get the hell outta my alley before I knock you into next week."

"Yeah, I'll never forget the time you got put in the corner when the teacher was droning on, and then he heard you say, real quiet-like, 'Shut yer clam hole, already.' Oh brother, the boys was laughing all day about that one!"

"Listen, I see a clam hole that needs shuttin' right now, and I'm gonna shut it for you if you won't."

"All right, all right," Aidan said as he took a step back. He now remembered the epilogue to the clam hole story, where Charles bloodied the nose of one of the laughing boys after school, misinterpreting their laughter as somehow making fun of him, when in truth they were just delighted at any insolence toward their teacher.

"You know what?" said Charles. "I'm late for a very important engagement with my supper. I'm just gonna take my . . ." A look of concern, then anger, washed over his face. He started pawing his way through the trash in the alley.

"Whatcha looking for?" asked Aidan.

"I don't need no help from the likes of *you*," muttered Charles, working through the furniture pile. "Just keep your goddamn hands off my money."

Aidan glanced down, and right next to his foot was a roll of bills. As he picked it up to give it to Charles, Charles raised his head.

"You *bastard!*" yelled Charles as he charged.

As they struggled in the alley, Aidan could tell that Charles was all fury and no technique. Aidan defended himself against the rain of blows until he saw his opportunity to throw the one punch he knew how to throw, one he'd actually been trained how to throw.

He landed a perfect left hook, and Charles fell back against the pile of furniture.

For a couple of beats, all the two boys did was catch their breath. Charles finally broke the silence.

"There is one thing I do like about you, Sullivan," he said, and he spit a rotten tooth into his hand. "I like that you're a southpaw."

CHAPTER 3

AIDAN PICKED UP THE WAD OF BILLS AND HANDED IT TO CHARLES. "I wasn't makin' off with it, you know." It occurred to Aidan that not much had changed since their school days, when Charles had always been inclined to assume the worst of others and illustrate that assumption with his fists. Aidan recalled talking to a boy in their class whose succinct comment, "Bit of an arsehole, that one," summed up what most boys thought of Charles.

"*Now* you tell me," said Charles, and he spit some blood off to the side. After a futile attempt to shake vegetable slime from the bills, he pocketed the money. "All right, let's call it even. Since you saved me from payin' for a dentist, I'll forgive you for almost sendin' me to jail." He strutted out of the alley.

"Charles!" Aidan called out, and Charles spun around. "Uh, I ain't had my supper yet either," Aidan stated quietly as he examined the grout between the sooty bricks in the wall, picking at it with his fingernails.

"And what is your *point*, Sullivan?" Charles asked in exaggerated tones.

"Well, if you know a place to get some supper, it's my treat." He looked at Charles, ready for the smart remark, the rejection. The truth was, he missed being with other boys since he'd had to stop going to school. A month ago, his mother's cough had worsened to the point of interfering with both her drinking and the sewing that paid their rent. That was when Aidan had known things were getting bad. When Maeve had asked him to return the unfinished piecework to its owner, he knew he needed to find a job, and that was the end of school. Charles wasn't much like Aidan's friends there, but he was better than nothing.

Charles crossed his arms and cocked his head to the side as he considered Aidan. "You know, if you're fool enough to want to spend your coin on my supper, I ain't fool enough to stop ya. I'm mighty hungry tonight, mind you. And I'm in the mood for a big dessert. Really big."

"Me too. Best part of the meal," said Aidan with a smile, and he let Charles lead the way.

They walked north, and at the point where the streets started to slope downhill, the buildings responded by becoming less and less reputable. Signs advertising what business was being conducted inside became less frequent, windows were grimier, trash bloomed in unswept corners. The smell of beer and whiskey conquered the stink of manure in the streets just as they arrived in Scollay Square.

Charles brought them to a saloon on a side street. After they indicated that supper was their interest and Aidan showed his ability to pay, the barkeep brought them crocks of what was probably beef stew, along with two short beers.

"I don't have to talk to you, you know. You didn't say anything about talkin'," said Charles between mouthfuls of stew.

"No, you're right, you don't have to talk. But you might want to slow down there. When's the last time you had a decent meal?"

"See, that's just the type a thing I don't gotta tell you." After shoveling a few more spoonfuls into his mouth, Charles added, "But there is one thing you could tell me if you're feelin' so chatty."

"Shoot."

"Back in that alley when you were hidin', before I gave you a free ride outta that pile of furniture, you sounded like an Irishman."

"I didn't say nothin' when I was hidin'," said Aidan.

"Yeah, you did. You said, 'Jaysus,' and there ain't nobody but an Irish that's gonna say that. But after that, your brogue flew the coop. Now you sound as American as P.T. Barnum. And you sure don't look Irish. So what the hell?"

"What's it to you?"

"Hey, I'm just makin' conversation. You want we should eat without talkin', fine by me." Charles resumed pushing food into his mouth at an impressive rate.

For the hundredth time, Aidan wondered how it was that Maeve, who looked as Irish as soda bread, could have given birth to him, with his cinnamon eyes and chestnut hair. How could he explain to Charles what he didn't understand himself? "My ma's as Hibernian as they come, born in the old country, a brogue you could cut with a knife. My little sister sounds just like her. I used to speak like them, but lookin' like I do, I figured out that speakin' your way, well, nobody can tell I'm Irish, and mostly that's a good thing in this city."

Charles grunted in what might have been his agreement at the wisdom of hiding Irish heritage. "Must look like your father, then."

"I wouldn't know," said Aidan as he looked out the greasy window.

"Yeah, well, you ain't so special—mine left town when I was three. Who needs a father, anyway?" Charles slurped his beer with bravado.

Aidan thought, *I do*. But rather than thinking of whoever fathered him, he thought of Dan Connolly—his sister's father, the one he wanted for a father. Some of Aidan's earliest memories were of Dan courting his mother, surprising them with a good cut of meat from the butcher, teaching Aidan moves from his amateur boxing days in the packed dirt yard. Dan had earned a good wage as a printer's apprentice, but before the wedding was to take place, there was an explosion of chemicals in the print shop, and Dan and another apprentice were killed. As the other apprentice was married, his widow received fifty dollars in compensation from the company, but Maeve got nothing except Dan's daughter growing inside her. Nothing was ever easy after that. Aidan was sure that if Dan hadn't died, today he would have been in school, practicing penmanship and long division, rather than hiding from the cops in a dirty alley.

"Hey, Sullivan, you with me?" asked Charles, snapping his fingers in front of Aidan's face.

"Yeah, sorry."

The boys ate, Charles outpacing Aidan by a fair margin. After a long pause, Aidan said, "Mr. Hamilton, you remember him, at the school, he wasn't half bad as a teacher, you know. A bit *boring*, like you told the class, but he was a good egg. He always—"

"Mr. Hamilton likes to pick up whores on North Street," said Charles as he swallowed the last spoonful of his stew.

"Really?" asked Aidan.

"Likes blondes," said Charles, and he clattered his spoon into his empty crock somewhat triumphantly. "And I'll have me another of them stews."

"You know, they ain't handin' out prizes for whoever finishes first," Aidan mentioned as he signaled the barkeep for more food. When the crock arrived, Charles dug in, but less voraciously than he had with the first.

Aidan broke the silence after he finished his own stew. "So you really saw Mr. Hamilton down by the waterfront?" he said.

"'Bout a month ago. And Bess, she works down there, she told me he's been payin' visits down there for years."

"You know a whore down on North Street?" Though Aidan had lived in the West End all his life, he had never set foot on North Street. It was the seediest place in all of Boston, the one place Maeve warned him not to go. Even Scollay Square was not a place that Aidan traversed on his own, but North Street didn't so much as pretend to offer anything but brothels and watering holes. Aidan was surprised and not a little impressed that Charles was on such familiar terms with the place and its employees.

"Uh-huh," said Charles as he ate.

"As in, you *know* her?"

Charles looked up, frowning. "Not like that, ya dunce. She just gives me tips on where to stay outta, which cops is the mean ones, like that."

"How do you end up being friends with a whore?"

"We ain't *friends,*" Charles said. "I sorta helped her out of a, well, a bad situation once."

Aidan waited for him to continue, but instead Charles said, "So what the hell did you do that you were hiding in that alley?"

"What did *you* do?"

"Nope. Asked you first."

"Well . . ." Aidan thought about the last month. It was hard to know where to start. "A few weeks ago, I was rushing the growler over on Summer Street."

"Shit for pay," commented Charles.

"Don't I know it." But it had been the only thing he could find. On almost every block in Boston, new buildings were going up or old ones were being torn down. Every day at noon, workers from construction sites all around the city broke for dinner, and boys were there to collect tin pails and dimes from them and run off to the nearby saloons for beer. The faster you could bring your full growler back, the better your pay, but Aidan had discovered a nickel was the most you could expect.

"But rushing the growler ain't against the law," Charles pointed out.

"Yeah, that turned out to be a sort of temporary thing. There was this older boy, Willy, he was rushing the can too—"

"Willy the Wind."

"How do you know him?" Aidan was beginning to think that Charles knew every shady character in the city.

"Willy's quite the recruiter."

"Well, we was just workin' together for a while, and he said he was thinkin' about gettin' outta the growler trade," said Aidan.

Charles pulled a bit of gristle from his mouth and flicked it to the floor as he continued to chew. "Willy don't rush the can except when he's lookin' for a new boy. What the hell would a near-grown mug like him be doin' workin' for nickel tips?"

Aidan looked away in mild embarrassment. Now it seemed obvious. Willy was by far the oldest boy at the site, and he never seemed in a hurry to run as many pails as he could like the others.

"Ah, don't feel bad, Sullivan. You ain't the first boy Willy ever duped. So what's his scam these days?"

"Well, he calls it 'The Clumsy Bootblack.' I'm the bootblack who blackens the mark's pant leg, then Willy moves in to lift his money clip when the mark gets all mad and tries to strangle me."

"Cute. Even with the strangling bit, sounds safer than his last scam."

"What was the last scam?" Aidan asked after a small hesitation, his heart sinking a little lower. He knew he should find out what he could, but a part of him didn't want to know any more.

"Well," started Charles with obvious enjoyment, "Willy would pick out some old crone in a busy crowd, and the boy would hop on the bicycle Willy gave him and run into her. The boy would stop and fret and moan all sorts of sorries while a crowd came around her to gawk, and then Willy would move in and have his choice of pockets."

Aidan said nothing.

"Don't you want to know why Willy ain't doin' that scam no more?" asked Charles with a little grin.

Aidan really didn't want to know, but Charles continued anyway.

"One day, the boy ran into a crone just like they planned, but the ruckus spooked a horse next to them, and the horse knocked him down and pulled its cart over the boy's leg. I ain't heard what happened to him after that, but the next day, I heard Willy was back at the construction site."

Aidan found that he'd lost his appetite for his stew. "Listen, thanks for tellin' me about what a great pal Willy is, but I think I know all I need to know now."

"Hey, I ain't sayin' he's a bad sort, I mean, as that sort goes. He ain't *tryin'* to get his boys in a mess. All I'm sayin' is, he ain't ever thinkin' about what's good for *you*." Charles wiped his mouth on his sleeve and pushed back his chair, slapping his hands on his thighs. "Best free meal I had in a while, Sullivan. See ya 'round." He stood up and walked to the door, then looked back at Aidan. "What? You ain't gonna keep following me around like a lost pup?"

Aidan joined him at the door and looked out. It had just started to rain. He flipped his collar up and pulled his cap down as far as it would go. "You know, working for Willy's just fine. I can handle him," Aidan said with irritation.

"Who's sayin' you can't?" Charles stuck his hands in his pockets and leaned up against the doorframe.

Aidan left the saloon, hunched over against the weather. Just before he turned the corner, Charles yelled from the shelter of the saloon doorway, "You still owe me dessert, Sullivan!"

Aidan shook the rain off his cap and entered the apartment, quietly in case his mother was sleeping. But when she heard the door close, she called out, "Aidan? Is that you, boyo?"

"'Tis. Are ya hungry? Where's the wee dormouse?" Aidan walked into the one bedroom that Maeve and Ella shared.

"She's across the hall at the McGarrity's, of course. She and those twins is as thick as thieves these days." Maeve was sitting up in bed, letting down the hem on one of Ella's dresses. She looked up. "Ya look soaked to the bone."

"Nah, I'm fine. Did Ella eat before she went across the hall?"

"Ya, I fed the lass," said Maeve. Aidan was hopeful—his mother was sewing and she'd put supper together for Ella. Last week she hadn't been able to cook at all. *Maybe she's really on the mend*, he thought.

"I can make ya supper," offered Aidan.

"Just put the kettle on," said Maeve as she snipped a thread.

Aidan put the water on the stove and then transferred the day's pay into the biscuit tin on the kitchen shelf. Supper at the saloon, including the beer, had run him fifty cents, but he still had a few dollars to contribute to the can, which already held four dollar bills and some coins. Even after paying the rent this Friday, they would still have plenty left over. The misgivings he'd had at the saloon about his job with Willy drifted away as he gazed contentedly into the biscuit tin.

"I'm glad you're home while Ella's out—I need to talk to ya 'bout somethin'," said Maeve as she shuffled into the kitchen, using furniture for support. She sat down gingerly at the table. "Have a seat."

After Aidan sat, Maeve gripped his hand across the table. "Ya done me proud, getting a job when I got sick. We ain't be eatin' so well since . . ." She trailed off as both of them thought of Dan Connelly. "Well, you're the man of the house now, and yer doing a right fine job." Maeve squeezed his hand, and Aidan smiled.

Maeve looked down at their clasped hands. "Ellen McGarrity was over here today. Such a kind woman she is, Aidan. She's been lightin' candles for me at St. Joseph's every week, prayin' for me recovery. Me and her had a cuppa tea while the girls played, and we got to talkin'." Maeve broke off at that point with a fit of coughing. When she could, she took a sip of tea and then continued. "Look, there ain't no easy way to say this, so I'm just gonna say it. Ellen said if anything happened to me, she would take Ella in."

"Ma, you're gettin' better! Nothin' is gonna happen. This weekend, I'm gonna take you and Ella—"

"Aidan, boyo, *listen*. Ellen said she would take Ella, but she won't take you."

Aidan said nothing.

"Ellen has her own two older boys, as you know, and they are eatin' her out of house and home, and both of them have had their run-ins with the law. I told her you ain't like that, you got a respectable job, you're a good boy, but she said all she could handle was my girl, and that was that."

Aidan stirred his spoon in his teacup, thinking about how his job with Willy could not in any sense be considered respectable.

"I dunna have it all figured out in my head, but I wanted you to know that you're not to worry about Ella if—"

"Ma, I don't want to talk about this no more. You're gettin' better. We're goin' for ice cream on Saturday!" Aidan brought his teacup over to the sink and emptied it, watching the tea run down the drain.

"Okay, okay, we're goin' for ice cream on Saturday," said Maeve. "I do feel better today, 'tis true. And Ella, with her sweet tooth, why the lass will follow you to the ends of the earth on the promise of ice cream." They both thought of Ella, how fortunate and how painful it was that she looked so much like her father, even had her father's penchant for sweets. For a while, Aidan thought that Dan had died never knowing that he was going to have a child, but one day years ago, he'd come across a package on the shelf of the closet. When he opened it, he found a small blue baby blanket, edged in satin, and a note in a yellowed envelope. Without reading the note, he pushed it and the paper wrapping to the back of the shelf and tucked the blanket under his mattress. Since then, after he was sure that his mother and sister were asleep each night, he would bring the blanket out, fold it, and use it as a pillow. He always woke before his mother and put it back under the mattress before she was up.

They sat in the quiet of the kitchen for a while. After a time, Maeve said, "And why were you so late comin' home? You're usually here half six the latest."

"Ran into an old mate from school. Took him out for supper."

"Supper! He must have been a good friend, you spendin' your hard-earned wages on 'im."

"Nah, not at all, really. Quite the hothead. But he ain't all bad."

"'Tis a fine—" Maeve started to say, but then she broke off coughing again. Her flailing hand upset her cup, and tea spread in a thin line across the table. When she couldn't stop, Aidan helped her back to bed, the forgotten tea dripping onto the floor.

CHAPTER 4

It was four days later that Charles saw Aidan again. Charles had been enjoying a nice stretch where he'd stolen nothing and paid for everything, which had left him a lot of leisure time. Sitting on the edge of an iron horse-water trough, he looked down and admired his new shoes. Part of his newly acquired funds had gone to the cobbler, and he was proud to be able to walk through the city streets without dirtying his feet like the younger urchins. With a smug grin on his face, he looked up, and just then, the crowd parted momentarily to reveal Aidan and Willy settling up for the day.

After Aidan handed Willy his bootblack kit and the two went their separate ways, Charles took off after Aidan and soon fell in step with him.

"Sullivan," he said with no inflection, looking straight ahead.

"Charles!" exclaimed Aidan. "Didn't expect to see you here."

"Word on the street is that Willy's newest boy's some guttersnipe named Artie."

"Yeah," said Aidan, looking at his shoes as they walked. "That's me."

"What's with the moniker?"

"Well, let's just say that Willy ain't a fan o' the Irish," said Aidan. "I'm headin' up Merrimac—you headin' that way?"

"Yeah, I was goin' that way anyway," said Charles, although he hadn't been headed anywhere at all.

"So," said Aidan, "how did you hear about who Willy was working with?"

"Well, *Artie*," Charles said as he strolled with his hands in his pockets, "I hear things. For instance, I hear that Willy and Artie been seen havin' a spat or two, disagreeing about how to divvy up the spoils."

Aidan looked over in surprise. "How could you know that? Weren't nobody that overheard us."

"Willy tells everybody that he's Willy the Wind because he can run like the devil, but most will tell ya it's more because he's such a windbag. He's down the waterfront most every night, running his mouth about his busy day when he ain't dumpin' whiskey into it."

"Well, I don't care. The money's good."

"But not as good as it should be, right? He ain't exactly a fifty-fifty kinda mug."

Aidan stopped walking and faced Charles. "I'm *aware* of that. One day he kept it all because he lost his shirt on a bar bet the night before. But I ain't got much of a choice. I'm the only one in my family that's bringin' in any coin, and I can't make it work on the goddamn nickels from rushing the bleddy *growler!*"

"Jesus, Sullivan, keep your shirt on," said Charles, but all the fun had drained out of telling Aidan about Willy. "Look, I know ya can't make a livin' doing work that's aboveboard. Wanna know what my last go at a real job was? Catchin' rats for the dogfights at the rat pit over on Fleet Street."

"What?"

"Nickel a rat. They need a ton of them. Each fight, a dog might take out twenty rats. And if you think rushin' the can was a lousy job, you ain't never caught rats. After a while, they say you get good enough to do it without ever gettin' bit, but I didn't stick with it long enough to find out. Got a bite that swelled up my whole arm, all red and white and festerin', and I was willin' to do anything else after that."

Aidan had no response to this. *Time to toughen up,* Charles thought but didn't say aloud. *Ain't never gonna make it otherwise.*

As they walked side by side, Aidan contemplated what Charles had just told him. He knew, as everyone did, that rat baiting was a big draw in the North End, and the job Charles described made sense— what man would catch the rats when he could pay a ten-year-old that was quicker and lower to the ground? Clearly, there were worse jobs than the Clumsy Bootblack, but Aidan wasn't sure if this made him feel better or worse. Either way, the image of Charles catching rats with his festering arm was one he was anxious to put out of his mind.

They made a turn and continued to weave their way through the West End, headed toward Aidan's tenement on Chambers Street. Unlike the business district, where street cleaners frequently carted away trash, here you had to watch where you stepped. The five-story tenements loomed over the narrow streets, and every alleyway afforded a view of drying laundry on the line. Whereas Washington Street was so wide that stores on both sides had awnings to shield the foot traffic, here the sun had trouble squeezing in between the dirty buildings.

When they reached the middle of a cross street, Charles stopped short and looked up at the tenement in front of him.

"What's up there?" asked Aidan.

Charles resumed walking without saying anything, but before they reached the end of the block, he said quietly, "I used to live there."

"Yeah?" said Aidan. "Where'd your family move to?"

"We didn't move," said Charles as he looked down the street and thrust his hands deeper into his pockets. "My Ma died there."

Aidan thought about this. "So, it was just you and your Ma when she died?"

Charles said nothing.

"You ain't got a home anymore," said Aidan, but it was more of a statement than a question. He saw Charles tense up, and immediately he regretted saying it.

"So now you're better than the likes of me? Fine," seethed Charles. He quickened his pace.

"That weren't even in the ballpark of what I meant. I just didn't know."

"Well, now ya do," said Charles testily, but less so than before.

They had arrived at Aidan's building. Aidan felt guilty at the relative opulence of his address. "I guess I'll see ya 'round," He started up the steps as Charles walked down the sidewalk.

"Hey!" shouted Aidan down the street. Charles turned around with exaggerated slowness. "Willy takes a dinner break one to two. I'm at Rosen's soda fountain over on Broomfield Street at half past one most days."

"Don't need your charity, Sullivan."

"Ain't charity. I owe you dessert, remember?"

Charles turned back around without responding and continued on his way. Aidan called after him, "Rosen's! Half one!" and he watched until Charles turned the corner, never once looking back. With a sigh, Aidan climbed the rest of the steps.

CHAPTER 5

For the rest of the week, Aidan sat at the counter at Rosen's from half past one to two o'clock. Each day, he periodically scanned the entrance for any sign of Charles, but so far he'd had all his egg creams alone.

Three days in, as the soda jerk delivered his drink and Aidan dug into his pocket for a coin, he heard a voice in his ear: "Put your money away, Sullivan, it ain't no good here."

"Hey!" said Aidan with a start. "How did you get in here?"

"I believe the door is the usual way," Charles said with a grin. He sat down on the stool next to Aidan. "Cherry phosphate," he told the jerk. He swiveled toward Aidan. "This your regular haunt?"

"These days. Lotta places they give you a hard time if they think you should be in school, but here they leave you alone. Truant officer don't come in much, neither." Aidan took a sip of his egg cream as the jerk set Charles's drink down on the counter. Charles took a roll of ones from his pocket and peeled one off the top, perhaps a bit closer to Aidan than was absolutely necessary.

"Can ya break a one?" Charles grinned as he handed the bill to the jerk, who rolled his eyes and headed off to the register.

"Okay," said Aidan, "so you're flush. Who's missin' their billfold today?"

"Hey, keep it down," Charles said as he looked around, but he was obviously pleased that Aidan had noticed. "Had a little piece of good fortune last night. New ship came into dock full of sailors lookin' for all the pleasures of the mainland, and I'd say they found 'em. 'Course, most is so desperate, being cooped up in a floatin' tin can for so long, that they don't exactly know when to stop, which works in my favor."

"So you're a lifter, like Willy?" asked Aidan in a low tone of voice.

"Well, in a sense, yeah."

"In what sense aren't ya?"

"Well," admitted Charles, "I believe Willy's marks are usually awake, if I ain't mistaken." He scooped up the coins that the jerk slapped on the counter and pocketed them.

"So you roll drunks," said Aidan, almost at a whisper now.

"I prefer to think of it as educatin' the intoxicated, but yeah," Charles said quietly.

Aidan thought this over as he pulled his egg cream through his straw. "So yours is really nighttime work. I mean, you can't be doing this in the mornin', 'cause most people ain't on a drunk at that time of day."

"Even more than that, it's gotta be dark."

"So wintertime it gets dark earlier, more hours to work in," postulated Aidan.

"Yeah, but when it's cold, not so many people end up takin' a whiskey nap in an alley," countered Charles.

"And Friday, Saturday must be your best nights."

"That," Charles agreed, "is surely true, and it don't matter the weather."

They both sat sipping their fountain sodas, thinking about the bounty that the city delivered in the form of inebriated citizens.

After a time, Charles said, "Why the hell do they call it an egg cream? There ain't no egg in it."

"Dunno. No cream, neither. But it's pretty good for a nickel," said Aidan as he finished his. "I better go find Willy. He'll want to make sure we get in a good afternoon of work before the rain sets in. Nobody wants a shoeshine in the rain, as he is ever so fond of telling me." Aidan smiled and slid off his stool.

The two boys walked out the door onto the sidewalk. "See ya 'round, Sullivan," said Charles, and he walked up the street toward the Common. Aidan walked down toward Washington Street. They had made no plans to meet again.

Most every weekday after that, they were both at Rosen's at half past one. Aidan always had an egg cream, but Charles picked something different each time from the large selection of drinks one could get for five cents. A couple of times, Aidan offered to pay for both, but Charles rebuffed him with a scowl. "Ain't so poor that I can't buy me a nickel drink," he muttered, sliding his own coin across the marble counter.

One day, after they gave their order, Charles said, "So how long you think Willy's gonna run this bootblack game?"

"Dunno. Haven't thought about it. It's workin' out pretty good, at least for Willy."

"How many times have the police figured out what you two are doin'?"

"Well, a couple times a copper chased Willy, but he's fast. Ain't seen no one yet who could catch him."

After a beat, Charles said, "Sully, I hate to tell you this, but I think your good thing might be closin' down soon."

Aidan looked at Charles with alarm. "What? Why? Why would he shut it down now, when we're makin' good coin?"

"Don't you see? This town ain't that big. Once he's called out a couple times on a scam, word gets around. Soon the police is gonna be watchin' every bootblack on the street, lookin' for the lifter to move in. Willy only runs a game for so long, then he shuts it down before he gets pinched."

"Well," said Aidan after a moment, "He'll just think of somethin' else for us."

"But it ain't a lock that you fit the part. What if his next scam needs a littler feller than you? Or some lame feller?"

"Or what if he just gets tired of me?" said Aidan, almost to himself.

"I'm just sayin'," said Charles, "Good to keep your eyes peeled for another situation." He finished his ginger beer and pushed his glass away. He looked up at the clock behind the counter. "Hey, it's almost two. You don't wanna be late for the Windbag. See ya 'round." He made for the door.

"Hey, I'm comin'." Aidan met him out on the sidewalk. They fell in step together. After a block, Aidan mumbled, "So I was thinkin', maybe me and you could team up to make some coin." He looked down at the gutter trash nonchalantly.

Charles looked skyward. He had thought it might come to this. What was the best way to let him down easy?

The truth was that over the last couple of weeks, Aidan had grown on him. Charles didn't usually talk much with other people. He sometimes exchanged information with other boys living on the streets, but he wouldn't trust them farther than he could throw them. A couple of months ago, Charles had emptied the pockets of an unconscious man and found not only cash but also, incredibly, a pocketknife with the initials "C.W." embossed on it. The chances of lifting anything that happened to have his own initials on it seemed so fantastical to Charles that he'd felt an urge to tell someone, to show them to prove that he was not crazy, not seeing things. But he'd had no one to tell. He ended up walking down to the waterfront seeking Bess, but he could not find her among the other whores walking the streets, and when he arrived in front of her building, he suddenly felt stupid and hurried away.

But Aidan was someone he could have shown the knife to. Aidan didn't expect anything from him, didn't have any information that Charles didn't already have, didn't seem like he would take anything Charles had left unguarded. Charles had stopped trying to figure out what Aidan's angle was and accepted that he didn't have one.

Unfortunately, taking him on as a partner was out of the question. Not because Aidan was green—he was, but he wasn't a dunce, and he could be trained. And not because he was Irish, which was becoming easier and easier to forget. It was because every day of Charles's life since his mother died was a lesson in how you shouldn't trust anyone. Anyone.

"Listen, Sully," Charles started as they turned onto Washington Street, "You ain't half bad and all, but I work alone."

"Why?" asked Aidan.

"Because when you depend on other people to save your bacon, sometimes they don't. Plus, if they screw up, they could bring you down with 'em."

"But they could save you, too. They could pull you outta your own screwup. I mean, it's possible, right?" Aidan looked over at Charles.

Charles flicked the brim of Aidan's cap, nearly causing it to fall off his head. "Rosen's, half one tomorrow," Charles said with a little smile, and with a quick about-face, he disappeared into the crowd.

In the end, Willy didn't have a chance to shut down the bootblack scam, because before he could, he was arrested. A few days after Aidan's partnership discussion with Charles, Willy had just lifted the fat wallet of a mark when the man suddenly spun around, knowing that he had been robbed. As he spun, he grabbed the first thing behind him, which was Willy's forearm. It happened so fast that neither the man nor Willy could believe that one had apprehended the other. As the shouting began and a police officer ran to the site of the commotion, Aidan stood frozen in fear, his hand still holding his brush in midair. A heated conversation ensued, during which Willy insisted that Aidan was his partner, but for whatever reason, the policeman didn't want to hear it.

Once Willy was hauled away, Aidan's knees began to shake, and he sat down on the pavement with his back against a building. In a few minutes, he felt a bit better. He realized that although he would not get paid for today's work, at least he'd inherited Willy's bootblack kit, which would allow him to earn legitimate money. But contemplating the wages he could expect to earn shining shoes, he felt deflated. And then he thought about Charles.

CHAPTER 6

Aidan headed down State Street toward the water, the last place he would usually go but the first place he knew he was likely to find Charles. Unlike colorful Washington Street, where commercial enticements reached almost circus proportions, State Street was drab and serious. Businessmen walked with good posture in and out of the granite buildings, bowler hats firmly set on brows, thinking of numbers and money. Still, Aidan was not entirely out of place, because peppering the sea of men were messenger boys of his age delivering packages and letters. He passed through that ocean of finance and prosperity, fourteen cents in his pocket.

When he reached the end of the street and turned onto Atlantic Avenue, the scene changed again. Here, the pewter sky that had underscored the seriousness of State Street seemed to cast a grimy pall over all the piers and the working-class people milling about. The primary activity was unloading the day's catch, to be sold right there on the docks and carted away, destined for the North End or Quincy Market. The stink of fish was overpowering.

Aidan was coming to realize how hard it would be to find Charles in all this commotion just as he saw Charles crossing the street toward him. "Hey!" Charles shouted as he wove his way between the steady stream of clopping horse-drawn carts. "What are you doing down here?"

In silent agreement, they turned up a street heading away from the waterfront, fists in their pockets as they ascended the slope. After a block or so, Aidan couldn't wait any longer. "Willy got pinched."

"Really?" said Charles, and despite his troubles, Aidan felt a small measure of satisfaction in being able to tell Charles something that happened on the street that he didn't already know. Of course, it had only happened half an hour ago.

"Mark felt his wallet leaving his coat or somethin'. He spun around and grabbed Willy fast as a rattlesnake and wouldn't let go for nothin'. Screamed his head off, and a cop came runnin'. Had Willy dead to rights, found the wallet on him and everything."

"He'll do time for sure, then." Charles stopped in front of a saloon, indistinguishable from all the others they had passed. "C'mon," he said, and they headed inside.

After dark, this establishment would be so full of drunken laborers and sailors that a boy would not be likely to venture inside, but now, when it was just before suppertime, it was only half full and its patrons only half drunk. Charles and Aidan took a scarred and sticky table near the door and ordered two short beers.

"So you're out of a job," Charles stated as they waited for their drinks to arrive.

"Got my bootblack kit," said Aidan halfheartedly as he tapped the box he had parked by his feet under the table. "At least Willy taught me how to shine shoes."

"Yeah, remember not to black the pants from now on," said Charles as the bartender put the beers down on their table, slopping some over the sides of the glasses. They paid and took a sip. Neither mentioned how little one could earn blacking boots, a nickel at a time. Aidan was itching to ask Charles again about working together, but he dreaded the rejection this time, since he could think of no other way out now.

Charles considered Aidan from across their table. "Listen, I know you want to team up, Sully. But just think about what happened today. Willy, did he try to protect you, or did he hang you out to dry?"

"Yeah, but Willy's a bastard, you said so yourself!"

"Okay, and what did you do when he got pinched? Did you try to distract the cops, help him get away?"

Aidan didn't respond. He hadn't tried to help Willy escape, even though Willy's arrest meant the end of Aidan's employment. Maybe what Charles had said was true—that when it came down to it, everyone was only out for himself. But no, he didn't really believe that, at least not in all cases.

"Willy wasn't worth savin'," he said finally.

"And you're sure I am?" asked Charles.

"Yes. Yes, I am," said Aidan without hesitation.

"What if I don't feel the same about you?" asked Charles.

"Then I ain't no worse off than I was with Willy," answered Aidan, and Charles had nothing to say to that. They drank their beers in silence for a while.

Charles looked out the window and wondered what he should do. Aidan's sick mother wasn't his problem. Charles could walk away, and Aidan would figure something out. Nobody had been there to help Charles when his mother died, and wasn't he here, living proof that you could make it on your own? He thought about the first winter, how the bitter cold had reduced him to begging for coins he would hand over to the flophouse. He recalled hammocks where the lice and bedbugs kept him up half the night, the groping hands of some man in the dark propelling him back into the freezing street on two different occasions. Shuddering, he forced himself back to the present, where Aidan was sitting across from him, not an orphan yet, not without a way to earn wages.

As he was considering how to turn Aidan down, he had another thought: If he said no now, would Aidan still want to meet him at Rosen's? Until this moment, Charles had not realized how much he looked forward to their meetings. Sometimes it was the only real conversation he had all day. More than the fate of Aidan or his mother, the possibility of losing his conversations at Rosen's propelled him to say, "Lemme think about it."

"Really?" beamed Aidan. "That's swell!"

"Hey, I ain't said yes, I gotta think about it."

"Yeah, but you didn't say no!" Aidan sat there, grinning like an idiot, and despite his misgivings, Charles had to smile.

"Say," said Aidan. "Come to my place tomorrow night and have supper with us. My ma said she would make beef stew with drop biscuits. She's finally feelin' good enough to start cookin' again, even said she can go out to do some shoppin' now."

"Probably your cookin' that made her want to get outta her sickbed," said Charles as he got up from his chair.

Aidan rose, and they walked to the door. "Half six, meet me at the steamin' kettle, and we'll walk up together," Aidan said, and they parted ways.

CHAPTER 7

THE NEXT MORNING, AIDAN SLEPT IN. HE HAD TOLD MAEVE HE HAD the day off, and she'd asked no questions. Now that she was up and about more, she must have noticed how much money was in the biscuit tin. If she wondered what good fortune had befallen Aidan at his job to earn him so much, she kept that wondering to herself.

When Aidan got up, he went out with Maeve's list of things to buy for dinner that night, stopping at the butcher and the greengrocer in their neighborhood. When he returned, she told him she had forgotten to put carrots on the list.

"Ach, I'll just make the stew without the carrots," she said.

"No, Ma, it's gotta be great, ya gotta have carrots," insisted Aidan.

"'Tis a fine thing to have a friend that is so *discriminatin'* in his victuals. Tell me, what wine shall we be servin' our visitin' royalty?" she said with a wry smile.

"I'll go get the bleddy carrots," said Aidan, ignoring her teasing.

"Oh, don't bother. I'm goin' out later anyway to talk to Mr. McGuire about gettin' some piecework to do again—there's another greengrocer right on the corner there. Not to worry, there will be carrots in the stew!" Her merriment was cut short by a fit of coughing.

"You're sure you're up to shoppin' now, right?" asked Aidan.

Maeve recovered and peeked at the rag she had held to her mouth before folding it quickly and tucking it into her apron pocket. "I'm fit as a fiddle, lad—go off and have yer fun on yer day off, but don't be late for this supper I'm makin' with special carrots for yer royal friend!"

After an afternoon of blacking boots, which yielded a disappointing forty cents in profit, Aidan packed up his brushes and headed over to Scollay Square. As he rounded the corner, he could see the steaming teakettle hanging over the door of the Oriental Tea Company. When Aidan was little, one of his favorite stories Maeve told was of the day that the kettle was unveiled. There had been a competition on New Year's Day to guess how much the kettle could contain, and a huge crowd, including seventeen-year-old Maeve, had gathered to see the answer revealed. Thousands of people had submitted their guesses in advance to the company, hoping to win a forty-pound chest of tea. But Aidan's favorite part of the story was when Maeve described the moment that they lifted the lid on the kettle to begin pouring the water in, and to everyone's surprise, out popped a young boy who had been hiding inside. Regardless of how old Aidan was at the time of the telling, Maeve always speculated that the "wee lad was just your age," and sometimes she went on to insist that he even looked a little like Aidan. She described how the crowd went wild when the boy appeared and how they cheered for him as he waved with both hands. Aidan always closed his eyes at this point, imagining that he was that boy and the crowd was cheering for him.

Charles was a bit late arriving at the kettle. "We'll have to hoof it," said Aidan, "or we'll catch it from my ma. She's been cookin' all afternoon."

As they made their way into the West End, Charles said, "You know, Sully, this damn stew better be good—you been buildin' it up ever since we ate at that place the first night."

"You'll be wonderin' how them saloons can call their swill by the same name."

Charles smiled and said, "So what the hell are we waitin' for—I'm half starved!" and they ran the rest of the way.

When they got to the tenement, they raced up the stairs, vying to get to the third floor first. Aidan knocked off Charles's cap and raced ahead of him when he stooped to pick it up. Laughing, Aidan burst into the apartment with Charles right behind him.

The smell hit them right away, but instead of the savory scent of Maeve's famous stew, it was the sharp smell of gin. Aidan stopped in his tracks and took in the situation. Maeve was at the kitchen table with her head resting on her arms, a bottle to one side of her, some paper on the other. She looked up slowly with red eyes swimming, her red hair unpinned and tumbled down on one side. When her eyes could focus and she saw it was Aidan, she started crying and put her face in her hands. Aidan moved closer and saw that the paper on the table was the wrapping that had contained the baby blanket. The note was out of the envelope, and the ink had mingled with Maeve's tears all over her hands so that she was unwittingly rubbing it onto her face.

Aidan looked around. It didn't appear that Maeve had found the blanket underneath his mattress. "Jaysus," he said, and he grabbed the bottle to throw it out the open window. Faster than he would ever have believed Maeve could move in her condition, she grabbed his forearm and brought her face close to his. Her eyes were bloodshot, and her gin breath was so overpowering it made him squint. "What was in the package?" she demanded. "Where is it? What was it?" Her grip became painful on his arm.

How could I have left the wrapping on the shelf? he berated himself. *How could I have been so bleddy stupid?* "It was . . . a little blanket. But it was all chewed up by the mice or somethin'. I threw it away."

"You threw away my baby blanket?" Maeve screamed at him. "Just who in the feck do you think you are? That was MINE! He gave it to ME!" She grabbed the bottle out of Aidan's hand.

"Ma, it had bugs in it. It was disgusting."

Maeve let go of his arm and pointed a trembling finger at him. "No. You wanna know what's disgustin'? This feckin' tenement, that's what. This hellhole with a stove for heat and a toilet down the feckin' hall. He was gonna take us OUTTA HERE. He had PLANS, for feck's sake. We were gonna be a dacent family together in a dacent apartment in a dacent part a' town, the four of us. Because he LOVED ME!" She sank to the floor sobbing and cradling her bottle like a lover.

Suddenly, Aidan remembered that Charles was there. He grabbed Charles's arm and muttered, "Let's go."

Once out on the street, Aidan walked as fast as he could back the way they had come, and Charles had to run a few steps to catch up with him. "Sully—" he started.

"Just don't say anything," Aidan snapped.

"Sully, people is drunk every day in this city. It ain't unusual."

"Yeah, but they ain't your ma, now are they?" he shot back.

They walked a while at Aidan's angry clip until they reached the Common, where Aidan plunked down on the first available park bench.

"What the hell use is it that she's feelin' better," said Aidan, "if she's drinkin' again? She ain't gonna be able to do work like that."

"Just because she fell off the wagon once doesn't mean—"

"You ain't never lived with no one that's got this problem, I see," spat Aidan. Then, less angrily, he continued, "Maybe you're right. I

want you to be right. I dunno what I'm gonna do if you ain't right."
He put his head in his hands.

"Why didn't you throw the paper away with the blanket?"

"I never throwed the blanket away. I hid it."

"Why'd ya keep it?"

"I dunno," said Aidan. After a pause, he said, "I guess I do know. I just did it at the time without thinkin' or nothin', but after a while, it came to me." He rubbed his eyes and sat up, arching his back over the bench to look straight up at the sky. "When Dan died, she never said nothin' to me about it. I came home from school, and some of the neighbors were in our kitchen, and one of 'em told me, but my ma was just starin' straight ahead, like she didn't even know I come into the room. Everyone was frettin' and fussin' over her, but all they could say to me was, 'Now stay out of her way, she's gonna have a rough time of it for a while,' and 'You be a good lad and help your ma out.' Nobody, not my ma or nobody else, ever stopped to think that I lost the only pa I was ever gonna get a chance to have."

Charles looked out across the Common, pretending not to see the single tear that ran from the corner of Aidan's eye.

Aidan rubbed the tear with the back of his hand and looked at Charles. "So I took the fecking blanket 'cause it was the least I deserved."

They both sat on the bench and watched the fading daylight.

As it got darker, Charles said, "You hungry?"

"Nah," said Aidan. "Lost my appetite."

"Wanna go make some money?" asked Charles.

"You serious? You're cuttin' me in?"

"I wanna see how you do. Give you a try. No promises or nothin'."

"You feel sorry for me. That's why you're doin' this," Aidan stated.

"Maybe. You comin'?" asked Charles to the air as he rose from the bench.

Aidan stood, and they walked out of the Common toward Beacon Street, headed down to the heart of all sin in Boston.

CHAPTER 8

Don't it have to be dark to do this kinda work?" asked Aidan as they wove their way through the streets.

"It does, but we ain't workin' yet—you gotta lotta learnin' and *observin'* to do 'fore I put my arse on the line with you."

Soon they entered Scollay Square, home to theatres of all stripes, saloons too numerous to count, and prostitutes for any taste. They walked in front of the Old Howard Theatre, feeling the heat from the sign spelling out "The Old Howard" in lightbulbs, a novelty in itself when electricity was still so new. As they proceeded, the brightness of the bulbs gave way to the anemic glow of the gas lamps on North Street.

In a part of the city where most streets were straight even if they were at odd angles to each other, North Street curved its way up from the waterfront like a snake. For any sailor coming into port in Boston, North Street was a meandering path of pleasure, with all the services he might require. Near to the water were places where you could store your bag of worldly goods for a fee, and after you lightened your load, every other storefront was a saloon, and every third building was a brothel. You could find a whore to do whatever you'd been dreaming of out at sea, or you could just drink until you couldn't stand upright, and there was never a night where business wasn't brisk.

Into this den of adult pleasures walked Charles and Aidan. Without realizing it, Aidan began walking a little closer to Charles.

"Now," began Charles, "alleys is where the opportunities are, but down here there's lots that could be goin' on in an alley, so you gotta be careful. The cheaper whores that work on their own, the ones that ain't with a whorehouse, they might be doin' some standin'-up business in any one of these alleys, and you do *not* want to interrupt them. You make any one of 'em mad enough, they'll make sure the cops are onto you, and then your goose is cooked."

"But . . ." said Aidan, unsure of how to phrase his question, "how are the whores in good with the cops? Don't the cops, you know, arrest them for what they do? I mean, it's against the law, whorin' and all, right?"

"Cops is frequent customers down here. Hell, they don't even have to pay." They passed by an alley emitting some human noises, and Aidan turned his head just in time to see the white uniform of a sailor pressed up against the violet gowns of a woman before they continued down the street.

"You ever, you know, think about using some of your profits you make down here for, you know, uh . . . with some of these, uh . . ." Aidan trailed off.

"No," said Charles firmly.

"Why not?"

"I'll show you later. And you better start focusing on why we're here, or I'll just go off and leave ya." The thought of Charles leaving him alone on North Street was tremendously helpful in focusing Aidan back on the task at hand.

After a tasteless supper in a cheap restaurant, it was dark enough to get to work. As they walked up and down the street, they cast furtive looks into alleys, their caps pulled down on their brows. Several times they entered one and heard a quiet sound that could have been someone shifting around, semi-conscious on a pile of trash, but instead turned out to be rats. After wandering around for more than an hour, they heard some conversation that stopped Charles. He peeked around the corner to view the scene.

"Got plenny a money," slurred a man as he simultaneously fumbled in his pocket and groped the woman.

"Yeah, I believe ya, but you ain't got what else it takes," she said, and she grabbed the man between his legs. "No wood in the shed. Next time, come see me earlier." She extracted herself from his grasp and swept out of the alley, almost bumping into Charles. "Ah," she said with a knowing look, "the vultures are waitin' already. If I thought he had more than a dollar, I'd wait him out myself."

The man in the alley slid his back down the wall with a moan until he was in a sitting position. "Goddamn whore won' take muh money, whassa . . ." he mumbled, and his head lolled to the side. Soon he began to drool, and then he slumped over.

"Capital. Here we go," whispered Charles. As they had discussed over supper, Aidan's job was to stand by the mouth of the alley with a stone in his hand. While Charles fleeced the pockets of the mark, Aidan would look for passersby that might interfere. If an interruption seemed possible, Aidan would begin to tap on the wall of the alley with the stone, and Charles would hide until it was safe to continue.

The job went off without a hitch. Although the man had fallen on his money-pocket side, Charles had no problem rolling him over without waking him. Charles pocketed the bills, and the boys strolled away from the alley. As Charles had explained over their supper, you never count your take until you're clean away, and you never run unless you're being chased. "Hardest part," he claimed. "Your whole body's saying two things: 'How much did I get?' and 'I better get the hell outta here!' But you can't listen. You gotta control yourself."

They walked a few blocks and then ducked into a side street. Charles unfolded the bills and took inventory in the weak gaslight. He looked up at Aidan. "That mug had a *fiver* on him." He showed Aidan the five and a one-dollar bill. They both grinned.

~

As was the deal that Charles had outlined, Aidan received a quarter of the profits for his part. After another hour, they found another mark who yielded two dollars, a much more typical take, according to Charles. When he declared them done for the night, Aidan balked. "That's it? But we're doin' great!"

"Yup. That's another rule I got: Don't get greedy. Can't do too many jobs a night without gettin' a little sloppy. There's only so many times you can roll the dice before it stops coming up in your favor."

Aidan thought that it was easy for Charles to be satisfied—he had more than five dollars in his pocket, after all—but he held his tongue. His profit was far more than he could make bootblacking for a full day.

"We got one more stop," said Charles as they headed down a side street. They came to an inn called Fore and Aft, a place for sailors and other transients to sleep that had a sooty saloon on the ground floor. They headed in, and Charles ordered beers at the bar. This saloon seemed particularly grimy to Aidan, even compared to the ones that they had passed in previous hours. There was a disheveled old man who had slipped from his chair and appeared to be asleep on the floor in the middle of the room, and two men up front were having a slurred argument. A glass fell off a table and shattered. No one moved to clean it up.

"Why celebrate here?" asked Aidan. "We passed a dozen places that was better than this hole."

"We ain't celebratin'. I'm answerin' your question of earlier." Charles took a sip of his beer. "You see that mug over there at the end of the bar?" Aidan looked over and saw a wreck of a man. He was young but seemingly crazy, talking softly to himself, swatting at imaginary flies. On the side of his nose was a large, tumor-like protrusion, and there was a smaller one on his jaw.

"Name's Gus. He's here all the time. A regular. Be here until the barkeep give him the boot. Wanna know what's wrong with him?" Aidan didn't answer. He knew Charles would tell him anyway.

"French gout," Charles said to his beer. "People say he was always down by the waterfront, sampling the goods. And that's why I don't spend my money down there." Charles took one more sip and walked out, closely followed by Aidan, who was suddenly far less enamored with the ladies of North Street.

"Listen," said Charles as they walked away from the waterfront, "you did all right tonight. I'm flush for a while—Rosen's is my treat tomorrow."

They walked in silence for a while, Aidan still horrified by the syphilitic man. When they reached Washington Street, Charles stopped. "It was good tonight, you know, good to have someone else around down there. I mean, not that I couldn't have done it myself, you know, but it was different. Good. You know."

But Aidan barely heard him.

When Aidan walked into the apartment, he was dead tired, even though it was only half past ten. Maeve was asleep, but Ella was up, playing with paper dolls she had cut out earlier in the day. "Whatcha doin' awake, ya naughty mouse?" Aidan asked her as he hung up his cap on the nail behind the door.

"I needed water, but I couldn't wake Mommy up. Then after I got me the water, I weren't so tired no more."

Aidan could smell gin and hear Maeve's soft, rattling snores. "Ya gotta get back in bed now. Go on, scoot," he mumbled as he rubbed his eyes.

"Ya gotta tell me a story," Ella insisted, sticking her lower lip out and twisting her red hair around her index finger. She looked up at Aidan with Dan Connelly's cornflower-blue eyes.

Aidan thought about the stories he could tell. As he looked at little Ella in her muslin gown with pink flowers at the collar, something Maeve had embroidered back in her better days, everything he'd done and witnessed that night suddenly seemed unbearably dirty. Standing before his sister, just having the memories in his brain of the prostitutes in the alleys, the drunks staggering from one saloon to the next, the man with syphilis—it felt like a violation. He was irrationally fearful that Ella could read his mind and see all the filth he had seen and the crimes in which he had participated.

"Get to bed now, or I'll fix it so you don't play with the McGarrity twins for a week!" he growled, and Ella scampered off to climb back in bed with Maeve. Aidan took his cap off the nail and went down to sit on the stoop, looking up at the moon, until enough time had passed that he was sure Ella had fallen asleep.

CHAPTER 9

THE NEXT DAY, CHARLES HAD BEEN SITTING AT THE COUNTER AT Rosen's for almost fifteen minutes when Aidan sat down next to him. Despite being kept waiting, Charles was still in fine spirits from all the cash filling his pockets. "What'll it be, Sully?" he joked. "As if I even gotta ask. Egg cream, my good man!" he called out to the soda jerk with two quick slaps of his hand on the counter.

"I ain't really thirsty," said Aidan.

"Horseshit. You ain't never gonna turn down an egg cream." Charles considered Aidan for a moment and then cocked his head a few degrees. "Hey, what the hell?"

"Charles," stated Aidan, and he paused. "I don't know about this workin' together thing."

Charles contemplated this. "Well, I thought this would come, but not quite so soon. All right, I know your take last night weren't enough for you plus your ma and sis. Twenty-five percent is more than fair, but I could go to a third if—"

"It ain't that."

"Then I repeat: What the hell?"

Aidan stirred his egg cream with his straw without drinking. "It's . . . the work. Not the work, really, but where we did it. And the work. The whole thing. It's so . . . it's like hell on earth down there," he finished, barely audible. He put his elbows on the counter and placed his palms over his eyes.

Charles started to protest but then stopped himself and thought about when he started to venture into North Street. Of course, he didn't go right from the relative comfort of living with his mother to working the alleys near the waterfront. It had been a slow slide. Still, had Aidan thought they would be strolling down the streets of Back Bay?

"Listen, you gotta go where the money is. Unless you can take a billfold in broad daylight without nobody knowin', the only way is to take it in the dark like we done. Plus, it ain't like you're a babe outta the cradle—what you and Willy done weren't no saintly act."

"That was different! Them marks was sober, regular business-men, and we was workin' in the light of day, with respectable folks all around. Even we was pretendin' to be respectable! Where me and you was . . . that place is horrible."

"It's horrible," Charles agreed. "But it's profitable."

The boys looked at each other, not sure what to do.

Finally, Aidan said, "Can we go to the Garden?"

They walked around the Public Garden without talking. After a while, Charles said, "I ain't been here in a helluva long time."

"I come here every day," said Aidan. "'Less it's rainin' or too cold. Ain't so pretty in the winter, but just look at it now. Why wouldn't you come here all the time?"

Charles kicked a stone from the path to the grass. "All these swells, puttin' on airs, lookin' down their noses. And if it ain't folks puttin' on a puss like they smell somethin' bad when they see you, it's the cops tellin' you that you ain't good enough to be here."

Aidan looked around. The people they were passing were indeed far better dressed then either of them, but they seemed engaged in their own conversations. Once, recently, he'd inspired a look of mild disgust when he had brushed up against a woman's skirts, but other than that, he didn't quite see Charles's point. Except, of course, about the police harassment.

"Well," admitted Aidan, "the cops sure do like to bounce you outta here if they see you takin' up the good spaces on the benches and such. But I know where to go if you wanna set a while and not be bothered. I'll show ya."

The boys walked to the end of the Garden near Charles Street, where there was a large tree near a monument that blocked the view of the street. They sat with their backs to the tree, looking out at the women with parasols, the barefoot children running on the grass in delight, the couples holding hands and waiting in line for the swan boats.

"You're tellin' me," said Charles, "that you don't feel like you don't belong here?"

"I'm tellin' you that I come here every day, more than any of these folks do. I know every monument—I've read every word on every one of 'em. I know what day the new flowers from the hothouse get put in the ground. I know what day they mow the grass. I belong here as much as anybody, maybe more, even if the cops can kick my arse outta here. They kicked me out a few times, but here I am, ain't I?"

Charles seemed to ponder this. He took out his pocketknife and started to whittle a Y-shaped piece of branch he found lying next to him. "So I suppose you been on them swan boats with all the fancy people?"

"Hell no," said Aidan as he plucked at the grass next to his shoe. "Ain't gonna catch me near any water deeper than a rain puddle."

Charles stopped whittling. "You're pullin' my leg, right? You live in a city right on the harbor, and you're afraid of the water? Jesus!" When Aidan didn't reply, Charles resumed whittling and said more carefully, "So, did somethin' bad happen when you was trying to learn how to swim or somethin'?"

"I never tried to learn how to swim. Nothin' bad ever happened, I just been like this since I can remember." Aidan took the grass he had plucked and flung it away from him like confetti, but most of it settled on top of his shoes. "You ain't afraid of nothin', I suppose."

"Everybody's afraid of somethin'," said Charles as he tried to shave off a knot in the branch.

"Yeah, and what's your thing?" asked Aidan, turning so he could see Charles better.

"Sort of a long story."

"I got nothin' but time."

So Charles told Aidan about how a year ago, he'd been caught stealing a sandwich from a restaurant with outdoor seating. One that had an owner who was paying above and beyond the usual graft to secure more police presence and who insisted on a robust prosecution of the street Arabs stealing his food. So whereas stealing a sandwich might normally have incurred probation in court, Charles instead found himself in Westboro at the State Reform School For Boys for a month of his young life that he would rather forget. He was originally supposed to be there for more than a year. "There was at least twice as many boys in there than the place was built for, plus rumor was they was gonna shut the place down, so they went through the files and let all them go that were there for status offenses and some of the littler crimes that didn't hurt nobody."

"What's a status offense?"

"It's something you done that wouldn't have been a crime if you done it when you was older, like playin' dice on Sunday, or bein' in the park after dark."

Aidan found a thin stick and snapped it in half. "So what was the scary part?" he asked.

"What wasn't scary about that place?" Charles answered. He tossed his whittled branch aside and slowly exhaled a deep breath.

"Mostly for punishment, they flogged you with a big wide leather strap. I got it twice while I was there, and that was the worst of it for me. But other boys, the older ones, that weren't enough for them, they was hard bastards, so they had other ways of dealin' with them. Really bad ways. Straightjackets and gags. Or they'd stick you in The Lodge and only give you bread and water for a week. But that wasn't the worst of it." He folded up his knife and put it in his pocket. "The guards said they weren't allowed to use the Sweatbox since ten years ago, but the older boys said they still had it somewhere in the building, that they never got rid of it. They said it's only twenty-one inch by seventeen inch, a long and skinny box, and when you get in, you can't even move. And then they leave you there, alone. For hours. And your hands and feet swell up, and you can't walk right when you get out. First I didn't believe them, that they ever used this thing—I was sure they was just tryin' to scare the new boys—but once I seen all the other stuff they done to them hard bastards, I started to believe it. I couldn't stop thinkin' about it, 'specially at night when I was tryin' to fall asleep. Even though I knew they didn't use it no more, probably didn't even exist no more. But I couldn't stop imaginin' it. What it would be like. How you'd struggle, and then you'd start to panic, and how nobody would come when you called."

Aidan's mouth hung open briefly before he shut it.

Charles said, "Scary enough for ya?" with a wry smile, but there was no smile in his eyes. "So whaddya say we talk about somethin' else?"

"Yeah. Jaysus. Yeah," said Aidan as he took off his cap and ran his hand through his hair.

They were quiet for a while, and then they talked of lighter things. The antics of a scrappy but entertaining boy in their school that they both remembered. The penny candy store with the nicest proprietor. The underground trolley they'd heard was to be built near where they sat, about which they had friendly disagreement. "Never gonna happen," said Charles. "Once they start diggin', buildings is gonna start cavin' in nearby. Can't be done."

Aidan wasn't so sure. "I bet they thought of that. Plus they're just gonna dig under the Common. Not like they're gonna dig right under a building. That'd be crazy," he admitted.

They walked into the Common along one of its many criss-crossing paths. "Hey, what time is it?" asked Aidan suddenly. They found a clock on a building that said five minutes of five. "We can just make it. Let's go. I gotta show you somethin'."

They made their way to the edge of the Common that fronted Boylston Street. Aidan sat down on the grass facing the street. "This is what you gotta show me? I seen Boylston before," said Charles, but he sat down.

"Ever been here this time of day?"

"I dunno. What's so special about this time of day?"

"You'll see. Just wait." They watched the commotion in the street—the logjam of horse-drawn carriages, the trolley cars packed like tins of sardines, the people weaving between traffic to cross to the opposite side. Several clocks began to strike five, each competing to be heard. Less than a minute after the sound of the last bell drifted away, the music started.

"Do ya hear it?" asked Aidan, smiling.

"Yeah. Who's playin'?"

"Look across the street." Aidan pointed to a set of double doors that had been opened to the street. A man sat at a grand piano, playing with great flourish. "Five o'clock he starts. Tryin' to get some mug coming home from work to buy one. Piano Row, that's what they call these two blocks that hug the corner of the Common. There's five different piano stores. Most of 'em advertise like this. But this one, he's the best. Listen."

The sweeping arpeggios of Chopin's No. 1 in C Major, otherwise known as the "Waterfall Etude," drifted over the trolleys and crowds and wafted onto the Common. The music was relentless, the notes traveling up and down the keys from low to high to low again, moving from major to minor to minor seventh, never pausing. The only music that Charles heard in his daily life was the occasional creaky fiddle tune seeping out of a brothel, accompanied by clapping and stomping on worn wooden floors. This piano piece bore no relation to that or anything he had heard before. The more he listened, the more the street noise fell away, until he was so focused that he could have been sitting in a room alone with the piano player. When the music ended, he felt a little wilting in his chest, as if he had dropped a Morgan dollar in the harbor, never to see it again.

Charles looked over at Aidan, who looked as content as a cat after polishing off a saucer of cream. The Public Garden, Piano Row. He could see it now, why it was hard for Aidan down on North Street. Aidan's Boston wasn't anything like his.

CHAPTER 10

THEY CAME TO AN AGREEMENT ABOUT WORKING TOGETHER WITHOUT much difficulty. Once Charles told him that he generally didn't go down to the waterfront more than once a week, Aidan felt better. He had been imagining wandering those streets every night, which seemed foul beyond tolerance. But Charles explained: Every hour you spent down there increased your risk of getting pounded by a thief who wanted what you had rightfully stolen or, even worse, getting pinched by the cops. And it was the meanest, most corrupt cops who ended up with the waterfront as their beat.

There were other rules, too. Charles focused on cash and generally did not get distracted by other valuables, although he did make exceptions, like when he spied the initialed pocketknife. And he stopped for the night when he felt he'd made enough, no matter how early it was.

These rules comforted Aidan. There was a formula to what Charles did that limited his time on the waterfront streets. And as much as Aidan wanted to avoid getting caught, Charles had a much clearer idea of what that was like. Aidan was counting on Charles's memories of the reform school to keep them both safe.

That Friday night, they met in front of the Old Howard. They made a few dollars—three for Charles, one for Aidan—and would have had more if they hadn't run into two older boys who moved in just as they identified a man who was out like a light, slumped against a broken crate in the shadows.

"Listen, the luck ain't with us. I'm not gettin' a good feeling about the rest of the night. We're done," Charles announced.

Aidan thought of the biscuit tin at home, not as full as he would have liked it, but not empty, either. Though it was not as if he had any say in whether he and Charles continued on tonight or not. They started walking away from the waterfront. "Where you headed now?" he asked.

"You know, no place. Why?"

"Well," said Aidan with some embarrassment, "um, last time we was out, I couldn't sleep when I got home, for hours. Doin' this just gets me all strung up, and I . . . I just wanted to know if you wanted . . . if you would come to my place. For a little while." He kicked a stone into the street as he walked.

Charles thought it over. "I dunno about your ma, Sully. But maybe we could set on the stoop for a while."

So they went to Aidan's building. Aidan sprinted upstairs and grabbed some day-old bread and hard sausage from the kitchen, and they ate on the stoop and looked up at the moon, visible over the row of buildings on the opposite side of the street. Charles cut the meat with his pocketknife, and Aidan broke the bread in pieces the right size for the wheels of sausage.

When the food was gone, they stayed on the stoop, sometimes talking, sometimes just surveying the night sky and listening to the occasional argument coming from an open window. Eventually, both boys were tired, and they parted ways. Aidan climbed the stairs to his apartment, where everything was still. Maeve and Ella were sleeping like spoons in their bed. Aidan lay down on his straw mattress in the main room and took out Dan Connelly's baby blanket. He refolded it, slipped it under his head on top of his thin pillow, and in thirty seconds, he was asleep.

And so it went. Through the rest of June and all of July, Charles and Aidan met at Rosen's Monday through Friday, where Charles let Aidan know which night they would be working, usually Saturday. As the weeks progressed, they began leaving Rosen's together to pursue the daytime diversions Boston could offer two young boys. On most good-weather days, Aidan was able to steer them toward the Public Garden for a spell. On rainy days, when they could afford it, they went to Austin and Stone's or one of the other dime museums down in Scollay Square. For ten cents you could see a freak show with tattooed ladies, two-headed animals, African pygmies, and other oddities. They never tired of the sword swallower, and they marveled over the trained goat who could play a hand of poker.

As much as they were on equal footing during the day, Charles called the shots on their work nights and Aidan was happy to comply. And though they had several face-offs with other groups of boys, most of which they conceded, they only had one encounter with the police. It was late on a Friday night, and after hours of scouting, they saw an alley with promise. After Charles had exited and the two were a half a block away, they slowed their pace.

"Hardly worth the—" started Charles, and then he stopped mid-sentence. Aidan could feel Charles tense up even as he continued to walk. Keeping his gaze straight in front of him, Charles whispered urgently, "Up ahead. Take a piss."

They turned into the next alley, and Aidan saw Charles take money from his pocket and stuff it between the slats of a broken crate. Then Charles unbuttoned his pants and stood in front of the brick wall. "C'mon, c'mon!" he urged Aidan, who did the same but was too confused and scared to be able to produce anything. A policeman appeared at the mouth of the alley.

"Well, if it ain't two little thieves out past their bedtimes," he said as he grabbed them both by the shoulder.

"We're just takin' a piss, officer, swear to God," said Charles plaintively.

"If this alley's yer toilet, what the hell were ya doin' in that other one? Couldn't have anything to do with that sailor lying in there, could it?"

"Yeah, we went to go use that one, but that sailor was in there taking up all the room, so we just went to the next one. Look, we ain't got nothin'. Spent our last on a couple of short beers, and we're headin' home now, swear to God." Charles took everything out of his pockets—slingshot, pocketknife, 35 cents—so that he could turn them inside out. With his empty hand he punched Aidan out of his frozen state so that he could do the same.

The policeman looked over the meager contents in the boy's hands and picked up the pocketknife for closer examination. "This here's a pretty nice knife for an Arab like you," he said suspiciously.

"Yeah, it's a beaut. My pa got it for me for my last birthday, put my initials on it and everything. I ain't never leave the house without it," he added with a faint note of pride.

The policeman narrowed his gaze, not fully believing that a boy as dirty as Charles had a pa and a house, but somehow convinced by Charles's confident tone. The fact was that Charles was an excellent liar. Even Aidan felt himself taken in by Charles's fabrication, starting to believe, despite the facts, that the two of them had in fact just been searching for a place to empty their bladders, that Charles would go home to his pa and perhaps get punished for being out so late.

The policeman slapped the knife back in Charles's palm. "Waterfront ain't the place for you to be takin' refreshment. I don't want to see you back here at this hour, or I'll run ya in no matter what ya got in yer pockets." He gave them both a shove, propelling them out of the alley, and they buttoned their pants as they scampered away.

They were three blocks distant from their run-in when Aidan finally spoke. "How'd you know he was behind us? I didn't hear nothin'."

"Dunno. Somethin' about the way a cop walks. Maybe he don't shuffle like most of the drunks down that way, or maybe he got some special copper shoes—I just know that sound."

"What'd you stuff in that crate?"

"One lousy dollar. All that for almost nothin'. I'll go back tomorrow morning and get it if it's still there."

After another block, Aidan asked, "Uh, Charles?"

"Yeah?"

"Can we stop up ahead for a minute? Now I really have to piss."

CHAPTER 11

August 1889

CHARLES COULDN'T HELP BUT THINK THAT IT WAS ALL GOING SO WELL until they killed that man.

July had slipped into August, and the brick and stone that made up the city sucked in the heat of the sun all day to slowly exhale it at night. People slept on roofs and fire escapes, trying to catch any breeze that made it through the gauntlet of tenements. Every window was wide open. The residential streets were crawling with little boys sent out with the family growler to get cold beer at their neighborhood saloon.

Charles was happier than he had been in a long time. He stored away any amusing or interesting incidents that occurred so that he could recount them to Aidan once they were together. He found himself eavesdropping on the conversations of others just for this purpose. Though he had less cash in his pocket these days, it didn't seemed to matter. What difference did it make? He was filled with an unfamiliar optimism. Though times were lean right now, he somehow felt, knew, that the future was bright, filled with possibilities. Somewhere in the recesses of his mind, he knew that Aidan wasn't quite as satisfied, but it was easy to ignore that when he was feeling so sure of all the good things to come.

"Problem is," expounded Charles as they took their shoes off in the Public Garden to cool their toes in the grass, "there just ain't enough people stupid enough to pass out cold in a nice, out-of-the-way place. Sailors do it sometimes 'cause they're all turned around, ain't familiar with all the twisty streets, can't find their way back to the flophouse. But most mugs that live somewhere in the city, they find their way home, those bastards." They both lay back in the grass with their hands under their heads, elbows pointing out.

"But you were doin' this before I met you, right? How come it worked better then?" asked Aidan.

"It didn't. It ain't never been enough so I don't hafta grab my dinner off a pushcart or look for supper in a barrel half the time." In truth, since he teamed up with Aidan, he had been forced to do these things even more often, but he never considered dissolving their arrangement. He didn't want to go back to the way it was before, whole days going by without a conversation, never sharing a meal or a drink with another soul.

"Listen," said Charles as they looked up into the branches of the tree above them, "all we need is a little better luck than we been havin'. It's gonna work out." And he really believed it. All this hot weather meant booming business for the saloons—beer consumption was always at its highest during the peak of the summer. Their luck was going to turn, Charles just knew it.

And their luck did turn, but not in the way that Charles predicted.

One humid Saturday night in mid-August, the boys were once again scouting without success. Aidan was beginning to doubt the viability of their whole enterprise, but he kept his thoughts to himself. In the mornings he had started to look around for a legitimate job, an effort he had chosen not to mention to Charles. If he did find a job, it would cut into their afternoons together. This isn't what Aidan wanted at all, but there just wasn't enough money dropping into the biscuit tin, no matter how many shoes he shined.

He told himself that there was really nothing to tell Charles—he hadn't secured a job, not even close. But the truth was that he was afraid to tell him that he was even looking, suspecting that Charles would lash out at him, considering this a rejection. In Aidan's fantasy, he would find not one but two legal jobs, and the two of them could work side by side. But so far he couldn't even find one. And Aidan wondered how Charles would fare working for someone who would tell him what to do. It didn't sound like Charles.

Charles decided to call it a night, and Aidan didn't protest. They ambled up the street, both of them glum and kicking stones off the sidewalk in frustration.

"It's early," commented Aidan.

"Yeah."

"Hungry?"

"Nah."

At the end of the block, the commercial district ended, and the West End began. They both stopped. "Let's keep walking," said Charles, and instead of walking to Aidan's tenement, they turned and entered the upscale neighborhood of Beacon Hill.

They'd only gone three blocks when Charles froze in his tracks and put his arm across Aidan's chest.

"What?" Aidan whispered. His heart started hammering in his chest at the thought of the police close at their heels—but then he remembered that they hadn't rolled anyone tonight. He strained to hear whatever Charles was hearing. And then he heard it: the not-too-distant sound of someone vomiting.

"C'mon," said Charles, and they crept to the end of the block.

As they approached, the sounds got louder and seemed to be coming from directly around the corner of the building. Then the retching stopped, followed by a moan, and then nothing. They both peeked around the corner and saw a man on one knee, bracing himself with a hand against the side of the building. Aidan could see the sweat that had darkened his white shirt in patches under his arms. The man sat and wiped his mouth with his hand, his jacket crumpled beside him. The stench of whiskey and bile sat heavily in the humid night air.

Charles pulled Aidan into the doorway of a tailor's shop. "This here's tricky business," he whispered to Aidan. "He's pretty out in the open." The side street where the man was sitting was neither a full-fledged street nor an alley. It was only wide enough to admit one vehicle going one way, and the broad sides of the buildings lining it were punctuated with doors, mostly service entrances.

"What are you doing?" whispered Aidan. "This ain't the waterfront. You said we was done, that we weren't having the luck tonight."

"I thought we was done. But this just fell in our laps."

"This is a respectable neighborhood." Aidan wasn't sure why this made a difference, but it seemed riskier to do their business here.

"And that mug is as drunk as a two-bit sailor. Listen, if he gets up and wanders home, it wasn't meant to be."

As they waited for the man to decide whether he would stand or topple, it came to Aidan that there was something very wrong with intentionally heading toward the sound of retching. To Charles, all sorts of sounds in the city nighttime spelled opportunity—a man pissing in an alley mumbling to himself, an argument between a john and a whore, vomiting—and Aidan had seen Charles's face brighten when he heard these noises. It seemed to Aidan right now that Charles made his living not in the street but in the gutter, and that Aidan had joined him there—had asked, almost begged, to join him there. But this could change. Tonight, on the stoop, they would talk. Aidan would get a pail of beer for the two of them, and he would make Charles see that if they put their heads together, they could find another way. They could start all over—they could be anyone. With this resolve, Aidan felt a weight lift off him, and now he was impatient for this business with the man on the sidewalk to be done, one way or another.

~

Ten minutes later, their patience paid off. A peek around the corner proved to Charles that the man had nowhere urgent to go. He was leaning up against the wall like a sack of potatoes, out cold. The door next to him, the one he must have come through, was partially propped open, and Charles could hear the sounds of an upscale drinking establishment—the clink of glasses and the din of conversation and laughter, minus the more rowdy eruptions of the waterfront saloons.

They had to move fast or risk someone else coming across their discovery. Aidan stayed on the main street, his alarm rock in his hand, while Charles moved around the corner, staying clear of the door. He delicately reached into the man's exposed pocket and drew out a fat roll of bills in a large money clip. He knew it! They were due for a break and here it was, what looked like the most money he'd ever taken out of a pocket in his life. But there was something else in the pocket, and after stuffing the roll of bills in his pants, he reached in again and drew out a beautiful and expensive ivory-handled folding knife, the type of knife that you'd see in a shop window at the very center, on the highest pedestal, surrounded by fine but lesser knives that served only to make this knife look more regal by comparison. Charles felt a little dizzy as he contemplated these twin prizes, but as exciting as the money was, it was the knife that mesmerized him, brought him back to the day he had stolen his pocketknife. Here was a knife ten times greater than that one, and it was as if Fate had set up this sequence of events: finding a good knife and having no one to tell, meeting a friend when you had thought you didn't need friends, and then being able to present this king of knives to your friend, so he could appreciate not only the beauty of the knife but the beauty of being able to share such good fortune.

He knew without a doubt that this knife should belong to Aidan, that Fate wanted it that way; it was crystal clear.

"Sully!" he whispered forcefully. Aidan appeared around the corner, and Charles opened the knife to display it in all its glory, glinting in the gaslight. It looked brand-new and sharp as a razor. "It's yours," he said, solemnly and with great satisfaction.

Aidan stepped closer to see the knife, but before he could even reach out for it, Fate added an extra event in the sequence that Charles had not foreseen. The man woke and grabbed Charles's ankle, and in surprise, Charles twisted to face him, which was when his other foot slipped in the vomit on the sidewalk. Losing his balance, Charles fell forward onto the man, and the knife slipped through the white shirt into the man's belly like it was a well-cooked yam.

Aidan watched in stunned silence as Charles scrabbled frantically to get off the man, but the man had now grabbed Charles by the arm and, despite the knife protruding from his gut, was holding on with an iron grasp. Aidan pried the man's fingers from Charles's arm and lifted him off the man. The cloth surrounding the knife was a blooming rose of blood. The man started wheezing and moaning.

"Jaysus, Charles, we gotta do somethin'!" Aidan exclaimed in a high voice that he didn't recognize as his own, but he could see that Charles was unsteady on his feet and his face was draining of color as he stared at the man's wound. "Holy Mary Mother of God," said Aidan, panicking, hyperventilating. He reached down and pulled the offending knife from the man's belly, and a rush of blood spilled onto the sidewalk. He dropped the knife in horror, realizing he'd just done more harm than good, and he felt Charles slump against his shoulder with a moan. "*Shit shit shit!*"

Aidan exclaimed. Never had he expected anything like this. As much as he'd imagined all the bad things that could happen to the two of them as they pursued their dangerous livelihood, in every scenario it was Charles who would figure a way out, Charles who would know the best thing to do in the worst situation you could find yourself in. But now Charles was unable to stand upright, undone by the sight of all that blood, and Aidan had no idea what to do.

Aidan yanked Charles away from the bloody scene and slapped him hard across the face. When Charles looked more focused, Aidan stared him in the eye and said, "We gotta go, *now*," and pulled him across the street. Walking even a few steps seemed to bring Charles around, and by the time they reached the other side of the street, he no longer needed Aidan's support. *All right*, thought Aidan, *now we'll get out of here, and Charles will feel right as rain and he will know what we have to do next.*

Just then, Aidan heard a woman scream from across the street. He spun around to face her even as he realized that this was exactly the wrong thing to do. She was standing in a doorway a few feet from where the man lay in his own blood, her hands to her face, mouth open. The woman looked up and locked eyes with Aidan, who was partially blocking her view of Charles. Aidan felt Charles tug hard on his arm, and they both bolted down the narrow street, turning the corner at full speed, but not fast enough to avoid hearing the woman cry out, "Lord in heaven, he's *dead!*"

They ran a few blocks, and then Charles pulled Aidan into an alley where they stopped to catch their breath. In their only lucky break of the night, they encountered no police officers or sober citizens in the blocks they ran.

"Jaysus fergive us, Charles, but what the hell are we gonna do?"

asked Aidan as he took off his cap and wiped his brow. He looked as if he were trying very hard not to cry.

"I've got a plan," Charles said evenly as he took deep breaths—but he didn't. He felt confident, however, that he would soon come up with one, and Aidan needed to think there was a plan so he didn't fall apart. Looking at Aidan straight now, he saw what their first step needed to be. "Sully, we gotta change these shirts," he said, and Aidan looked down to see what Charles saw. There were two smeared, bloody handprints on the front of Aidan's shirt, as if the man had grabbed him from behind, although Charles figured that Aidan must have wiped his own hands on his shirt without realizing it. Charles's shirt was even bloodier.

"All right, we go to your place, and you grab us a couple of shirts." It wasn't much of a plan, but Charles had from here until Chambers Street to come up with the next step.

When they reached Aidan's building, they went around back and plucked two shirts off the clotheslines that were about the right size. Aidan went to stuff the bloody shirts in the tenement's trash barrel, but Charles grabbed them.

"I'll get rid of these. You don't want these near your place," said Charles, and Aidan nodded stupidly. "Okay," he continued, "you wanna stay low tomorrow—don't go out and black no boots or nothin', no runs to the store for your ma. Tell her you ain't feeling good if you hafta. Then meet me . . ." Charles stopped to think. "There's a pawn shop right on Fulton near Richmond. Tomorrow, four o'clock."

"Why are we going to the waterfront?"

"Because we're gonna go talk to Bess."

CHAPTER 12

It was early spring of the prior year, right before his time in reform school, when Charles met Bess for the first time. She had long been a fixture down by the waterfront, as long as any prostitute lasted before succumbing to violence or disease or just becoming used up. Bess's most marketable attributes were her long golden hair and her impressive bosom, which made up for a face that, in repose, was hard and hatchet-like, with beady eyes and a straight, grim line for a mouth.

In her neighborhood, those who could not command much of a rate used public places to ply their trade. Almost everyone else in the business was associated with a brothel, but a few, such as Bess, ran their own business out of their tenements with select repeat customers.

Bess was smarter than the average whore, so it came as a surprise when she found herself in a delicate situation against which she had taken every precaution. Despite her preventive measures—the insertion of both a copper penny and a sponge soaked in tansy oil prior to every work night—her predicament was undeniable.

One night not long after Bess's discovery, Charles darted into the backyard of a tenement to evade an older boy trying to establish some ground rules about thieving territory. He went rooting around near the fence for something to hide behind and found a pile of clothes that he could drape over himself, but when he went to shake them out to eject any resident vermin, he found that there was a woman's body still wearing them. A faint groan emanated from the heap of fabric.

While he was trying to decide what to do next, he heard a thin and steely command: "Help me up."

Had she asked him rather than told him, had she sounded pathetic and weak, Charles might have responded differently, but he found himself bending to grab her arm and pull her up before he could even consider any other response. As she stood and leaned on Charles, a putrid smell wafted up from her body, and Charles gagged.

Following her directions, he helped her up the one flight of stairs to her tenement and settled her on her bed. Given the grimy neighborhood, this room was decorated in a surprisingly fine style. Sheer fabric was strung from the tops of the four-poster bed, and a stuffed chair was covered with a fancy brocade. There was color everywhere, from the garnet bed covering to the saffron chair to the woman's deep violet skirts. He felt sure he had never seen fabrics in these colors. Even in the limited lamplight of the room, the effect was dazzling.

"What's your name?" asked the woman, although it sounded more like a statement than a question.

Charles looked over at her and was unsettled to see a beautiful head of golden hair piled above a face that could have belonged to a drill sergeant.

"Charles," he answered, unconsciously straightening his posture.

"Well, Charles, it was lucky for me that you come along when you did. And now I'm gonna ask you to do somethin' else for me." She paused to take a couple of breaths, and her eyelids fluttered with pain. "I got a situation that old Doc Pearson helped me out with, or so he told me, but seems he made things precious worse.

The stink of these bloody rags got so close as I had to put 'em out in the yard barrel, which is where you found me. Guess as I overestimated my ability to haul my arse back up the stairs." She reached for a silver flask on the table next to the bed and took a sip with a trembling hand, but to Charles she seemed as sober as a judge, and he thought whatever was in the flask wasn't doing much to numb her pain.

"So I need you to run me a little errand, Charles, and I'm prepared to pay you somewhat generous. I need you to track down that bastard Pearson and bring 'im here, irregardless of how drunk he is." She fumbled for her purse in the night table drawer. "There's two grog shops on Richmond where he parks his arse, one's the Lion Arms, and two doors down is the Wheel and Rudder. Always with the top hat, likes to fancy himself a bit of a dandy, and carries his black bag with him, advertisin' his callin'." She took a five- and a ten-dollar bill out of her purse and closed it.

"This fiver will be right here waitin' for you, free 'n clear. But Pearson ain't gonna come unless I pay him up front, so I gotta trust you with this sawbuck." She handed him the ten-dollar bill. "Now, I ain't got no fancy education, but even I can figger that sawbuck is worth more'n that fiver. So I send you outta here, most would keep walkin'. You might be the type that'd sell your granny for less. But Charles, I wouldn't send for that bastard Pearson unless I had one foot in the grave. So if you keep walkin', you might as well put a gun to my head and pull the trigger." She held out the ten-dollar bill for him to take.

He looked into her face, set like stone against the pain. As he approached her bed, he could smell the stench he'd encountered when he first helped her up. He could see the blond tendrils that had escaped from her piled hair and were now plastered darkly to her sweating temples. He took the money from her without looking away from her eyes.

"I'm Bess," she said.

~

Once Charles was out in the street, he looked at the bill in the yellow gaslight. It was the biggest denomination he had ever held. For how long could this feed him?

Charles was disoriented after his zigzag escape from the boy chasing him, so he randomly chose a direction that he hoped would lead him to a place he would recognize. In a few blocks, he came upon Richmond Street, where he paused. When he left Bess's building, he could have walked the other way and never have encountered Richmond Street. And yet he had walked in this direction.

He headed uphill and soon came upon the Wheel and Rudder.

The bartender pointed out Doc Pearson when Charles asked for him, a portly man with watery eyes sitting with two other men, and indeed Charles could now see his black bag parked next to his chair.

"Doc Pearson?"

"Yes, my boy, how can I be of assistance?" he inquired without looking at Charles as he took a sip of whiskey from a smudged glass.

"Bess needs ya. Says you gotta come. I got your pay up front she gave me."

"Bess . . . yes. Treated her recently for some female complaints. I hear, by the by, however, that there are few complaints about her from the male populace!" Pearson and his companions found this uproarious.

By the time their laughter had died back, Pearson seemed to have forgotten that Charles was standing beside him. "Bess is poorly," Charles stated, "and you gotta come now." He pulled out the ten-dollar bill and waved it in front of Pearson's face.

"Well, gentlemen," said Pearson after he downed the last of his whiskey in one gulp, "it appears that duty calls." He went to snatch the bill suspended before him, but he grabbed thin air as Charles pulled it just out of his reach. "Bess said to pay you when we get there," Charles improvised.

Pearson donned his top hat and followed Charles out of the saloon, weaving slightly.

Bess had fallen asleep while they were gone, but she roused as they entered her rooms. Pearson approached her bed. She stared at him with malice.

"Young Bess, it would appear you have not been taking care of yourself," he said as he placed his bag at the foot of her bed and fumbled with the clasp.

"Pearson, you bastard, this is your doing, and don't pretend it ain't," she said through clenched teeth.

"That is a matter of opinion, but what is a matter of pure fact is that you will receive no further treatment without further payment, and your young squire here refused to hand over my fee until we were standing before you. He's a mistrusting sort." Charles handed over the bill, and Pearson looked at it tenderly before pocketing it. Addressing Charles as he swayed, he said, "All right, young street Arab, it's time you crawled back into the hole from whence you came. Be off."

Bess reached under her pillow and drew out the five-dollar bill. When Charles went to take the money, she didn't release her grip on it right away, and Charles looked up to find her locking eyes with him. She held on to the bill for a heartbeat and then let it go.

One night a week or two later, Charles saw Bess on the street.

"Well if it ain't my young squire," she said as she folded her arms in front of her.

"Doc Pearson fixed you up, I can see."

"Lucky he didn't finish me off. I ain't exactly sure what he done, and he let me know I was too ignorant for him to bother explainin', but at least he give me some laudanum for the pain. But the hell with him. I'm back to work, and it's you I owe."

"You don't owe me nothin'—you paid me a fiver, remember?"

"I'd like to think my life's worth a little more'n a fiver, Charles." She started to walk away, but after a step, she turned back. "You come see me if you need some help. I know some people in this town," she said a little cryptically, and the flat line that was her mouth curled up on one side in what might have been a smile.

When Aidan woke up the day after that bloody night with the beautiful knife, at first he didn't remember anything, and it seemed like any other morning. But as he lay on his mattress, it came back to him in a rush, and his stomach started to hurt. He told Maeve he must've eaten some bad oysters last night and stayed curled up in bed for most of the morning, listening to the light rain hitting the windows. He tortured himself by replaying last night's events over and over in his mind. Of particular agony was the image of his hand pulling the knife out of the man's belly, how there was some initial resistance but then it slid out with ease, as if it were greased, and of all the blood that flowed out after it. How could he have thought that removing the knife would give the man relief, make his wound better in some way? But he hadn't been thinking straight. How stupid it seemed now. He might as well have slit the man's throat while he was at it.

The rain stopped sometime in the afternoon, and after an eternity, the hour to meet Charles arrived.

When Bess answered the door, she looked at Aidan skeptically. "Your note didn't say nothin' about bringin' 'round your friend here."

"We're in the fix together. This here's Aidan," said Charles as he jerked his thumb over his shoulder.

"Well. Come on." She moved away from the doorway to admit them.

Now that the rain had passed, the sun streamed in through Bess's windows. The raindrops on the windows glittered like crystal, and all of Bess's colorful fabrics were glowing. Aidan was struck stupid by the sight. The only other place he'd seen colors like this was the stained glass in St. Joseph's with the morning sun behind it, back when Maeve was well and would take him and Ella to church.

Charles stood with his cap in his hands, looking down as he fiddled with the brim, rubbing the edge where it had started to fray.

"So let me speed this up 'fore I grow old," Bess said as she settled herself in the saffron-colored chair. "You two are in some trouble. I trust it ain't that the truant officer pinched ya."

"We rolled some swell and ended up killin' him," Charles said in a rush.

She stared at them, and for a moment it looked as if she were going to laugh, but if that had been her impulse, it died in her before it came to fruition. "How the hell did you two kill a man?" she asked incredulously.

"He had a knife," Charles mumbled.

"He pulled a knife on ya? Why, that's self-defense, a nasty mug pullin' a knife on two innocent little pups. Ain't no judge—"

"Bess," Charles stopped her. "He was out cold, and I took his knife outta his pocket and splayed it to show Aidan, and I fell on him."

Bess considered this for a moment. "You said he was a swell— you sure 'bout that?"

"He was dressed pretty fine and had this knife like I ain't never seen, plus he had this." Charles took the money clip out of his pocket and held it out to Bess.

From the moment they entered Bess's rooms, Aidan had been distracted by the surroundings. The vibrant colors, the smell of perfume, and just the idea of being in a prostitute's bedroom—the very room where she earned her living, that very bed!—not to mention the association with St. Joseph's—it all made his head spin. To add to the distraction, in the afternoon August heat, Bess was wearing only a lace-trimmed chemise and satin corset on top, and just her under-petticoat below. He could neither look at her sizable bosom nor avert his gaze very far from it. All these elements caused Aidan to only half-hear the conversation between Bess and Charles, despite its importance to his future, but when Charles produced the money clip, he snapped out of his fog.

He stared at Charles. "You didn't say nothin' about no money."

"Yeah, well, I was too busy worrying about the bloody handprints on your shirt. Jesus, Sully," Charles huffed.

Bess took the money clip and said, "Christ, you two are like an old married couple." She turned the clip over in her hand, and Aidan could see some sort of encrusted jewels winking in the sunlight. She tossed it back to Charles. "That clip weren't bought at no five-and-dime. D'ja count it?"

"Ninety-seven," said Charles without emotion.

Aidan was dumfounded. "You couldn't remember to tell me about ninety-seven dollars?"

"Sully, for the love of Christ, shut yer clam hole."

Bess picked up a fan from the side table and began to fan herself languidly. "So the bad news is that I don't know nobody that can get you off for murder. You grab a loaf of bread, even steal a lady's pocketbook, maybe I know somebody could get you probation, keep you outta reform school. But killing a mug, even a tramp, I don't got no favors to call in like that, and if I did, I'd save 'em for myself. And your mug weren't no tramp. The good news is that you got some scratch, which is gonna help you get outta town."

"Outta town?" Aidan repeated. "We gotta leave?"

Charles turned to Aidan. "What did you think? Do you think we're gonna wait around and hope that lady that spotted you ain't gonna tell the cops?"

"Someone spotted ya?" interjected Bess. "This story just keeps gettin' better, don't it? Aidan, Sully, whatever they call ya, you'd do good to face the fact that you're gonna be leavin' city limits. Question is, are you goin' to Westboro, or someplace where they don't use the strap?"

Aidan walked over to the window to press his forehead against the pane. This was just too much to fit in his head. He looked down on the street and saw the ash man and his horse-drawn cart. The man emptied two ash barrels into the cart, neither the man nor the horse seeming to mind the billowing cloud that plumed up with these deposits. They were both coated with a fine layer of ash. The man spoke into the horse's ear, and the horse moved a few yards to the entrance of the next building, where there were three more ash cans. Aidan admired how the man didn't need to touch the horse to get it to move along. He wanted to be that man, to trade places with him, so that he could be an old ash-covered worker with a steady job and a horse that would listen to him, and the old man would have to be an eleven-year-old boy who had killed a rich swell.

"I know we gotta leave," Charles said to Bess earnestly. "I been to Westboro, and I'll drown myself in the harbor before I go back there. But I don't know where to go. That's where I was hopin' you could help out."

Bess thought for a moment as she fanned herself. "How old are the pair of ya?"

"I'm twelve, and he's almost."

After a pause, Bess walked into her tiny kitchen and faced its window. Arms crossed, she looked out at the brick wall of the tenement next door. The boys fidgeted in the main room, unsure of how much time Bess would need in the kitchen to devise what they hoped would be their salvation.

After a while, she came out of the kitchen. "I think I got an idea. I ain't sure it's gonna work, but I'll wager that you ain't got a better plan." She resettled herself on the saffron chair. "It's gonna require that you two are brothers, I'll say that." The boys looked at each other. Aidan shrugged. They looked back at Bess, ready to go forward.

"And his name," she said, turning her gaze to Aidan, "ain't gonna do. Don't know how he ended up with that one anyway — don't look like there's a drop of Irish blood in 'im."

Charles said, "He's already got his cover name for when he wants to pass—it's Arthur."

"That'll do. Charles and Arthur . . . it's Wheeler, right?"

"Yep," Charles said with a look of fledgling hope on his face.

"But you spent time up in Westboro. They got a record of you up there, can't be connected to that. We'll change Wheeler to . . . Weston. Charles and Arthur Weston."

Aidan heard all this as if he were in a dream, the kind where events are happening all around you that you can't influence, where you reach out to grab someone's shoulder and your hand goes right through.

Bess said, "I need a little time to think about it. You two clear out of here for a little while. Leave that clip somewhere somebody's gonna find it. Then use some of that wad—not too much—to go get yourselves some cheap clothes, something that looks different than whatcha got on, or really whatcha had on last night. Looks like anything clean and new will be a damn good disguise. Come back half past five." Bess stood up from her chair.

"We can't pawn the clip?" asked Aidan.

"Well, you can if you're keen on tipping off the police," she said humorlessly. She looked at him as if he were a friendly dog that was proving too stupid to train.

Charles grabbed Aidan by the arm and pulled him toward the door. "Half five, Bess, we'll be back," and they were gone.

When they reached the sidewalk, Aidan turned on Charles. "You know, you coulda told me your plan included me leavin' home. Leavin' my sick ma and my baby sister."

"Yeah, and how would that have made anything any better?" Charles shot back.

Aidan kicked a bottle on the sidewalk, but it just spun in a circle, refusing to smash against the base of the gaslight as he had intended. "Easy for you—what are you leavin', your favorite alley? You say that we gotta leave like it's *nothin'*!"

Charles stopped in his tracks, and Aidan stopped alongside him. "Fine. I'll go. You stay. Let me know if they dust off the Sweatbox up in Westboro." Charles resumed walking.

In a flash, Aidan's anger ebbed away, replaced by the reality of the trouble they were in and the fear that Charles would leave him to fend for himself. "No, wait," he said as he caught up to Charles. "All right, you're right, we need to leave. But for how long? And what am I gonna tell my ma?"

"I don't got them answers yet. Let's just wait to hear Bess's plan. Then we'll figger it out."

Charles ducked into the next alley and left the clip on top of a barrel. When he emerged, they looked around for a place that sold ready-made clothing. By the time they walked out of the shop, it was time to head back to Bess's.

She let them in and handed Charles a note in an envelope. "Bring this to Reverend Stryker at the Old South Church. Don't give it to anyone but him. You." She pointed to Aidan. "You got an address?"

"Chambers Street, Number 47," he said.

"I'll send a note when it's all set up. In the meantime, wash your faces, for Chrissake, and get a haircut, short. And stay out of trouble, and out of sight." She stood there, stonefaced, and said nothing more, and the boys realized that they were being dismissed.

～

As the boys began the long walk to Back Bay, Charles realized the envelope Bess had given him was not sealed, and he showed Aidan.

"Read it," urged Aidan, and Charles read aloud as they walked. It began without a greeting:

> *For as long as we have been acquainted, I have not once asked for a favor, but I find myself now in need of one. Two brothers, ages eleven and twelve, have recently become orphans—*

"Orphans, huh?" interrupted Aidan.

"You'll get used to it," said Charles, and he continued:

> *and without strong guidance from the home, they have fallen into some trouble. In this matter, I need your help before they fall farther. If you would come to my home this evening, I should like to discuss this in detail and, I hope, convince you of the worthiness of my cause.*
> *B.*

"Don't tell us much, do it?" Charles said as he folded the note and put it back in the envelope. "Other than wherever we're goin', we're brothers, and we got no parents."

"She ain't lyin' about the fallin' into trouble part," Aidan observed.

"You know what?" asked Charles. "That's some pretty fine writin' for one of her kind, don't you think? Bet most of these whores down here can't spell more'n their name." The penmanship was a little shaky, with some blobs of ink at the end of a few words, but there were no spelling mistakes, and the hand was fine and feminine.

"Maybe one day she could be something else, get outta here," said Aidan.

"Nah. Once you start working down on the waterfront, you're tainted. Ain't no one gonna take ya."

CHAPTER 13

IN LESS THAN A WEEK, EVERYTHING WAS IN PLACE.

After delivering the note to Reverend Stryker, the waiting began. They didn't see each other except when Charles would come around Aidan's tenement once a day to see if Bess had sent a message. On the third day, Aidan produced a note that simply read:

Come at noon tomorrow. B.

Bess outlined the plan from her saffron armchair.

"You two are brothers, recently orphaned. Your family minister appealed to Stryker 'cause Stryker knows the superintendent over at the Boston Farm School. That's your story, and you damn well better remember it. Stryker went to see Bradley two days ago and convinced him to take the two of ya. You're leavin' tomorrow, so tonight you pack up."

"Where is this place?" asked Aidan.

"Thompson Island, out in the harbor."

Island. Harbor. Water. Charles glanced at Aidan. He looked like he'd stopped breathing.

Bess continued, "You two need to spend some time before tomorrow gettin' your story straight. Everything—where you lived, what your ma was like. When you get there, don't be chummy with the other boys, or you'll screw up your story. If you get caught, it's all on you—I ain't associated with this at all, and Stryker will just say some woman pulled the wool over his eyes and disappeared into the wind."

Charles thought about this and said, "So Stryker is just doin' this as a favor to you?"

"That and seventy-five of your dollars that I'm donatin' to the church."

"Seventy-five! That's pretty steep," grumbled Charles.

"I convinced him to take the boat over to see Bradley personally and get him to put you ahead of a bunch of other boys that applied weeks ago. I'd say you got off cheap. Stryker can fix his leaky church roof, and everybody's happy. You ain't gonna need money there anyway. You go to school, you farm, you learn the trades. It's all spelled out for you. You just do what they say, and you'll be fed."

"How do you know about this place?"

Bess got up and walked to the window that looked out onto the street. "I had a nephew. My sister come on hard times and she had to send him there when he was thirteen."

"What's it like?" asked Charles.

Bess ran her finger slowly down the windowpane. "I never seen it. She didn't let me see the boy since he was a tot. Seems I ain't in the right profession. I thought of goin' there anyway to see him, now that he wasn't with her, but he mighta told her. He wouldn't even have knowed who I was."

She spun around and faced Charles, hands on her hips. "You gonna give me seventy-five, or are you gonna take your chances with Boston's Finest? Your funeral."

Charles stood and counted out the bills. After Bess grabbed the money and managed to find a place for it in her already overtaxed corset, she handed him a piece of paper from her writing desk.

"Everything you need—where you gotta be tomorrow and

when," she said. "And there's one more thing. This place, this Bradley—he don't take the bad ones. Boys as done even some stealin', they don't get in. They wanna get these boys before they get tainted on the streets. So they hear about your rollin' a drunk, doin' time in Westboro, it's all over. You see? It's more than just keepin' a secret about knifin' that swell. You gotta keep your whole past a secret."

Charles looked over at Aidan, who was staring off into space with glassy eyes. He punched him in the arm, and Aidan stood, looking a little disoriented.

When they reached the door, Bess said, "Good luck on ya. Don't bungle this."

Charles ducked his head a bit. "Bess, I dunno what to say but thanks. You're savin' our lives."

"Well, now we're even, ain't we?" she said neutrally.

As Aidan shuffled past her, he looked at her bashfully and said, "Thanks, Bess."

Bess looked at him as if she might revise her untrainable-puppy conclusion, but she said nothing more as they left.

Charles proceeded down the sidewalk with Aidan, his thoughts rising like kneaded dough. An island! That sounded like a grand adventure—coves to explore, rafts to build. They'd have to have sailboats there—why, they probably had to teach sailing, being on an island. And swimming! Walking in the humid August heat, Charles was almost giddy at the thought of jumping off a pier into cool, clear water without commercial boats around to foul it. And food! No more stealing, no more poking around trash barrels. Meals prepared, hot when you sat down—sitting down every day to eat *at a table*, for Chrissakes! And a bed, a real bed, dry even when the rain came down in sheets. The same bed every night, yours, no one having the right to roust you from your spot. And a pillow! The thought of a pillow, his pillow, clean and soft, holding the gentle impression of his head from many previous nights, was perhaps the best part of all. No—who was he kidding? The best part was going to be the food.

He had all but forgotten that Aidan was even walking beside him.

Aidan was so full of things to say to Charles, some contradicting others, that he found he couldn't say anything. There was no way in hell he was going to an island. There was also no way that he would let Charles go and leave him behind. He hated Charles for getting him into this. He knew he had gotten himself into this. He wanted a fresh start far away, but he didn't want to leave Maeve and Ella. Was it crazy to throw his lot in with Charles, and did he even have any choice at this point? And with all that, there was no time to think about any of it. The boat—*A boat! Holy Mother of God!*—left tomorrow morning, and he was sure Charles would be on it. Aidan rubbed his temples as he walked. How could he do this? How could he not?

Aidan glanced at Charles. Whatever he was thinking about was putting a grin across his freckled face. Meeting Aidan's gaze, Charles grabbed him around the shoulders and gave him a joyful squeeze.

Without thinking, Aidan pushed him to the sidewalk, landing Charles on his back.

"A fecking *island*." Aidan stood over him, hands on hips. "Do you have any idea in that tiny knowledge box of yours what this means for me? Do you have your head so far up your arse that you can only think about how grand it will be for you to finally sail the open seas? *I can't do this.*" He was shaking with rage.

Charles started to get up, and Aidan put his boot on Charles's chest, staring down at him in anger, his fists clenched. "Tell me you at least understand this."

Before Charles could respond, they both heard, "And what might be goin' on here, laddies?" They looked up into the face of a curious police officer, and they both paled, suddenly remembering the crime that brought them to this moment.

"My brother here," Charles said, laughing and pushing Aidan's foot aside, "he's got a bit of a temper—ain'tcha, Artie? Thought I was puttin' the moves on his girl, but I swear, officer, she's the one that's sweet on me. That ain't my fault, is it?" He stood and brushed himself off.

"I suppose not. But I won't have you brawlin' on my sidewalk. You take it home to your mam and resolve your differences in her parlor, not here."

"Yessir," Charles said respectfully, and he grabbed Aidan's arm as they departed.

When they looked back and could no longer see the policeman, they both let out a long breath.

"Jaysus," said Aidan.

"We gotta get outta sight. Bess says we have to work out our story—where can we do that?"

"If you're thinkin' about my place, my ma will be there. She ain't goin' out these days." Aidan looked around nervously.

They discussed and rejected all the public places they normally frequented.

Aidan finally said, "How about wherever you slept last night?" Lately Aidan had started wondering, as he lay in his bed at night, where Charles was, what he was lying on, what he was covering himself with when it was raining.

"Yeah, all right," agreed Charles, though clearly only for lack of a better idea. They reversed course and ended up in an alley on a street that was unfamiliar to Aidan. On the way, Charles had picked up some small stones and put them in his pocket.

"Why the stones?" asked Aidan.

"You'll see."

About halfway down the alley, Charles stopped. "Home sweet home. Well, at least for the past couple of nights."

Aidan looked around. There was an old straw mattress, a little dirty but in surprisingly good shape, wedged between two ash barrels. Charles sat on one end and gestured for Aidan to sit on the other.

"Wonder why someone got rid of this mattress," Aidan wondered out loud.

"Could have somethin' to do with the big blood stain on the other side."

Aidan felt a little ill.

"Okay," said Charles as he made himself more comfortable, "before we get into gettin' our story straight, let's put this water thing to bed. These islands, out in the harbor, they're bigger than you're thinkin'." In truth, Charles had no idea how big the Harbor Islands were or specifically how big Thompson was, but he figured that it had to be pretty big to have a school and a farm—plus, he knew he had to be completely confident with Aidan to get him past this water problem, so he had no qualms about filling the gaps in his knowledge with whatever came into his head. "So we get there, and you can stay far, far away from the shoreline. It'll be just like Boston—you know there's water nearby, but you don't hafta get near it, right?"

Aidan nodded.

"So all you gotta do," continued Charles, "is just get there. Now this is one short trip, I'll tell you." Never having been on this trip or even in a boat, Charles nevertheless was sure of this fact because he had seen Thompson from the harbor on clear days. When he'd first started spending his leisure time on the docks, he had asked some laborers there about the landmass he could see in the distance, and one of them had eventually stopped working to rest his back and pointed out Thompson, only a mile away.

"How long are we in the boat?" asked Aidan anxiously.

"Why, you'll be there before you know it! And the minute we step onto that island, ain't no Boston cops gonna be spotting us. Hell, there ain't no cops there at all!" This seemed like a pretty safe guess. "Just think about it, Sully—no more looking over your shoulder, no more creepin' around at night. We can just do what you're supposed to be doin' when you're twelve! I bet they have a baseball team! Maybe they even grow all them pretty flowers you love so much in the Public Garden!"

In one fluid motion, Charles reached into his pocket, drew out his slingshot and a stone, loaded it, and hit a rat that Aidan hadn't even noticed was sniffing near his shoe. The rat squeaked and ran off, almost before Aidan realized what had happened.

"I see why you picked up them stones," he said with a shudder.

"Okay, so let's figure out who we are now. You and I are brothers. Of course, I'm the elder. When's your birthday?"

"Eighteenth of November, '77."

Charles counted on his fingers. "Irish twins," he concluded with a grin. "Lucky you ain't closer to my age, then we'd have to change your birthday. Okay, our ma's name is Margaret."

"Not Maeve, huh?"

"Sully, we ain't Irish. So we go with my family's names."

"What about something different than either one of our mas, just to be fair?"

"Listen, I'm glad you brung this up. You are a shitty liar, Sullivan, and I am about to teach you how to be a better one."

Aidan didn't even think of protesting. He had never been good at lying point-blank, but he had noticed on many occasions how effortless it seemed for Charles. If there was ever a time when he needed to learn the art of lying, it was now, and he had confidence in his instructor.

"The first trick is to use the truth as much as possible inside your lie. For example, if a copper asks me where I was today and I ain't got a good excuse for today but I had a grand alibi for yester-day, I just tell him about yesterday: 'I went to the Cyclorama today, officer, and all them scenes of Gettysburg was somethin' to see, let me tell you!' Sure it ain't true I done that today, but I just shift the day in my mind, and then if he asks me somethin' else—'And how long was you there for?'—I don't have to think up some new lie. I just tell him the truth. The truth about yesterday, that is. Which brings me to the second trick, which is that you try to start believ-ing your own lie."

"But you know you're lyin'. How can you do that?"

"I can't describe it no better than that. But I think you're gonna be doing this a lot startin' tomorrow. You gotta look people real direct in the eye and tell them a story that some part of you is buyin' into, like it's what you want to believe so much that you start thinkin' it's true."

"I dunno."

"You're gonna know, all right. You're gonna get a lot of practice."

Aidan and Charles talked on and on for hours, trying to think of every detail of their fictitious lives as brothers—where they lived, what they did for Christmas, where they went to church, who did what chores. Aidan got used to the occasional slingshot attacks on the rats, and after a while, the rhythm of their conversation was unbroken by the whizzing of stones across the alley and the result-ing squeaking and scurrying.

The more they solidified their story, the less solid Aidan's real life seemed. He felt his own history fade away like words written in sand being erased by the incoming tide. Maeve, Ella, St. Joseph's had never happened. He had never taken communion, wasn't even Catholic. His mother had not come from Ireland. He had insisted on keeping Dan Connelly as their mother's suitor after their—Charles's—father had departed, convincing Charles that having an Irishman in the picture would be helpful. That way, if Aidan were to ever let anything Irish or Catholic leak out accidentally, they could blame it on Dan's influence. They also kept Aidan's apartment in their history, since Charles had been inside it but Aidan had never seen the interior of where Charles lived. But not much else of Aidan's past survived the cut. He began to miss Maeve and Ella even though he had not left town yet.

After a while, the boys got hungry. Charles left to buy some food, and when he came back with their supper, Aidan asked, "How much money you got left?"

"Had a little before we acquired that money clip, so even after we had to give all that to Bess, I still got about twenty two dollars."

"Charles, I need twenty of that."

"Very funny, Sully."

"I ain't pullin' your leg. First off, you ain't never give me my cut of the ninety-seven. And second, what are you gonna need with all that money at the school? Like Bess said, we'll be eatin' for free."

"So what do *you* need it for?"

"I ain't takin' it to the island. Listen, I am trustin' you eight ways to Sunday for this whole thing. Now you gotta trust me that I need this for somethin' important."

Charles stared at Aidan for a few moments. Then he dug the money out of his pocket and gave it to him.

As they started to eat, Charles said, "You know, for a minute I thought Bess was gonna say that I needed to change my first name too."

"I'm glad she didn't," Aidan said with his mouth full. He swallowed before continuing. "I got enough stuff to keep in my head without havin' to remember to call you somethin' else."

"But if I had to, I'd stick with my initials. They was meant to be—the pocketknife tells me so." Charles had told Aidan of the pocketknife story and its initials during one of their many times at Rosen's.

"So instead of Charles, you might be a . . . Chester?" suggested Aidan.

"Not on your life."

"Clarence?"

"Do I really look like a Clarence?" Charles chewed a while. "I got it. Chauncy."

"What the hell is the difference between Chauncy and Clarence?"

"Chauncy, why that's the name of a man that's gonna go places. You see, Chauncy's strollin' down the Commonwealth Mall linkin' arms with a Lillian or a Josephine. He's always wearin' a top hat—he don't even own no bowler. He's a man of business, a tycoon or a bank president or a lawyer. He's got power, so much that he ain't gotta show it—people can just see it comin' off him like a vapor. *That's* Chauncy for ya. And Clarence, he's the clerk in Chauncy's office that's always tippin' over the ink pot by accident, wreckin' all the paperwork."

"Yeah, well that cap of yours ain't no top hat, my friend," Aidan pointed out, though he was taken with the picture Charles had painted.

"Well, I ain't grown yet, but maybe I'll change my name when I am. With a name like Chauncy, I could see where I'm going," said Charles with a grin. "Chauncy Weston. He'd own a whole block in this town."

"So that would make me Arthur Weston, brother of that rich son-of-a-bitch."

"Play your cards right, and I'll let you live in my brownstone over on Marlborough. That is, until we find us some beautiful wives. Then you gotta get your own place."

"It's a deal," said Aidan, and they shook on it.

Aidan went home after it got dark and they couldn't think of anything more to populate their new collective history. As they had planned and horse-traded the details of their fictional past, it had started to seem like an adventure to Aidan, and he'd become relaxed, almost giddy, with any thoughts of their crime pushed to the furthest corner of his mind. But his high spirits dribbled away on his walk home. By the time he reached his front stoop, he could barely lift his feet to clear the steps.

Maeve and Ella were propped up in their bed, Maeve trying to help Ella sound out the words in a book between bouts of coughing. "Smart as a whip, that one," Maeve said to Aidan as Ella went off to use the toilet in the hall. "Sure is lookin' forward to startin' at yer school in the fall. She told me today how you're going to walk her to school on the first day." She smiled and held Aidan's hand as he sat beside her on the bed. "And now why might you be lookin' so down in the gutter? 'Fraid Ella will do better than you at school, eh?"

Aidan managed a weak smile.

"Oh, that won't do at all. Ya better tell me what's on your mind before your face sticks that way."

"Well, it's good news, actually."

"Sure and I could tell that by the way you look," Maeve said dubiously.

"I got a job." Aidan concentrated on remembering the explanation that he and Charles had devised that afternoon. "A really good job. As an apprentice to a cabinetmaker. Won't make money for a while, but he's gonna put me up. Then after a year, I'll start pullin' a salary, a small one. But it's in New York. I'm leavin' tomorrow, Ma." Aidan couldn't continue with the rest of the details he and Charles had discussed. He had never lied quite like this to his mother, and he found he could not look her in the eye.

Maeve lay against her pillow for a while, looking at Aidan not looking at her. For once her concentration was not broken by her hacking cough, though Aidan wished for any interruption at this point. Finally she said, "I see."

Aidan couldn't respond.

She put her hand on his cheek and turned his head toward her.

"I thought I had at least two more years until you left to find your way in the world. But I can see that you're not going to wait until you're fourteen like most boys, are ya now?"

"I can't, Ma. I mean, I can't miss this opportunity, you know." Aidan could feel a prickle of fresh sweat under his collar.

He looked at his mother, lying in bed. Her skin was almost the color of the pillow. He realized he hadn't paid much attention to her or Ella in the past week, since that night when he pulled the knife out of that man's belly. But if he were being honest with himself, it had been much longer than that since he'd thought about his family except to wonder whether he was bringing enough money home for them. And now there was no more time; he'd wasted it all. Tears pooled in his eyes, and he felt on the verge of confessing everything to his mother, the dam of lies crumbling under the rushing waters of the truth.

Just then Ella came running into the bedroom and scampered up onto the bed. "Them Rubinowitz boys was all lined up for the toilet—I nearly wet meself waitin'!" She crawled next to Maeve and clung to her despite the heat.

Aidan lay down next to Ella, sandwiching her between himself and Maeve. "Ma," he said quietly, "tell us about growin' up in Ireland."

And so Maeve told the old stories that both her children had heard many times, but this time, Aidan asked questions—"How old was the dog?" "Was Uncle Liam married yet?" "What happened to the bicycle?"—and this caused Maeve to remember some stories she hadn't told before. Ella fell asleep, but Maeve kept telling stories, and Aidan kept listening and asking questions until after midnight. Maeve finally fell asleep in the middle of telling the story about the old tomcat in the pub, and Aidan kissed her and Ella before he left the room.

He sat for a long time at the kitchen table with a piece of cheap stationery in front of him. Maeve always kept a few sheets with matching envelopes in the kitchen drawer, though this was the first time that Aidan had cause to use one. When he had worked out in his mind what to write, how to say what needed to be said without telling any more lies, it was only a few sentences.

> *Dear Mrs. McGarrity,*
> *I am leeving this morning and I hope to better myself by doing it. I can't ern no more money for my ma for a whyle. Please take care of her and Ella. I will come back when I can.*
> *Aidan Sullivan*

He folded the note up with the twenty dollars he'd taken from Charles, sealed it all in the envelope, and slipped it under the McGarritys' door. Then he climbed into his bed and cried as quietly as he could.

In the morning, Aidan woke before Maeve or Ella and packed the few things he needed, All of his clothes fit in a large flour sack, and besides that, he didn't have much else: a harmonica Dan Connelly had given him for one of his birthdays, a baseball glove also from Dan, a few other odds and ends. He retrieved the baby blanket from underneath his mattress and shoved it to the bottom of the sack.

When Maeve woke, she gathered all her strength and cooked Aidan a large breakfast and packed up some cold ham and biscuits in wax paper for later in the day. They didn't talk much over their meal. After the eating was done, they hugged their teacups in a silence broken only by Maeve's rag-muffled coughs.

Finally Maeve said, "I been thinkin' of all the boys I know that left to go apprentice. Minnie's boy Frankie, he went with that cooper. And Patrick Moran with the printer. Now Patrick sends home a pretty penny to his ma. But they was fourteen, finished with schoolin'. I know you been made to grow up too quick on account of me being sick. I knew for a while now that you would go. But I thought I had more time." She pressed her apron into the corner of one eye, but her voice was steady.

"Ma, I'm comin' back. I don't know when, but this ain't good-bye forever." Aidan gripped her hand but couldn't look her in the eye. When *would* he be back? Would his troubles just blow over in time? Would he have to wait until his appearance changed—till he shot up a few inches, grew a beard? None of his questions had answers. But he recalled what Charles had said about lying: You had to look the person in the eye and start believing what you were saying. "We will be together again, Ma. I am coming back," he said with conviction, and he locked eyes with Maeve.

And Maeve was comforted; Aidan could see she did believe him. And seeing her belief, he believed it too.

PART II
Island

Main Building
Boston Farm School, Thompson Island

CHAPTER 14

SUPERINTENDENT CHARLES H. BRADLEY SAT AT HIS BIRD'S-EYE maple desk, gluing newspaper clippings into his leather-bound scrapbook. He carefully applied the thinnest sheen of mucilage to the next clipping—just a small paragraph, only as big as two postage stamps—and placed it squarely on a new page. After fanning it a bit with his hand to speed the drying of the glue, he uncapped his fountain pen and made a note in his tiny, spidery hand, squeezed into the margin above the paragraph: *Boston Herald, August 18, 1889.* Merely a mention of the school band playing at Faneuil Hall last week, entertaining visitors from many states, undeterred by the heat and humidity even in their high-collared uniforms. But Bradley clipped and secured every printed mention of his school, no matter how brief, and had done so since his arrival eighteen months earlier.

It was understandable that Bradley thought of it as his school, since his authority was absolute and there was no other industry on the island. Certainly he answered to the board of trustees—but unlike most other schools, the Farm School was supported entirely by charitable donations, so he was beholden to no one in government. It was this fact, more than any other, that had inspired him to leave his post at the State Primary School in western Massachusetts and move here with Mary. It was Mary who had first pointed out the advantage of that freedom, how they could be liberated from the Commonwealth's purse strings and do what was in the best interest of the boys.

Ah, Mary! What had he done, he asked himself (and not for the first time), to deserve the blessing of marrying Mary Chilton Brewster? No one else had ever understood his passion for education. Bradley's father and mother were Vermont farmers and had been surprised to learn that their only son was not interested in a life of agriculture. But when Bradley met Mary at the State Primary School, for the first time he'd been able to speak without restraint about the challenge and thrill of forming young minds, of setting boys on the path of virtue and temperance and productivity, of steering them away from the temptations and evils of city life. Instead of receiving diplomatic murmurs of agreement when expressing these views, he was charmed to find that Mary returned his enthusiasm note for note. It was obvious to Bradley from the first of these conversations with Mary that he would marry her.

As Bradley looked up from his scrapbook, movement at the bottom of the hill caught his eye through the window. When he first was given a tour of the building, it puzzled him that of all the rooms, it was this one that was the superintendent's office. Others were grander or centrally located. But the first time he sat at the desk, the reason became clear: From his seat, he had a perfect view of the curving road leading down the steep hill to the wharf, and of the wharf itself, which was the official entry point to the island. From here he could see everything arriving onto the island and everything leaving it, and so it was that he saw the two new boys disembarking the steamer.

An unsettling feeling crept up on Bradley as he watched the two boys sling their sacks over their shoulders. The meeting with Reverend Stryker last week had been odd, though Bradley couldn't put his finger on why. It was not the first time applicants had been accepted before the board had a chance to meet; the superintendent could approve applicants if he deemed there to be urgency in removing the boys from a dangerous environment. And certainly Stryker portrayed the situation of these boys in those terms—their only remaining parent just recently passing, the concern that they would quickly fall into the bad elements of their neighborhood. Last fall, Stryker had made a similar plea on behalf of Francis Burr, who now had the highest grades in the Second Class and was looking likely to win the flower garden prize next month.

And yet . . . the Burr family had been in Stryker's congregation for years, while these Weston boys belonged to a different church with a different minister. As Stryker explained it, this minister had come to him, knowing that he had arranged for the placement of Francis, and had begged him to make the appeal to Bradley. It all made sense, and it so happened that the boy at the top of the admissions list had a mother that seemed a bit ambivalent about sending her boy off. She was the overprotective type, in Bradley's estimation, and was likely to want to take her boy back at the slightest change in her financial situation, regardless of the contract she would be required to sign—relinquishing all claims to her son until he was placed out after graduation—before they accepted the boy. Bradley had been struggling with this application and what his recommendation to the board would be on the very day that Stryker came to call. Accepting two boys at this point would put them one over their limit of one hundred students, but Will Thayer would be leaving next week for his apprenticeship at the telegraph company. So what was the problem?

Perhaps the problem was with Stryker himself, thought Bradley. Stryker had been a visiting minister on Sunday mornings since before Bradley's tenure, and in comparison with the other visiting ministers, he struck Bradley as . . . what? Disingenuous? That was too strong a word. But maybe not as . . . holy as one might expect. Something about his demeanor was just a little more secular than seemed proper for his position. And yet Bradley really had no choice but to welcome him into both the chapel and the office. Stryker had a wealthy congregation, several members of which were substantial donors to the Farm School.

Bradley pushed his meeting with Stryker from his mind, as it seemed a puzzle for which he could find no answer. As was his habit when he was unsettled, he turned his mind to the thing of which he was sure: the boys at the school. The boys were all. They were why he rose in the morning, were usually the last thing he thought of at night. He felt enormous responsibility for the whole island, as if God himself had entrusted a small nation to his care. He felt humbled by the enormity of the task, and in his prayers at night, when he and Mary knelt together beside their bed, he always asked God to guide him in raising these one hundred young men.

But as with most things in life, God had not given Bradley the most detailed road map. Of all the things for which he was responsible—what the boys would learn in school, what they would eat, how much time would they spend working, sleeping, playing, praying—the one that weighed most heavily on him was the question of which boys would be included in the one hundred on the island. Reading the current literature only served to confuse him more. Was Francis Galton correct with his theory of eugenics, that the elements in the blood predetermine one's character? Or did Charles Loring Brace have the right answer—bringing children out of the city, transporting them on orphan trains to faraway farms so that their characters could be righted by their environment? Everything seemed to hang in the balance. If he believed Galton, he would spend more and more time screening applicants and their parents, looking to exclude those whose heredity would thwart any attempt to produce an upstanding citizen. If he believed Brace, he would simply accept the most needy, perhaps even those who had begun their descent into sin and could benefit most by being set on the path to righteousness.

As the scientific debate raged on, the board was clear in its overall position: acceptable applicants were found among the worthy poor, not the vicious poor. Board members universally agreed that the Farm School's ability to freely select its population was critical to its success. Indeed, at the State Primary School, Bradley had seen at close range how a degenerate youth could poison the ranks. Soon after Bradley first arrived there, a boy named Johnny McFarland slithered into the population and immediately started exerting his influence on his fellow students. A rumor started and persisted that Johnny had spent some formative years in New York's Five Points neighborhood. Theft among the boys rose precipitously, grades dropped, punishments increased. It was as if Johnny were a vector for delinquent behavior, culminating in a fire set in one of the classrooms, which, fortunately, was extinguished before it could spread. He and another boy, Paul Harkins, a boy who had never before been in serious trouble in his three years at the school, were found to be responsible for the fire and were sent to Westboro. Bradley had heard nothing about them after that. But it troubled him now. Had Johnny been doomed to become a criminal because of what his blood contained? Or had his experiences in Five Points, if that rumor were even true, transformed an innocent child into a moral deviant? And what of his partner in crime, Paul? Was he fated to eventually become vicious, or was it only his exposure to Johnny that had infected him?

One thing was clear: Regardless of why boys like Johnny turned out the way they did, to mix them into a population of virtuous boys was to risk, maybe even guarantee, contamination. Public reformatory institutions in Massachusetts had failed again and again in decades past, and they were failing now for this very reason. The Farm School, meanwhile, had prospered, a model of efficiency and control since 1832, primarily because they could afford to pick and choose who would attend. The mantle of responsibility weighed heavily on Bradley. He sometimes felt he was one applicant away from bringing down the school like a house of cards. When that burden felt too great, he had to remind himself: His contract stated that he could personally expel any boy at any time with only a rudimentary explanation to the board, and even that could be given after the boy's departure. So far, he had not had occasion to do this, but he was ever vigilant in examining the ranks for trouble, as if looking for the first signs of cholera or smallpox.

Outside his window, the boys meandered up the hill with Mr. Fielding, the groundskeeper who had brought them across on the steamer. Bradley was irritated to see Fielding pointing to all the buildings that were visible from their path—the boat houses, the small corn house with its upslanted sidewalls, the stock barn, the storage barn. He had spoken to Fielding about this before. The new boys were generally too stunned to take much in, and Bradley had requested that they always be brought to his office posthaste. But Fielding still could not resist giving a tour on the way, his words flowing around the boys and off into the air without leaving any impression.

Just then, Bradley heard a squeal of delight from down the hallway, immediately followed by a shushing. He checked his pocket watch—must be Henry's nap time. He resisted the impulse to walk down the hallway just to see his little face, the face that could now smile back a drooling, one-toothed smile. Mary would not tolerate Bradley throwing him in the air or tickling his round belly before naptime, insisting it took twice as long to get him down when his father did such things.

Henry would have been charming enough to capture Bradley's heart no matter when he was born, but he brought special joy to his father because his birth seemed an omen confirming their decision to come to the island. Bradley and Mary had been married for several years when the Farm School offered him this job, and during those years, they had both been somewhat surprised that Mary had not conceived. To Bradley this seemed all wrong—how could two people who were so committed to the education of children not be able to have children of their own? Try as he might, he could not believe that this would be God's plan for them. It was only weeks after they arrived at the school that Mary found she was with child. Though Henry was obviously conceived on the mainland, in Bradley's mind, it was God's way of telling him that this school, this island, was where he was meant to be.

That Henry was a boy only further strengthened Bradley's belief that God was confirming his choice. How would he have raised a girl on an island of one hundred adolescent boys?

Fielding had finally made his way to the building with the two new boys; Bradley could hear them entering through the main door on the floor below. He closed his scrapbook and stored it in the bottom drawer of his desk, then took a deep breath to push away his irritation at Fielding for taking so long—he had delayed a trip into Boston so that he could meet with these boys when they first arrived. But he needed to put that behind him now because this meeting was critical to getting these two boys off on the right foot.

As he heard the three sets of feet creak up the staircase, he willed himself to conjure up an image of the life these brothers had left behind less than an hour ago. He didn't need to review their file to remember their sad and familiar story: mother recently dead of an unspecified fever, father unknown to his sons, penniless. Before the boys could even get used to a world in which their mother no longer walked and breathed, they had left the only city they had ever known and found themselves in a place that, while a mere mile away, might as well be in the Dakota Territory for all the resemblance it bore to the West End.

Across this desk he had seen the dirty faces of more than a dozen boys during their first hour on the island, and not one of them looked like he fully understood what was going on. And yet Bradley looked forward to these meetings with a feeling that, before coming to the island, he had only experienced kneeling in a pew.

It was the feeling of a new beginning, the first day of a new life. This wave of feeling had come over him at an almost painful level when he first held Henry in his arms and smelled his infant head, a sensation so intense that he had to close his eyes until it receded. All his introductory meetings with new boys since Henry's birth had brought back an unconscious scrap of memory from that day, and sometimes Bradley thought he could smell Henry's sweet baby scent while he was lecturing them, though more often, the smell of the boys themselves would dominate the room.

A knock at his door brought Bradley back to the present. Here he'd been reminiscing about his baby boy and had not quite finished his mental preparation for this meeting. Well, there was no help for it now. He smoothed his vest down, straightened the papers on his desk, and bid Fielding to enter with the new boys.

CHAPTER 15

THE MOMENT AIDAN STEPPED OFF THE WHARF AND ONTO SOLID LAND, he clenched his fists in an effort not to burst into tears of relief. His most fervent desire at that moment was to move away from the beach and curl up on the ground until all his trembling subsided. But before he could act on this desire, Charles had wrapped his arm around his shoulders and was steering him up the gravel path behind the steamboat pilot. The cold sweat that had run from Aidan's forehead into his eyebrows during the tortuous ride now trickled into his eyes, blinding him with its salty sting. His rubbery legs gave out, but Charles tugged him upright before his knees hit the ground. "You made it, Sully. It's a walk in the park from here on out," Charles whispered to him. "Land as far as the eye can see."

Aidan rubbed the sweat out of his eyes and looked around as he walked. It was true what Charles said: The land extended to both the left and right, and straight ahead of them was a steep hill. But soon his eyes were saturated with the view, and that was when his nose took over. Nowhere he'd been had ever smelled like this, even the Public Garden. Every city dweller was all too familiar with the smells of hay and manure, but here those things smelled fresher, in part because there was so much fresh air with which it could mingle. That was it, Aidan decided—it wasn't so much the smell of honeysuckle or grass as it was just the vast quantities of fresh air:

endless, clean air that wasn't funneled through narrow streets and alleyways and airshafts, picking up the stink of humans living too close together. How had he breathed before?

Now that Aidan was able to walk without assistance, Charles loosened his grip on him and took in their surroundings.

"What the hell is all that noise?" he hissed into Aidan's ear. He glanced left and right but couldn't seem to divine the source. "Christ, that's gonna drive me off my nut. Do you hear that god-damn racket?"

Aidan turned his focus to the sound around him, and he immediately heard it—slow, raspy screeching, getting lounder and softer in waves, coming from the fields around them. *Must be some kinda bugs*, he thought, and with Charles's sense of hearing, he could understand how it was making him crazy. But there were other things, too. Songbirds, invisible in the high trees, were singing their hearts out with all sorts of notes that bore no resemblance to the low cooing of pigeons he associated with birds. Off to his right he saw a group of boys laughing as they entered a long, low building, and then he heard the squawking of what could only be several disgruntled hens—even a city dweller like him could identify that sound. Somewhere in the distance he heard the lowing of a single cow. He looked over his shoulder back to Boston, where he could make out a few of the taller buildings, just to verify they had only traveled a mile and hadn't landed on some island a thousand miles from nowhere.

Up ahead, the pilot was droning on about the difference between the stock barn and the storage barn. He suddenly looked back and noticed that the boys were several yards behind him. "C'mon with the two of ya, we're makin' our way to Superintendent Bradley, and he's expecting ya. Hop to it."

The boys made strides to close the gap, but when the pilot continued up the path, Charles pulled Aidan back and whispered, "Okay, I'm doin' the talking in front of this Bradley guy, see? You still ain't feelin' aces on account of that boat ride, and so you ain't got a lot to say. I'll handle this. *Arthur.*"

"Yeah, sure," mumbled Aidan. It was no stretch to say he was still wobbly.

Soon they arrived at the building at the top of the hill. Its broad, symmetrical front of red brick and white columns was formal and imposing. The land was not level until you were right next to the house, so the building's four stories seemed even taller upon approach.

"This here's Bulfinch," said the pilot, gesturing to the structure in front of them. "Named after the fella that designed it, not the bird. Over there's Gardner Hall. The superintendent will go over all this with ya. Speakin' of which, better get to it," he finished, and he tugged open the door.

Once they started up the main staircase, Aidan tried to get a feel for the layout of the building but became immediately turned around. Everywhere there were corridors and doorways, hallways leading to other landings or stairways. The further they tunneled into the building, the darker it became, since most doors were closed and there were few hallway windows. By the time they reached their destination on the third floor, he wasn't sure he could even find his way back to the front door.

After knocking and instructing the boys to remove their caps, the pilot swung the door open, and they all squinted as the sunlight from the room barreled forth. The man behind the desk rose to greet them, but they could only see a silhouette, the light streaming out from behind a tall figure. He motioned them in, and once inside, Aidan could see his features. He had a kind face, with eyes that sloped down slightly, giving him a somewhat naturally apologetic look. It was hard to imagine this man being angry or loud. Aidan immediately felt even worse about the deception that he and Charles had created, and he dropped his gaze down to his shoes.

"Ah, Mr. Fielding," Bradley said as he rubbed his hands together and raised his eyebrows, "what have we here?"

"May I present," said Fielding with an exaggerated little bow, "the Weston brothers."

"You, I will wager, are Master Charles Weston," Bradley said as he held out his hand. Charles shook it as he looked Bradley in the eye and said, "Indeed I am, sir."

"And that would make you Master Arthur Weston, would it not?"

"It would," Aidan said sheepishly, and he offered a damp hand.

"Please have a seat," said Bradley as he gestured to the two chairs set up in front of his desk, and he settled into his own seat. He asked Fielding to wait outside in the hall. *Jaysus*, Aidan thought. Charles had assured him that after the boat ride, everything would seem easy, but Aidan hadn't really thought about how it would feel to look people in the face and tell lie after lie.

Once seated, Bradley did not launch into his speech but instead gave the boys a moment to settle in. He thought about how what he had read in the folder compared with the flesh and blood version in front of him. They didn't look much like brothers, but there was often more than one father in these situations. It struck him as odd that Charles seemed dirtier and scabbier than Arthur. Then again, with that cocksure attitude he'd felt in the boy's handshake, Charles was bound to be more of a scrapper than his brother, who was perhaps just a more fastidious boy, relatively speaking. The more he looked at them, in fact, the more he believed that these two did not come from the same father. But he was relieved to find that he did not detect in either boy the delinquent aura he always feared he would find across his desk—the miasma that had seeped out of Johnny McFarland, and which every teacher at the State

Primary School had sensed on that boy's first day. A little wrinkle in Bradley's brow smoothed and relaxed.

"Today," he began, "is the first day of your new life." He put his elbows on his desk and made a steeple with his hands as he continued. "Your new life will have more schedule and rigor than you are likely used to. You will rise earlier, work harder, pray more frequently, and bathe more often than you ever have before. The ringing of the bell will instruct you that it is time to end one activity and begin the next. You will have no choice in what you do during school and work times. In the summer, you will be in bed for the night before it is even dark, and you will be well glad of it, you will be that tired." Bradley paused for a minute to let this sink in, looking at Charles and then Aidan, both of whom were attentively listening to every quiet word.

"On the other hand, you will have free time before dinner and before supper, and you will find that you have resources far beyond what you've had at home with which to entertain yourselves. You will have a bed of your own with clean blankets and linens, which will be clean because you and the other boys will launder them. You will have three meals a day made almost entirely with foods grown or raised on the island—foods grown and raised and harvested and served by you and the other boys. You will wear a school uniform and shoes, which will always be in good repair because you and the other boys will mend them when needed. You will learn some or all of these jobs and perform them when you are told, and you will become a cog in the wheel that turns to make this island a self-sufficient haven. If you abide by the rules, you will never want for any necessity, never be cold at night, never go to bed hungry, always have medicines and proper care when you are ill. You will learn enough to be employed in the outside world at age fourteen, and I will personally secure your first job for you. I believe every boy on this island thinks this is an excellent arrangement. Some find it difficult to adjust at first, but often those are the ones that ultimately appreciate the benefits the most."

Bradley paused again to see if he had lost the boys yet, but it did appear that they had been paying attention and were now turning all this information over in their minds. He was tempted to continue past this point—there was so much more to say, for them to know—but he decided that to pursue anything more than his parting instructions would be pushing his luck.

"You will call me and all male instructional staff either 'Mr.' with their surname or 'sir.' Similarly, you will address the matron, my wife, as 'Mrs. Bradley' or 'ma'am,' and the same for all female instructional staff. Mr. Fielding, our groundskeeper, is simply 'Mr. Fielding,' and despite my preference, the boys have a long tradition predating my arrival of calling Mrs. Culligan 'Cook,' which she apparently tolerates." Bradley stood, and the boys also rose and picked up their sacks of possessions. "If you have an issue that cannot be resolved by other staff members, you may come to see me if I am in my office."

Mr. Fielding opened the door at that moment, as if on cue.

Bradley checked his pocket watch. "Mr. Fielding will escort you to Mrs. Bradley, who will get you settled in time for dinner at half eleven. Good morning, boys," he said, glancing back up at them with a smile.

As the boys were walking to the door, Charles stopped short. "Mr. Bradley? Sir?" he asked.

"Yes, Master Weston," Bradley replied.

"My brother here, Arthur my brother, he ain't so comfortable with, uh, water. The harbor, I mean. Fielding here said somethin' about daily swim lessons? Can he, maybe, not do those?"

"If your brother *isn't* comfortable around the harbor, the swim lessons that *Mr.* Fielding mentioned can be adjusted at first to bring him along at a modified pace." Turning to his left, he continued, "Master Arthur Weston, you are not the first lad to arrive on these shores with a fear of the water, but every boy who graduates from the Farm School has learned the basics of swimming. Indeed, one of the boys who felt as you do came here as a nine-year-old. That boy is almost thirteen now, and he is our instructor of the boys that fear the water. You will find him quite understanding of your situation. And you will also learn over time to speak for yourself, as I am sure you are every bit as capable as your brother. Perhaps more so in the grammar department—we shall see." He put a reassuring hand on the boy's shoulder and looked into his eyes. He saw more than the usual amount of misery there, and he wondered if he could ever really fathom the lives all these boys had to live before they arrived on his island.

"Off we go," said Fielding, ushering the boys out of the office. "We don't want to keep the matron waitin', now do we? She has plenty to do, I'll tell ya that. Busy she is, and now two more to settle. Come along." Bradley watched as the three of them disappeared down the stairs. *Be good*, he said to them inside his head. *Do what you're told here. Turn your lives around.*

As he descended the staircase, Charles felt far more relaxed than he had prior to the meeting. Bradley would not pose a challenge, he thought to himself confidently. Nice fellers always wanted to believe the best about people, and Charles would be sure that the best of the Weston brothers was what Bradley would see and hear about. Hell, maybe that's who he and Aidan would become—the nice Weston brothers, never in no trouble, rescuing kittens outta trees and such. This was their fresh start if there ever was one. No reason they couldn't become model American boys now that they didn't have to roll drunks anymore.

Fielding brought them to the matron's sitting room, furnished with a small settee and a rolltop desk, but the matron was not there.

111

"Ah, probably putting little Henry down for a nap down the hall. Plant yourselves on that settee and don't move a muscle. I'll be back straight away," said Fielding, and he left the sitting room, closing the door behind him.

"So, whaddya think so far?" asked Charles as soon as the door clicked shut.

"I can't believe we was standin' in Boston an hour ago," said Aidan. He ran his fingers through his hair.

"I know! Things here is so different, it's like we just got off two days of travelin' out West on the Orphan Train. They got buildings just for chickens and cows to wander around in, for Chrissakes."

"It's like that primer we had in school a couple years ago—*Mary and Jack Down On The Farm*. With their dog Jip chasin' the hens and all. But I didn't think anyone really lived like that. Well, around here at least."

"Listen, when the old lady comes in, we gotta make it so that we don't get separated, see?" Charles said. "I dunno if they're in the business of splittin' up brothers, but we gotta make sure they don't. We can say that it would just be too upsettin' to be split up, as we just been made into orphans and all."

"Yeah, absolutely," said Aidan, twisting his cap in his hands. Looking up at Charles, he said, "You really think they might do that? Split us?"

Just then, the door swung open, and a small but energetic woman swept into the room with a pile of linens in her hands. "Good morning, Weston brothers. As you may have guessed, I am Mrs. Bradley, matron here at the Farm School. I am in charge of everything having to do with living in this building. All activities under my watch must be done neatly"—she stopped briefly to plunk half the pile of linens into Aidan's arms—"and efficiently," she finished, landing the other half in Charles's arms. She looked into both their eyes intensely, making an impression even deeper than her introductory words. Though only half a head taller than the boys, she projected a calm yet militant attitude that was impossible to ignore. Her dark brown hair swept up to a complicated bun, and no stray hairs dared to break loose from the pack. Her plain visage was unadorned by any cosmetics or jewelry, save the ivory silhouette brooch at her high collar. Despite the heat and her brisk movements in a dress that reached the floor, she showed no evidence of perspiring.

She began to slowly pace back and forth in front of the boys as she continued. "Outside of your trade learning, all your indoor moments will be in this building. There are three dormitories, six classrooms, the dining hall, and the chapel, all under this roof. And the entire staff of the school also lives here, so you will never be far from those who are in charge." Here the matron stopped and fixed her gaze on Charles, who fought the urge to look down.

Not quite the easy mark as her husband, he thought. *Christ, if she stares at Sully like that for long, he's gonna crap his trousers and confess everything.* He made a mental note that they should avoid this woman whenever possible.

"In your hands," the matron resumed, "are your bed linens, towels, night clothes, and school uniforms. You will eventually be measured for new uniforms. Until that time, you will make do with these. Now we proceed to the East Dormitory." She swept between the two boys, nearly spinning them around, and proceeded out through the doorway. They quickly shouldered their bags and scurried to catch up.

In the dormitory, Mrs. Bradley walked them to a stripped bed at the very end of the room. "As you may or may not know," she began, "your arrival here puts us one over our normal level of one hundred boys, and thus we do not have two spare beds. However, in five days, a boy will leave the island for his placement, so this arrangement will be quite temporary. I'm sure as brothers you've shared a bed for at least part of your life, so this will be nothing new."

Aidan looked over at Charles in surprise, but Charles clamped his hand on Aidan's shoulder and faced Mrs. Bradley. "Ma'am," he assured her, "it will be just like old times."

Mrs. Bradley narrowed her eyes again as she considered Charles. "Hmmm," she murmured. She looked as if she were making a mental note about Charles, and not a good one.

"Ma'am?" ventured Aidan.

The matron's focus swiveled to Aidan. Charles breathed a silent sigh of relief.

"What are we supposed to do with these here sheets?" Aidan asked.

"Under each bed, there is a wooden box that has been made in the carpentry shop by a student here. They were specially designed to fit under these beds. Each boy that leaves bequeaths the box to the next occupant of the bed. This box will hold all your clothes, linens, and other personal possessions. Any staff member can examine the contents of any bed box at any time. This seems like as good a time as any to review what is not allowed to be in your possession: weapons of any kind, including pocketknives; alcohol or other illicit substances; tobacco products; matches; fireworks; or any printed material you could not read sitting next to your mother, God rest her soul. Cards are permitted, but gambling, whether with real money or tokens representing money, is forbidden. Dice are not permitted." By the end of her litany, she had crossed her arms in front of her and returned her gaze to Charles. "Store everything but your uniforms and towels, which you are to bring with you to our next destination."

Aidan slid the box from beneath the metal bed frame, and he and Charles inspected it. It was long and narrow so that it could be removed from either the side or the foot of the bed. It was all right angles, tight and sanded smooth. Aidan ran his hand over the top and down the side before opening it. As Charles leaned down to place his bed linens inside, he noticed words carved into the lid's underside: *Joe M. 1886. G.T.+D.S. Go Beaneaters!*

"Come along, Masters Weston, we've a lot to do before the dinner bell," said Mrs. Bradley, and she swept out of the room. Charles and Aidan trailed behind.

They arrived at a room on the ground floor adjacent to the kitchen, and before Mrs. Bradley opened the door, the smell of dinner being prepared hit Charles like a boxing glove, rendering him ravenous.

"Is that chicken?" asked Aidan, inhaling deeply, an almost religious expression washing over his face.

"With boiled vegetables and potatoes," Mrs. Bradley said. "But you are in here first," she added as she opened the door.

Along the walls were a dozen galvanized metal tubs. In the center of the room was a table holding a tin bucket full of soap pieces. Near two of the tubs were two boys, from the looks of them a bit older than Aidan and Charles, who were holding the valves open for two of the tubs.

"Boys, this is Horace Warwick and Thomas Bowditch, in Second Class. Our new students—Charles and Arthur Weston, respectively," the matron said, gesturing to them with an upturned palm. "Masters Warwick and Bowditch are in their houseboy rotation, and although I am familiar with every houseboy job, I did not know that it took two houseboys to run two baths."

Bowditch and Warwick looked at their shoes. "Yes, ma'am," one of them mumbled.

She fixed them with a piercing stare for a moment and then relented. "Each boy on his first day has a thorough bath, including the vigorous use of soap. For boys younger than ten, I assist them with this—and you can be sure that if I am not satisfied with *your* results, I will rerun your bath and assist you as well."

Charles shuddered at the thought of this woman scrubbing behind his ears as he sat naked in eight inches of water.

"I'll be back in fifteen minutes, at which time I expect you to be dressed," said Mrs. Bradley. She turned to the houseboys, who had stopped running the water. "You two, I believe your schedule calls for setting tables next door, if I'm not mistaken," she intoned in a voice that clearly implied that she was not mistaken.

"Yes, ma'am," they said in approximate unison, and they made to follow the matron out the door. But when a teacher approached her in the hallway and the two women engaged in conversation, the houseboys ducked back into the bathing room and went over to the tubs.

"Enjoy yer baths, ya dirty bastards!" one said quietly. They grinned as they each took what looked like thin pieces of rope out of their pockets and threw them into the tubs. The one who hadn't spoken knocked Charles's cap off his head and laughed before they both sauntered out and closed the door.

Charles and Aidan peered into the tub closest to them and saw a small snake frantically swimming around the flat metal bottom.

"Jaysus, is that a *snake?*" Aidan said.

"Goddamned bastards," Charles muttered. He thought for a moment. "Hey, open that window."

As Aidan opened the window, Charles rolled up his sleeve and went to grab one of the snakes.

"What if it's poisonous?" asked Aidan, clenching his fists to his chest like a girl.

"They wouldn't put poisonous snakes in their pockets," Charles said as he made another swipe, sloshing water around in the metal tub.

"What if they thought they was the nonpoisonous kind but they was wrong?"

"Then they'd be dead," Charles said as he victoriously held up a snake. It writhed in his pincer grip, and Aidan gave him a wide berth as he walked over to the window and tossed it out.

"Wanna give it a try?" Charles asked with a wry grin, gesturing toward the other tub.

"Uh . . ." started Aidan. "I mean, you already did one—now you know how to do it an' all. You ain't gonna let a rank amateur take over now, are ya?" He flashed a hopeful smile.

"For you, little brother, I'll wrestle this here python to the ground. But you owe me." In three more swipes, Charles secured the second snake and then flung it out the window.

"We better get to it," Aidan said, "or Matron's gonna be here before we're done." He tossed Charles a lump of soap from the tin pail.

"Yeah, that look of hers could hard-boil an egg—I don't want no trouble from that quarter."

They undressed back-to-back, averting their eyes until they had lowered themselves into the shallow water of their respective tubs. They didn't say anything for a while, each lost in his own thoughts.

After a few minutes, Aidan cupped some water and lobbed it in Charles's direction. "Better get scrubbin', brother—you got more work to do on that front than me. And you don't want Matron helpin' you out, do ya?"

"I already made a solemn vow that she ain't never gonna see my pecker, and I suggest you do the same," Charles said as they both began to lather up the soap.

After they were done washing, the water was a grayish-brown, but they were loath to leave it for their rough towels.

"Charles?"

"Mmmm?"

"You think we should tell Matron about the snakes? Or tell Bradley?"

"No dice, Sully. This you gotta know." Charles sat up straight in his tub and faced Aidan. "We do that, we ain't never gonna be able to stand our ground. This is between us and them. We just gotta learn the ropes here, learn who we can trust. But that don't include no adults."

Aidan considered this and understood the truth of it. "But what if we can't trust no one? What if they're all bastards like Bowditch and Warwick?"

"Could be. But we already know there is someone here we can trust."

"Who?" Aidan looked puzzled. "Who can we trust?"

Charles smiled his lopsided smile at Aidan. "Each other."

CHAPTER 16

Aidan and Charles had just finished pulling on their uniforms and were finger-combing their wet hair when Mrs. Bradley came to collect them for dinner.

The din from the dining hall could be heard from the far end of the hallway. When they walked in, it seemed to Aidan that the boys, clad in identical blue uniforms and moving every which way, were writhing around the room like the snakes from the tubs. He fought down a shudder. Mrs. Bradley pointed to a table near the door with unoccupied chairs, and Aidan and Charles went to sit down.

When all the chairs were taken, Mrs. Bradley rang a small bell that she took from her apron pocket, and the boys quieted down quickly. "Master Pickering," she called out, "please say grace."

A pudgy boy at the table next to Charles and Aidan stood and bowed his head, eyes closed. "Bless us O Lord for these thy gifts which we are about to receive from thy bounty through Christ Our Lord Amen," he rattled off loudly and with no punctuation.

A boy with straw-colored hair leaned toward Aidan and whispered, "Anyone that takes too long with grace is gonna catch it with the boys after dinner." He smiled conspiratorially.

"Dinner may be served," stated Mrs. Bradley. The screech of chairs being pushed back in unison, scraping on the wooden floor, made Aidan and Charles jump. One boy from each table went to fetch platters of food from the adjacent kitchen, and talking in the hall resumed, though more quietly than before.

Aidan said to the boy who had whispered to him, "Do the boys who take too long servin' the food catch it too?"

"Nah, they're just motivated 'cause they don't get to eat until their table's served." As if to illustrate, the serving boy for their table plunked down a platter of chicken and a separate plate of potatoes and vegetables, exclaiming, "Dig in, men!" He sat and proceeded to take his own advice.

"I'm Bill Dutton, Third Class," said the straw-haired boy, and he shook Aidan's hand. "I bet you'll be Third Class too, or I'm a monkey's uncle." Bill started to pile food onto his plate. "And you are . . .?"

Aidan felt a reminder kick under the table from Charles. "Uh . . . Arthur Weston. And this here's Charles. My brother. Charles."

Charles nodded to Bill.

"Brothers, huh?" said Bill. "We only got one other pair of brothers, but they're years apart. You two look almost the same age."

"We was always in the same class at school, eleven months apart and all. I'm sure they'll do the same here," said Charles as he started to eat.

"Well, depends how ya test," said the serving boy at the head of the table, his mouth full of chicken.

"For cryin' out loud, Tink, can ya shut your piehole when you got grub in there?" Bill shook his head and gestured with his fork toward the boy, whose hair was red as pure copper. "That there slob is George Tinkham, Tink to anyone who can stand his table manners. Honestly, Tink, you're puttin' me off my food."

"Keep yer bloomers on, Betty," said Tink, wiping his mouth with his napkin and turning to Charles. "I ain't as bad as he makes me out to be. But I got my priorities, and this here pullet is at the top of my list right now." Tink reached for the platter of chicken and helped himself to another piece. "Cook boiled it just right, with the rosemary and onions, God love 'er. I just might hafta marry that woman some day." All the boys at the table guffawed.

"So, Tink," said Charles, "what did you mean about testing? With the classes and all?" He was trying to look nonchalant, but Aidan could see that he was worried.

"Today or tomorrow, they'll give ya both a test to see where ya place," said Tink from behind a mouthful of potatoes. "Most place with their age—First Class is fourteen and up, Second Class is thirteen, Third Class is twelve, and so on. Unless of course you ain't in First School."

"What's First School?" asked Aidan, unable to conceal his anxiety.

"Jeez, nobody went over this with you already?" said Tink, punctuating his question with a stifled belch. "Twelve years and up is First School, eleven and down is Second School. How old are the pair of ya?"

"I'm twelve, and he's eleven," said Charles.

"I'll be twelve in November," added Aidan.

Bill whistled. "Well, that will be interesting, now won't it?" Addressing Tink, he said, "What if one ends up in West and one in East?"

"What . . . what are you talking about?" asked Aidan, now becoming agitated.

"Sorry, must sound like we're talking in Morse code. It's just that because of the way your ages are . . . okay, so *First* School is for the older ones, that's for First Class, Second Class, and Third Class. And 'older ones' means twelve and up. We all sleep in East Dormitory. *Second* School, that's the youngers, eleven and younger, they're in West Dormitory. Fourth Class, Fifth Class, and Sixth Class. So you see? They could split you, one to First School, one to Second School. You'd sleep in different rooms, and your school and work schedules would be completely different too. Be a bit rough to be split up that way right off the bat."

"But they already gave us a bed in East, with the older ones" said Aidan. "Don't that mean—"

Tink interrupted. "All that means is that the empty bed was there. Just temporary."

Aidan stared at Charles, barely able to contain his panic.

Charles turned to Bill. "What do we have to do to stay together?"

"All right, listen up. You both wanna be in First School—better privileges, not sleepin' next to a bunch of bedwetters. So you both gotta try to ace that test. And you gotta talk to Bradley. He's in charge of the school; the principal doesn't wipe her nose without askin' him. Go to Bradley's before the test is graded, before you even take the test, and tell him you gotta stay together, make somethin' up if you have to, so at least if you both crap out on the test you'll still be together. With the bedwetters," Bill added with a grin.

"We ain't gonna crap out," said Charles firmly, but Aidan wasn't so sure. It had been so long since he had been in school. Would he remember anything at all? And Charles—he had never been a good student. Was it possible that Aidan would place in First School and Charles, even though he was older, would be sleeping with the bedwetters?

"You boys better eat up," offered Tink as he tipped his chair back, his own plate clean as a whistle. "In about three minutes, all us serving slaves is gonna take up the plates whether they still got food on 'em or not."

"Master Tinkham, chair legs on the ground," said Mrs. Bradley from across the room.

"Yes, ma'am," said Tink as he lowered his chair. He whispered to the boys at the table, "I don't care how well *she* cooks, I ain't marrying *her.*"

Bill regarded Charles and Aidan's worried expressions as they tried to finish their meal. "You look pretty tight over all this. It ain't that bad. The level of smarts they're looking for ain't that grand. Most of them that don't place with the others their age are the kind that got kicked in the head by a horse. You gotta relax, or you're gonna freeze up on the test."

Mrs. Bradley rang her little bell, and Tink rose with the other serving boys and cleared the plates, leaving Charles's and Aidan's for last so they could shovel in the last forkfuls of food.

"Thanks, Tink," said Aidan with his mouth full.

"Eat faster next time," said Tink, but he was smiling.

"Ladies," Bill called down to the two boys at the end of the table, breaking up their conversation, "you ain't been very sociable to our two new boys up here."

"If I could only convince this Irish knucklehead that boxing ain't a proper sport, I'd have plenty of time for the niceties," said one, a tall boy with a big nose.

The other, a smaller boy with jet-black hair, threw up his hands in frustration. "They've had the bleddy Queensberry rules since '67, fer cryin' out loud." His nose would be considered small under any standard, Aidan thought, but it looked especially so in comparison to that of his conversation partner.

"Well, give it a rest for a minute. Charles, Arthur, this is Salt and Dec. Or as they are known in their student files, Robert Saltonstall and Declan Moore."

"You two in Third Class?" asked Salt.

"Now that's a bit of a touchy subject at the moment," said Bill, "but they're aiming to place in Third and dodge Fourth."

"If you're gonna talk to Bradley, make sure to trot out yer best grammar," said Dec in a gentle brogue as he folded his napkin. "If he thinks ya can speak dacent, you're more likely to dodge Fourth."

"And across from Salt we have Mr. Sumner Burke," continued Bill, gesturing to a thin, gangly boy with large ears and a prominent Adam's apple. "Sumner don't say much, which is a bit of a relief with all the arguing that the rest of these mugs do."

Sumner looked over at Charles and Aidan and gave a quick nod of his head.

"Bill's understating that situation a bit, by the by," said Salt as he craned his neck to see what was taking so long with the dessert. "He means that Sumner don't say nothin'. At all. At least outside of the classroom—and even in class he ain't made to talk much anymore."

They all looked over at Sumner, who gave the slightest of shrugs and commenced tearing at a cuticle.

"No one better to tell your secrets to," commented Dec. His words had an unsettling effect on Aidan that he hoped was not apparent.

Tink arrived at the table with a pan of pound cake still warm from the oven. "Pound cake!" said Salt, and he pointed at Bill. "I told ya! You owe me two bits."

"It was just pound cake three days ago," said Bill, looking miffed. "I thought for sure it would be gingercake today."

"You still owe me. You ain't gettin' out of it," said Salt as he cut into the pound cake.

"Lads, yer all goin' to hell with this gamblin', don't ya know," remarked Dec as he took his slice of cake. "I've a mind to tell Tink's ladyfriend the matron in order to save your souls."

"Where are you from?" asked Aidan of Dec, and he received another kick under the table.

"Boston," Dec said with a grin. "But if you're askin' where I was born, 'twas County Kildare—Newbridge, to be exact. I left when I was a wee lad, so I don't remember it much."

Hearing Dec's voice was like hearing music for Aidan, it sounded so much like his mother—the brogue that went from light to heavy without warning. It was like being rocked in a cradle. He felt a stab of homesickness for the first time since they had arrived on the island.

"Well, at least we heard of Boston!" said Charles, and he looked over at Aidan with eyes clearly reminding him not to say anything Irish. "You want some milk, Arthur?"

"Milk would be capital, brother," said Aidan as he looked back at Charles. *I won't,* he assured Charles without a sound. *I won't bring us both down.*

An hour of scheduled outdoor play followed the midday meal, but it was too hot for any organized sports. The six boys lay about under a maple tree, watching some of the younger ones play tag. In the shade of the shadow cast by Bulfinch, some of the older boys were seeing who could handstand for the longest time, and near them, another group was trying to make blades of grass sing between their thumbs.

"What happens after this?" asked Charles.

"One to half two is work for everyone," said Bill as he twirled a stick between his fingers. "This time of year, it's nothin' but farm work. Sweatin' your balls off in the sun. Then at half two, it's either school or trade. Me and Tink, we been working in the field this morning, as you can probably smell—well, with Tink, anyway—so it's school for us in the afternoon. Dec and Salt did their school in the morning, so they'll go blacksmithin' while I'm takin' a nap at my desk."

"Nope, it's the print shop for us now," mumbled Salt, lying flat on the ground with his eyes closed. "We rotated out of blacksmithin' last week, remember? Christ in a handcart, it gets hot down there—they ought not to do blacksmithin' in August. Print shop's a dream compared to that oven."

"So you could get a job in one of them print shops in Boston some day, for real pay," said Aidan. He thought of Dan Connolly, dropping by after work with his hands stained black.

"True enough. There are worse jobs, I'll wager," Dec said.

"You'd do better to work on hiding that Mick accent of yours than to learn the finer points of print set," said Salt as he lobbed a small pebble at Dec. "Weren't that long ago that you couldn't walk down the streets of Boston without seein' a NINA sign in every other storefront." Aidan remembered asking his mother years ago what NINA stood for when they saw a sign in a bakery window. She refused to answer, and they finished their walk home in silence. It was Dan Connolly that told him later, when Maeve was out of earshot, that the sign meant "No Irish Need Apply."

Just then, a bell mounted on the side of Bulfinch was rung by Mrs. Bradley, who seemed to have appeared out of nowhere. Boys began to peel off down the hill or back into the building, but Charles and Aidan stood still, unsure where to go. The matron swooped in.

"Master Weston and Master Weston, for now you are to shadow Master Dutton in his farm work. When the bell rings at half two, you may follow him to the his classroom, where I will meet you." As she looked at the two of them, Aidan felt as if he were a bug mounted on a straight pin and found it hard to break her gaze.

"Well?" she asked. "Off with you now. Mr. Fielding does not favor tardiness." She gave them a small shove, and they ran off down the hill.

"Matron said we're to shadow you," said Aidan when they caught up with Bill.

"Well, despite those puny city-boy muscles, I'll wager the two of you can keep up with me today," Bill said with a grin.

After grabbing burlap sacks from the barn, they got down to the monotony of weeding beneath long rows of staked tomatoes. Aidan chatted easily with Bill about farming while Charles said nothing except a burst of profanity when a roughly pulled weed landed a spray of dirt in his mouth.

When they had reached the end of a row, Aidan asked Bill, "So, how long you been here?"

"Three years and four months," Bill answered, and it was as if a cloud passed over his formerly sunny disposition. Aidan looked over at Charles, who shrugged a shoulder, signaling his equal ignorance of what had just happened to change Bill's mood. The three of them weeded in silence until the Bulfinch bell rang.

CHAPTER 17

An hour and a half later, Charles found himself engaged in a battle far more difficult than pulling weed after weed in the August sun—more difficult, in fact, than anything he could recall in recent memory. It was painful and arduous, and he felt he had no chance of winning. He was in an epic struggle to stay awake in class.

When they met Mrs. Bradley at the classroom, Charles thought for sure they would be given the test for placement on the spot, but she instructed them to take a seat.

"After the bell at 1700 hours, when the classrooms are empty, you will be given the test. I advise you to use the time from now until then to refresh your memory of academic subjects," she suggested.

But Charles could not focus on Miss Wilhelmina Cuffing's droning voice as she discussed the thirty-eight states and eight territories. "The area of land between the states of Kansas and Texas is an Unorganized Territory in the shape of a cooking pot. As you can see, here is the handle . . ." She pointed to a map tacked to the wall, but Charles's eyes involuntarily rolled up into his head. He was sitting near the back of the hot, airless room, and he could have gotten away with a brief nap with his hand on his cheek and a locked elbow, but he was actually trying to pay attention in case geography was on the placement test. He looked over at Aidan, who was sitting two rows away looking sleepy but essentially awake. Unlike Charles, Aidan didn't appear to be in danger of falling off his chair in a public display of lost consciousness.

Charles tried to remember the last time he had actually gone to school. To the best of his recollection, it was around March or April of the previous year, during a particularly cold and rainy week that included bouts of unseasonable sleet. He had been suffering from a head cold and needed to warm up and dry out. But his mother had died just months before, and he was nervous that someone from the school would figure out that he was on his own and try to place him in an institution. So when the sun had come out later that week, Charles had ended his academic career for good. Or so he'd thought.

Just thinking about how little formal learning he'd had made fresh sweat break out and seep into his already-damp collar. How could he be placed with these other Third Class boys, one of whom was now actually raising his hand and correctly identifying the Utah Territory? The part of the map they were talking about just looked like a bunch of boxes to Charles, except that one that looked like a face, and he didn't even know the name of that one. Just then, the teacher pointed to the face, and Aidan raised his hand. "The Montana Territory?" he ventured.

"Correct, Master Weston. Very good for your first day," she said, and a few of the boys sniggered, but Aidan looked pleased.

"Now that you all have memorized the territories, I regret to inform you that they will become states in short order. In February of this year, President Cleveland signed into law the Enabling Act ..." But Charles couldn't listen anymore, even if the Enabling Act was the first question on the placement test. What did this have to do with his life? The only good news was that school was only for two and a half hours a day, according to Bill. The farm work, well, that was going to be a pain in the arse, but any half-wit could do it, and at least there was a purpose to it. And the trade learning—why, that would be the best of all. Nobody would take a chance training a street Arab for a trade back on the mainland, but here he was like anyone else, just a boy who should be taught how to make a living.

After what seemed like a century to Charles, the bell finally rang, causing the classroom to erupt in activity. Boys poured out of all the classrooms and into the yard. As Charles followed the crowd into the hallway, he felt the heavy hand of the matron on his shoulder. The test! In his stupor, he had managed to forget about that and everything else except his desire to get out of this stuffy building. When the last boy left the classroom with a smirk for Charles and Aidan in their captivity, Mrs. Bradley walked them back in and directed them to desks at opposite ends of the classroom.

"You have one half hour. When the bell rings for supper, you must hand your test back to me. If you are done early, review your work, and then you may hand your test in early." She took a seat at the teacher's desk and sat with impossible ramrod posture.

Time, which in the preceding hours had progressed at the rate of a garden slug, now raced ahead. Charles proceeded sequentially, working out quick guesses for the questions he wasn't sure of, which was most of them. He snuck a look over at Aidan and could tell he was further along in the test. Fresh sweat broke out on the back of his neck. When the bell sounded, he had just started the last page.

As they brought their papers up to Mrs. Bradley, Charles remembered what Bill had advised. "Ma'am? We would like to talk to the superintendent about our placement. He did say we could, uh, talk to him sometimes, if it was, um, important."

"You may come to his office at seven this evening. I happen to know that there is another boy who has arranged to talk to him at that time. Now, off to supper before all the food has been devoured by your classmates." She parceled out a meager smile, but it was nothing that would encourage Charles to revise his opinion of her.

Just before seven, Charles and Aidan navigated themselves to the door of the superintendent's office. Already waiting there was a freckled younger boy, sitting opposite the door with his back against the wall. Charles and Aidan sat down next to him.

"What're you here for?" asked Aidan.

The boy stared straight ahead as if he hadn't heard. After about a minute, when Aidan had given up on him and was opening his mouth to say something to Charles, the boy blurted out, "I'm aimin' ta visit my ma and my little brother."

"You're gonna ask Bradley if you can go back to the mainland? For the day?" asked Aidan. Was that even possible? Not that Aidan would set his foot in a boat if he didn't absolutely have to, but still.

At that moment, the door opened, and all three boys looked up at the superintendent in his doorway. From this angle, he looked tall and imposing, but his voice was gentle. "Master Jackson, please enter."

Without a word or a glance at the boys, Jackson stood and entered the office, a grim and determined look on his face. As soon as the door closed, Charles and Aidan moved to the other side of the hallway, flanking the door, and attempted to listen to the conversation inside. They could hear the soft murmuring of Bradley's voice and the higher sound of Jackson's, escalating in pitch a bit as the conversation wore on, but they were unable to make out any distinct words.

"Sounds like it ain't goin' Jackson's way," Aidan whispered to Charles. "You think he's gonna get his visit?"

"Bradley's soft. He'll give in."

After another few minutes, they heard the scraping of chairs on the oak floor and they scuttled back to their original spot across the hall. As the door opened, Bradley was saying, ". . . will personally post a letter to her, encouraging her to make coming here for the next Visiting Day a priority." Jackson crossed the sill, and they could see the vertical tracks that his tears had plowed down his dirty cheeks. He didn't look at the boys as he walked past, his fists jammed into his pockets.

Bradley looked expectantly at his remaining visitors. "Masters Weston?"

As they rose, Aidan murmured in Charles's ear, "Not so soft after all."

"Your visit is conveniently timed," Bradley said as he sat at his desk. "I have in front of me the results of your test this afternoon. But first, you may discuss with me the purpose of your visit." He laced his fingers across his vest and leaned back in his chair with a mild expression on his face.

Charles rubbed his hands on his thighs and then looked up at Bradley. "See, Mr. Bradley, me and my brother, we're eleven months apart. Heck, we're practically twins. Always been together in school, nobody split us. And we're hopin' you can see into your heart to keep us together here, too. I know we ain't—uh, aren't—exactly the same kinda student, but Arthur here always helped me study."

It was impossible to tell by Bradley's unchanging expression how much impact Charles's speech was making.

"Arthur's the only family I got left, sir," he added. And though it was a lie, technically, Charles said it with more conviction than Aidan had ever heard in his voice, and he met Bradley's gaze with eyes open and honest.

Still expressionless, Bradley addressed Aidan. "And is this how you feel?"

Aidan had not expected to speak during this meeting, and he almost flinched when Bradley addressed him. "Uh, yes, sir." Feeling that this utterance was paltry in comparison to Charles's impressive oration, he dug around in his mind for what he could say. "Being here is . . . so different. Everything is different. Not bad, I'm not sayin' that. But Charles is the only thing I recognize here." Once out of his mouth, it seemed a strange thing to say, but he couldn't think of any way to modify it.

Bradley looked down at his desk and straightened the papers on it until they were at right angles. After a moment, he looked up and cleared his throat. "This is not a situation I have encountered here during my tenure. While several pairs of brothers have arrived on my watch, they were not close in age and thus were placed separately. Furthermore, I recognize that given your ages, the pair of you are on the cusp of being in both separate classes *and* separate schools. Highly unusual."

He picked up the boys' tests from his desk. "If I were to interpret the results of these tests strictly and without regard to your age or personal situation, Charles would be in Second School and Arthur in First, with the irony being that the elder brother would be in the younger school." He paused for effect. "But it is not my habit to interpret these test results in isolation."

Aidan tentatively exhaled.

"In fact, it was never my plan to split you between schools. I am not without a heart," he added.

Charles started to say something, but Bradley held up his hand. "However, there is the question of which school is appropriate for the both of you."

Not the bedwetters, not the bedwetters, Aidan chanted in his mind.

Bradley stood and walked to the open window, which was conveying the slight breeze coming up from the water. "I am not in favor of placing a boy in a class that is too difficult for him. But neither do I favor placing a boy in a class where the work is too simple: this leads to boredom and troublemaking. I must take into consideration the personality of the boy, as far as I can divine it." He walked over and leaned against the front of his desk directly opposite Charles. "I have decided to put my trust in you, Charles Weston. Despite your lackluster test and poor grammar, I see in front of me an intelligent boy whose lack of academic knowledge is not due to a lack of ability. You will have to work at it, but I believe that you can do the work of Third Class. I am never wrong when I see intelligence in a boy." And Bradley placed his hands on Charles's shoulders, looking him square in the eye.

Aidan stole a look at Charles's face. He appeared disoriented. Aidan imagined it was the first time anyone had expressed something so positive about Charles, at least in such certain terms. Charles sat there, mouth slightly open, unmoving, even after Bradley removed his hands and returned to his desk chair.

"So you will stay where you were temporarily placed in the dormitory, and you will both be in Third Class together," Bradley said. He stood to indicate that the meeting was drawing to a close, consulting his pocket watch and then the view down to the wharf. "It appears you have missed out on the evening swim. The boys are returning already. Go along and meet the matron outside." With a snap, the pocket watch closed and slipped back into Bradley's vest.

After their mumbled thank-yous and good-byes, the boys headed down the creaky oak staircase.

"I guess he is soft after all," Aidan said.

Charles didn't reply and kept descending the stairs.

Fifteen minutes later, the boys were unpacking their few possessions and placing them into the bedbox beneath the bed. The dormitory hummed with the noise of dozens of boys milling about—cracking wise, hurling mild insults, horsing around—and yet it was all done at modest volume levels so as not to incur reprimand.

"Merton Poole," said the boy sitting on the bed next to them, and he stuck out his hand. His voice had a nasal twang, and his hair had more cowlicks than seemed possible on one head. "They call me Poole since Merton don't roll off the tongue. I don't hafta ask if you're the new brothers."

"Arthur and my brother Charles," said Aidan as he shook with Poole.

"Matron probably gave you the palaver on the bedboxes, but what you really gotta know about them is that a lot of the boys buildin' 'em built in a false bottom for your . . . more importantly stored items, shall we say."

Charles removed the few things they had put in the box already and tapped the bottom. "Seems pretty solid to me."

"Push around the edges and see if you can flip it up," suggested Poole as he used a comb to clean under his fingernails.

Charles pushed down around the perimeter of the box floor until it angled up toward him. As he pried up the floor, the boys could see blocks of wood secured to the true bottom, separating compartments of different sizes. Two were big enough to store a book, others were smaller.

"Hey, that's clever!" said Aidan.

Charles saw something in the smallest compartment, and he reached in to retrieve it. "An arrowhead." He showed Aidan.

"Last fellow left you a little somethin', huh?" said Poole as he looked over. "Lots of arrowheads on the island. All the boys is always scoutin' about for them. The best ones end up in the Reading Room under glass—you should go see 'em. Reading Room is open to all the boys on Sundays."

Charles put the arrowhead back. "So the matron don't know about the false bottoms?" he asked Poole.

"Nope. Not all of the boxes have 'em—you two got lucky. And Matron and them don't hardly ever look through 'em. Trick is, you gotta never give 'em a reason to get curious about what might be in your box." Poole set down his comb on the nightstand between the beds and stretched, letting out a loud yawn and a small fart. "Better load 'er up and put that panel back down before she rides in here on her broomstick."

Charles remembered his pocketknife he had been carrying around in his boot all day. He took it out and stored it in the compartment next to the arrowhead. He turned to Aidan. "Anything of yours for storage?"

"Not yet," Aidan said, and together they lowered the panel and pushed it into place.

Charles and Aidan had already washed up and changed into their nightclothes, having observed and copied the others who had chosen to only wear their cotton drawstring pants. Even with the open windows, the dormitory was still warm from body heat of the boys, but at least without a shirt, it was tolerable. As they sat on their bed, Charles's attention was drawn to the bed opposite theirs, where a boy their age was being harassed by older boys for wearing his nightshirt fully buttoned. Despite the younger boy's insistence that he wore it for protection against the mosquitoes, the older boys were coming up with increasingly more fanciful and rude explanations for his unorthodox nightwear. Even when the young boy's protests stopped, the taunting continued.

"Those ones is pretty rough on him," Aidan commented to Poole.

"They ain't the worst," said Poole as he lay in his bed, now reading a book.

"Who's the worst?" asked Charles, thinking of Bowditch and Warwick and the snakes.

Poole put his book facedown on his belly. "Well, you'd think that some of them big brutes in First Class would be the worst, but First Class ain't bad. They're all tryin' to keep their noses clean 'cause Bradley's gonna find 'em a job on the mainland this year. Hell, some of them is hittin' the books for the first time in their life, tryin' to get high marks to impress him. Anyway, they ain't gonna get in trouble over some little shaver. It's Second Class that has some you want to avoid. And all of them seem to revolve around that gentleman playin' Klondike over there." He pointed down the row of beds to a blond boy near the end.

"He don't seem that bad from here," commented Charles.

"What's his name?" asked Aidan.

"Caleb Hart, and he don't seem that bad until he do, and then you'll see him different." With that, Poole picked up his book and started reading again.

Caleb Hart was among the fairest people Charles had ever seen. His short-cropped hair was so blond it looked translucent on his scalp, and as he hunched over his cards, it was hard to distinguish where his back ended and the white drawstring pants began. It was clear that he wore a shirt for his outside work, but there was a raging sunburn on the parts that the shirt had left exposed. Almost all the other boys sported body parts that were dark brown from a summer's worth of sun, but Hart's red neck was peeling, and his pink face gave him an angry look, even though he was in repose, placing ten on Jack.

"Bowditch and Warwick," Charles said to Poole, "are they some that revolve around this Hart?"

"Uh-huh," said Poole, absorbed in his book.

Charles tried to locate Bowditch and Warwick in the room, but he couldn't. Many of the boys were lying down, reading a book or trying to sleep already, a forearm across their eyes, despite the drone of activity. It was odd to see these older boys sleepy and ready for lights-out while the sun was still blazing away outside.

It was just past seven thirty when the matron arrived, announcing her presence by calling out, "Count off!"

One by one, the boys barked out sequential numbers. As the calls were launched, books were placed on night tables, bodies slid under sheets, eyeglasses were lifted off noses. By the time the last number was shouted into the humid air of the dormitory, all boys were horizontal, including Aidan and Charles, who had decided to sleep head to foot. Charles let Aidan have the only pillow.

"As you must know," said the matron to the rows of recumbent boys, "you have two new students among you. Accordingly, all students will renumber tomorrow morning before breakfast." A few groans went around the room. "Lights out," she commanded, and the boy nearest to each oil lamp extinguished it.

The room became still; all the boys seemed to be waiting for something. And then it came: the sound of "Taps" being played by a bugle somewhere outside the building. *Day is done, gone the sun . . .* Charles listened to the music, a string of slow, mournful tones that seemed to him as if they belonged at a funeral.

As soon as the last note faded away, the silence in the dormitory was broken by settling-in noises: boys turning over in their cotton sheets, bed frames squeaking, a pillow being punched into a more desirable shape.

Charles looked across the room at the landscape of lumpy forms on beds. How could they be tired? Despite a certain soreness in his shoulders from the weeding, he felt more awake than he had all day. He couldn't remember the last time he had fallen asleep before midnight. The hours until he might be able to doze off stretched out before him.

"Hey," he called out softly to Aidan.

"Hey," Aidan responded.

"You sleepy?"

"Not on your life."

A book whizzed through the air and hit their bedframe. "Put a cork in it," grumbled a voice from the opposite row.

Aidan motioned for Charles to reverse his position so they were no longer head to toe. The bed was just wide enough to hold their shoulder spans as they lay on their backs, forearms pressed together. From this position, they could whisper low enough to avoid the wrath of the other boys. Poole assisted in covering their voices by emitting a steady, wheezy snore.

"Think we can slip outta here?" whispered Charles.

"Did you notice that there gentleman?" Aidan pointed to a bearded man that had settled into a straightback chair at the far end of the room near the door. In the fading light, he was whittling a block of wood with his chair tipped back to rest against the wall.

"How long you think he stays here?" wondered Charles.

"I guess we're gonna find out."

For a while, neither said anything. Soon there was a chorus of young-boy snores, and at least one or two taking what pleasures their hand could provide. Charles and Aidan looked at each other with expressions of mild disgust.

"Ain't no goddamn privacy in this place," grumbled Charles.

"Jaysus," said Aidan in agreement.

When the only sounds left were that of sleep, Charles said to Aidan, "You know, you gotta be pretty impressed with what we done today. You crossed the harbor, we ain't got beat up by any of them big Second Class mugs, and we landed in the same class. Tomorrow's gonna be like rolling off a log!"

"I can't believe I got in that boat."

At the wharf, Aidan had seized up as if his boots were nailed to the dock. Charles had been forced to drag him for several feet to get him to the end of the gangplank, and once in the boat, he'd had to peel Aidan's fingers from his arm.

"Wouldn't have looked too good to leave my little brother back on the mainland," Charles said, grinning.

They talked in low tones into the night, reviewing their day, comparing their impressions. The snakes in the tub doubled in length in their retelling, and the weeds multiplied. Aidan slid his baby blanket out from underneath the pillow, where he had surreptitiously stashed it earlier, and he rested his head on it. They discussed which of the questions on the placement test were most unfair and whether there was even a chance that any of the teachers would be pretty. At some point, the night watchman left his tilted chair, but by then the boys had lost their motivation to escape. Finally tired, they fell asleep.

In their quarters, the matron and the superintendent were kneeling beside their bed.

"Dear Lord," Bradley finished, "watch over Mary and Henry and all who work here, striving to better these young minds. And bless each and every boy, that he may overcome his past and fulfill his purpose according to your Heavenly Plan. Amen."

After they had climbed into bed and put out the lamp, they reviewed their day together in the darkness.

"Laundry's running out of bluing," Mrs. Bradley said.

"Already on the list," said her husband. "Did you put the new boys at Dutton's table for dinner?"

"Just as we discussed. He took them in, of course." Mrs. Bradley unbuttoned the top button of her high-collared cotton gown; it was just too hot to have it fastened around her neck. She made a mental note to button it again in the morning light. "That Dutton will turn out to be a fine young man."

"Quite so," her husband said. Then he added, "I put both brothers in Third."

"They did that well on the test?"

"Not quite. But they'll rise to the challenge. Sticking them in Second School didn't seem right."

"I suppose." Mrs. Bradley thought about her experience with the boys that day. What was it about Charles? Arthur, now there was the demeanor she was used to—confused, scared, not sure what to say or who to trust. But Charles . . . he was too confident, too smooth. "That older one, Charles," she said. "There's something about him."

"Yes. I saw it too. Smart as a whip. He has a real opportunity here."

"No, it's as if he's . . . hiding something. Pretending that everything is fine."

"Well, perhaps everything is fine with him."

"Nonsense. Not one of them that arrives here has everything fine with him."

"Well, perhaps he is our first. Or perhaps he is just too proud to let us see how he really feels." Bradley turned on his side.

Mrs. Bradley remained lying on her back. "I'd like to see their file tomorrow."

"Of course, my dear."

Soon Bradley's breathing deepened and slowed. Mrs. Bradley stayed awake for a while, staring straight up at the ceiling as the dusk seeped in.

CHAPTER 18

THE SOUND OF THE BUGLE PLAYING "REVEILLE" REACHED INTO Charles's dream and tried to pull him out of his deep slumber. In his dream, he was sleeping in the Public Garden on a park bench, but the park bench was really a bed, the most comfortable bed in the world. Somehow he knew that the police had been barred from the park and that he could sleep undisturbed. The only annoyance was a mosquito buzzing in his ear, which grew louder and more insistent, and ultimately he realized it was the goddamned bugle.

Aidan had appropriated the pillow to put over his head, but Charles grabbed it away from him and ignored Aidan's protests. Finally the bugle's intrusion stopped, and Charles's body began to relax. He tried to reenter his dream about the bed in the park.

All around them, the boys were stirring. Feet hit the wooden floor and shuffled around, there were yawns and murmurs and the grunts that went along with stretching. At the far end of the room, someone stubbed his toe and said "Sonofabitch!" under his breath. Charles, halfway back to the park bench of his dream, barely heard them.

"Good morning, Master Weston and Master Weston," rang out Mrs. Bradley's voice from the foot of their bed. "It is time to rise and shine."

Aidan managed to mumble something that might have been

"What time is it?" but also might have been just moaning. Charles moved only to put his arm over his exposed ear.

Then came the loud clang of something being struck against the metal frame of their bed, three times in rapid succession. Charles and Aidan bolted upright, Charles crying out "Goddammit!" His exclamation further startled Aidan, who fell to the floor in his confusion, banging his head on the nightstand on the way down.

The matron regarded them calmly, a dented stick slightly smaller than a baseball bat gripped firmly in her right hand, as if this was just the reaction she'd expected. The other boys—who, Charles now noticed, were gathered all around her—were laughing and pointing. "I've been told that this is an unpleasant way to be woken up. In the future, it would be best if you rose with the other boys when you hear 'Reveille.' And Master Charles Weston, that will be two demerits for taking the Lord's name in vain."

The matron spun around, and the boys cleared a path for her like the Red Sea parting as she swept out of the room.

Aidan rubbed the back of his head and got up from the floor as the boys dispersed. "Did we fall back asleep for that long?"

Poole was digging out his uniform from his bedbox as he answered. "Matron expects every new boy is gonna try to sleep in. Happens to all the new ones. She'll come in with that stick every day 'til you start gettin' yourself up with the rest of us. The record is four days."

"What's a demerit?" asked Charles.

"Yeah, I forgot to thank you for that bit of entertainment. It ain't often we get to see someone cussing out the matron, not that we don't all wish we could. Five marks—demerits—in a week, and you're demoted to Purgatory for a while. Bradley calls it "disciplinary isolation," but nobody else does. And if you think the Second Classers was rough on Bainbridge about his nightshirt, well, you ain't seen nothin' 'til you seen them have their fun with a Purg."

"What happens when you're in Purgatory?" The phrase "disciplinary isolation" put Charles on alert. *Is that like the Sweatbox?*

"They make ya eat separate and sit separate in class," said Poole. "Can't go to ballgames and such. Believe me, you don't want it." Charles had to suppress a laugh.

Poole had now finished getting dressed and was lacing up his boots when Charles realized that once again he and Aidan were lagging behind what all the other boys were doing. They scrambled to put on their uniforms. Everything seemed turned around in this place—they all got in bed when it was still light out and got out of bed before the sun was fully up. Back in Boston, everything important occurred after dark.

Poole stood and pulled the cuffs of his shirt fussily, his neat uniform at odds with the cowlicks in his hair, which seemed to have multiplied during the night. "My advice?" he asked rhetorically. "Make sure you get a second cup of coffee at breakfast before the pitcher's empty." He joined the flow of boys streaming out of the dormitory.

Charles and Aidan were among the last to enter the dining hall, but no one was sitting when they got there. Before Charles could ask what was happening, Mrs. Bradley called out, "Size up!" and a great shuffling and murmuring ensued amongst the boys, who were still yawning and scratching themselves.

The tallest boys placed themselves against the wall near the doorway, starting a human chain that trailed behind them. There were drowsy discussions and half-hearted horseplay as the boys sorted themselves out by height in the orangey light of the rising sun. Charles and Aidan hung back until the line was mostly established, then walked alongside it to see where they would fit in. When Aidan squeezed into his place, Charles kept walking down the line, and he realized it was the first time they had been separated since coming to the island.

Mrs. Bradley went down the line, periodically placing her hands on the heads of two adjacent boys and switching their sequence. Conversations were snuffed out as she approached, as if her presence sucked up the oxygen required to converse. She stopped in front of Charles and placed her hand on his head. She considered him closely, making him wish he could back up, but his back was already against the wall.

"Uh, am I in the wrong place?" he asked. "Should I switch? Ma'am?" he remembered to add. He could feel sweat surfacing under his arms.

"Oh no, Master Weston, you were very clever to get yourself to this particular place," she said, and she slowly removed her hand and walked on.

She knows, Charles thought as he closed his eyes, feeling his bowels loosen in fear. *No, she can't know, how could she know, what could she know? Nobody knows except us and Bess. She's just a suspicious old witch, trying to get me to spill the beans, and I ain't falling for her voodoo act.*

"Hey, you all right? You don't look so hot. You ain't gonna puke all over my boots, are ya?" Pickering, orator of the brief grace before yesterday's dinner, was standing next to Charles in line, looking slightly nervous.

"Naw, I'm shipshape," said Charles, and he took a deep breath and exhaled slowly. A couple of cups of coffee and he'd be ready for the matron, whatever else she had to dish out today.

Charles was intent on relaying the morning's experience with the matron to Aidan as soon as they could find a moment alone. He was so focused on this idea as they left the dining room that he was the only boy who failed to see the St. Bernard puppy barreling down the hallway at full speed. Too late he heard the cries of "Quincy, dead ahead!" as other boys jumped out of the way. The dog ran into Charles's leg as if the leg were not there, spinning him around and knocking him to the ground. From his vantage point on the ground, he saw the dog maintain his gait until he reached the end of the hallway, where he tried in vain to stop his momentum on the smooth floor before slamming dramatically into the wall.

"You all right?" asked Aidan as he helped Charles up.

"Why'd they let a pony in the building, fer Chrissakes?" he answered, but his reply was drowned out by Mrs. Bradley's reaction. "MR. FIELDING!" she called out the window in obvious irritation.

Fielding appeared behind her in the hall and lunged for the puppy.

"Mr. Fielding, I have been *very* clear with you that Quincy is to remain outside until after the morning bell, when all the boys are either in school or in the Gardner Building!"

"Yes, ma'am, but he ran inside when the boys opened the door to go out to the yard." Quincy started licking Fielding's face with his large, rubbery tongue.

"Quincy is a purebred St. Bernard and thus is quite trainable. It should be within your abilities to train this animal to stay with you."

"Yes, that should be possible, ma'am, but someone forgot to tell Quincy that he's trainable." As if to illustrate this point, Quincy took this moment to break free of Fielding's grasp and joyfully prance around the hallway. One of the smaller boys backed up against the wall in fear, which Quincy took as a cue to rear up and plant his enormous paws on the boy's shoulders, knocking him to the floor.

"Mr. Fielding!" the matron exclaimed in a higher octave.

With considerable effort, Fielding managed to move Quincy out the door, but not before Quincy lifted his leg to the oak newel post. The matron rustled off in a huff to find the nearest houseboys on cleaning duty. As soon as Charles and Aidan had exited the building, Tink caught up with them.

"Hey, you know why they call that pup Quincy?" he asked them. "'Cause whenever he sees some nice woodwork or furniture, Quincy's gotta Market!"

Dutton came up behind Tink and knocked his cap off with a flick of the brim. "Ain't no one found that joke funny since you thunk it up, dunderhead." He grabbed Tink's cap from the ground and ran, with Tink giving chase right behind him.

Charles and Aidan sat down in the shade of a tree in the yard. "Listen," Charles murmured, "Matron . . . it's like she knows something's fishy about us. She gave me the stink eye when we was sizing up, and she said . . ." But now it sounded flimsy. A look? What had she really said? That he had found the right place in line? Maybe that's all she meant. He realized if he tried to explain it to Aidan, it would come out sounding like he was jumping at shadows, imagining things that weren't there.

"What'd she say?" asked Aidan.

"Nothin'. Well, not nothin', but nothin'. The important thing is that our story is rock solid. You're my brother Arthur, we ain't never had a pa, our ma just died of a fever. You get asked somethin' where you ain't sure what the answer should be, you just clam up and look at your boots like you're just too full of grief to know your arse from your elbow."

"What about you? Ain't you at all afraid that you're gonna slip up?"

"Why? You think I'm gonna?"

"I didn't say that. I just . . ." Aidan leaned his head back against the tree trunk with a sigh and gazed up at the branches. "Never mind."

They sat in silence for a while, until a small stream of boys began to walk around the corner of the building.

"Where do you think they're goin'?" Aidan asked Charles.

When they rounded the corner, they saw that every boy on this side of the building was in some way tending to one of the large, rectangular flower beds set in the lawn, Fielding presiding over the whole scene like a monarch. Quincy had been tied to a post, and he wagged his tail furiously in the dust whenever a boy passed near him. Most boys were toting pails of water from the pump near the building or pulling weeds. As Charles and Aidan walked between the beds, they could see a marker in each bed with a boy's name on it.

"Hey, each one of these belongs to just one boy!" said Aidan. "Do you think you and me are gonna get one?"

"Ain't you gonna have enough weedin' and plantin' to do with Fielding?" Charles surveyed the boys working their plots. "Why the hell would any of these mugs want to do extra farm work? And in their free time! They musta been kicked in the head by one of them cows."

When he turned back to Aidan, he realized he was standing alone. Aidan was heading over to Fielding. Charles trotted to catch up.

"Mr. Fielding, what does a boy have to do to get a garden?" Aidan said to Fielding.

"That boy would have to demonstrate an interest in having a garden, and I'd say you just qualified." Fielding suddenly looked up and shouted to a smaller boy watering his bed. "The dirt, Leighton! Water the dirt, not the leaves, and slowly! You're gonna wash that plant clear out of your garden and down to the wharf!" He looked back at Aidan. "Little shavers don't have a lot of horse sense. Let's hope you can do better."

Fielding walked them over to a forlorn plot. Flowering plants were indistinguishable from the weeds that choked them, and the flowers had been deprived of water for so long that it was hard to determine their original color. "This one here is available. The boy who planted it was First Class, and he knew he would be placed out midsummer, so I'm afraid he let it go to pot. Quite a sorry sight. I'm fairly certain you can't make it look any worse," he added.

Aidan and Fielding began an earnest conversation about the maintenance of garden plots—watering methods, tilling tools, times during the day when the boys were permitted to work on their gardens—which interested Charles as much as the teacher's lecture on the Dakota Territory. When they began discussing the transport of manure from the fields to the gardens for soil enrichment, Charles slapped Aidan on the back and without a word proceeded back to the yard. *Brother or not*, he thought to himself, *I ain't standin' around listenin' to a conversation about cow shit.*

Charles saw Salt leaning against the building and practicing a trick where a coin moved across the knuckles of his right hand. He beckoned Charles over.

"Heard you got spun by the pup this morning," Salt said, his eyes back on the moving coin.

"What about it?" Charles snapped.

"Keep your shirt on, Slugger," said Salt. He flipped Charles the coin. "Didn't mean nothin' by it."

"Sorry," Charles mumbled. He examined the Indian head on the penny while he tried to think of something to say. "So, uh, what's that dog doing here anyway?"

"Been a month since Bradley brought him over from the mainland. Big row with the matron about it. He brought it for Henry, but the matron was fumin' about how St. Bernards are too big for a little tyke. Seems like Matron's got a point, since Quincy's head is about the size of Henry now."

"Who's Henry?"

"He's their babe, born last fall. Matron's lying in was a blessed time for all the boys. The principal and one of the teachers filled in for her, but even all put together, they weren't near as bad as Matron with them eyes in the back of her head and that witchy sense of when you were thinkin' bad thoughts. You got the Devil in ya, she'll find it."

Charles found it both reassuring and unnerving to hear that others also believed Mrs. Bradley could see into a boy's soul.

Salt held out his hand for the penny, and when Charles returned it, he went back to practicing his trick. "Hey, did Fielding tell you about the standing bet he has about Quincy?"

"Nope."

"Fielding thinks that dog is just too damn stupid to learn a single trick. Any boy who can teach him somethin'—sit, lie down, roll over, you know—Fielding'll give him a dollar."

"No foolin'. A whole dollar for one trick?" *How hard can that be?* Charles thought.

"Sounds like a cinch, huh? Plenty have tried it. Nobody's collected yet. Lester Adams said he taught Quincy to piss himself on command, but since Quincy does that most times he's happy to see someone, it was sorta hard to prove Lester was controllin' it."

It occurred to Charles that he wasn't sure what money could buy here on the island. For the last year and a half, he had spent most of his earnings on food, occasionally on clothing and a place to sleep if necessary. All those things were provided here. He was about to mentally file this question away—he was sure that if he kept his ear to the ground, the answer would turn up eventually without his having to admit that he didn't know something. But then again, here he stood, toeing the dirt with nothing else to say. What did he care if Salt thought he was a dolt?

"Salt, this might be a queer question, but whaddya do with money here?"

"Well, Bradley would tell you that it's for your bank account."

Charles laughed. "Yeah, like I got a bank account."

"Well, not yet, but you're gonna. Bradley will set up an account this week in the school bank for you and your brother. Anything you brought with you, you put in to start it up, if you got anything."

Charles frowned. "Let's say I brought some cash with me. Why would I give it over to Bradley and trust that I'd ever get it back?"

"You think it's safer on your person? In the false bottom of your bed box? How many other boys know about them false bottoms? I'll answer that for you: all of 'em. But not all of 'em are above rooting around in the new boy's bedbox to see what he brung with him. Most here ain't tryin' to do you harm, but all it takes is one to clean you out. And the first question Bradley's gonna ask is, 'Son, why didn't you deposit your money in the school bank?'" Salt did a decent impression of Bradley as he quoted him, hands clasped together, eyebrows knitted together in concern.

It was a question of who to trust; Charles could see that now. Bradley, or the likes of Caleb Hart and his followers. As much as Charles had an innate aversion to trusting adults, he would cast his lot with Bradley. In this case.

While Aidan was talking to Tink during dinner, Charles pocketed a few pieces of the roast in one of the handkerchiefs that had been issued to him with his uniform. Later, while he was picking corn and Aidan was off trussing tomato vines, he heard Quincy barking playfully, and he emerged from the cornrows to see what was going on. Several boys were dragging burlap sacks of weeds across the field, and Quincy was nipping at the bags. Charles trotted over to the scene.

"Take this pup off your hands?" he offered.

"He's all yours!" the tallest boy insisted, and the others laughed.

Charles took Quincy around the far side of the cornfield, where he was shielded from view. Quincy was already aware that something tantalizing resided in Charles's pocket, and he had come with Charles eagerly.

Slowly, Charles took a piece of the roast out of his pocket, and he could tell that he had Quincy's full attention. Quincy danced around as if the ground were too hot for his paws, his eyes never leaving the bit of meat.

"Quincy," Charles said, "you want this?"

Quincy responded with an enthusiastic wagging of his thick tail and a small stream of urine.

"I ain't givin' you this for old Lester Adams's trick, ya pisser. Now pay attention. Quincy, sit!" Charles held the piece of roast high between them.

Bladder empty, Quincy's wagging slowed its tempo and he gave a little whine.

"*Sit*, Quincy, *sit!*" Charles commanded.

Quincy gave a throaty bark and lunged for the meat, knocking Charles to the ground, where he hit the back of his head on one of the many rocks that had been culled from the cornfield. As Charles lay on the ground, seeing stars, Quincy ate the meat in one quick gulp, licked Charles's greasy hand, and then ran off.

"Stupid, mangy—" but there he had to leave off, the pain in his head was so great. He rolled on his side and put his hands over his eyes and waited for the hurting to let up.

After about a minute, he felt well enough to sit up, and after another minute, he stood. How much time had passed? He shook his head, disoriented. He had better get back with his fellow corn-pickers before Fielding noticed he wasn't there.

As he rejoined his group, they were heading to the barn with a handcart full of what they had picked. The boys were in good spirits, full of a seemingly unlimited supply of jokes about male anatomy that could be illustrated with ears of corn. As they approached the barn, one of the older boys looked over at Charles and said, "Hey, new boy, you ain't lookin' so good. And what's in your hair?"

Charles felt up where he had hit his head, and in addition to feeling a lump already swelling, his hand came away wet. Without thinking, he brought his hand down, and the last thing he saw before his vision swam and the sunlight dimmed was his own bloody fingers.

∼

Charles woke up on a hay bale in the barn, the boys crowding around him. "Look, he ain't dead!" one exclaimed. There were some disappointed murmurs.

"For the love of Pete," said Fielding, "I *told* you boys he weren't dead! Now give him some room, you're breathin' up all his air." Reluctantly, the boys backed up a pace or two.

"Harvestin' ain't been this much fun since Pratt got bit by that copperhead!" said a voice in the crowd, inspiring others to reminisce fondly about that day until their conversation was interrupted by the Bulfinch bell.

"Off with you, now. Except you, Cantrell, double time up to Bulfinch and get a glass of water for poor Weston here." Cantrell sprinted off, happy at the prospect of missing the start of class as Fielding sat on the bale next to Charles. "Quite the egg on yer noggin there. Care to tell me how it came about?"

Despite the fog in his head, Charles was able to avoid the embarrassing truth of his failed dog-training efforts. "Tripped on a root, hit my head on a rock."

"Musta been a mighty whack to make ya faint dead away."

Charles was happy to let Fielding think it was the blow to his head that had caused him to faint.

"Well, just set quiet 'til that water comes," said Fielding. He slapped Charles on the knee before standing up and leaving the barn.

Charles lay on the hay bale and thought of how hard it would be to do anything but lay on the hay bale right now. All his energy seemed to have leached out of him. He thought of Aidan, now in class and probably wondering where Charles was, but he lacked the strength to even keep thinking about that.

After a while, Cantrell showed up with his water. "Cook also sent this for you to clean up your bean." He handed Charles a dripping wet rag along with the glass. Charles sat up and drank down half the glass of water, suddenly aware that he was wildly thirsty.

Cantrell rocked back on his heels. "Helluva way to get out of an hour of class, but whatever it takes, eh?"

Charles drained his glass and handed it back with a grunt.

"Cook'll flay me if I don't get this glass back to her, but the rag's a keeper." Cantrell trotted out of the barn and up the hill to Bulfinch.

Charles did his best to clean up his hair without looking at the rag. When he thought he'd done the best he could, he tossed the rag behind the bales of hay and then was startled to hear a low growl emanating from where the rag had landed. The growl came closer and got louder, and the hair on Charles's neck stood on end. Finally, from the shadows there emerged a scrappy dog, mottled brown and black. He stopped still as a statue and locked eyes with Charles, his growl backing off but still simmering.

They stayed frozen in this position until Fielding rounded the corner into the barn. "Lucifer! Go on with ya! Git! Thought I heard him. He didn't bite ya, did he?"

"Naw, he didn't do nothin'." Lucifer slunk back to wherever he was hiding before.

"Well, good, because that woulda been one heck of an afternoon for you. Attacked by a rock *and* a dog." Fielding smiled.

"He bites?" Charles asked. Oddly, once Charles had been able to see the dog, his nervousness had dissipated. Maybe it was because the dog was smaller than his growl had led him to believe.

"Bit a Fifth Classer last month. Bradley's been after me to put him down—Lucifer, not the Fifth Classer"—Fielding grinned—"but he's right hard to catch. Every time I set my mind to it, it's like he knows what I'm thinking and slinks away." Fielding leaned up against a post and scratched his beard. "'Tween you, me, and the lamppost, my heart ain't in it. I've no problem putting down a beast that's in pain, not to mention the animals we raise for slaughter. But Lucifer, he's one smart bugger. Don't feel right to snuff him out, even though he's mean as a snake. Ah, I must be gettin' soft in the head." Fielding shooed the whole subject away with his hands. "You're lookin' much improved. I've a few things to take care of down by the wharf, and then I'll see you up to your classroom."

Charles realized he was feeling better—good enough that he could proceed up to Bulfinch himself—but why rush going to class? He could wait for Fielding. He stood up gingerly but felt no dizziness. Just then he heard a low, almost imperceptible growl, and he turned to find Lucifer out of his tunnel of hay bales again.

Charles looked down and crossed his arms. "Can't stay away, huh? I dunno what you want from me." But as he said it, he realized that he still had pieces of roast in his pocket and that Lucifer was undoubtedly smelling that roast. "Ah, I'm onto you now. Well, this here was supposed to be training roast, but my dog-trainin' career ain't lookin' aces right now." He pulled the handkerchief from his pocket and unwrapped the meat. Lucifer stopped growling. "You poor bugger. Always lookin' over your shoulder so as you don't get caught. You an' me both, we're too smart for that, ain't we?" Charles tossed Lucifer the meat, and Lucifer caught it in midair, making short work of it without taking his eyes off Charles.

"You ain't so bad as they're makin' you out to be, are ya?" mused Charles, and he took a step toward the dog. Lucifer exploded in a fury of snarling and barking, and after the dog was sure this display registered, he turned tail and retreated down his hay tunnel.

"Oh sure, take my roast and then snap at me!" Charles called after Lucifer, but he understood. Just because someone gives you food doesn't mean you can trust him.

CHAPTER 19

AFTER A BRIEF DETOUR TO THE ICEHOUSE FOR A CHUNK TO PUT ON his head, Charles was escorted to the classroom by Fielding. He could see the look of relief on Aidan's face from across the room. Charles kept himself awake in the stuffy room by running the rag full of ice back and forth on his neck when he felt in danger of dozing off. It wasn't until the bell rang to end class that Aidan could talk with Charles.

"What the hell happened to you?" Aidan asked before they even left the classroom. "That Cantrell feller said you split your nut wide open on a boulder fallin' down a ravine."

"That story seems to have gotten a bit more grand with the retellin'. Did he mention how Florence Nightingale herself was tendin' to my wounds?"

"It ain't funny. He said they was thinkin' about takin' you to a hospital on the mainland."

"The only medical help I got was a glass of water and a rag, and that came from Cantrell. What a goddamn fabricator. I oughta kick his arse."

"I couldn't make heads or tails of what the teacher was sayin' 'til you walked in. Jaysus." Aidan let out a long breath as they sat under their tree in the yard.

It dawned on Charles how worried Aidan had been and that it

had been more than a year since anyone had worried about where he was. This feeling was so unfamiliar and overwhelming that he couldn't say anything for a while.

When the moment passed, Aidan said, "So what did happen to you?"

"I told Fielding I tripped on a root and hit my head on a rock."

"But . . .?"

"Well, the rock part is true. But there weren't no root. Listen, I know you ain't gonna tell any of these other mugs, but I was tryin' to train Quincy, and he knocked me straight down onto that rock."

"Quincy! You sure you didn't come up with that idea *after* you hit your head?"

"Fielding'll pay a dollar if you can teach him a trick."

"Based on that egg on your head, seems like it's worth more than a dollar."

"I'll give you that. I pulled a weed yesterday that looked smarter than that dog."

Several boys passed by Aidan and Charles, heading around to the back of the building. Charles watched them until they disappeared. "You gonna go work some cow shit into your garden?"

Aidan picked up a leaf and twirled it by the stem. "Nah. Cows take the best shits after supper. I'll go then." They leaned back against the tree, saying nothing, side by side, content.

Aidan tried to cram just a few more weeds into his overflowing sack as he knelt in his flower bed after supper. He wondered if some of the plants in his sack should have stayed in the garden. He was operating under the general principle that the thriving plants were weeds and the dying ones were not, but there seemed to be exceptions to the rule.

"Determined to take out every dacent-lookin' livin' thing, are ya?" said a voice with a familiar brogue.

Aidan twisted to see Dec leaning on a shovel behind him. "It's too easy to grow the things that *want* to grow here," Aidan said as he stood.

"An' haven't you just summed up the whole idea of gardening." Dec took inventory of Aidan's patch of dirt. "To be sure, it's a wasteland. I've a few marigolds to spare if you've a mind to tart it up a bit."

"I'll take anything." Aidan slapped at a mosquito on his forearm. "These buggers are eating me alive. Don't they bother you?"

"Ah, there's another thing I can give you from my garden. A bit of Declan Moore's Mosquito Dissuader Plant, commonly known as peppermint. Ya rub the leaves on your skin."

"Cow manure and peppermint—it's a wonder they let you into the dormitory at night," said Aidan.

"Now that's the beauty of gardenin' this time of the evenin'— swim's right after. We'll all be smellin' like harbor water when we turn in."

Aidan laughed nervously. "I'm more of a bathtub bloke, to tell true. Think I'll stick to gettin' clean indoors."

"Nah, nobody uses them tubs except for their first day an' then when it's cold—and I do mean cold. Last swim's sometime in October. Watch ya don't freeze your stones off."

"But . . . but . . . ain'tcha got a choice in the matter? What if I don't want to go to evening swim?"

"If it's choice you're wanting, you came to the wrong island." Dec's chuckle had a bitter edge. "Hope you like chapel, boyo."

Just then, the Bulfinch bell began to ring. Fielding called out for all the boys to line up and count off. Dec clapped Aidan on the back and said, "And if you're fearing the water, then it's John Balentine you'll be seeing down by the wharf."

After count off, there was some delay up in the front of the line.

Aidan looked around as boys started up quiet conversations and realized that Salt was behind him. They were separated only by one boy, who was currently occupied with digging earwax out of his ear.

"Say, can I switch with ya?" Aidan asked the digger.

"Sure, we're same height anyway." The boy swapped places with him and resumed his work.

"Salt," said Aidan, looking down.

"Arthur Weston. How's Day Two treatin' ya?"

"Yeah, well, you know, it's all right. But I got a question for ya. About somethin' Dec said."

"Shoot."

"Well, just now he said somethin' about having no choice, and that he hoped I liked chapel, but then it was time for count off, and I didn't have time to ask him what he meant." Truthfully, he might not have asked Dec even if he'd had the time. He sensed an anger lying just beneath Dec's comments that he didn't want to provoke.

"Hmm, and it's only Tuesday. He usually doesn't get all feisty until Wednesday. Tomorrow's chapel day, you see, and that tends to gets his nose outta joint."

"You go to church on Wednesdays instead of Sundays here?"

"Wednesdays and Sundays. Twice on Sundays, actually." Salt smiled the smile of the first one to deliver bad news.

Jaysus, Aidan thought to himself, *wait 'til Charles hears that*. "So Dec don't like services?"

"Not these services. You see, being of the Irish persuasion, the poor bastard was raised Catholic, and he don't like going to regular church. I says to him when he first got here, 'It ain't like they're makin' you go to the Jew church where they wear them girlie shawls and speak that gibberish,' but then he says to me, 'What if they made you go to Catholic church and it was all Latin and flingin' incense about and eatin' them wafers?' and I had to admit he had a point."

Aidan thought about St. Joseph's and the stained glass windows, and right then he wished he'd gone to Mass more often, or at least once right before he left for the island. "So they make you go, even if you ain't Protestant?" Now Dec's reaction to the idea of choice here at the school made sense, total and complete sense, to Aidan, who would now have to go through the same experience—except no one here other than Charles knew he was Catholic. With a sense of growing agitation, he realized that he would have to pretend that he was familiar with Protestant services, something he and Charles had failed to cover when syncing up their stories the night before they left.

"'Course they make you go. I told Dec, 'You think you feel bad, what about that poor bastard Ben Hausmann,' but some people just don't want to be cheered up. The Irish is a moody race, I tell ya."

"There's a Jew here?"

"Yeah, and when he showed up, he had a big powwow with Bradley. Some of the boys was listening through the door, and Hausmann put it to Bradley that Jews don't believe in Jesus! I mean, that's about as basic as it gets!"

"So how can that be a religion if they don't have Jesus?"

"Exactly," Salt said with satisfaction just as the line started moving down toward the wharf.

As he walked, Aidan thought about Dec and Ben Hausmann and himself and maybe other boys here, all sitting and listening to what would be considered false religion, maybe even heresy, back in their old neighborhoods. How his mother would feel if she knew what he would be doing three times a week. Did Dec's mother know? Was she alive? How could Ben's family let him be here—did they even know that he would be forced to attend Christian services and pray to Jesus?

When the line of boys rounded the bend, the water came into full view, giving Aidan's stomach a lurch. He turned back to Salt as he walked. "Dec said I would be seeing Balentine when we got to the wharf. Which one is he?"

"Balentine, eh? You skittish in the water?"

"Maybe."

"Tiny should have some sympathy for that. I'll introduce ya."

But as it turned out, Salt's services were not needed, because Bradley himself was at the wharf to intercede. Once the signal to break formation was given, most of the boys stripped naked and charged into the water within thirty seconds, leaving a handful on the beach with Bradley, including Charles, Aidan, and a tall, gangly boy with a blush of acne across his forehead.

"Arthur Weston," intoned Bradley, "I'd like you to meet John Balentine, Third Class. He will be your swim instructor for as long as necessary. As I mentioned before, Master Balentine had similar concerns about the water when he first arrived here, so he will be most able to assist you." Bradley clasped Aidan's shoulder with one hand and Balentine's with the other, forming a human bridge between the two as if to cement their new relationship. Looking pleased, he led Charles away, though Charles clearly would have preferred to stay.

Aidan and Tiny walked to the far side of the wharf, where there were no boys in the water.

"Gotta be honest with ya," said Tiny, looking over at Boston on the horizon, "it's a mixed blessing to be put with me."

"Whaddya mean?" *Not an inspiring start*, thought Aidan nervously.

"Well, it's grand that they ain't makin' you plow into the water like all the others, but all of them are seein' you here with me. It's like advertisin' the problem you got. Some like to see who's weak, if you know what I mean." They sat down on the pebbly sand, feet just inches away from the water's edge.

"Like Caleb Hart?" Aidan looked at Tiny for reaction.

Balentine looked at Aidan and gave a wry grin. "Second day and you already heard about Hart, huh? He mess with you yet?"

"Nah. Just heard about him."

"He usually waits 'til you settle in." Tiny went back to looking at the Boston skyline.

Aidan wondered if he could talk to Bradley about declining swim lessons. Wasn't this supposed to make him feel better, not worse?

Tiny sighed. "Well, down to business. For most of the boys, this here is the best part of their day, maybe next to eatin' or strokin' themselves at night. They can horse around, be loud, cool off. Joy to the world. They don't even notice that they're gettin' clean. But for us, it ain't never gonna be like that. It's just another thing we gotta do. Just another chore to get through."

Aidan felt himself sinking into despair, dragged down by the anchor of Tiny's gloomy demeanor. He waited for instructions on how they would begin this chore, but Tiny just stared out across the water.

"So . . . how are we gonna start?" Aidan asked tentatively.

Tiny looked over at him with a faint expression of surprise, as if he hadn't expected Aidan to still be there. "Right. Well. I'll show ya. First you gotta get rid of them clothes." Tiny began undressing, folding his clothes into a neat pile on the beach.

When Aidan got down to his trousers, he hesitated. He looked over to the other side of the wharf, where he saw more naked bums than he had ever seen in one place. Not one of the boys seemed to mind this exposure. Aidan couldn't see Charles, but he wondered if he was as uninhibited as, say, the boys jumping off the wharf, testicles protectively cupped in their hands only at the last possible moment before hitting the water. Aidan looked to the beach: only Fielding and the industrial teacher, Mr. Croft, were supervising the swarm of boys. For once, the matron was nowhere to be found.

Aidan finished undressing and stood with one hand in front of his genitals, unable to relax his arm down to his side just yet.

Tiny went over to the end of the wharf, reached underneath, and pulled out a thick, shoulder-high stick.

"What," joked Aidan, "you're gonna push me in the water with that stick?"

Tiny looked at the stick as if he were considering this alternate use. After a moment, he said, "It's got these marks on it, see?" Aidan walked over to see the stick. The marks cut into the wood started about knee height and continued up the stick every two inches or so. "First day, up to the first mark, second day, second mark, and on like that." Tiny reached under the wharf again and brought out a small wooden bucket. "'Til you can get all the parts of you that stink into the water, you use this bucket to rinse off."

Aidan looked at the highest mark on this stick, which was about level with his jaw. *No feckin' way*, he thought, *I am ever going to be in this harbor up to my throat.*

Tiny waded out to his knees and plunged the stick into the water so that the first mark was just visible. Some boys from the other side of the wharf were gathering and chuckling. One of them pointed and said something Aidan did not catch, which caused the others to all laugh together. Tiny began to look irritated.

"If you ain't up to this mark and rinsed off by the time swim is done, you and me are staying out here 'til you are. And if you don't like four of them pointin' and laughin' now, wait 'til a hundred of them are all lined up and got nothin' to look at except us."

Aidan walked slowly into the water. To his ankles was all right. This was how deep his bath water had been the day before. The next step was more difficult. The water lapped up against his shins, making him flinch. Sweat broke out on his brow. He heard Tiny let out a sigh.

In an instant, all his agitation combusted into anger. This was the sympathetic teacher for those who were afraid of water? This was the surefire method of curing his problem? To have this gloomy arsehole tapping his toe, looking like he lost a bet and got stuck with this job? Aidan's rage spilled over and found its target.

"Listen, Balentine, or Tiny, or whatever they call you, I don't know who pissed in your tankard, but you are a shit swim teacher. Maybe you oughta try pretending that you don't hate this, or me, or this harbor. If you have any recollection about how it feels to go through this, you might want to dredge up them memories and try to help me, 'cause now it's you that's makin' this take so long because you are *no goddamned help!*"

Up close, Aidan could now look directly into Tiny's close-set eyes, but Tiny had trouble meeting his gaze. Looking away from the wharf, Tiny said softly, "It's me."

"What's you? It's you that's the arsehole? I couldn't agree more."

"It's me that they're laughing at." Tiny's voice was almost a whisper. "Most of 'em forgot. I go into the water every night, make sure I ain't the last one in, horse around, laugh, nobody notices I don't go in past my waist. I get wet all over, I look like I been out deeper. But then at supper tonight Bradley tells me I got a new job. You're my new job. And now they remember. You want me to remember how it feels to go through this? How I puked on the boat ride over and it wasn't five minutes after we landed before the whole island knew? How two Third Classers carried me near the water my first week and pretended to throw me in and I pissed myself? Trust me. I'm rememberin' it now."

"I'm sorry." Aidan cast around for something else to say. "I really think they're laughin' at me, to be honest." They both looked toward the wharf, but the boys had gotten bored and had drifted away. "See, we ain't *that* interestin'."

Just then, Charles rounded the end of the wharf and came wading into the water toward them. "Well if I didn't see it with my own peepers, I would not believe it."

"What?" Aidan said, but as he looked down, he realized with amazement and a bit of horror that his knees were fully covered by harbor water. In his anger, he must have strode toward Tiny without realizing it.

"How'd ya do it?" asked Charles.

Aidan replied, "I had a good teacher."

Tiny smiled.

Just after Bradley settled into his desk chair after walking up from the wharf, there was a knock at his office door. "Enter," he said with some irritation. The boys' evening swim was when Bradley liked to catch up on the remaining paperwork of the day. With the window open, he could hear the boys enjoying themselves in the water as the day of farm work was rinsed from their bodies. There were board members who were concerned that such frequent bathing would be harmful to the boys' health, but Bradley had seen no evidence of this. To the contrary, in fact—it seemed to keep the lice at bay, and few could argue that the smell of one hundred boys in the summer was not improved by this practice. He had come to think of the evening swim as a sort of natural daily baptism, and he imagined the boys' souls coming out of the water a little cleaner than when they went in. Last October, his first autumn on the island, he'd found himself saddened when the water became too cold for this evening ritual, and on the day in April this year when it had begun again, he had felt a great satisfaction.

This time of evening, however, was also the favored time for the teachers to approach him with the issues of the day, since all female staff were required to be within the confines of Bulfinch to prevent them from exposure to the nakedness down by the water. It was rare that Bradley could get through even one piece of correspondence without a knock at his door, and it seemed that this evening would be no exception.

But it was Mrs. Bradley who entered this time.

"Mrs. Bradley," he said. "A pleasant surprise!"

"Good evening, Mr. Bradley." She stood before his desk with ramrod posture. When they first arrived on this island, they had agreed for propriety's sake that they would address each other as Mr. and Mrs. Bradley except within the confines of their bedroom. At first this was awkward, especially when they were alone, but by now it was reflexive.

"How can I be of assistance to the matron?" he asked.

"I would like to see the Weston boys' file, as we discussed yesterday."

"Ah, yes, the Masters Weston." He retrieved the file from his desk drawer. "I've pressed Balentine into service for resolving Arthur's fear of the water. They're at it now." He glanced at the file briefly before handing it to her. "Just what is it that you are looking for in this file?"

"I shall know when I find it," she said as she took the file and sat across the desk from him to peruse it.

Bradley mentally reviewed the contents of the file, which were so sparse that he could recall everything known about the Weston brothers: their West End address, no living kin, their recently deceased mother a regular churchgoer and a teetotaler. He couldn't imagine what Mary would find that would not be to her liking.

She looked up. "Where is the Affirmation of Character Letter?" For applicants who were orphans, the school typically requested a letter from a neighbor or friend of the family attesting to the boy's Christian values and upstanding behavior.

The letter. He had never heard back from Stryker after their meeting. "Stryker didn't have one when he came here. I requested that he obtain one and put it in the post," he said, bracing for his wife's response.

"But he hasn't yet. So we only have Stryker's word?"

"And the word of the boys' minister."

"Whom you have never met."

"My dear, why would Stryker lie? He is a minister, for goodness' sake."

"Why would he not provide an Affirmation Letter? He provided one for that other boy."

"Burr. Yes. He must have forgotten this time. I shall write him this evening and remind him, if it pleases you, but is it really necessary at this point? The boys are here. If we don't have an Affirmation Letter a month from now, we aren't going to ask them to leave." Bradley came around from his side of the desk and sat next to Mary. "In my nine years of working with boys of this age, I have seen all sorts, and I can tell you that Charles and Arthur are good boys." He grasped Mary's small hands and held them, looking into her eyes.

"And in my ten years of working with boys of his age, I have seen my share of lying, and I can tell you that Charles is hiding something." She pulled her hands away.

"But what could that be?" Bradley implored. "Their mother isn't really dead? Their father didn't really abandon them? They secretly have a fortune? You can see as plainly as I that they are poor and undereducated boys, and I don't believe they would be here if they had any other choice. Let us accept this and put our efforts toward molding them into fine, self-sufficient young men."

The matron took a deep breath. "All right. I will defer to your judgment on these boys, Mr. Bradley." Bradley could hear what silently followed that sentence. *You haven't changed my mind. I will still be watching them.* But at least the conversation was closed for the time being.

"How has little Henry been today? I haven't seen him since after breakfast." Henry was always a subject on which they could agree.

Mary smiled for the first time since she'd entered the room. "He has the new nurse wrapped around his little finger, I'm afraid. She'd spoil him rotten if I didn't intervene now and again."

"Well, thank goodness you are there to put a stop to that," Bradley said softly as he reached for Mary's hands, and this time, she did not pull away.

After a moment, Bradley stood and tugged his vest down. "And now I'm afraid I must get back to this correspondence. But I will be in to see Henry before he goes down for the night."

When Bradley reached the other side of his desk, Mary was standing but had made no move to leave. "Is there something else?" he asked.

"Yes. Well, perhaps not. I'm not sure."

"Mrs. Bradley, I must note in my journal this unusual day on which you were not sure of something." Bradley smiled.

His smile was not returned. "I have heard some disturbing conversations concerning Miss Turner."

Bradley's smile faded. They had only just hired Miss Turner three months ago. Her references were impeccable, and her enthusiasm for educating rivaled that of the Bradleys'. Mrs. Bradley, however, had objected to her hire on the grounds that she was too attractive. With her glossy chestnut hair, blue-green eyes, and petite form, she was indeed far prettier than any of the other teachers. And while all the teachers were unmarried, only twenty-year-old Miss Turner was in her prime.

"What is the nature of your objection?" Bradley had asked his wife when Miss Turner had applied.

"I have dozens of objections, and they are all in First and Second Class."

"Mrs. Bradley, they are mere boys!"

"You think of them as boys, but some of them can have the thoughts of men."

In the end, Bradley had dismissed his wife's concern as irrelevant and had insisted that since not every teacher was willing to live year-round on an island, they could not afford to turn away such a qualified applicant based on her looks. The only concession Mrs. Bradley was able to obtain was that Miss Turner would teach the youngest class.

"How is her instruction?" Bradley hoped for an academic issue.

"Superior. Sixth Class has not received such excellent grades since you became superintendent, and they have the fewest demerits of any class."

"So the concern is . . . of a personal nature?" Bradley asked with a sinking feeling.

The matron hesitated. "It may be premature to bring this issue to you. What I have heard is essentially just chatter from the other teachers." She paused as they both remembered Miss Turner's first weeks here, how the other teachers had taken an instant dislike to her based on her youth and beauty, how they had made her feel less than welcome. "I'm sorry to have wasted your time," she concluded.

"Not at all, Mrs. Bradley. As you know, I like to keep my ear to the ground on all issues pertaining to my staff. I trust you will come to me if you hear substantiation of this chatter?"

"You can rest assured, Mr. Bradley, that I will."

Once the matron had left, Bradley let out a little sigh, relieved that he did not have to hear the details of the teachers' chatter. It was better not to know some things, he felt, until there was a need to know.

CHAPTER 20

WHEN THE BOYS FILED OUT OF BULFINCH AFTER DINNER THE NEXT day, Aidan slapped Charles on the back and with a wordless smile headed off to the flower gardens. As Charles settled himself against the tree in the yard to brood a bit about being left alone, he noticed Bill, Sumner, Tink, and Salt in a huddle not far away. After a minute, the huddle broke, and Bill headed over with the two others close behind.

"Looks like your brother left you for a rose bush," said Bill with a grin. "Not a gardener, I take it?"

"Cow shit ain't my cuppa tea," Charles grumbled.

Bill stuck his hands in his pocket and looked over toward the gardens. "Well, if you can grab your brother on the way, we got somethin' to show the two of you."

Once Aidan joined them, they walked single file between the garden plots, and at the end, Charles saw what he had not noticed yesterday—that there was a tall privet hedge that ran along the back of the garden area, and in the middle of the hedge was an arch-shaped passageway to the other side. Charles was the last of the boys to pass through, and when he emerged, he felt odd and off-center. He recalled a time, years ago, when he'd had a high fever and everything in the tenement—windows, door, table, stove—had taken on strange proportions and dimensions. Now, looking out over this vista, things also didn't seem the right size. At the end of a grassy slope he could see a row of a dozen evenly spaced houses, but they looked too small—the nearby flagpole towered above them, many times higher than the tiny structures. Each house was different in some way—different door, or windows, or trim—and most had plants or little bushes carefully tended around their foundations. At this distance, it was hard to tell how big the houses were. Could a boy fit in one? An adult? Were they for animals? If this island were for girls, he would have thought they were dollhouses.

Aidan looked equally puzzled. "What are all them little buildings?"

"That," Bill answered proudly, "is Cottage Row."

They trotted down the incline and arrived in front of one of the cottages, this one yellow with white trim. "This here's ours—Laurel." Bill slapped the side of the building. "She ain't the biggest or the fanciest, but she ain't the humblest either." Charles could see that the door was just tall enough to admit most of the older boys here, but that any adult would have to stoop to enter, a thought that pleased him.

"Yeah," Tink added, "the humblest would likely be Deer Horn over yonder," and he gestured to the second to last cottage on the left. Two boys were prying boards from the side of the house. "That's the second time this summer they're tearin' off a chunk of that place, tryin' to make it bigger. Why they built it so damn small in the first place is anybody's guess. You stuff even four boys in there, they're smellin' their own farts it's so close."

"And thank you, as always, Mr. Tinkham, for that cunning description. Sometimes I do not remember why we let you buy any Laurel shares in the first place," said Bill, trying not to smile.

"Musta been my good manners, but it's clear you ain't got any. You gonna invite these Westons inside, or do they have to cool their heels in the side garden?"

"Right this way," said Bill as he entered the cottage first.

Inside there was a table and chairs and a small warped bookcase with an oil lamp on top. Pinned on one wall was an array of battleship pictures that looked like they'd come from a magazine. Salt opened windows in the front and back to let the breeze air out the stuffy room. They sat down around the table.

"It's grand," said Aidan. "So . . . whaddya do here?"

"Well," said Bill as he sat and tipped his chair back so that it rested on the wall, "when you have shares in a cottage, that's where you can always go. The others that have shares is gonna treat you fair, and vice-a versa. Any bad blood between you, we settle here at this table. Some mug outside of Laurel does you wrong, this ain't a bad place to plot your revenge. Plus we play the other cottages in sports on the weekend."

"Here's also 'bout the only decent place to study," added Tink. "Rule is, if one of us is studyin', anybody else in here's gotta shut their trap. You ain't gonna get that kinda cooperation in the dormitory. And some of them in other cottages come to practice their instrument."

Charles frowned. "What kinda instrument?"

"The school band?" prompted Bill. "Christ, Bradley didn't tell you much, huh? This place had the first school band in the country, Bradley told us."

"You're awful proud for someone with a tin ear. They wouldn't let you into the band if you paid 'em," teased Salt.

"*Anyway*," said Bill, glaring at Salt in mock annoyance, "the point is, the cottages is a place you can go when you don't want to be with all them other mugs." Bill gestured with his hand toward the window, indicating all the others on the island. "Plus, we have been known to scare up the odd game of poker from time to time."

"Oh, Mr. Dutton!" Tink called out in falsetto. "You young men aren't *wagerin'* in there with coins or tokens standin' in for any *money*, are you? That would be strictly against school rules!" He cooled himself with an invisible fan.

Salt laughed and threw his cap at Tink. "You're off your nut, Tinkham."

"I ain't speakin' to you, ya traitor," said Tink as he threw the cap back. "Starlight my arse."

"Ladies, ladies, let's keep it civil," intoned Bill. He turned to Charles. "You see, Salt here owns two shares of Laurel, but he's puttin' them back up so he can buy two in Starlight, so he can be with Dec."

"And I hope you will be happily married for a long time," said Tink to Salt.

"Shut it, Tinkham. We been over this about twenty times."

"Can you two pantywaists pipe down for a minute so I can explain this?" Bill tilted his chair back down to the floor.

Aidan interjected, "Ain't Dec part of Laurel?"

"He's been on the island the least outta all of us," Bill explained. "He only got here a little more than a year ago, and by the time we figured out we wanted him, Starlight had already hooked him. They're all right over there, not a bad cottage if you can't be in Laurel. Your dormitory mate Poole is over there. But they got shares up for grabs 'cause Will Thayer's leaving end of this week, and Thayer agreed to sell his shares to Salt."

Charles thought about this. "So you're offering the shares to us?"

"Shares is bought, not given. Two dollars a share."

"Who says we got four dollars?"

"Who says you don't?"

Tink frowned at Charles. "Ya know, if you're gonna be—"

Bill cut him off. "Tink, we talked about this. We decided."

A silence intervened while Charles and Aidan contemplated the situation. They could hear the sounds of the other cottages—laughter in one nearby, nails shrieking as weathered boards were pulled off of Deer Horn, a door opening and slamming shut and boys racing each other back to Bulfinch.

Bill addressed Charles. "Listen, we're makin' an exception here for the two of you mugs. Laurel's always had four members: me, Tink, Sumner, and Salt. But the two of you is blood, and we don't wanna split ya."

"Well, I'm in," declared Aidan.

Charles looked at him with surprise. "We ain't talked about this, brother."

"What's to talk about? It sounds grand."

"We'll take him without ya," said Bill, "if you're really not interested."

"No," said Charles quickly. "I'm in too."

"Thought so," said Bill, and then a smile widened his face. "Welcome to Laurel."

Swim that evening had come early to accommodate chapel services. A damp-headed procession of boys shuffled into the chapel from the hallway, single file, and filled the pews in their pre-established height sequence so that the shortest boys were up front. Mr. Bradley was already there, elevated by a platform and obscured from the chest down by a podium. He arranged papers fussily, smoothing his mustache as he reviewed something from the top page, turning up the wick on the podium's lamp to see the words more clearly. He looked out over the boys filing in, scanning the crowd until he found the boy he was looking for.

Charles had managed to fall back after count off so that he was next to Aidan, walking on tiptoes to evade detection by the matron. Salt had also swapped with the boy between him and Aidan so the three of them could shuffle along together. Just as Aidan was about to sit down, Dec entered the pew in front of him, bent his right knee, and crossed himself. Before he was even finished, Bradley's voice boomed out above the din of the boys.

"Master Moore, may I remind you, again, that we do not genu-flect in chapel." Bradley's hands gripped the side of the podium and he stared down at Dec peevishly.

"'Tis a habit hard to break, sir. Dreadful sorry." Dec ducked his head in a gesture of respect, but Aidan noticed that his brogue was thicker than he'd heard it so far, right-off-the-boat thick, like Maeve when she was in her cups. He looked up at Bradley, who did not appear satisfied with Dec's apology.

"One demerit, Master Moore," said Bradley as he made a note on one of his papers.

Salt leaned in and whispered to Aidan, "Pretty much every week they go through this. Bradley's bent on squashing the Irish Catholic outta Dec, and Dec is just as bent on stayin' a Pope-lovin' Mick. But he does it all meek and respectful-like, so Bradley can't do nothin' but slap a demerit on him. Which Dec don't care about." The boys sat down and tried to get comfortable on the hard wooden pew. "And Dec goes out of his way to get the best grades in Third Class. Always in the top three. Anytime you can't find him in his garden, he's usually over in Starlight hittin' the books. It's just another way he's stickin' it to Bradley, like showin' him that he can be as Irish as the Blarney Stone and still be as smart as a whip." Salt stated this proudly, as if besting Bradley was something he himself had done.

"Don't he get put down in Purgatory after a while with all them demerits?" asked Aidan. Yesterday, Aidan and Charles had noticed the large chart in the dining hall with a row for every boy and a column for every day of the month, newly updated with their names and the demerits Charles had received for his profanity in front of the matron. Aidan had noticed that Dec had a fair number of marks.

"Most every month he's almost at the maximum, but he ain't never gone over. He keeps track. He ain't gonna give Bradley the pleasure."

Just then, Bradley cleared his throat several times, and the chatter of the boys died away.

"Good evening. Through the grace of God we gather here tonight . . ." Almost immediately, Bradley's voice faded into a background murmur for Aidan. Salt had told him as they marched up the hill from evening swim that although on Sunday morning there was a visiting minister from the mainland, it was just the superintendent on Wednesday and Sunday nights, and that Bradley's nights were generally a mix of biblical lessons on good character and a few school announcements. The trick, Salt had advised sagely, was to perk up for the announcements, which could be something important like a baseball game organized for the weekend or a special dessert for Sunday dinner.

With Aidan's mind free to wander, it gravitated to Dec's defiance. Here Aidan sat, raised as Irish as Dec and sitting one pew away, but while Dec would stick his thumb in the eye of anyone trying to tell him that he should cover up his heritage or his religion, Aidan was striving to do just that—deny his upbringing and his church. He thought of Maeve, how she would have liked Dec, would have approved of his resistance, would have been proud of him on behalf of Ireland. What did that make Aidan? Would Maeve be ashamed of what Aidan was doing? He had been so busy since he and Charles had landed on the island two days ago—had it really only been two days?—that he had not had a chance to think much about Maeve. But now he missed her sharply, and he missed their small tenement, where he could be who he was, not have to worry about whether his voice had a hint of brogue or whether he would remember to answer to a name that wasn't his. Suddenly the burden of being Arthur Weston doubled in weight, the yoke heavy on his shoulders, and he wanted to crawl onto his old straw mattress in the West End and fall asleep, never again to see these ninety-nine boys for whom he had to pretend that he had a brother, didn't have a mother, and had never put a communion wafer on his tongue.

Aidan sat, trapped in his misery, as Bradley droned on. Eventually the superintendent wrapped up his discussion of Proverbs 22 and paused, clearing his throat as he looked through his papers on the podium. Salt nudged Aidan, and all the boys shifted in their seats. "My trip to the stationers' in Boston, which was postponed last week due to inclement weather, transpired yesterday, and I have procured the sorely needed new composition books for the Second School and other various school supplies. While there, I also purchased new stationery with which you may write to your families. As usual, you may purchase these items, as well as stamps, at the School Store."

And then, Aidan started to feel a little better as a plan formed in his head—a plan of which he was pretty sure Charles would not approve.

It wasn't until right before supper the next day that Charles and Aidan had a chance to meet with the boys down in the Laurel Cottage. Both boys dug in their pockets and tossed crumpled bills on the scarred table. Charles had offered to lend the money to him, but Aidan's mother had secretly slipped some dollar bills into his baseball mitt before he left, now enabling him to pay his own way.

"All right, then. Tink, as our treasurer, will see that these here funds get to the Laurel account in the School Bank."

"Or," said Tink as he pocketed the bills, "I could give it to Webber and ask him for a bottle of somethin' refreshin' and some of them girlie postcards."

"Use your own funds, you deviant," said Bill.

"Who's Webber?" asked Aidan.

"Webber," said Tink dreamily with a goofy smile on his face. "He's the mug you wish was your best friend."

"Webber's the mail carrier," Salt explained. "First Class, straight as an arrow, which is why he got the job in the first place. He goes over to Boston every day, finds his way over to the big old post office there, and gets our mail, maybe does some other errands for Bradley or the principal."

"He's the only boy who gets to leave the island on his own," Bill added.

"And nobody's watchin' him!" Tink leaned forward in his chair and slapped the table. "He could be goin' anywhere, buyin' all manner of interestin' items! Except it's damn near impossible to convince him to stray from the path. That mug don't have an adventurous bone in his body. I'll tell you," and here Tink tipped his chair back and knitted his arms behind his head, "if I was the mail carrier, I'd show a bit more flexibility toward all us boys trapped on the island."

"Tink," said Bill with a smile, "the one job you ain't never gonna get is mail carrier. Bradley picks someone with a conscience, and as of yet, you ain't grown one."

"What Tink and Bill have failed to mention," Salt interrupted, "is that Webber did indeed bring back some mighty interestin' picture postcards at the beginning of the summer."

"Which nobody outside of First Class has been able to see," Bill shot back. "I don't believe it. Webber's got too much pole up his arse to do it."

"Yeah," agreed Tink, "Webber don't have the balls required for such a maneuver."

"Lester Adams says he's getting them when Thayer leaves this week and that he's gonna let Second Class boys see 'em for a fee," said Salt, sticking to his convictions. "And in one of 'em, the lady forgot to put nothin' on under her chemise."

"One of them thin summer chemises? Jesus!" Tink exclaimed, suddenly a believer. "Lester's startin' this next week?"

"How much is he gonna charge?" asked Aidan.

Charles scowled and hit Aidan on the arm. "It's horseshit. Them First Classers is just blowin' smoke. Don't believe it."

"Now I find that downright interesting," Bill mused. "Presented with the same palaver, we got us two brothers that are drawin' the opposite conclusion. I think I'm gonna like havin' the two of you in Laurel."

"But they ain't really in yet, of course," said Tink, nudging Bill.

"Right you are, Tinkham, which brings me to why we are here. There's a little something that everyone in Laurel has to do in order to be accepted into the fold, as it were."

Charles frowned and looked at Aidan, who suggested, "Let's just hear what it is."

"Wise counsel," noted Bill. "Okay, here it is: You gotta borrow something from one of the teachers."

"That don't sound so hard," said Charles cautiously.

"And when I say borrow, I mean the kind where the teacher don't know you're doin' the borrowing."

"Ah." Charles smiled.

"What are we takin'?" asked Aidan, less pleased than Charles about this turn of events.

"It's your choice. And don't worry, you'll return it after a couple of days. The only thing is, it's gotta be a personal item, and you gotta steal it at night when they're sleeping."

"Sneak into a teacher's room at night and steal somethin'?" said Aidan. "How many demerits do you get for that?"

"None," said Tink. "If you don't get caught."

"We'll do it," said Charles.

"Wait a minute," began Aidan.

"May I speak with my brother outside for a moment?" Charles stood and grabbed Aidan's arm.

When they were far enough away from the cottage, Aidan asked, "Ain't we in enough trouble already? What happened to keeping our noses clean, to being the Weston brothers who ain't ones to get into a scrape?"

"Yeah, well," said Charles, kicking a stone out of his path, "that's pretty dull."

"Dull? Ain't that why we came here?"

Charles was silent for a moment as they continued to walk aimlessly in the field. "Sully, this place, there's things about it that are just capital. My stomach ain't been so full since I don't know when, and even sharing a bed with the likes of you, it's damned comfortable. Plus I ain't got nothin' to worry about. Everything is all planned out for you here. But that's sort of the problem too. There ain't no choice. Everything is 'line up' and 'count off,' and the bell rings and you gotta hop to it. March from here to there. No talkin'. You cussed? Demerit. You late to breakfast? Demerit. Last week nobody but nobody told me what to do."

"Last week you ate somethin' outta the trash barrel that made you puke."

"I know, I know—I said this place has got its good points! What I'm sayin' is, there's only so much I can walk in a straight line without goin' off my nut." Charles thought for a moment. "So back in the cottage, you were plenty interested in payin' to see that girlie postcard. You think that ain't in Bradley's big book of rules? You think there ain't a demerit waitin' for you if Matron finds you doin' that? You ain't so saintly yourself," Charles concluded somewhat triumphantly.

Aidan started to defend himself, but then he stopped. Was it really that different? If tomorrow Lester Adams asked for his last dollar to see the girl wearing just her gauzy underclothes, wouldn't he do it, even if it meant a demerit? Or ten demerits? He knew he would, without a doubt.

"But it's stealin'," Aidan said, but with weakening conviction. "That's what we came here to stop doin'."

"It ain't stealin'. We're gonna give it back. And all the boys here done it."

They had walked in a circle and were now approaching Laurel

again. Charles stopped and made one last appeal. "Back in Boston, you begged me to cut you in on the waterfront work, where we was skulkin' around in the dark with drunks and whores, stealin' cash, and every night we coulda ended up in the paddy wagon. Here, Bill's askin' you to tiptoe down the hallway and lift a comb off of a chest of drawers, and the worst that could happen is someone makes a little mark with a little fountain pen in a little book."

"It's not a little book, it's a big chart in the dining hall." But even to Aidan, this sounded ridiculous. "Okay, fine, you win," he conceded as they reached the cottage door. "And one thing's for sure: Weren't never a Farm School boy who was better suited to the task than you."

~

They worked it out quickly before the supper bell, picking from scraps of paper in Bill's hat.

Aidan picked first. "Ya got The Coffin!" proclaimed Tink merrily. Aidan and Charles had already discovered that their teacher Miss Cuffing was known by this name among all the Second Classers.

Charles was next. "Miss Turner!" breathed Tink weakly as he pretended to faint dead away.

"I'll trade ya," said Aidan quickly.

"Wouldn't you like that," responded Charles with his crooked grin.

Aidan had pointed out Miss Turner to Charles when they were filing in for chapel last night. "Lookit that," he whispered, possibly to Charles or possibly as an involuntary utterance, as he saw her for the first time. Dressed in the same drab fashion as the other female staff, she nevertheless stood out to Aidan like a glowing coal in a pile of ash. The dim kerosene light that made unflattering shadows on the other faces only served to highlight Lydia Turner's high cheekbones and flawless skin. Walking behind The Coffin, who stood nearly six feet, Miss Turner was diminutive and graceful, gliding while the others shuffled, arranging her hands prettily in her lap when she sat, in contrast to the others who shifted and scratched.

"She's a mite better lookin' than The Coffin, huh?" mused Charles before he was distracted by the matron, who was admonishing two young boys in the front pew.

"A mite?" Aidan was once again baffled by Charles's lackluster response to the fairer sex. After several weeks working with Charles down by the waterfront, he could understand the lack of attraction to the women there. All the cleavage there that had so mesmerized Aidan had lost much of its appeal when he began to appreciate the tired faces under too much paint. But here, how could Charles, almost a year older than Aidan, fail to appreciate Miss Turner?

"It's settled, then," said Bill, donning his cap. "Tonight you both do the deed. Right after breakfast tomorrow, we all meet at Laurel, and you show us what you got."

"What about the night watchman?" asked Aidan.

"You gotta wait him out," said Tink. "He leaves sometime after eleven to do the rounds outside."

"Good luck on ya, Brothers Weston," said Tink. He slapped them both on the back and made for the door with Salt behind him.

"Hold up, one more thing," said Bill. "After dinner tomorrow, we're all here studying for the test."

Charles frowned. "Ain't that more like an individual choice?"

"Not at Laurel. You're representin' our cottage now, and Laurel don't have no eedjits in the ranks."

Aidan grinned and put a hand on Charles's shoulder. "Laurel's gonna be good for you, brother."

CHAPTER 21

AIDAN'S "BORROW" WAS EASIER THAN HE HAD ANTICIPATED.

While they waited out the night watchman, Charles whispered some pointers to Aidan. "Don't breathe too noisy, or you can't hear nothin'. In the dark, you gotta be all ears. You listen for any change in The Coffin's breathin' or shiftin' around. You think she's wakin' up, you freeze. Don't turn around and look to see if you been made. Just freeze until she sounds like she's back asleep. Get the first thing you can, and get outta there."

"What if she does wake up?"

"Say . . . I dunno, you got lost lookin' for the toilet, you're new here, you're sorry, then run. But that ain't gonna happen. This is easy."

They were silent for a while, listening to the night sounds of all the boys around them and the crickets chirping outside. They heard the whinny of a horse in the distance. Eventually they dozed, but their sleep was light and brief, their minds buzzing with the job ahead of them.

"Sully." Charles was the first to see that the night watchman was gone. He nudged Aidan's shoulder. "It's time."

As soon as he was alone, Charles started to think of all the things that Aidan might do wrong. As the minutes wore on, he became convinced that Aidan was not up to this task, and he strained to hear sounds of running or shouting that would confirm his fears. After what seemed like an unnecessarily long time, Aidan crept back into the dormitory.

"What the hell took you so long?" whispered Charles.

"I thought I heard Quincy roamin' around."

Quincy. Charles had forgotten about him. "But he sleeps outside."

"Yeah, well, we ain't even been here a week, so for all we know he sleeps inside sometimes."

"But he wasn't really there?"

"Naw. At least I didn't see him."

Charles wished he could know for sure that Quincy was outside, but there was nothing to be done about it now.

"What did you get?"

Aidan showed Charles a thin book of poetry. "Right off her night table. Turns out The Coffin sleeps like a rock. I tripped over a shoe, and she never moved. Plus her snores were drownin' out any noise I made." Aidan slipped the book under their pillow. "Your turn. Watch out for St. Bernards."

Charles crept down the hallway. Bill had drawn them a map showing the way to the room that each of them needed to find, and Charles made it there quickly. Once inside her room, he was surprised to find it well lit by the moonlight. Thick curtains that would have blocked the light were thrown back, and Charles found it strange that anyone would choose to fall asleep this way when the curtains could have been closed.

On a chest of drawers he could see a comb, a hand mirror, and a silver filigree hairpin. He picked up the hairpin, turning it around in his hand slowly. *This would certainly do*, he thought.

A little wave of disappointment washed over him. This was likely the only time he would be doing something exciting on the island, and it was turning out to be so easy. Short of running into Quincy on the way back, it felt like taking candy from a baby. There was something about his life of crime that he missed, the way his heart would pound with both the fear of getting caught and the thrill of getting away clean. *Well, there's nothing for it now,* he thought with a silent sigh, and he moved toward the door.

Lydia Turner shifted in her bed, rolling over toward the moonlight, and it was then that Charles saw the locket around her neck.

Now that would be a prize, he mused. To be able to tell Bill and Tink that he had taken the necklace from around her neck while she slept, why, that would be legendary. Generations of boys in Laurel would hear the story. And Charles could even see the clasp, lying on her chest exposed, rising and falling with her breathing. This, he knew, was meant to be.

As quiet as a cat, he put down the hairpin and approached her bed. He leaned down, without touching the bed, and reached out. As he gingerly released the clasp, the smell of rosewater wafted up from the bed and made his head feel strangely fuzzy. The clasp came undone, and now came the most difficult part: slipping the chain from the back of her neck. As he patiently and gently pulled on the chain with the locket in the palm of his hand, he noticed her hair, the color of dark, shiny pennies, not pinned back as it was during the day but spread out across the pillow in little waves. Another gentle pull, releasing the chain another inch, and he saw her night clothes, not buttoned to the neck—in fact, not buttoned at all that he could see—and the tiny beads of sweat in the thumbprint shallow at the base of her neck, rising and falling with her breath, breath he could hear now that he was so close. He felt dizzy, forgot what he was doing for a moment, then remembered and resumed, more roughly than before, forgetting that rushing a job like this was the kiss of death. His head swam with the smell of roses and the sight of those tiny beads of sweat, and he had to brace himself on the bed with his other hand, which is when Lydia Turner moaned and turned toward Charles.

What happened next was a moment in Charles's life that he

would replay countless times in his mind, both before and after he became an adult.

Lydia Turner did not open her eyes—at least, not wide enough that Charles could see them—but she reached her hand up and pushed her fingers into the hair behind his ears. Palming the back of his skull, she pulled him toward her and whispered, *"Cole . . ."* as she brought his face almost to hers. The last few inches between them were bridged as her head came off the pillow and her mouth reached out, parted, to meet his.

It was then that Charles understood.

He understood why Tink and Aidan would pay their last dimes to see Lester's postcards. He understood why boys in the dormitory would take themselves in their hand at night even though they knew that others could hear them. He understood the first thing on every sailor's mind when his ship docked in Boston. And it was because this—his lips on Lydia Turner's mouth, her tiny tongue parting his teeth—was like fire and candy and a soft pillow and a lit fuse, and it was like none of those things because it was like absolutely nothing he'd known before. He wanted to stay like this, to do this and keep doing this, forever.

It was just then that Lydia Turner realized whom she was kissing, or rather, whom she was not kissing.

The hand that had been pulling him toward her reversed course and pushed his face away as the other hand yanked the sheet to her chin with a little yelp. She sat up and backed away to the headboard, and the hand that had pushed him away now covered her mouth in horror.

Charles remained frozen in a stupid half-sitting, half-standing position, his mouth still open, his breathing labored and his sleeping pants tented. Though he had always been quick with a glib line to get himself out of an unexpected situation, he could think of absolutely nothing to say at this moment. He stared at her, his mind an empty bucket.

"Why are you here?" she hissed.

Charles couldn't remember.

When he would replay this whole experience in his mind periodically throughout his life, this was the part he would edit. Sometimes he would find a way to convince her that he was a better choice than this Cole person, whoever he was, that his charms deserved at least another kiss. Sometimes he appealed to her sense of pity, playing up the orphan angle, convincing her that he just needed to be held. Every once in a while, he would just explain the truth of why he was there, and she would understand, giving him a peck on the cheek as he left that would linger just a little longer than a peck.

But what really happened is: he stumbled out of the room, slightly bent to accommodate his tented pants, and stubbed his toe on the door on his way out.

It was more than a quarter of an hour before Charles returned to the dormitory.

"*'Oh, where were you Sully?'*" Aidan minced in a whisper. "*'You took such a long time.'* Where the feck did *you* get to?"

Charles said nothing as he climbed into bed. He had been surprised to calculate after the fact that he had probably spent no more than a few minutes in Lydia Turner's room, and that the kiss he would never forget had taken no more than two seconds. The remainder of the time he had spent sitting on the top step of the stairs, trying to sort out in his mind what had just happened as well as willing his private parts to revert to their normal state.

Aidan punched him on the arm. "Hello? Did you hit your head or somethin'?"

"Naw."

"Well, what happened? Did you get anything?"

Charles opened his hand to reveal the locket. Aidan picked it up. "That's a beaut. I think I seen her wearin' that in chapel." He put it back in Charles's hand. "Okay, and now you're gonna tell me what happened that's makin' you act so queer, even if we hafta stay up all night."

"You can't tell nobody, not Bill or Dec or no one. Understand?" Charles proceeded to tell Aidan the whole story, minus his graceless exit.

Aidan regarded Charles critically. "You ain't blowing smoke up my arse, are ya? She grabbed you by the hair and stuck her tongue in your mouth?"

"She didn't think it was me! She thought it was some mug named Cole. Probably dreamin' about her beau on the mainland."

Aidan thought about this. "She grabs your head and pulls herself off the pillow? She weren't sleepin'."

"What are you sayin'?" Charles was still having trouble thinking straight after his experience.

"She musta thought you were someone named Cole *on the island*. Someone she was expectin' tonight."

"*What?!*" Charles exclaimed a little too loudly, causing Poole in the next bed to mumble something and turn over. They waited until his wheezy snoring resumed.

"Maybe that does make some kinda sense," Charles admitted after having a moment to think about it. "Maybe that's why the curtains weren't drawn. She weren't trying to sleep."

"She wanted to *see* him. Jaysus."

They both stared up at the ceiling until Charles broke the silence. "What if she tells someone I been in her room at night?"

"But she's thinkin' that you know her secret. She's gotta be more afraid that you're gonna tell on her. I don't think she's gonna make a peep."

Of course, Charles thought. He should have figured that out—would have, if his brain weren't so foggy. "Sully, I gotta get me some shut-eye. Christ, what a night." He rolled over to face the wall.

After a minute, Aidan said, "Charles?"

"Yeah."

"What was it like—you know, kissin' her and all?"

"Well, you know what it's like to kiss any old girl, right?"

"'Course," Aidan lied.

Charles turned to face Aidan to make his point. "Well, it weren't nothin' like that." And he rolled back to face the wall again.

CHAPTER 22

No one at the breakfast table could put off talking about the previous night's adventures until they got to Laurel.

"You got it with you?" Tink asked both of them, to which they nodded.

"What is it? Give us a look, why don't ya," implored Tink through a mouthful of fried egg.

Bill intervened. "Not on your life. We wait until we're in the cottage to see what they got. Too many eyes here. But congratulations, Westons, on your success. A toast, boys!"

They raised their coffee cups as Bill said, "To carrying on the fine traditions of Laurel Cottage!"

"And what traditions might those be, Master Dutton?" said the matron, appearing, as she customarily did, out of thin air.

Without missing a beat, Bill swiveled his head around to face her. "Well, ma'am, it is our expectation that the Laurel boys will be highly ranked on today's math exam. Our final study session is after dinner this afternoon, down at the cottage."

The look on Mrs. Bradley's face revealed neither disbelief nor approval. "Well then, I look forward to reviewing all of your grades personally," she remarked, and with a rustle of skirts, she moved on to another table.

"Nicely done," said Charles with admiration as Bill took a little seated bow. The smooth lie, the unflappable transition, was an art that Charles had practiced with a variety of adults in his time living on the streets. He knew all the components: the relaxed facial expression, the steady tone of voice, the direct gaze innocent as a lamb. Bill had nailed them all just now with the matron, and seeing that, Charles's estimation of him increased a notch.

"But you know we do expect Laurel to ace the math exam, right?" Bill cocked his head.

"Of course we do," said Aidan as he turned to Charles. "As you may know, brother, the best lies are ones that contain a lot of truth."

"Yeah, I heard that once," said Charles as he stole the last of Aidan's bread and jam in retaliation.

When the 7:00 a.m. bell rang for their break before work, the boys wasted no time in getting down the hill to Laurel Cottage.

Aidan showed his book of poetry first. "I thought The Coffin just made *us* read Longfellow," said Salt. "Hard to believe she's readin' it for pleasure herself."

"When do I put it back?" asked Aidan.

"You can do it at the end of school," Bill assured them both. "Coffin will be grading the exams. She always does it right away after we hand 'em in."

"And what about, uh, Miss Turner?" said Charles, realizing with embarrassment that he was blushing at the mention of her name. He hoped no one would notice. "She gonna be busy then too?"

"Probably," Bill said as he thumbed through the Longfellow book and then put it down on the table. "Speakin' of that lovely lady, what did you grab of hers?"

Charles brought out the locket. Tink whistled. "Looks like this is worth a pretty penny. Too bad we can't sell it."

"Something this rich, I'm surprised she'd ever take it off," said Bill as he held it. "You took this off her night table?"

"Yeah," muttered Charles, scuttling his plans to brag about removing it from her neck.

"Okay," Bill announced, "you mugs passed muster, and now you're officially Laurel boys. That was some excellent purloining you done."

"Borrowing," corrected Tink.

"Exactly," said Bill, pointing at Tink without looking at him. He handed the locket back to Charles. "You better get this back to her on the double."

"I plan to," Charles said, although he dreaded the idea of going back to that room and potentially running into Lydia Turner again.

All morning, the sun beat down on the island mercilessly, and even with the front and back windows open, Laurel Cottage was an oven by the time the boys came in to study. The breeze off the water usually gave relief on the hot days, but today the wind was lazy and refused to blow up the hill. Farm work was suspended a half hour before dinner when one of the Fifth Class boys vomited from heat exhaustion while picking tomatoes. Fielding found jobs for the farm crew in the shade of the stock and storage barns until the bell rang for the midday meal.

In the cottage, Charles stared at a bumblebee buzzing outside the window, hoping it would fly in and provide distraction from the fractions on the paper in front of him. He was the only one sitting around the table that did not have his head down and his pencil scratching out numbers. Bill and Tink conferred quietly on an answer and then resumed their independent work. The bee flew off across the field, much to Charles's disappointment.

Charles flinched as he felt the blunt end of a pencil inserted in his ear. "If we all pass the exam and you fail, what fraction of Laurel will be dunces?" said Aidan in a low voice as he removed his pencil.

"Funny." Charles put his elbows on the table and rubbed his eyes with his index fingers.

"C'mon," whispered Aidan. "Work the last two problems here, and we'll compare answers."

Charles arched his back in an attempt to peel his sweat-damp shirt from the small of his back, and as he did, the clasp of Miss Turner's necklace in his pocket dug into his thigh. All day he had been trying to avoid thoughts of Miss Turner, but now, with no physical labor or conversation to distract him, memories of last night intruded. With profound embarrassment, he shifted in his seat to accommodate the increasingly tight fit of his pants. He prayed that he would not have to stand anytime soon.

He picked up his pencil and attacked the next problem with vigor in an attempt to distract himself. A combination of checking each answer with Aidan and periodically digging the point of his pencil into his forearm ultimately resolved his problem before the bell rang and they all stood to leave.

With a promise of all his desserts for the whole weekend, Charles convinced Aidan to return the locket to Miss Turner's room after returning The Coffin's Longfellow book. After class, Charles stood lookout at the end of the hallway while Aidan entered and exited the rooms in quick succession. In less than a minute, they were done and heading down the stairs to join the other boys in the yard. Now, if Charles could just manage to refrain from physically embarrassing himself while naked during evening swim, he would consider today a total success. His strategy for avoiding this embarrassment was to jump from the wharf into the deepest, coolest water at the first indication of trouble and, if necessary, stay there as long as was allowed.

But his strategy proved unnecessary due to the grease pole. On the side of the wharf was fastened what looked like a flagpole that ran parallel to the water, installed each year on the day after Arbor

Day and stored back in the boathouse right before Halloween. It was periodically rubbed with rendered animal fat during the summer, providing daily amusement for the boys trying to walk it to the end. Those that made it would attempt to grab a red rag tied loosely to the end of the pole before they plunged into the water.

So far, Charles had not even made it to the halfway mark on the pole. He watched the efforts of other boys from his place in line on the wharf, trying to discern what worked and what didn't. It looked like those who splayed their feet outward like a duck did the best, and small steps worked better than long ones. Such was his concentration that he had no room for thoughts of Miss Turner or anyone else on the island, including Aidan. Aidan had gone off with Tiny to the other side of the wharf, as was the pattern now, and each day Charles was a little more comfortable with being split up during evening swim. And after all, if they had to be split up, wasn't this the best time for it? To his way of thinking, after a day of sweating in the fields and sitting in a stifling classroom, there was nothing better than to plunge below the waterline without a stitch of clothing between you and all that cool, swirling water. Four days ago had been the first time he had ever been fully submerged in water, and it was even grander than he had imagined. As much as he wanted to stick with Aidan, he couldn't bear standing next to him and Tiny, knee-deep in the surf and just waiting for evening swim to end.

Charles thought the Fourth Classer now starting on the pole would make it to the end, but he changed his mind when the boy started clowning for his friends on the wharf. He began to walk backwards without guarding against the most serious mishap a boy can make on the pole. Before anyone could warn him, his feet slipped off opposite sides of the pole, and, after landing on it as if he were straddling a horse, his mouth a perfect ring of pain and shock, he slipped into the water and sank like an anchor.

Charles looked back to shore. The industrial teacher, Mr. Croft, pulled off his boots, and some boys in line for the pole began diving off the wharf to rescue the unfortunate boy. It looked like Mr. Croft was trying to ascertain if someone would find the submerged boy before he had to get wet.

Charles looked back to the water, and indeed an upperclassman had already brought the boy to the surface, where he was coughing up harbor water. But something nagged at Charles's brain, something he had seen just now that had set off an alarm bell in his brain, and yet he couldn't put his finger on what it was. Not here— not out on the wharf or in the water. He looked back to shore. Croft was shading his eyes to verify the rescue, and the boys on the beach were cheering and pumping their fists in the air. Yes, the shore—something had been amiss on the shore when he had first looked back. What was it? He turned his head a little farther, and he saw it, the feeling in his head clicking into place like tumblers on a safe—yes, this was the bad thing: Caleb Hart, Bowditch, and Warwick were moving as a group toward Aidan's side of the wharf.

Before Aidan and Tiny could even make it to dry land, the boys stood in a line to block them. Aidan looked around frantically for Charles but couldn't see him. Caleb spoke first, and even through his fear, Aidan couldn't help but notice that Caleb was one of the few boys on the island whose voice had changed to a low adult pitch. The sound was strangely soothing, a weird contrast to the menacing look on his sunburned face.

"How goes the swim lesson, ladies?" Caleb took a step closer, and the others followed suit.

"We ain't botherin' you. We ain't doing nothin'," said Tiny, looking at his feet, as if that line of argument would improve their situation.

"Oh, you're bothering me all right. Just the fact that you

pantywaists are on my island bothers me. And it seems to me, Balentine, like you're not really making very good progress with the new boy. So I'm taking over, and you are excused from your duties today."

Tiny's face showed conflicting feelings—relief that he was not the primary target, and guilt at the thought of abandoning Aidan. He opened his mouth to make some sort of protest, but Caleb cut him off. "Don't even bother. Take him," he said to Bowditch, who grabbed Tiny by the arm and walked him away, leaving Warwick and Caleb facing Aidan.

Caleb stepped forward again, and six inches from Aidan's ear, he purred, "Now let's cure this little fear of yours."

Before Aidan knew what was happening, Caleb had grabbed him under his arm, and Warwick had yanked him off his feet by his ankles. The coordination was almost graceful, indicating that they had either discussed how they would execute this plan or that they had done this to other boys before. They began to swing Aidan back and forth, parallel to the waterline.

Since the moment that Charles had seen Caleb and company talking to Aidan and Tiny, he had been trying to make it off the wharf, but the cheering and congregating boys had blocked his way. Resisting the urge to push boys into the water, he moved as fast as he could down the wharf. Once he cleared the throng of boys and was running at top speed, he saw Caleb and Warwick swinging Aidan over the water. He tackled Warwick at the knees moments after Aidan had been released, Aidan's stiff, petrified body sailing out to land on his back in four feet of water.

"Sully!" Charles cried, forgetting Caleb and Warwick, and he ran out to grab Aidan. Aidan fought him blindly, not knowing who was grabbing his arm, and they wrestled in the water for a few moments, Charles trying to get Aidan's head above the waterline. When he saw Aidan's ears were above water, he yelled, "Sully, it's me! It's Charles! It's me!"

Aidan stopped struggling and grabbed Charles by the shoulders with rubbery hands. "Get me outta here," he said weakly.

Charles walked Aidan to shore like a sober man dragging his drunken friend along in Scollay Square. As they cleared the surf line and Aidan fell down on the sand, dazed and coughing, Charles realized that the crowd on the wharf had turned 180 degrees to witness at least part of Aidan's ordeal. Instead of cheering, as they had for the grease-pole rescue, they were quietly murmuring. Charles bent over, hands on his knees, and breathed heavily as he looked around for Caleb and Warwick, but they were nowhere in sight.

Bill, Tink, and Dec emerged from the crowd and ran over to kneel beside Aidan. "What the hell happened?" asked Bill of Charles.

"That bastard Caleb Hart is what," said Charles between labored breaths.

"You all right, boyo?" asked Dec, leaning over Aidan.

"Sure an' I've had better days, now," mumbled Aidan, unconsciously matching Dec's brogue. Alarmed, Charles looked at Dec to gauge his reaction. Dec frowned in confusion, then shifted his gaze to Charles. *Goddamnit*, thought Charles. This was just the sort of thing he had been worried about when Aidan had started hanging around with Dec. All that Mick talk was a flame pulling Aidan in like a moth. This confirmed what Charles had thought from the start: no good would come of that association. Luckily, Bill and Tink were deep in conversation about Caleb and his deserved comeuppance, so Charles was sure that no one but Dec had heard Aidan speak.

"I think my brother's makin' fun of that accent of yours," Charles ventured.

"That true?" said Dec, neutrally and not entirely rhetorically.

By this time, most of the boys, as well as the instructors, had formed a circle around them. Mr. Croft pushed to the front of the circle. "What's happened here?"

Bill answered before Charles could speak. "Arthur here just went out a little too far. Got a little cocky on the swim lessons, but no harm done. His brother reeled him back in." Bill's look to Charles broadcasted clearly: *We'll deal with this ourselves.*

"Are you all right, son?" Mr. Croft asked, leaning down toward Aidan.

"Yessir." Aidan sat up and pushed his hair out of his eyes. "Just a bit deeper than I was expecting out there."

"Well, all right then. I will inform Superintendent Bradley of these two incidents right away. Strange that they would happen almost at the same time. Curious."

Charles thought it was anything but curious. He was sure that Caleb had used the commotion from the pole accident as his cover, seeing that the instructors were all preoccupied. He wondered if Caleb would have struck at all if the pole accident had not occurred. Had he been waiting all week at evening swim for the right moment?

Later on in the dormitory, Bill, Tink, Salt, and Dec arrived as a group at the foot of Charles and Aidan's bed.

"So who the hell," asked Bill, "is Sully?"

A brief silence ensued.

"Whaddya mean?" asked Charles, stalling for time. *Did I call Aidan 'Sully'?* He could not remember doing it, but how else would Bill have heard that name?

"You called Arthur 'Sully' when you were pullin' him outta the drink. Now that you're Laurel Boys, seems like we should know about this nickname business."

"Oh, sure, Sully, yep, that's what we called him at home," said Charles as he plumped up the pillow on the bed, needing just a few more seconds to organize his thoughts around the new set of lies into which he was headed. "Forgot all about that."

"So, how'd he get that moniker?" asked Tink, sitting down on the edge of the bed, clearly hoping for an entertaining yarn before bedtime.

Charles was now prepared. He took a breath. "Well, as it turns out, that's an interesting little story, if you boys got a minute."

Dec sat down on Merton Poole's unoccupied bed and made himself comfortable. "I got time for this," he said, a bemused expression on his face that Charles didn't like.

"See this?" Charles showed them his missing tooth on the right side of his mouth. "That weren't no dentist who yanked that out. Guess who took care of it for me."

"Your brother?" asked Salt.

"With a left hook that knocked my arse into next week!"

Poole arrived back from his evening ablutions and shoved Dec over to make room for himself. "Arthur clocked you?"

"Indeed he did. 'Course, he started the whole thing. Tried to take some money I lucked into."

"The hell I did," said Aidan. "You just went off half-cocked, like you always do, assuming the worst."

"Yeah, well, he taught me a lesson that day. You see, none of you know this, but my brother's had a few boxing lessons."

"From who?" asked Bill.

Charles started to answer, but Aidan got there first. "You see, my ma—our ma—had a beau for a while, used to be an amateur boxer. Taught me some moves. Charles here just didn't have the *aptitude* for that kinda instruction. He was always off getting into trouble while I was busy *improvin'* on myself." Aidan was clearly enjoying himself now.

"Well anyway, it was hard to stay mad at him 'cause that tooth he knocked out was rotten. Just that very morning our ma was saying how she didn't know where she was gonna find the money to get my tooth pulled. So we ran home to tell her the good news. And she turned to Arthur and said, 'Well ain't you a regular John L. Sullivan!' See, this was just after Sullivan and that Mitchell feller went toe-to-toe over in France, and we'd been talking about it all week. And I guess the name just stuck. He was Sully from that point forward."

"The Boston Strong Boy!" said Tink wistfully. "Last month, after Sullivan beat the tar outta Kilrain, Bradley brought us three different newspapers over from the mainland. Boys was fightin' over who would read them first. Seventy-five rounds they went, bare-knuckle!"

"So your ma wasn't mad that you'd been fighting?" asked Poole.

"Naw," said Aidan with a faraway look in his eyes. After a heartbeat, he looked at Charles. "Remember when we came up the stairs that day, how we smelled her famous beef stew?"

"She always did cook the best beef stew, Sully," said Charles kindly, allowing Aidan to rewrite the scene, substituting the savory smell of stew for that of gin.

"With the carrots. Always with the carrots. And biscuits still hot out of the oven. She'd been cooking all day, remember?" Aidan implored Charles, grabbing his forearm. "Remember how she cooked all day because she knew it was our favorite?" Tears sat in the corners of Aidan's eyes.

"I remember. I do. She had it all ready for us the minute we walked in."

The mood became solemn. There were now almost a dozen boys circled around Charles and Aidan's bed listening to the story, and each one of them knew of the circumstances that had brought the brothers here, circumstances that echoed some of their own family tragedies.

"You miss her," Bill said. Several boys nodded slightly, involuntarily.

Charles let Aidan answer. "Very much."

~

Charles and Aidan assumed that no one other than those involved had seen Caleb and Warwick throw Aidan into the water. But there was another witness.

Earlier in the evening, Bradley had been preparing notes for an upcoming board meeting, but the stuffy heat in his office, combined with the tedium of the work, had given him a headache. He closed his eyes, relieved to block the view of the ledger books on his desk, and leaned back in his chair. Without his sense of sight, his hearing took over and brought him the happy sounds of evening swim. He felt a surge of envy. *Oh, to be jumping off the wharf into the cool water right now,* he thought to himself. The breeze that usually made it up the hill to his office window had failed to materialize that evening. He walked to the window and opened it a few more inches in what he recognized as a futile attempt to cool off the room. He gazed down the hill at the boys, and he felt his headache ease a little.

He heard rather than saw the pole accident. He was looking at the younger Weston boy and Balentine to the left of the wharf when he heard the change in the boys voices, heard a degree of urgency indicating trouble. He looked to the shore. *What the blazes is Croft doing?* Nothing, as far as Bradley could see. If this wasn't resolved in the next minute, Bradley would have to consider if he could sprint down to the water in time to do anything useful.

But suddenly he heard the boys cheering. *Well, no thanks to Croft.* And then he saw Caleb Hart, recognizable from his platinum-white hair at almost any distance, and two other boys move to the other side of the wharf.

There was something clearly sinister about the intentions of this group of three. All other eyes down by the water were preoccupied with whatever had happened in the main swim area—he could hear their familiar three cheers and a tiger—but Hart's group was bearing down on Weston and Balentine.

What Bradley saw next made him feel mildly ill. Though witnessing the harassment of one of his boys was certainly uncomfortable, the truly painful part was knowing that the perpetrator was also one of his boys.

He saw it all as if he were watching actors on a stage from the cheapest seats in the hall, the players tiny, but his view unobstructed. He saw the tackle—that could only be the older Weston—and then saw Caleb and the other boy slink away, blending into the crowd.

As soon as it was over, Bradley went back to his desk and pulled Caleb Hart's file. Since his arrival, he had tried to read several files each week to familiarize himself with the boys. He saw the small check on the corner of the file indicating that he had already read Hart's, but nothing stood out in his memory about it. As he leafed through it, his heart sank. If there was ever a file depicting the right boy for the Farm School, he was holding it. Good student back on the mainland, churchgoing family, father deceased years ago, mother destitute but devoted to her only child. The Character Affirmation letter was from a minister Bradley knew, glowing with praise for the parents.

He threw the file on the desk and closed his eyes against the headache that had come back with a vengeance. What was the use of reading the files? He had made his way through more than half of them, and now it seemed a colossal waste of time. He wished that he, not the previous superintendent, had been the one to interview Mrs. Hart and her son. Would he have sensed cruelty in the boy? Or had the boy not been cruel yet—could something, some experience on the island, have turned him? Or was it simply time that was the alchemist?

He heard Croft knock at the door, undoubtedly anxious to describe this evening's events in a way that would absolve him of any neglect. Bradley bid him to enter as he replaced Caleb's file in the drawer. Croft had seemed like a fine fellow when Bradley had first met him, but over time, Bradley had come to see him as lazy and inattentive. How, Bradley thought as his headache rose to new heights, could you ever know the nature of a person from the start?

CHAPTER 23

At breakfast the next day, Aidan's spoon stopped midway between his oatmeal bowl and his mouth.

Dec and Tink were engaged in an argument that had escalated to the point where Bill was trying to mediate before the matron gave them all a demerit for excessive volume. This allowed Aidan to nudge Charles's elbow undetected.

"Lookit," Aidan murmured, and he gestured with his chin to the demerit chart on the wall.

"What? The chart?" Charles didn't see any new demerits on either of their names.

"'Bout halfway down, first column. Last name Thomas," Aidan said to his bowl.

Charles squinted and scanned down the list of names until he came to it. His mouth briefly hung open before he quietly said to Aidan, "Talk in the yard."

With the bell signaling the end of breakfast, they filed outside. Dec called to Aidan, "Hey, Sully, ya comin' down to Starlight for your first clarinet lesson this morning?" During band the day prior, the bandleader had asked both Charles and Aidan to consider learning clarinet, explaining that the band had lost two clarinetists when the last two boys were placed out. Charles had truthfully pleaded a tin ear, which, fortunately for everyone, he had not been asked to prove, but Aidan had accepted and only found out later that Dec also played clarinet.

Aidan gave Dec the thumbs-up as Charles dragged him to a quiet corner of the yard.

"It can't be him," Charles stated flat out.

Aidan raised an eyebrow. "And why is that?"

"There has to be some grown feller here on the island named Cole or something."

"Naw," said Aidan with a growing smile. "I'll bet my hat on it. Miss Turner's man ain't a man at all—he's a First Classer."

"You're bettin' your hat on the notion that Miss Turner is droppin' her drawers with a fifteen-year-old student on this here island?"

"Could be fourteen, even."

"Why would she do it?" Charles could all too well imagine why a boy would want such an arrangement, but a beauty like Lydia Turner wanting one of the students?

"I dunno. What other choice has she got here?"

None of the women Charles had seen working the waterfront had shown any enthusiasm for their job—only for the money it provided. He had heard men discussing with their hired pleasures how their wives wouldn't give them what they needed. This pretty much summed up what Charles had known about women and sex before he had come to the island. The idea that a woman could want what men wanted, could feel what he had felt in the rose-scented darkness of Lydia Turner's room, was a thought he was just getting used to. He realized that the most intoxicating part of his two seconds of paradise with her was the strength of her want—her delicate hand gripping his skull with surprising force, pulling her own head off the pillow, the way her tongue worked its way past his ignorant lips and teeth. Charles put his hand in his trouser pocket to hide the growing result of reliving these memories.

"And think about it," added Aidan, "she musta been expecting some kinda boy. If she was waiting for, say, Mr. Croft, she wouldn't have thunk it was you."

Charles thought of Mr. Croft's pendulous belly and hair slick with fragrant Macassar oil. It *was* hard to imagine Lydia kissing Charles for two seconds thinking it was Mr. Croft.

Aidan slapped Charles's arm. "Hey, we gotta see this Cole Thomas. We gotta get Dec or Bill to point him out. The lucky duck."

"But we can't let on why we wanna know," Charles insisted.

"'Course, brother. Your secret's safe with me. And as long as you don't take that hand outta your pocket, you probably won't give your own self away."

Soon the bell rang for a lineup, a deviation from the normal schedule of farm work right after Saturday breakfast. This morning, Bradley stood at the head of the line, hands clasped behind his back, projecting his voice to penetrate the murmur of the crowd.

"As I'm sure I needn't remind the First Class," he began as the hum died off voice by voice, "this morning marks the end of Master William Thayer's laudable matriculation here at the Farm School and the beginning of his adulthood. He begins his apprenticeship at the telegraph company on Monday after spending the weekend settling into his new living quarters on the mainland. I speak for all the staff here at the school when I say we have every confidence that Master Thayer will lead a good Christian life and make us proud to list him as an alumnus. We will now proceed to the wharf after lineup in reverse order—First Class at the head of the line today."

Once they had cleared the decline of the hill and were on flat land, two of the boys at the front hoisted Thayer onto their shoulders and began a round of "For He's a Jolly Good Fellow." Fielding was waiting on the steamer, and Thayer's one suitcase and small box of possessions were loaded onto the boat. All the boys gathered in a semicircle on the beach to hear Thayer's final words, which seemed to go on and on.

"But," Thayer concluded at long last, "the thing I'm gonna miss the most is these dunderheads in First Class. You're a grand bunch. And I'm sure gonna miss cleaning your clocks at baseball!"

With that, five of Thayer's friends rushed up to the wharf and delivered manly expressions of their friendship: clapped handshakes, back slaps, ruffling of hair.

"For cryin' out loud," grumbled Charles into Aidan's ear. "Will he get on the boat already?"

"Hey, I gotta hunch," said Aidan, oblivious to Charles's complaints. "Let's go talk to Bill. He's right over there." Aidan pulled Charles along until they were positioned next to Bill.

"So, Bill, who are them mugs up there with Thayer?"

"Well, let's see," said Bill as he squinted to see better. "That's John Pedgrift on the right of him with Lester Adams, and on the left you have Webber, the mail carrier—remember, we told you about how he—"

"And who else?"

"Well, also on the left is Cole Thomas and Phillip Scott."

"Thomas, he's the one with the black hair?" asked Aidan.

"Naw, he's got that dirty straw-colored hair, sorta like Charles."

"As a matter of fact," said Aidan, smiling now, "just yesterday I tapped Charles on the back only to have him turn around and it was that one instead. Easy to mistake the two, don't you think?"

"From behind, sure," Bill agreed.

Or, Charles thought, *in the dark.*

CHAPTER 24

Aᴋᴛᴇʀ Tʜᴀʏᴇʀ'ꜱ ꜱᴇɴᴅᴏꜰꜰ, ᴛʜᴇ ᴡᴇᴇᴋᴇɴᴅ ᴘʀᴏᴄᴇᴇᴅᴇᴅ ᴏɴ ɪᴛꜱ ɴᴏʀᴍᴀʟ course. Saturday-afternoon baseball was the pinnacle of every summer week. Most boys tracked the progress of their beloved Boston Beaneaters in the *Boston Post* that Webber brought back from the mainland every day. The better the Beaneaters did that week, the more frenzied the game on the island that Saturday.

Charles and Aidan sat with the Laurel boys near home plate on felled tree trunks long since denuded of any bark by years of young backsides. The morning cloud cover was dissipating, much to everyone's relief. Tink attempted to explain to them the game schedule, but all Charles could really understand was that the infield and outfield teams were each comprised of two cottages, and that Laurel's turn was not this week. This week, it was Tritonia and Elk vs. Starlight and Crescent, Laurel rooting for Starlight to support Dec and Salt.

"So what happens after this?" asked Charles, bored by the game. Since his mother died, there had been no room in his life for games with other boys, not that many—or really, any—had invited him to play any games before.

"Well," said Bill as he clapped for a Starlight batter stepping up to the plate, "the game will end maybe by three, and then we have a stretch before Town Meeting at four. They're gonna schedule Herbert Smith's trial date today."

Tink frowned a bit as he thought. "Did Herbert get arrested before or after you two landed here this week?"

"Arrested?" Aidan's eyes widened.

"Bill, these guys weren't here when it happened—that was last Sunday."

"That's right. Remember how Bradley was none too happy about having an arrest on the Sabbath? Then his whole Sunday evening service had to be about the holiness of God's day. What a sleeper that one was—"

Just then, Merton Poole, much to everyone's surprise—including, it seemed, his own—hit the ball far into the outfield. At first too stunned to even move, he stared at the ball sailing high into the sky until his teammates shoved him toward first base. Bill and Tink were on their feet cheering with most of the other boys until the outfielder caught Poole's ball just as Poole tripped over the base.

Aidan pulled on Bill's shirtsleeve as they sank down again onto the log. "What did Herbert do? Who arrested him? Is he in jail?"

"Jail? Naw, not anymore. They sprung him pretty quick."

"What did he do?" repeated Charles.

"Now, Bill, I do believe you are stringing these poor fellows along now. Look at them. You'd think they were being hunted by the law themselves with them panicky looks." Tink looked amused.

Charles laughed nervously. "I, uh, it's just that I thought that Boston's Finest wouldn't walk the beat over here. Ain't they got better things to do?"

"Well, it will probably make you feel a bit better to know that Pickering was the arresting officer."

"Pickering?"

As the teams changed sides on the field, Bill explained about the Cottage Row Government. Aidan listened attentively as Bill laid out the structure—boy police officers with a boy Chief of Police, boy lawyers, a boy judge, and so forth—but Charles could not get beyond his initial reaction.

"So you're telling me," he said, interrupting Bill, "that this is all set up by the boys?"

"Uh-huh." Bill whistled and clapped as Salt caught a foul ball.

"But Bradley makes 'em do it?"

"Nope. He's in favor of it, you know, for the civics-lesson aspect of it. Learning about government and all. But it's driven by us. Boys before us thought the whole thing up."

Charles pretended to watch the game, but his mind was trying to believe what he had just heard. A hundred boys on an island, free to do whatever they wanted as long as it evaded the detection of the staff. No police, no courts, nothing more serious being risked than demerits on the chart in the dining room. So why, why in the world, would they choose to create these things from the adult world, watching and spying and punishing?

Aidan interrupted Charles's thoughts. "So you ain't told us yet what he done."

Tink pulled a grave face. "Well, it was pretty serious. It don't bode well for Herbert's future. A step on the road to depravity; next stop, a murder in cold blood—"

"He stole Harry Leighton's stash of marbles," Bill said, clapping as the teams changed sides again.

Charles was incredulous. "Pickering arrested him for stealing marbles?"

"*Allegedly* stealing marbles," insisted Tink. "Dutton, you ain't giving poor Herbert the benefit of the doubt."

"Well, what the hell were all them marbles doing in Herbert's bed box then, including Harry's special yellow aggie he got from his brother last Visiting Day?"

"I'm just following the law in this here country: innocent until proved guilty. Shouldn't you know that, being the prosecutor and all?"

"What's a prosecutor?" asked Aidan.

Tink answered for Bill. "Why, Bill's the lawyer that's gonna prove that Herbert done it. Good thing he already made up his mind that Herbert's guilty."

"How'd you get to be the lawyer?" asked Charles.

"Elected," said Bill. "But my term's almost up. Every three months, they have new elections, and you can't run again—gotta give some other boys a shot."

Bill and Tink then started a long conversation about who had been in the various government posts since their time on the island, and Charles and Aidan lost interest, not knowing any of the names.

Charles turned to Aidan. "Can you believe they didn't have no cops or courts and then they just went and made them?"

"Sure." Aidan didn't seem surprised. "Ain't you ever played cops 'n robbers? They're just playin'."

"It don't bother you that there's a police force here on this island?"

"It ain't a *real* police force. Just don't steal no one's marbles." Aidan cracked a smile, but Charles was having none of it. Aidan's voice dropped to a whisper. "You ain't worried that they're gonna find out . . . you know . . . are ya?"

"Naw. How could they?"

"So what's the problem?"

Charles couldn't quite find a way to explain to Aidan that he was bothered by the idea that the boys had *chosen* to govern themselves in this way. When Bess told them about this place, he'd imagined he would escape everything that troubled him—hunger, poverty, worry. And while the eating and sleeping had been as grand as he thought it would be, he had not anticipated the restrictions. Lining up, marching single file, and, of course, the bell. The goddamn bell, bolted to the side of Bulfinch, ringing to call the boys in from the farm, back from evening swim, announcing dinner and supper and every other thing that had to be done according to the hands on the clock. And now, to find out that there were courts and coppers here, it just seemed like he hadn't really escaped at all—just traded one set of demands for another.

He was saved the burden of explaining all this to Aidan by an outfielder catching the last fly ball, ending the game. The boys in the crowd surged to their feet as if they were a many-legged animal, moving as one.

Prior to Town Meeting, Charles ranked Bradley's Wednesday chapel service as the most boring experience on the island, followed closely by certain lectures in The Coffin's class. But Town Meeting gave The Coffin some stiff competition. If he couldn't understand why the boys had chosen to create their own government before, he was even more amazed as he endured the meeting. Between the taking of attendance, the reading of minutes from the previous meeting, and the discussion of other mind-numbing administrative issues, Charles waited in vain for something interesting to arise. At the end of the meeting, Herbert Smith's court date was set for next Saturday, and finally the meeting was adjourned, leaving almost an hour of free time before supper.

With some ham wrapped in a napkin, both stolen from the dining hall, Charles headed down to the barn. Every day at dinner, he pilfered some meat, and then found some time to sneak off in the afternoon and feed Lucifer. He was careful that the other boys, including Aidan, didn't see him take scraps from the table or head off toward the barn, although he wasn't sure why. There was nothing wrong with what he was doing, and yet he did not want anyone to know.

The barn was cool and dusty. It smelled like hay and animal sweat and leather, and the horses shifted in their stalls when they sensed a person entering their midst. Charles clicked his tongue as he had done every time he came to the barn with meat. He was trying to get Lucifer to associate that sound with meat and with the giver of that meat.

"Lucifer!" he called out in a loud whisper, and he clicked some more. "Lucifer!" He walked around the barn to places the dog might be hiding.

He heard a low growl behind his back, and he smiled.

Turning around slowly, he said in a low, soothing voice, "Is that any way to treat your best friend?"

Lucifer stopped growling but stood at rigid attention, his fur bristling on full alert. Each day, Lucifer growled a little less when he encountered Charles, but it was still the way he announced his presence. It was almost as if he hid and waited for Charles to be looking the other way so that he could appear behind Charles as if from thin air.

"So I bet you think I have something for you, huh? Well, it so happens that they were having a special on ham today. I hope you like ham." He removed the napkin from his pocket as he talked. "I had some for dinner, and I thought, now, who else might enjoy some of this? And you came to mind, yes you did."

He clicked his tongue and tossed a piece to the dog, who caught it in midair without taking his eyes off Charles. "But that weren't the biggest piece, my friend. I was hoping you might do a trick for me." He paused. "Sit. Sit, Lucifer. *Sit.*"

On all the previous days, Lucifer had remained standing in his rigid position when asked to sit, and Charles had eventually given him all the meat anyway, at which point Lucifer had slunk away. Charles knew he couldn't get near enough to Lucifer to push his hindquarters down in demonstration, so he held out little hope that this would work. But he was in no rush. No one knew what he was doing, so no one could laugh at him if it never worked.

Lucifer relaxed just a tiny bit, and he sat.

Charles clicked and threw him the rest of the meat, of which Lucifer made short work. "Good boy! Good sit!" he said. He resisted the urge to walk toward Lucifer to pat him on the head or scratch him behind the ears. Lucifer had made it clear that he wanted a good two or three feet between them at all times, and Charles respected that boundary.

Lucifer crept away behind a pile of wooden crates, and Charles sat down on a bale of hay. "Well, it sure was nice dining with ya. Same time tomorrow? We got chapel tomorrow, twice, if you can believe that, so I ain't exactly sure when I can show up."

Much to Charles's surprise, Lucifer poked his head out from behind the pile of crates.

Charles buried his excitement and didn't move or change his tone of voice. "I know. Chapel twice on Sunday. More's the pity. Seems like a bit much to me too, but I don't got much choice. We gotta play the cards we got dealt, right?" A grin spread across his face. He felt an enormous satisfaction that Lucifer had returned. It was possibly the happiest Charles had been on the island.

"Who the devil are you talkin' to?" Fielding strode in through the door that Charles had left open.

"N-nobody," stammered Charles. Lucifer skittered away as Charles stood and jammed his hands in his pockets.

"You're sitting on that bale, nattering on to nobody." Fielding crossed his arms.

"Well, not nobody, exactly. Um, I was talking to Lucifer."

"Lucifer! Did he have a go at you? Snap at you? Bradley was right, I should have taken care of that business—"

"No! He ain't all bad! He's comin' around, Mr. Fielding. He don't have to be put down."

"Weston, that dog has been nothing but mean since he was a young pup. You been here only a short bit—you don't know him. A leopard doesn't change its spots, son. He's bad news waiting to happen. You stay away from him."

"Okay, but just give him some time. You been putting off putting him down for a while—just wait a while longer," Charles pleaded.

"I'm not makin' any promises," Fielding insisted. But Charles could see that he had influenced him, at least a little.

"So who was it that got bit by Lucifer?"

"It was Percy Tisdale in the Fifth Class. Gash all down his thigh, a nasty wound. He was lucky the infection was minor. Usually with dog bites it's much worse. A dog's mouth is a dirty place. You talk to Percy and ask him about that day, and maybe that'll convince you to keep your distance from that animal."

"I think I'll do that, Mr. Fielding."

"Well, come on out of here and join your chums up the hill. I'm headed up that way myself, just need to grab something from around back of the barn."

Charles headed to the door after Fielding. When he was sure Fielding was out of earshot, he whispered, "See ya tomorrow, old friend," right before he cleared the door.

It seemed that there were more holes than Aidan had fingers.

Dec and Aidan sat in two mismatched chairs in the Starlight Cottage, each holding a clarinet, as Dec tried to show Aidan which holes needed to be covered.

"You're holding it like it might bite ya," mumbled Dec as he shifted two reeds around in his mouth. "I've held mine quite a bit, and you can rest assured it never has done so." He moved Aidan's ring finger to the proper place. "Now you're right as rain. Don't move a finger."

Dec handed one of the reeds from his mouth to Aidan and demonstrated how to secure it with the ligature. "Treat your reed like the fine lady she is, nice and gentle. Bradley don't order these too often from the mainland."

They worked through a C scale, first in unison, then Aidan alone.

"Dec, I sound like a cat in heat."

"Ah, but to a tomcat, that's a fine sound indeed." Dec grinned. "You don't sound bad at all, actually. You should have heard me when I started. All the barn cats jumped into the water and started swimming to Boston just to escape the noise."

Together they worked through an F scale. "You master that bugger," said Dec, "and we can start you on 'Grandfather's Clock.' That's in F."

Aidan laid his clarinet down on the table and arched his back to stretch. "Hey, will ya play me something? Salt says you're awful good."

"So it's inspiration you're looking for now, is it?" Dec played a little trill while he thought. "Ah! I've thought of one. I think this might be just your cuppa tea."

It started out so soft and slow it took Aidan a few beats to recognize it. Once he did, he couldn't help but close his eyes so he could hear it better. No noise from beyond the walls of the cottage could be heard above Dec's playing, and Aidan found it easy to forget where he was. The wooden chair he was sitting in started to feel like his chair at the kitchen table in the West End, and he was remembering Maeve singing this song, "Molly Malone," the song that was beloved by a whole country, a song he heard hummed by the baker behind the counter and whistled by the ice man as he rode up the street. And that one time, when Maeve had sung it as she and Dan Connolly danced round and round in the front room. Dan wouldn't sing with her, insisting he was the only Irishman who could not carry a tune, so he just looked at Maeve as she sang, and they tried not to bump into any furniture, both of them smiling like there would be a law against it tomorrow. Aidan had been too young to remember anything before or after this scene, or even why everyone was so happy that evening. But all the details were still clear—the pin his mother had secured in her copper hair, how Dan had a handkerchief that stuck out of his trouser pocket and waved like a little white flag as they spun around. How Aidan had felt that everything was just perfect.

He realized that Dec had come to the end of the song and had stopped playing a few moments ago. The silence seemed louder than the music. Reluctantly, he opened his eyes and felt that his lashes were wet. Dec's face was a foot away from his, and he was staring at Aidan.

"Yer a fecking Irishman." Dec pointed a slim finger at the bridge of Aidan's nose.

"What?" Aidan rubbed his eyes with the heel of his hand as he felt his bowels quiver. "What the hell are you talking about?" *Jaysus Jaysus Jaysus*, he thought as his mind spun around frantically, stupidly. *Charles will kill me. He will just kill me.*

"I knew it!" Dec folded his arms in triumph. "I knew it!"

Aidan could feel dots of perspiration pop out on his forehead. "Knew what? What is there to know? There's nothing to know."

"Let me tell you a fact of life, laddie. No one, but I mean *no one*, cries when they hear 'Molly Malone' if they ain't Irish."

"I ain't crying! It's just that you play so good."

"Jaysus himself doesn't play good enough to coax tears from any boy by the name of Weston. But Sullivan, on the other hand . . . well, that's a horse of a different color. *Sully.*" Dec looked smug, like he hadn't a shred of doubt.

"You can think what you want, but I know what I am." *And what is that, exactly?* Aidan wasn't even sure anymore. He gripped his trembling hands in his lap.

"Fine, boyo, if that's the way you want it." Dec moved toward the door. "Let's see what the boys of Laurel think."

"No!" Aidan stood up so quickly he knocked over his chair.

Dec walked back to the table and sat down, tipping his chair back so that it rested against the wall. "I'm listening," he stated.

"Dec, you don't understand."

"I will concede that point."

"First, I want to know how you figured it out." If he could just stall for a little time, he could try to figure out how much he had to tell Dec in order to satisfy him.

"Well, in a way, you have Fielding to thank. Every time he's deciding who's gonna do what farm work, he's always gotta be the comedian. Whether it's planting the potatoes, weeding the potatoes, harvesting the potatoes, he's always gotta act like he don't know who he's gonna pick, and then it's, 'Why, Master Moore, I believe this would be a good task for you!' like the thought just came to him. One day Fielding's gonna wake up with a potato up his arse."

Despite the situation at hand, Aidan had to smile at that one.

"So," Dec continued, "yesterday I was harvesting the new potatoes, and what a bleddy pain that is, getting them out with a pitchfork without bollixing up the plant for the fall harvest, but even with the tough jobs, after a while you get into the rhythm of it all, and your mind is free to float where it wants. And where it wanted to float yesterday was all the little ways that being a Hibernian on this rock is a crap deal."

"Like chapel when Bradley gave you demerits for genuflecting."

Dec brought his chair down from its tipped position with a thud that made Aidan jump. "Exactly. No flies on you, Sully. So out in the field, I was forking potatoes and thinking about being Irish here, and you floated into my mind. I figured out that you remind me a bit of one of my brothers—not the looks, but something else. Then I started thinking about how Charles calls you Sully and how you spoke in brogue when he fished you outta the harbor—"

"I what?" Aidan had no recollection of this.

"Well, you'd just had a near-death experience in a puddle, so you'll be forgiven for not remembering everything you said," said Dec. "So to sum it all up, all these thoughts were circling around, and they just came smack together, and I was 99 percent sure. But 'Molly Malone' was the linchpin—a nice bit of quick thinking on my part, I'll say."

"You could be a police detective."

"Like the world needs another Irish policeman. Okay, I've done my bit, and now I want to know why you are pretending to be something you ain't."

Aidan took a deep breath. "So I'm Irish."

"Yes," said Dec patiently.

"But the thing of it is, well . . . Charles ain't. Different fathers and all." He paused, hoping this was enough, waiting for Dec's reaction.

"Now that's pretty easy to believe. But what I don't believe is that you two coulda been raised for any amount of time under the same roof and have you come out with a brogue and him not."

"Okay, okay. We ain't got the same ma *or* da. He ain't my brother." Aidan felt like he was falling off a cliff and couldn't see where he would land.

Dec thought for a moment. "So you're pretending to not be Irish *and* pretending to have a brother. I've gotta admit, you are not really clearing this matter up."

A breeze blew in through the cottage window, cooling Aidan's sweating face, and riding in on that breeze came the entire story, as if God himself sent it down from the heavens, exactly what he should tell Dec. Allowing him to confess who he was without revealing what they'd done. Just like Charles had instructed in his tutorial on lying: laced with the truth, just changing a detail here or there. He took a deep breath.

"My ma was born in the Old Country, but my father was some American son of a bitch I never knew. I guess I get my looks from him, more's the pity. But Charles, well, his father was never in the picture, and his ma died a few years ago, so he was living in whatever alley he could find until I met him. Which was that night I knocked his tooth out."

"So that tooth story was true?"

"I did indeed perform that bit of dentistry in the alley. With a left hook." He allowed himself a little smile. "So eventually, I brought him home to have a real supper." The next part, while untrue, was not so hard because he had already rewritten this story with Charles in front of the boys in the dormitory. In Aidan's mind, it was now almost as if Maeve really had been at the stove stirring the beef stew when he and Charles walked in. "My ma, well, she has a big heart, and when she heard that Charles was living in the out-of-doors and had no family, why, she insisted that we take him in." Even to Aidan's ears, that sounded a little rash. "Well, you know, after she got to know him and he came back a few times. Plus he was working and bringing in some coin, which helped us out."

"So he was sort of like your brother."

"*Exactly.* And everything was grand for a while." He thought of the days when the biscuit tin on the shelf was full of money, when he and Charles would sit out on the stoop late at night after they had finished their work. "But my ma, well, she was sick. Consumption, you know."

"Fecking curse of the Irish," Dec murmured.

So far, what he had said was basically true, except for Maeve taking Charles in. But that could have happened. Now, however, came the part in his tale where he started to feel very bad about lying. Aidan sent up a little prayer asking forgiveness for what he was about to say.

"My ma . . . she passed recently."

Aidan paused, but Dec sat motionless, waiting for him to go on.

"And me and Charles had nobody, and Charles was ready to go back to living on the street, but I couldn't do it. To him it was nothing to lie on a dirty mattress and fend off the rats while you wait to fall asleep, but I . . ." He shivered, despite the heat, at the thought of sleeping with those big rats skittering around him.

"Jaysus," breathed Dec, barely audible.

"But we agreed we would stick together. No matter what. So we said we was brothers so nobody would split us up. And since Charles couldn't pass for Irish if there were a hundred dollars riding on it, we agreed that I would be, well, not Irish."

A silence settled over the cottage as each boy sat with his thoughts. Dec appeared to be absorbing all this new information, while Aidan was enormously relieved that he had reached the end of his story and it had all hung together. He only hoped that Dec would not ask any questions, especially about how they'd finagled their way into the school. He didn't want to have to navigate around Charles's prostitute guardian angel and her minister friend-or-possibly-lover.

Finally Dec spoke. "I'm glad you told me. Here I was mad as a wet hen thinking that you were hiding your Irish because you were embarrassed. Wanted to get ahead in life without people looking down on ya, expecting ya to drink yer wages and have ten children ya can't support and what have you. But I understand it now. Jaysus, sometimes I can't believe this island can stay afloat with all the sad stories on it."

The bell started ringing up the hill for lineup and dinner. As they rushed to pack up their instruments, Aidan said, "Listen, Dec, it's real important that nobody knows about this. Even one more boy knowing makes it more likely that the story will get back to Bradley, and he ain't gonna be too happy to know that we lied to get here. He might throw us out."

Dec snapped his clarinet case closed. "You told the right person. Half the lads here couldn't keep a secret if their lives depended on it, but you don't have to worry about me."

As they ran up the hill to make it to lineup, Aidan realized he wasn't really worried about Dec telling other people. A much bigger concern, however, was how he was going to tell all this to Charles.

Toward the end of evening swim, Charles and Aidan convened on their driftwood log. Adequate progress had been made with both Tiny's marked stick and the grease pole, and both boys were satisfied with their accomplishments. They looked out on the boys horsing around in the water, splashing and jumping on each other's backs, doing handstands and playing chicken.

Aidan was trying to find a way to tell Charles about his revelation with Dec but couldn't find a way to begin.

"What were you up to before supper?" he finally asked. Maybe Charles would ask him the same question and he could just report exactly what happened in Starlight Cottage.

"Nothin'," Charles said.

"Nothin'? Well, you musta been doing somethin'. Were you down at Laurel?" Aidan hadn't seen him down at Cottage Row.

"Nope."

"Well, where were ya?"

"I wasn't nowhere, okay? I don't gotta report back to you every time I blow my nose, fer Chrissakes." Charles picked up a small stone and hurled it into the shallows of the water.

Aidan had grown to expect that Charles would lash out at him every once in a while, learned that his temper was something that needed to find a target periodically. But this time it gave him an excuse to withhold his conversation with Dec.

"No, you're right," Aidan agreed, finding his own stone and lobbing it into the lapping surf. "You don't gotta tell me everything."

CHAPTER 25

Aᶠᵗᵉʳ DETERMINING WHETHER EACH PEW HAD THE SAME NUMBER OF boys (two did not) and figuring out what animals the water stains on the ceiling of the chapel most closely resembled (horse and pigeon), Charles was so desperate for distraction that he actually started listening to the visiting minister's Sunday sermon.

". . . and so it is written, 'the Lord had regard for Abel and his offering, but for Cain and his offering he had no regard. So Cain was very angry, and his countenance fell.' It is here that we see the emergence of evil in man. Even before his act of violence against Abel, it is his anger against God's judgment that reveals his true nature."

Horseshit, thought Charles. He recalled this story from his sporadic visits to church with his mother, one of the few interesting stories in that whole big book. *Who wouldn't be angry with God for that?* Perhaps the story had stuck with him because the minister had pointed out that there is no explanation as to why God rejects Cain's offering. Of course, the man blathered on with his own ideas about how Cain was lazy and brought God inferior goods, but there was no actual evidence of that in the Bible. What if Cain's offering was top-notch and God just rejected him anyway? Nobody standing in the pulpit ever saw it from Cain's point of view. *Besides,* thought Charles as he looked at the minister, *this harp polisher wouldn't know evil if it snuck up behind the podium and bit him in the arse.*

Charles had been out of sorts ever since his conversation with Aidan at evening swim, although he didn't really know why. Last night, he and Aidan had slept in separate beds for the first time now that Thayer had left. Merton Poole had taken on the task of horse-trading beds with the other boys so that Charles and Aidan could end up next to each other. Although they had talked all week about how comfortable it would be to have their own beds, Charles had slept poorly. As he was falling asleep, he'd wished he were out in the barn, curled up on a couple of hay bales, listening for sounds of Lucifer moving around in the dark.

After morning chapel and dinner, Charles and Aidan went their separate ways without a word.

"Hey, Sully, you gonna tend that garden of yours today?" Dec called out as he headed that way, seeing Aidan leave Bulfinch.

"Be there in a little while."

Once he was sure that Charles wasn't around, Aidan trotted down the incline to Laurel, holding his school satchel close to his body in a way that he hoped looked unobtrusive. He startled a bit upon opening the door to see Sumner at the table. He had expected to find the cottage empty; most boys seemed to want to be outdoors after the confines of morning chapel.

Sumner nodded at him without a sound and resumed his letter writing. *Well,* thought Aidan, *at least I won't have to worry about him telling Charles what I'm doing.*

Aidan opened his satchel and brought out his school inkpot and pen, as well as his first and only purchase from the school store: two sheets of stationery and an envelope. Only now did he realize he had left himself no room for error, since he would need both sheets. He should have bought more paper in case the ink ran down the pen and blobbed his words, as happened frequently in composition class. Well, there was nothing for it now—he'd just have to be careful.

But the more pressing problem, he soon realized, was what to say. For days he had been putting together the elements of this letter in his mind, but now those elements skittered away like a shy animal every time his mind approached them. He looked over at Sumner, who was writing at an impressive clip, a pile of several sheets to his left already filled. Apparently everything Sumner didn't say came out in his letters.

Sumner felt Aidan's stare and looked up. Aidan immediately averted his gaze down to his empty paper.

After a few more minutes, Aidan began.

Dear Ma,
I am fine hear. I been thinking about you and Ella alot.
The food is real good and there is plenty of it so you dont
have to worry none. I don't have no money to send you but
I hope I will someday. I hope your coff isn't too bad. I am
learning alot. Dont worry about me.
Aidan

His stomach was in knots. He realized that he now had three separate fictions he needed to maintain: the one that Bradley and most of the boys knew, the one Dec knew, and the one Maeve knew. A little over a week ago, none of these stories had been written yet, and Aidan had never told a lie he hadn't copped to in the confessional. Even working with Charles had not required that he lie to Maeve, since she drew her own assumptions and hadn't asked questions.

He dipped his pen in the inkpot to start on the other piece of paper, his stomachache easing a bit as he wrote to the only person with whom he could be truthful.

CHAPTER 26

Soon Charles and Aidan found that the wonder and tension of what each new day would bring was replaced by the comfort and monotony of knowing what the day would entail. All weekdays were the same with the exception of Wednesday, when there was evening chapel, and Saturday dangled out in front of the week like candy in a storefront window. They learned the art of dozing during Sunday-morning services without drawing attention and to anticipate the special dessert after Sunday supper.

They both attended Herbert Smith's trial, where it was proven, to no one's surprise, that Herbert Smith had in fact stolen Harry Leighton's collection of marbles. The defense attorney, Francis Burr, was a year ahead of Bill but had little talent for public speaking and did not seem to have prepared much in the way of a defense. Charles noted that Bill referred to notes on a single handwritten sheet of paper on the table but that Francis had nothing in front of him. As soon as Bill walked over to Harry with a small box in his hand and asked if Harry could identify the marbles found under Herbert's bed, the end came swiftly. Superintendent Bradley watched the entire trial from the back of the room and left without a word when it was done.

Over supper that night, the boys congratulated Bill on his win. "Another feather in your lawyer cap," proclaimed Tink, openly chewing meatloaf. "You're gonna be leaving some awfully big shoes to fill next month."

"But to be fair to old Francis," insisted Salt as he poured himself some more milk, "that was a pretty easy win, weren't it?"

"Not necessarily," said Bill in lawyerly tones.

"Whaddya mean?" asked Salt. "Okay, supposin' you had to switch with Francis. How would you stick up for Herbert? See, I betcha you couldn't."

"Well, you'd be losing that bet. I could defend Herbert if I had to, even though he's guilty as sin."

"How you gonna defend someone you know is guilty?" asked Charles.

"Well," said Bill to Charles, "let me catch you up on civics class, since you're so interested. Turns out that every mug out there deserves an excellent defense—even the guilty ones. Just because I believe he's guilty don't actually mean that he's guilty. He's only guilty when the judge or jury decides."

"What if he confessed to you?" asked Charles.

"Even then, I gotta use the law to try to get him off."

"Like how?"

Bill put his fork down to devote himself fully to Herbert's defense. "Okay, I might say, 'Harry, did you see Herbert take your marbles?' and he'd say, 'Well, no.' And I'd say, 'Now, everyone knows they were found under Herbert's bed, but did you or any other mug see Herbert put them under there?' and Harry would say, 'Well, no,' and I'd say, 'Do you know if Herbert's got anyone that don't like him so much recently?' and Harry would say, 'Well, everybody knows about that big fight he and Frederic Adams had last week,' and I would say, 'So Herbert's got at least one boy on this rock that might want to make him look bad, is that what you're saying?' And so on. See?" Bill took up his fork again and made up for lost time with his meatloaf.

Charles had speared a piece of potato, but it was suspended in the air at the end of his fork while he thought about this. "So you ain't saying that Frederic did it, but that he coulda."

"Exactly right, Weston. And then you keep driving on with it if you can—ain't it true that Frederic is in the same dormitory as Harry, in fact, ain't his bed even closer to Harry's than Herbert's is, etcetera, etcetera."

"So maybe Frederic did do it." Charles put his forked potato back on his plate, lost in thought.

"Nah, Herbert did it." Bill grinned and pointed his knife at Charles. "But I had you goin' there, didn't I?"

Tink and Salt clapped and hooted for Bill until the matron came over to threaten demerits.

As August eased into September, the Weston brothers became used to the idea that everyone believed their concocted history. Even Aidan responded automatically to The Coffin or the matron when they called out for Master Weston, and his confidence that Dec would not divulge his confession appeared to have been warranted. And it was easier on both of them now that all the boys had taken to calling Aidan "Sully."

As the first weekend in September approached, the boys' chatter turned to Visiting Day. Mealtime conversation centered around which family members were anticipated to visit and what items they would likely bring. Mothers were apparently the most frequent visitors and could be relied on to bring something edible. Older brothers came infrequently but often brought contraband items, especially brothers who were alumni of the school.

One evening, the boys of Laurel Cottage were engaged in an after-supper study session, to which Aidan had once again dragged Charles. He had found Charles at the far end of the flower beds, in deep conversation with a younger boy.

"Dontcha remember how Bradley is expecting your grades to be good?" asked Aidan as he and Charles walked down the hill.

"That's his problem," Charles grumbled as he waved away a mosquito.

"So who was that little shaver you were chumming around with?" asked Aidan.

"Name is Percy Tisdale."

"Why were you talking with him?"

"Ain't it enough that I'm gonna waste an hour studying geometry with you? Do I have to tell you everything?"

"Geography."

"What?"

"The test is on geography tomorrow, not geometry."

"Really?" Charles's surprise seemed genuine.

"Do you ever stay awake in class?" asked Aidan, exasperated, as he handed Charles his satchel.

"Not if I can help it." They had reached Laurel, and Charles held the door for Aidan. "After you."

Moments later, Dec, Tink, and Sumner arrived.

"Announcing our special guest," Tink proclaimed with an elaborate waving of his hand, "Master Declan Moore, who would rather study with real men than the ladies of Starlight Cottage."

"Not to mention that Poole is practicing his bleddy French Horn in there," added Dec.

"Where's Bill?" asked Charles.

"Off being irritable by hisself, I believe," said Tink as he tossed his books on the table. He cracked his knuckles and arched his back in a long stretch before throwing himself down noisily in a chair.

Aidan had noticed that Bill had been unusually quiet during dinner and supper that day. "What's eating him?"

"'Tis Visiting Day this weekend," said Dec as he pulled a chair out from the table. "Best to steer clear of him 'til it's over."

"Why?" asked Charles.

Dec started to answer, but Tink got there first, apparently as interested as Charles in delaying the study of geography. "It's like this: Bill's father died when he was young, and his mother remarried a total son of a bitch. Managed to have twin babes with him while he wasn't knockin' her around, and then she died when Bill was nine. She weren't cold in the ground before the son of a bitch got Bill on the first steamer over to the island. The little ones, boys both of them, they was too young to come. Needless to say, the lout never came to visit, didn't write. By the time Bill had his week off in the summer and went looking for the little ones, there weren't no trace of them or the father. Their place was rented to someone else, and that family had never heard nothin' about who lived there before."

"Bill had thought his wee brothers would end up coming here too," added Dec. "Another year, and they would have been old enough. But they never showed. Spittin' image of their ma, according to him." A silence settled over the cottage as they all contemplated the half brothers that reminded Bill of his dead mother and how Bill would probably never see them again.

"So, to summarize," said Tink lightly, breaking the silence, "Bill hates Visiting Day because it reminds him of who ain't coming for him. Day after, he'll be fine again."

"Well, we ain't got no one coming for us neither," said Charles.

"Most boys' families can't come every time," said Tink. "My ma couldn't come last month."

"I think it's different when you know there ain't *never* gonna be no one," said Aidan.

After a slight pause, the boys all reached for their books.

Charles had figured that despite their recent arguing, he and Aidan would stick together during their first Visiting Day, but he was surprised and annoyed to discover that Dec's family appeared to have adopted Aidan for the day. As the passengers had disembarked from the steamer, the band had played several rousing songs. Aidan had gone to compliment Dec on his playing as Dec's family approached, and after a brief introduction, Mrs. Moore's forcefully maternal personality simply swept Aidan up with Dec and his two little sisters. Aidan seemed all too happy to attach himself to this family, and he promptly forgot all about Charles.

The more Charles thought about this, the more irritated he became. What had happened to them being brothers? Sticking together? He conveniently forgot his recent disagreements with Aidan and assigned all the blame for his isolation on Aidan and Dec's mother, ruminating on how unfair the situation, pushing aside the faint thoughts that his own prickly personality might be the main reason he was so often alone. Instead of admitting that he wished a family would allow him to tag along on Visiting Day, he focused on his conviction that he wouldn't want to be with any lousy Micks and that Aidan was a traitor for leaving him to fend for himself.

When he became bored with repeating these sentiments over and over again in his head, he headed down to the barn. The bacon he had pilfered from the breakfast table had leached its grease through the napkin, and it made his fingers slick when he put his hand in his trouser pocket. Through repeated use, the napkin had become a collage of meat stains and was disgusting enough that Charles had actually noticed its condition and made a mental note to steal a replacement.

As he reached for the barn door handle, he heard the ping of metal. Peeking around the corner, he saw Bill leaning up against the side of the barn, winging pebbles at an empty milk canister.

"Hey," he said.

Bill glanced over his shoulder. "Weston," he returned grimly, winging another pebble.

At this point, Charles wished for something appropriate or clever to say, but nothing came to him. The truth was that during the time he had spent living out on his own, trusting no one, other boys had been refining the art of conversation amongst themselves without even being aware of it. Charles, on the other hand, had only developed the ability to interact with adults: shopkeepers, the police, Bess. With other boys, if the situation didn't call for something smarmy or angry, he often couldn't find much to say. He liked Bill the most of all the boys he'd met, in fact, because Bill was always in command of the conversation—starting it, maintaining it, making it easy for everyone around him to know his part.

Except for today, when Bill was clearly not in the mood to command anything except the denting of a milk canister.

Charles considered just entering the barn and getting on with his Lucifer business, but instead he sat down next to Bill, leaving a respectful yard in between them, and stared at the canister. After all, Charles had nothing but time today.

After several more pebbles made their flight, Bill spoke first. "No visitors?"

"Ain't got nobody who even knows we're here."

"Least you got your brother." Bill threw a larger rock this time. It made a satisfying, low-pitched ping as it found its target. Both boys could see the dent from where they sat.

"You'd think. But he's off with Dec's family." Just saying it made Charles mad all over again.

"No, sir! He left you on your first Visiting Day?"

"That he did." Bill's incredulity was most gratifying. Just having someone understand what an affront this was made Charles feel better.

They could see small groups of people dotting the hillside, a few small children running after each other in circles. It was odd to Charles to see women and children roaming around here.

The delighted screams of little siblings were shrill in his ears. He couldn't wait for Visiting Day to be over.

"They'll be ringing the bell for the assembly soon," said Bill, his dark mood lifting. "Think we have time to grab some sand from the beach for your brother's bed?"

CHAPTER 27

JUST LET ME RINSE MY HANDS OFF AT THE SPIGOT," SAID AIDAN AS he stuffed the last weeds into the sack.

"No time. Just brush 'em off on your pants." Charles grabbed Aidan by the forearm and pulled him up from the flower bed.

"So now suddenly you're Mister Punctual? What's with you? Last Town Meeting, I had to drag you."

"Yeah, well, I'm a convert now. Let's go."

They joined the ragged stream of boys heading toward the assembly hall in Bulfinch.

Once the meeting began, they sat through the usual administrative droning. Charles sat with his back unsupported by his chair, his leg bobbing up and down.

"Will you quit it?" whispered Aidan into his ear.

"What?"

Aidan put his hand on Charles's knee. Charles brushed it off gruffly but stilled his leg.

Soon the agenda turned to filling the positions being vacated this month. The mayor, a First Classer named Pedgrift, called out the positions to be filled. First up was the judge, and when that position was filled, Francis Burr's position was next.

"Now, who is interested in becoming the defense attorney to replace Burr?" said Pedgrift.

Charles stood. "I am," he announced, clenching his fists.

There was a general murmuring in the crowd. Pedgrift's voice rose above the din. "Usually boys is here a while before they sign on with Cottage Row Government."

Charles cleared his throat. "I been here five weeks, and I'd do just as good a job as anybody here." He looked around to see if anyone would challenge him and saw that Bradley stood, arms crossed before him, at the side of the hall. Bradley nodded almost imperceptibly at Charles before they broke eye contact.

Bill stood. "I second the motion."

Once Bill had seconded, there were no others that wanted to challenge Charles. In truth, the coveted positions were the police and, to a lesser extent, the judge. The attorney positions required preparation work for the trials, and attorneys lacked the power to arrest or sentence other boys, which was the fun part. So Charles's election happened swiftly and without fanfare, though it did not go unnoticed by Aidan.

"So now you're part of the government," commented Aidan as they left the building after the meeting. "The government that you couldn't believe any boys would start."

"Yeah, well, things change. I got my reasons."

"Ones you ain't gonna tell me about."

Charles didn't say anything.

"Fine," said Aidan. "You just keep to yourself. Don't let no one know what you're thinking. For the first time, you got a brother and ninety-eight other boys you could be pals with, but what a grand idea to shut them all out. Brilliant." Aidan abruptly headed off to the gardens, leaving Charles with a desire to say something—either a snappy retort or an apology, he wasn't sure which—but without the words to say it.

After Caleb and his followers tossed Aidan into the water, Charles expected an escalation of some sort—either retaliation by the other Laurel boys or more organized bullying. But neither happened. Aidan had been shoved, "accidentally," in the yard a few times by Warwick and Caleb, and Bowditch had tripped him when he was carrying a full watering can to his flower bed, all of which Charles heard about after the fact. But as a group, the boys seemed to have lost the coordinated focus they'd shown that evening on the beach.

Which was not to say that Caleb and his group were not busy. Nearly every day, one could observe a boy in Third Class suffering through their attentions. Boys in the lower classes were mostly left alone because Caleb sought out boys near his own size. But any boy in Third Class who stuck out in any way made a nice target.

Today all the Laurel boys stood in the yard and watched as Caleb, Bowditch, and Warwick launched their attack on John Stonecypher. Caleb had cornered him against the rough bricks of Bulfinch, and Bowditch and Warwick were shielding the action from the monitors. Charles and Aidan didn't have to ask why this boy was a target—they had heard him stutter in class.

"That ain't right," muttered Charles. "Nobody ever tries to stop him?"

"What, you're gonna stick your neck out for Stonecypher?" asked Salt.

Charles didn't reply. In truth, he didn't care about Stonecypher's plight at all, but Caleb's assault on Aidan down at the shoreline was very much on his mind. Charles had, in fact, been waiting for Caleb to challenge him in some way, and he had resolved that when that happened, he would do his best to beat the living hell out of Caleb. But Caleb never made a move toward Charles, nor had he done anything to Aidan when Charles was present. Charles's recent difficulties with Aidan hadn't diminished his desire to knock Caleb down a peg. In fact, the more irritated Charles became with Aidan, the more he wanted to take it out on Caleb.

Charles looked around. Mr. Croft was brokering peace between two feuding Fifth Classers, and the other monitors were too far away to see what was going on in this part of the yard.

Charles broke ranks and started to walk over to Caleb.

"What are you doing?" asked Aidan, but Charles ignored him. In quick succession, he shoved Bowditch aside to clear the path and shoved Caleb.

"You bastard!" cried Bowditch, grabbing Charles around the neck, but Caleb called him off.

"Weston," Caleb said with eerie calmness. "What kind of a fucking half-wit are you?" He looked almost happy.

"Not every Third Classer's gonna take your crap, Hart."

"Well, this one is," he said, and he turned back to Stonecypher. "Cat got your tongue?" he asked, pursing his lips and giving Stonecypher a few little slaps on the cheek.

Charles's lunge was aborted when Caleb grabbed Charles by the throat and slammed him up against the bricks.

"It ain't gonna happen here, Weston. But tonight, 'round the back of the storage barn at half midnight, you're gonna be there, and you and I are gonna settle this." The pressure of Caleb's hand around Charles's windpipe caused his field of vision to narrow at the edges, and he started to hear a faint ringing in his ears. But a moment later, Caleb's hand relaxed and moved to his shoulder in a friendly gesture, just before Mr. Croft pushed Bowditch and Warwick aside.

"What's going on here, gentlemen?" Croft asked suspiciously, hands on his wide hips.

Caleb's mild expression never changed. "Just settling our differences, sir. Weston here is rather headstrong, but I think perhaps I've persuaded him to my way of thinking."

"Weston?" queried Croft, anxious for this to be confirmed so that no further action on his part would be required.

"Can't quite say I'm persuaded, Mr. Croft." Charles tried to match Caleb's expression through gritted teeth.

"Well, as long as your discourse is civil. I'm sure you'll come to some resolution."

Charles was pretty sure that the resolution wouldn't be of the type Croft was suggesting.

～

"I'm coming tonight," whispered Aidan as they waited out the night watchman in the dormitory that evening.

Charles turned over in his bed, his back toward Aidan. "Suit yourself," he said neutrally, but he felt a little glow of satisfaction.

When the time approached, they saw Caleb and Bowditch, who slept closer to the door, slip out. Charles counted to one hundred before he and Aidan did the same. As they passed Cantrell's bed, he stirred from sleep briefly to give them the thumbs-up. Before the bell had rung for supper that night, all of the Third Class had known about the night's face-off, and many had fallen asleep that evening anticipating the news of the outcome spreading from boy to boy before the breakfast bell.

Caleb and Bowditch were waiting for them outside the storage barn. "I'll give you credit for showing your mug, Weston. You got a set of balls on ya." In the moonlight, Caleb's platinum hair almost seemed to glow. It was practically a beacon that one could follow in the dark like a kerosene lantern.

"Let's get on with it," muttered Charles, rubbing his neck. The more he thought about what they were doing, the stupider it seemed. Any fighting he had done in his life had been in the heat of the moment, when his temper had flared or he had been attacked. In the yard this afternoon, seeing Caleb close in on Stonecypher, he'd had the same surge that had propelled him to tackle Caleb on the beach. He would have taken on five Calebs at that moment. It was as if there had only been room in his mind for one emotion and no room for thoughts at all, as if rage had taken up the space that might have housed concern for getting hurt or getting caught. But this situation at the storage barn was like a boxing match: planned in advance, without any anger to push him over the edge. He could only hope that Caleb would goad him enough that he would be able to fight.

All four boys flinched and looked westward into the dark as they heard the sound of the night watchman stumbling over something and cursing. They could see his lamp bobbing in the distance as he progressed across the field. "Quick, inside," Caleb whispered, "'til he goes 'round the other side of the island." The boys slid silently through the doorway and to the far side of the barn, where, one by one, they realized that they were not alone.

Charles, the first through the doorway, tried to make sense of what he was seeing, tried to understand the whole picture, but all he could really see was a leg. A beautiful white leg, glowing in the light of a lantern set on the floor. A leg that started with a foot in a tiny leather boot, but which continued on up the curved calf without a stitch of clothing on it, bent prettily at the knee, proceeding equally unclad up to the thigh, where it met a crush of bunched-up skirts—though not before displaying what could only be a bit of perfect, pale buttock. Just when Charles thought the leg could not be more beautiful, the heel of the little boot braced against a bale of hay, tightening the muscles in the calf and thigh. Involuntarily, Charles took a little breath and held it. To his ears, there wasn't a sound in the barn.

He had never seen an actual woman's leg above the knee before.

Into his field of vision came a hand that grabbed the perfect thigh roughly, and like a horse whose blinders are removed, Charles suddenly had panoramic view of the whole picture. Lydia Turner's auburn hair tangled in hay and her fingers equally tangled in Cole Thomas's hair, Cole with his trousers pooled at his ankles and his face buried in her neck. Sound returned to the barn: a moan from Cole, a gasp from Miss Turner as she saw the boys, and then Caleb's voice saying, "Thomas, you fucking dog, you."

Without a word, both Cole and Miss Turner hurried to right their clothing as Charles, Aidan, and Bowditch stared, frozen in various expressions of disbelief. Caleb's smile, the way he crossed his arms and tilted his head to one side, gave the impression that this was the kind of thing he would expect to come across sooner or later, and that somehow it was to his advantage.

Miss Turner was still finger-combing hay from her hair when Cole began his negotiations. "Listen, Caleb, this is something best kept just among us boys, don't you think?" He tried to assume the attitude of a First Classer speaking to a Second Classer, but everyone in the barn could feel that the balance of power had gone the other way.

"Well," mused Caleb, rubbing his chin in exaggerated concentration, "that is one possibility, assuming there's something in it for me. On the other hand, it really would be the right thing to do to just go straight to Bradley."

Without thinking, without realizing it was going to happen, Charles blurted out, "No!" So immediately did he regret this that he clapped his hand over his mouth as if to prevent the already-uttered word from leaving it.

Caleb turned to Charles with an expression that could, in the dim lantern light, be interpreted as appreciative, so gentle was his smile. "Weston, I was truly on the fence about whether Thomas here should pay me for my silence, but you've helped me make my decision." And with that, he strolled out of the barn, trailing a grinning Bowditch and a quietly protesting Cole.

When the sound of the departing boys had been swallowed up by the night, Charles turned back to Miss Turner, now standing before them. She could not easily pass without him stepping aside. Charles realized this was his last chance to say something to her.

Did she recognize him from the night in her room? Did she appreciate his stupid attempt to stop Caleb from turning them in, or did she hate him as the catalyst of their exposure? He couldn't tell from her expression. She drew herself up to her full height, no taller than Charles, in an attempt to retain a scrap of dignity.

Charles plucked a piece of hay from her hair that she had missed and moved to let her pass. She quickly left the barn without looking back.

Aidan exhaled and leaned against the barn wall. "Jaysus. I can't believe that just happened." Charles came to lean on the wall next to him, and they stared at the farming tools stacked against the far wall. A cricket in the barn chirped a slow and rhythmic pulse, out of time with his fellow crickets outside. They stayed there for a while, each lost in playing back these events in their mind, rolling the scene forward to what would happen tomorrow.

"Hey," said Aidan, nudging Charles with his shoulder, "at least you didn't get the crap beat outta ya." He ventured a little smile.

But Charles knew he had lost the fight with Caleb, as sure as if he were bleeding on the barn floor.

CHAPTER 28

By THE TIME BREAKFAST PLATTERS LANDED ON TABLES THE NEXT morning, every boy in the school knew some version of what had happened in the storage barn the night before. As the story was passed to the young boys, it became more innocent to accommodate their limited understanding of relations between men and women. Those boys came away with the impression of impassioned kissing or muffled rustling under a blanket—something they might have witnessed or overheard in their homes back on the mainland. But with the older boys, the tale grew in graphic detail, some describing Miss Turner's complete nudity, her moans of passion loud enough to wake the horses, her insatiable lust that Cole could only begin to satisfy.

A few First Classers badgered Cole for details, but when they were met with silence, they backed off. The majority of the boys gave him a wide berth, knowing that he was likely in serious trouble. This did not stop them from endlessly talking about Cole and Miss Turner; they just made sure that Cole did not overhear them.

Cole moved through the routine of his morning like a man awaiting his execution. Every boy was aware that Caleb Hart was not at breakfast, and they imagined him conversing with Bradley while they all ate their eggs and toast. When Cole was plucked from lineup after breakfast by the matron, no one was surprised, least of all Cole.

Out in the yard, conversations bloomed in small groups, and the boys from Laurel Cottage were no exception.

"So Bainbridge said her naked arse was pointin' up in the air," said Tink urgently to Charles and Aidan. "You sayin' that weren't the case?" His expression telegraphed his hope that Bainbridge was telling the truth.

Charles had refused to confirm anything other than the basic facts, and Aidan had remained mostly silent on the subject. Charles stared at Tink until Tink looked away and spit on the ground. "Well, I'll just believe what I want to, then," he said to no one in particular.

"No," said Aidan, and all eyes in the group swiveled to meet his. "This ain't right, Charles. You go around sayin' nothin', and these stories are growin' wilder and wilder. Hart and Bowditch can't be trusted to tell the truth." He turned to Tink. "No, her arse weren't naked, and she weren't pointin' it to heaven. She weren't makin' loud noises or talkin' dirty. We were there for two seconds before they called it quits, so nobody saw much of nothin'."

After a brief silence, Tink said, "That ain't as fun as what Bainbridge is sayin'."

"You see?" Charles fumed to Aidan. "They don't want the truth. They want the Bainbridge version. They want to make her out to be a whore!"

"Well, ain't she?" asked Salt. "She couldn't keep her bloomers on, had to go and deflower poor Thomas." He and Tink guffawed.

"You wouldn't know a whore if you stepped on one." Charles pushed past him and headed off down the hill. Aidan followed as Salt called after them, "And you would, Weston?"

Charles plunked himself down on the bench outside the henhouse, out of view of the boys in the yard but near enough to

Bulfinch to hear the bell for lineup when it came. Aidan sat next to him gingerly.

Without looking at Charles, Aidan said, "Everyone says Bradley's gonna make her leave the island, no matter what the boys say. It ain't gonna change anything."

"Then why'd you try to tell Tink that Bainbridge was makin' all that up?"

"Yeah, that was sorta stupid, I guess. You're right—they don't want the truth."

Charles grunted in agreement, but he was appeased. That was something that always impressed him—how Aidan could admit a mistake so easily, as if it didn't cost him anything. Charles could rarely do it at all, and when he did, it gave him almost physical pain, as if he were wrenching an arrow from his gut.

After a moment of picking at the splinters in the bench, Charles said, "They're making her out to be like one of them alley sluts down by the waterfront. But she ain't like that." He thought of the smell of roses in her room that night, her clean hair in wavelets on the white pillow. So much nicer than having all that straw in her hair last night. Why couldn't she have just kept meeting Cole in her room? Then this never would have happened. And then he had an uncomfortable thought.

"Sully, what if it was because of me? What if she didn't feel safe meeting him in her room anymore after I found her out? What if that was why she started meeting Cole outside?"

"This ain't your fault."

"What if it is?"

"You know whose fault this is? Hers. Didn't look like Cole was forcin' her to do anything. She made the choice. She had to know this could happen."

"But if it weren't for Hart, that bastard, she'd be getting ready to teach class right now instead of packing her bag."

"She was playin' with fire, my brother. She was lucky it was you in her room that night. Another boy mighta turned her in, and she'd be long gone by now. It was probably gonna happen sooner or later."

Charles sighed. Aidan was right, and for the first time since they were in the storage barn last night, he felt a little better. A little less angry—at Caleb, at himself, at Cole, at everyone who had conspired to take his first kiss away from the island.

Superintendent Bradley had given up hope that his headache would recede before it really took hold. He sat at his desk, fingertips to temples, and waited for Mrs. Bradley to come back with some breakfast if any could still be found in the kitchen.

When Bradley opened his door to see Caleb, he could only think of the cruelty the boy had shown throwing the younger Weston brother into the harbor. When Bradley had called Caleb to his office the morning after that incident, Caleb had calmly admitted to what he had done using euphemistic phrases—"horseplay," "clowning around," "ribbing"—that cast his actions in the light of typical boyhood high jinks. Even Bradley was almost persuaded that he had overreacted. But as he replayed the event in his mind, he could once again feel that there was nothing lighthearted in Caleb's actions. When Bradley announced the punishment incurred, Caleb had accepted the demerits and the extra chores with an easy grace that did nothing to allay Bradley's concerns about the boy.

But Bradley always gave every boy the benefit of the doubt—outwardly, at least—and thus he welcomed Caleb into his sanctum and listened to the boy's quiet disclosure with his practiced expression of benevolent neutrality. By the time Caleb was finished, however, Bradley could only hope that his facial expression had held, because he felt anything but neutral inside. After a few clarifying questions, Bradley thanked and dismissed him. When the door had clicked shut behind Caleb, Bradley sat numbly, unmoving in his chair.

Was it lies? What would Caleb's motivation be to lie? After all, he had admitted to breaking curfew, sneaking out of the dormitory after the watchman had left, seeking fresh air when he was unable to sleep. Any boy knew that was a multiple-demerit offense. The boy he'd implicated, Cole Thomas, was a class above him, old enough to leave the island. Bradley had found Thomas an internship at a printing press two months ago, but Thomas had pleaded to remain on the island. He'd found Thomas's reasons for turning down the internship vague, but another First Classer had been more than happy to take the job, so at the time, Bradley had thought no more of it. But as he thought about it now, Thomas's actions seemed to support Caleb's claims.

All of which was a convenient way of thinking about everything but that which horrified him the most: Lydia Turner. His decision to hire her. Against his wishes, the memory came back to him: how he'd shaken her hand and welcomed her as she stepped off the steamer, how delicate and refined she'd looked standing on the rough wood of the wharf.

From a position of complete stillness, he bolted from his chair and stepped into the hallway. He cornered the first boy he saw and asked him to send the matron to his office.

"You look unwell," Mary Bradley commented as she took a seat, but she refrained from further comment and waited for her husband to speak.

They listened to the tick of the pendulum clock until Bradley could decide how to begin. "There has been an accusation." A few more ticks of the clock filled up the pause. "One that may not surprise you." Three more ticks. Bradley cleared his throat. "Miss Turner has been accused of . . . interfering with a First Classer. Cole Thomas." Bradley extracted a white handkerchief from his jacket and mopped his damp brow.

"Mr. Bradley, I must confess that something of this nature was the subject of the chatter among the other teachers, and I feel remiss in not bringing this to your—"

"I do recall our discussion. I understand that you felt those rumors were not substantiated at the time. But more importantly, even if you had brought it to my attention at that time, it would not have prevented the damage from being done. You are blameless in this matter." He did not broach the subject of whether *he* was blameless in this matter.

"Is it possible that the rumors and this accusation are both false?" asked Mary, although nothing in her expression gave any indication of hope.

"It is possible. Nothing would please me more." He thought of it: Hart a liar, fitting with his cruel behavior toward Weston at the wharf; Lydia Turner, his hiring decision, innocent and virginal, remaining here as the instructor who gets such good grades from the youngest boys. "But I cannot permit myself to live on this hope if it is false. Please bring Thomas to my office."

The interview with Cole put to rest any hope. When questioned about his involvement with Miss Turner, he freely, even boldly, admitted it, confessing his love with evident relief. Inwardly, Bradley groaned. She has well and truly infected him, he thought. The boy cannot see how her immorality has laid claim to him. It is like the opium pipe that appears to deliver on its promise of heaven even as it drags you to hell.

Cole wished to prolong his discussion with Bradley, endeavoring to know the fate of Miss Turner, making his desire to remain with her, on or off the island, known. But Bradley ushered him out. Mrs. Bradley, who had been waiting outside the door, entered and stood by the desk. Bradley could see she had heard every word from the hallway. The pain in his head crescendoed.

"Could you bring a bit of breakfast?" he asked.

After she had gone, the thought that commandeered his mind

was: *All that effort and worry about screening the boys, and all this time it was a teacher that was the bad seed.*

Any change in routine was amply noted by the boys, and this is what they observed on this day: the superintendent left mid-morning for Boston and didn't return until late. The boys in Miss Turner's class were put on double farm duty and had no class that day. Miss Turner did not emerge from her room, and a houseboy brought midday dinner to her. After lights out in the dormitory that evening, the boys nearest the window heard activity outside and went to the window in time to see Miss Turner making her way down to the wharf, accompanied by Mr. Fielding. Word spread through the dormitory, and several more boys, including Charles, went to the windows. The night watchman pretended not to see the boys get out of their bed. Cole Thomas lay in his bed staring up at the ceiling, no expression on his face.

Charles came back to his bed and sat glumly with his elbows on his knees. Aidan sat up on his bed so that their knees were almost touching.

"Hey," Aidan said in the voice that all the boys instinctively learned to use in the dormitory, the one that was pitched just low and soft enough that the person next to you could hear you but the person one bed away could not.

"Hey," returned Charles in a monotone.

"You did everything you could to protect her."

"'Course I know that. You think I don't know that?" His belligerent words were reflexive; his heart wasn't in it.

"Well, the way I see it, once you done everything you can think of to do, you can rest easy." And with that, Aidan got into bed and closed his eyes.

After a while, Charles did the same.

CHAPTER 29

By THE END OF THE WEEK, A NEW TEACHER HAD ARRIVED TO REPLACE Miss Turner, and most boys agreed that the superintendent must have placed a premium on homeliness in his search. Miss Fowler had facial features that seemed to belong to several different people—small eyes, a medium-sized nose with an awkward bump, large lips resembling twin earthworms sleeping side by side. Her nasally drone could be heard from outside her classroom even with the door closed.

During free time before Town Meeting that Saturday, Aidan and Dec were in Starlight Cottage for what was becoming a regular music lesson.

"Ya sound bleddy awful today, Sullivan. Let me have a look at that reed." Dec inspected Aidan's mouthpiece. "It's in a bit of rough shape, but the main problem is it's too high up." He loosened the ligature and lowered the reed slightly. "Try it now."

Aidan played a partial scale. "Thanks. Even I can tell it sounds much better."

They played through one of the band pieces, Dec breaking into harmony for the last two measures for his own entertainment. "You're really not half bad when your reed's not all bollixed up," he said. "I'd not have thought you'd come along as fast as ya did. Maybe you can join the band for performances—probably not this next one in October, but maybe the one after."

"October? The band's performing for Visiting Day again?"

Dec started to break down his instrument as he spoke. "Oh, that as well, that slipped my mind, but what I meant was the performance at Faneuil Hall."

"The band is going to the mainland to perform?" Aidan removed his reed and stored it in its little wooden box.

"Bradley must have announced the dates this summer before you got here. But indeed, we are."

"I bet you'll sound capital. Wish I could hear you play."

"Your wish is my command, Mr. Sullivan. You *are* going." Dec snapped his case shut.

"What?"

"Everyone's going. For all the big performances, the whole school goes."

Aidan sat with a piece of his clarinet in each hand, frozen. *Back to the mainland. On the boat. Jaysus.* He couldn't tell if he was more frightened of traveling across the water again or showing his face in Boston.

"What the divil is with ya?" asked Dec. "Wait—the water. You're not keen on taking the steamer over, are ya?"

"You could say that." Aidan jammed the remaining pieces of his instrument into the case, possibly not all in the right places, and squeezed it closed. "You think I can get out of it?"

"Listen, boyo, you live on an *island* now. You have to face the fact that every once in a while, you are going to have to travel that one wee mile over to civilization. I mean, didja think that you would just come here and die an old man without ever leaving?"

Aidan hadn't given this a thought until now. Ever since stepping off the steamer more than a month ago, his concerns about the water had been focused completely on evening swim.

Dec gave up on getting an answer to his question. "C'mon, let's get our horns up to the dormitory before Town Meeting." They exited the cottage, the bright sunlight dilating their pupils painfully. Squinting, they made their way up the hill. "The fact of the matter is, you'll cross on the steamer that day, you'll return, and nothing bad will have happened. So what have ya got to worry about, eh?"

Aidan knew from experience that it was pointless to try to explain an irrational fear to a rational person.

For Aidan, Town Meeting was neither here nor there. He had no objection to it and also no interest in it. To him it was just something that you did here, like studying history or hoeing weeds. So he couldn't understand why Charles seemed to have such strong reactions to all things related to the Cottage Row government. First Charles was outraged at its very existence, and then he volunteered to become one of their lawyers. And it was clear that Charles didn't want to talk about it. Back in Boston, before they had come to the island, Aidan had thought that he understood Charles. They were friends—one would have to say best friends—and while Charles had built a wall around himself with other people, he hadn't been that way with Aidan. Somehow coming here had changed that, and it didn't seem like it could be fixed.

All the Laurel boys had been together as they filed into the room for Town Meeting, but then Aidan and Charles had become separated. Aidan sat with Dec and Salt, bored silly by the meeting, until Dec nudged him.

"What's your brother doing?"

Aidan looked over at Charles, standing among the sitting boys, facing the boy-mayor sitting at the head table. Aidan recognized the expression on Charles's face—it was his *go-ahead-and-challenge-me* look. Before Aidan could ask Dec what was happening, the mayor spoke.

"Defense attorney don't ask for trials. Prosecution does. Why would you want to bring your, uh, client to trial if he hasn't been accused of anything?" The mayor looked irritated, but Charles was undeterred.

"I want to clear my client's name. Everybody thinks poorly of him, and he don't deserve it."

"So who's this client, anyway?" Once the mayor had spoken, all ears waited for Charles's response.

"Lucifer."

All the boys started talking at once, the room humming with discussion. Even the boys at the head table—the mayor and his constables—were talking among themselves until the mayor remembered that he should be bringing order to the meeting. He banged his gavel on its pedestal several times.

"Order! Order! Hey, shaddup!" In a few moments, it was quiet enough to proceed. "Weston, you're saying that you want to bring a dog to trial."

"Yep."

"To clear his name."

"Yep."

The mayor thought about this. "Hey, Hinkley—you okay with this?"

Prosecutor Ralph Hinkley, recent replacement for Bill, stood from his seat in the crowd. "S'okay with me."

"All right. Next Saturday—Town versus Lucifer!" As the gavel banged, conversation erupted in the room.

Aidan looked at Charles, still standing, now with his lopsided grin decorating his face.

Dec elbowed Aidan. "'Tis an odd thing your brother's doing, eh? From the look on your face, I'm gonna say he didn't mention this to you beforehand. I'll wager not a boy will miss the trial next week."

Aidan turned to Dec and asked, "Who's Lucifer?"

~

Within the hour, some loquacious boy found his way to Mr. Fielding to tell him about next week's trial. An hour after that, boys started trickling down to the barn to catch sight of the now-famous, soon-to-be-tried Lucifer, but Fielding was having none of it.

"I'll not have any of you boys bitten by that godforsaken cur," he proclaimed as he roughly ushered them out of the barn and shut the door behind him. "You stay away. I don't care what that crazy Weston boy is up to—that dog is dangerous. Now git!"

Aidan, Charles, and the rest of the Laurel boys all gathered in the cottage. "So let me see if I understand all this," began Aidan. "You been teaching this wild dog some tricks, and you think that proves he ain't mean and they shouldn't take a rifle to him."

"He ain't wild. He ain't off living in the woods like some . . ." Charles struggled for a comparison. "Like some wild dog or somethin'. He wants to be with people. That's how come I could train him."

"But how are you gonna prove that he ain't dangerous?" asked Bill. "Even a dolt like Ralph Hinkley will be smart enough to call Percy Tisdale to the stand, and Percy will probably be more than happy to drop his trousers and show everybody that scar on his leg."

"Actually, I'm countin' on that." Charles grinned.

"That makes no sense," said Aidan.

Bill studied Charles. "You know something we don't know."

"See you at the trial," said Charles. He got up from the table and left the cottage.

"Your brother's pretty good at keeping stuff to himself when he wants to, ain't he?" commented Bill.

You have no idea, thought Aidan.

CHAPTER 30

It's too bad that ain't one of the textbooks we're supposed to learn something from this year," observed Aidan dryly as he lay on his bed, flipping through one of Poole's magazines. Charles was bent over a civics book he had stolen from The Coffin's classroom on Monday, reading as if it were a story of adventure on the high seas or a daring train robbery. He grunted in response to Aidan and kept reading, occasionally pulling out a well-worn folded piece of paper from the back of the book and making a note with a short stub of pencil. All week he'd been at it. Aidan was quite sure Charles had never spent so much time in front of an open book.

Finally, the day of the trial arrived. Attendance was not mandatory, but most trials attracted a fair number of boys. For the more interesting trials, wagering added an extra level of interest. Merton Poole set the odds and collected the bets prior to the trial. Since Poole had begun fulfilling this responsibility last year, his math grades had improved—much to the pleasure of The Coffin, who was unaware of how Poole was practicing his basic arithmetic.

Wagering on Lucifer's trial hit a new record. "Over 60 percent of the boys got some hide in this game!" Poole proclaimed to those around him as the boys filed into the room. He had set odds for Lucifer's acquittal at 6 to 1, but a surprising number of bettors had faith in either the dog or in Charles.

Aidan filed in with all the Laurel boys, plus Salt and Dec. As they took their seats, he heard other Third Classers discussing the case in the row in front of him.

"That Weston mug's got fire in the belly—he'll run circles around Ralph," claimed Cantrell.

"Don't matter how clever Weston's palaver is—that dog has a record of bein' vicious. How's he gonna explain that away?" retorted Pickering.

Aidan looked to the back of the room and saw the superintendent, the matron, and Mr. Fielding standing against the wall. Was this good or bad for Charles? Mr. Bradley looked peeved. Bill had mentioned that Mr. Bradley had repeatedly asked Fielding to "take care of the problem" but that Fielding had never gotten around to doing away with Lucifer. Was Mr. Bradley now irritated with Charles as well as Fielding?

After a prolonged effort to quiet the crowd down, the judge had Charles and Hinkley make opening statements, limited to two minutes each.

Sweating visibly, Charles glanced one more time at his creased sheet of notes on the table and began. "Wasn't too long ago—" His voice came out in a raspy squeak, and he stopped to clear his throat as the boys laughed. When they were quiet again, he restarted. "Wasn't too long ago I found out that Mr. Fielding was aimin' to put Lucifer down. But I got to know Lucifer, and he isn't a bad dog. He's a scared dog, and he knows nobody likes him. But he isn't bad inside, and he don't deserve to be shot." He sat down abruptly and wiped his forehead with his sleeve.

Hinkley stood and shoved his hands in his pockets. "I don't hate this dog or anything, but he ripped up old Percy pretty good, and I don't feel like I could ever turn my back on him. Even Mr. Fielding keeps us away from him. Maybe he don't need to be shot. Maybe Mr. Fielding should take him on the steamer to the mainland and dump him somewhere in Boston to fend for himself. But if he stays here, what if he goes for someone's neck next time? He don't belong on the island with all us boys."

The judge allowed some time for the murmuring of boys comparing these opening statements before he brought the gavel down. "Call your first witness, Ralph."

"I call Mr. Fielding."

Hinkley went through a brief summary of facts with Fielding: Lucifer was mean since he was a puppy, he had bit Percy Tisdale, Mr. Bradley had asked him more than once to put Lucifer down. Aidan thought Fielding looked pleased to be the center of attention and seemed to want Hinkley to ask him more questions, but Hinkley was not one to drag things out and was quickly done.

Charles approached Fielding's chair. "Has Lucifer ever bit anyone except Percy?"

"Not that I know of," said Fielding.

"Don't you think you'd have heard about it if he'd bit someone else?"

Fielding thought about this. "You're probably right. But he's snapped at me and some of you boys plenty of times."

"Was he pretty close to you when he snapped?"

"Well, sure! He's gotten right up to me and done it, mean little bugger." Fielding straightened in his chair a bit. Aidan thought he almost looked proud to have survived the dog's dangerous advances.

"So he was close enough that he *could* have bit you—and he chose not to," said Charles.

Fielding didn't say anything.

"Thanks. That's it." Charles took his seat back at the table.

Bill leaned over to Aidan and whispered, "Now that there was a nice piece of work by your brother." Aidan felt a little flush of pride.

Fielding, looking confused, proceeded to the back of the room and stood next to Bradley.

Hinkley called Percy Tisdale as his next witness and got right down to business.

"Tell us about the day that Lucifer bit you."

Percy scratched his neck and shifted uncomfortably in the chair. "Well, it sure was a beautiful day that day. Saturday. In the spring, um, maybe April. First nice day in a long time. Everyone itchin' to get out and explore the island. You know, after bein' cooped up all winter."

Hinkley crossed his arms. "Can you get to the part about the dog?"

"Um, right. Well, I was walkin' along, mindin' my own business, and Lucifer just come outta nowhere and attacked me." Percy scratched his neck some more.

"Where did he get ya?"

"Well, everybody knows it was my leg, here." He rubbed his left thigh.

"Can you show the court your scar?"

"Okay." Percy was shrugging his suspenders from his shoulders when Charles stood suddenly. "Objection!"

The judge looked surprised. "About what?"

"Inflammatory."

"Well I don't think Percy here is going to burst into flames, Weston." The crowd had a good laugh at Charles's expense.

Charles's hands balled into fists by his side, but he kept control of his voice. "What I mean to say is that seein' Percy's scar is gonna, uh, prejudice the court against Lucifer."

"Seems like it oughta. Overruled. Sit down, Weston."

Charles's hands remained in fists, hanging at the sides of his chair when he sat. His face looked neutral, but Aidan could tell he was seething.

Percy was so thin that once his suspenders were no longer on his shoulders, his pants dropped comically to his ankles. He seemed to know this would happen, and he waited until all eyes were on him to do it. When the laughter died down, everyone in the room focused on the long, jagged scar on the inside of Percy's thigh. Percy had clearly enjoyed the attention up until this point, but now he began to look somewhat uncomfortable.

"You can pull 'em up, Percy. Your witness, Weston."

Charles strode to the chair as Percy snapped his suspenders back in place and sat. Though Charles was now looking directly at him, Percy looked out the window and scratched his neck, which was by this time quite red.

"Where exactly were you when all this happened?"

"I don't exactly remember."

"Huh. So you remember the weather, the month, but you don't remember where you were."

"Well, it weren't too far," said Percy nervously, looking to the back of the room where the superintendent was.

"Huh. Do you remember talkin' to me a few weeks ago about all this?"

"Uh-huh." Percy picked at his cuticles.

"Do you remember telling me you were far up the shoreline when this happened?"

Percy said nothing. Every boy in the room, even Aidan, knew that "far up the shoreline" was beyond where any boy was allowed to go unsupervised.

"So which is it?"

Percy moved on to a different cuticle.

"I've been doin' a bit of reading about somethin' called perjury, Percy. Turns out it's a real bad thing to lie in a court of law. Much worse than just lyin' to people on any old day. You could be in some serious hot water for lyin' to this court." Aidan didn't see how this could be true, since this was a court run by twelve-year-olds, but it seemed to have an effect on Percy, who was now jiggling his leg nervously. "So even if you been lyin' about somethin' all this time, that really ain't a big deal. We've all done it before, even me. It's natural." Charles paused here for a heartbeat. "But if you lie today and leave that chair, that's a whole different ball of wax. You'd be lyin' in front of the matron, the superintendent"—and here he leaned in closer—"in front of God, Percy."

Aidan had to cover his mouth with his hand to prevent his laugh from escaping. No one else thought this was amusing—the room was deathly quiet—but Aidan knew that Charles could give a rat's ass about all things religious.

Bill leaned over to Aidan and whispered, "You think it's funny, but he's done it. He's a natural—brilliant."

And indeed, Percy cracked.

Out tumbled the story of how Percy had been exploring the shoreline alone, had somehow not noticed that he was far beyond the allowable boundaries—"musta been spring fever and all," he posited—and had climbed atop a large boulder sporting a dirt-filled crevice in its side that was so deep it had sprouted a small tree. Percy slipped off the boulder and snapped the sapling off with his boot, and the jagged wood edge ripped through his trouser and into his leg. As he limped back to the buildings, he concocted the story that Lucifer had done it so he wouldn't have to explain where he had been.

Charles was not done with Percy. "Why did you choose Lucifer?"

"Well, everyone knows he's mean as sin. Weren't no stretch of the imagination to believe he done it."

"Did anyone question your story at the time?"

"Not a one."

Charles walked back to his table, and Percy scooted out of his chair with evident relief, but before he could take his seat among his classmates, Mr. Bradley's voice rang out from the back of the room. "I'll see you in my office after supper, Mr. Tisdale."

The boys then looked to Ralph Hinkley, who was frowning. "Your next witness?" asked the judge, but Hinkley shook his head. "Prosecution, uh, rests," he said glumly.

Without waiting to be asked, Charles said, "I call Lucifer."

It took several bangs of the gavel to quiet the boys' response to that. "You're gonna question a dog?" asked Hinkley.

"Your Honor," said Charles to the judge, "just give me five minutes to get him up here, and you'll see."

The judge made a pretense of considering this, but it was clear that the boys were dying to see whatever spectacle would result from bringing Lucifer into the room, and the judge was no less curious. Finally, he said with feigned restraint, "I'll allow it," and the boys cheered. Aidan turned to look at the back of the room and saw Fielding and Bradley conversing intensely, culminating with Bradley waving Fielding away, shaking his head.

Charles was off like a shot out the door, and the conversation among the boys never flagged in his absence. Some were badgering Poole to change or augment their bets, but Poole refused. Others were recounting personal experiences with Lucifer and interpreting them in light of the new information. Neither Bradley nor the matron made any attempt to quiet them.

Dec said to Bill, "Mister Former Prosecutor, is it your professional opinion that our boy has kicked the prosecution's arse?"

"It would appear so, but our boy is taking a gamble by fetching that dog. It's like he won the bet pool with a great hand of poker, and now he just went double or nothing."

It took Charles a minute or two to convince Lucifer to enter the room, despite the bacon he was dangling. Lucifer did not stop his low growl even as he advanced upon the meat, a growl that could be heard in the utter silence of the room as every boy stared at the dog. Aidan had not yet seen Lucifer and was surprised at how small he was, his back not even two feet off the ground.

Charles had been walking backward and making a soft clucking sound, but now he stopped and said, "Lucy, sit!"

Lucifer dropped his rear end to the ground and gobbled his reward.

Charles slowly knelt down while retrieving another piece of bacon from his pocket. Some boys gasped to see how near he was to the dog, within easy striking range if Lucifer decided to lunge.

"Lucy, shake!"

Lucifer held up a paw and rested it on Charles's open hand. As soon as the bacon was in his mouth, both the hand and paw retracted. Lucifer began a low growl. Aidan could see sweat trickling down Charles's temple and darkening the back of his shirt.

"Lucy, lick," Charles said as he placed more bacon on the flat of his trembling hand. Lucifer delicately snatched the meat and ate it, but then came forward and licked Charles's palm several times. A collective "oh!" rose from many of the boys. Aidan could see that the last had not really been a command—Charles was just showing that Lucifer was tame enough to eat from his hand—but it had given the impression that Charles was controlling all of what Lucifer did.

Loud enough for at least some of the boys to hear, Charles said, "You're a good dog." And he led Lucifer out of the room.

Conversation escalated to a fever pitch, and the judge made no attempt to quell it. Aidan looked over his shoulder to the back of the room. Fielding was talking with the matron, but Bradley stood rigidly, no expression on his face.

When Charles came back, wiping his greasy hand on his trousers, conversation died down. He said, "The defense rests," and sat down in his chair.

"Final arguments. Ralph, you first," intoned the judge.

Hinkley thought for a minute before he stood. "Weston's got a nice parlor trick there, but how many of us have bacon in our pockets all the time?" He paused as the boys murmured. "Maybe Lucifer didn't bite Percy, but that don't mean he isn't dangerous. You all heard him growling. Maybe he likes Weston, but say he decides he don't like you. How would you feel walking in the dark one night and hearing that growl behind you? He don't belong on the island."

Hinkley sat as Charles rose, and after a few bangs of the gavel, it was quiet enough for Charles to speak.

"Sounds like Hinkley's afraid of his own shadow. One thing he didn't mention is that life is full of dangerous stuff. We got snakes on this island. Pickering's allergic to bees. Heck, Percy ripped his leg open on a *tree*." The boys guffawed. "Lucifer's no blind baby kitten, I know. He growls a lot. And he's not pretty. But he's not really mean on the inside. He's scared. And I proved that he's trainable. He's getting to trust me. He can change. You gotta give him a chance." Charles looked like he had more to say, but then he sat down.

Minutes passed as the judge conferred with the jury members. Bill was confident. "He's won for sure. He made that cur look like an obedient pup."

"Woulda been better if he hadn't growled the whole time," observed Salt.

"I'm with Bill," said Tink. "He showed that Percy's been lyin' the whole time, that weasel. Everyone's been thinkin' that dog's vicious for months, but everything they been thinkin' was built on a lie."

Aidan thought about this. "But can everybody really forget what they thought about him, just on account of that lie being shown to be a lie? Are people really gonna turn on a dime like that, reverse what they felt about him?"

"I think they could," said Bill. "I think some are gonna see Lucifer in a whole new light."

This idea, the sudden reversal of opinion, bothered Aidan for some reason, but before he could think on it, the gavel went down, and the room fell silent.

"Jury," said the judge, "you reached a decision?"

The foreman stood. "We have, Your Honor. On the charge of being dangerous enough to be put down, we find Lucifer the dog," and here he paused for dramatic effect, "guilty."

The judge did not pretend to have any control over the crowd at this point. Chairs were knocked over as boys jumped to their feet. They stood, yelled, cheered, booed. A few approached the jury and began to argue. Aidan looked to the back of the room and saw the matron, but Fielding and Bradley were gone.

Through the din, the boys heard the bell ringing for lineup, the only sound that could pierce through the noise. Slowly, the boys filed out, getting in their last exclamations about the trial before they exited in order to avoid demerits for talking during lineup.

Charles made no move to join the exiting boys. Aidan sat down next to him as the last boy left the room. They could hear Fielding administering count off outside. Aidan knew they would be demerited for their absence, but he stayed with Charles, discarding idea after idea of what he could say.

The door opened to reveal the stern countenance of the matron. "The superintendent would like to see you in his office."

"Grand," said Charles under his breath. The boys rose to follow her. Charles crumpled the lead-smudged paper that had been his constant companion for the past week and threw it viciously at the trash bin near the door, where it bounced off the wall and landed on the floor.

The boys took their seats across from Bradley's desk. Aidan knew that he was an interloper here, that Bradley only wanted to see Charles, but the superintendent didn't seem to object to Aidan's presence.

Bradley cleared his throat and tugged his vest downward. "Master Weston. Master Charles Weston, that is. I see you have the support of your brother, which I will allow. This time." He paused. "Today you engaged in an effort to clear that dog's name—a failed effort, but an effort nonetheless. Frankly, I cannot fathom why you would undertake this effort. Furthermore, you knew the outcome you desired directly opposed my wishes pertaining to that dog. And yet you persisted."

Aidan looked over at Charles, expecting to see him examining his shoes. Instead, Charles was locking eyes with Bradley, one hand fiercely squeezing the other in his lap. *Jaysus*, thought Aidan, *can't he ever back down?*

Bradley continued. "I'm going to be perfectly honest with you. I found—"

"You coulda stopped this trial before—" Charles interrupted.

"*Silence.* You have done all the defending you will do today. As I was saying, I found your arguments . . . persuasive." Bradley let the word hang in the air. "I did not initially favor this trial at all, but I was curious to see what you would do with it. In your months here, you have not shown much interest in any-thing—until, that is, you became part of the legal branch of the Cottage Row government. I found this encouraging, and I was further encouraged to see the commitment you showed to your cause, however misguided I believed it to be. But most of all, I was impressed by your defense itself. You did quite well for yourself in there."

"But I lost," said Charles bitterly.

"The verdict was against you, that is true. But Lucifer did not lose." Bradley leaned forward and put his forearms on his desk with his fingers knitted together. "I have decided to intervene. I have never done so before in these trials, but I no longer believe that Lucifer is the threat I thought him to be. I will lift his death sentence, to use the legal parlance. You will continue to work with him, to socialize him so that he will cease growling at the boys and scaring them. You should also know that if Lucifer does attack anyone here, including you, his death will be swift. I am putting my trust in you that that will not happen."

"Yessir. And sir?"

"Yes?"

"It's Lucy. Not Lucifer anymore."

"Ah, a rose by any other name . . . You are aware that the dog is not a bitch?"

"Yessir. But he answers to Lucy now, and him bein' called by the devil's name ain't, er, isn't helpin' with the boys."

"Point taken. You may tell Fielding your dog has been officially renamed."

Bradley excused them and they headed down the oak stairs. They could hear the boys milling about in the yard, and they knew Charles would be swarmed once they emerged from the building. Aidan punched Charles's arm. "So you won after all. Except not how you wanted to."

Charles pushed open the heavy door, and the sun poured over them like stage limelight. "This weren't a bad way to win."

CHAPTER 31

The following Saturday was Visiting Day, but by Thursday, Charles had already become irritated with Aidan, anticipating his defection to Dec's family.

As they filed into class that afternoon, Aidan commented to Charles, "You were awfully quiet at dinner." Tink had gone on about Sumner's older sister, whom Tink claimed was quite a looker, and how he hoped she would visit on Saturday, giving him an opportunity to woo her, but Tink's goading had failed to get Sumner to utter a word. Charles had been almost as silent.

"Yeah, well, I can't say I enjoyed myself too much on last Visiting Day, no thanks to you."

"You're sore that I went off with Dec."

Charles slammed his satchel down on his desk. "Now why would I be sore that my own brother abandoned me on *family* day?"

"Okay, I was in the wrong. I didn't think about it. It was just that Dec's ma reminded me of . . . well, you know." Aidan sat at the desk in front of Charles. "It felt like family."

"*I'm* your family here."

"Yes," Aidan conceded. "Yes, you are." He nudged Charles's shoulder. "This Saturday, me and you are gonna stick together like glue. We're gonna watch all them people get off the boat, and when everybody's got someone, well, I'll have you and you'll have me.

Why, you won't be able to get rid of me. I'll be eatin' off your plate, wipin' my nose with your kerchief, followin' you into the crapper, wipin' your—"

"Okay, okay," said Charles, trying to maintain his frown. The Coffin began slapping her ruler on the desk to signal the beginning of class. "Go find your seat, you nutter."

Due to the threat of rain, heralded by ominous, sooty clouds rolling in across the water, the customary band concert to greet the Visiting Day steamer was moved to inside Bulfinch. As the boys lined up and marched down to the wharf, a few fat drops of rain pelted a boy here and there, but the clouds seemed reluctant to let go of what they had.

"Don't you think it's a bit cruel to make every one of us come down to greet the boat?" Aidan said to Charles. "I mean, lookit Bill over there." Bill was kicking the sand with the toe of his boot, cap pulled low, his hands shoved in his pockets. He looked at the ground in a crowd where most everyone else was craning to see the visitors coming down the wharf.

Charles grunted. "Salt says even though the visitors are supposed to send a letter that they're comin', sometimes people come unannounced. Plus, Bradley don't want all the extra work of figuring out who should meet someone off the boat. And—"

Aidan gripped Charles's shoulder, hard.

"What the hell, Sully?" he asked as he followed Aidan's gaze to the wharf, where he saw a woman offering her limp, downturned hand to the superintendent. "Who is—" But then she turned so that her hat brim tipped up just enough to reveal her face. *Bess.* "We've got to get down there. C'mon!" Charles said, and he started to push the boys in front of him aside.

"Wait." Aidan grabbed his arm. "I been writing her."

"What?"

Aidan dropped his voice to a whisper. "I didn't ask her to come! I never thought she would take it in her head to come. I just wrote her with letters to get to my ma."

"Why didn't you tell me?" hissed Charles.

"I thought you'd be mad. Say that I was takin' a risk. And I was, I know. But you don't know what it's like, leavin' your ma behind."

"What if Bradley or someone had asked you who you was writing to?"

"I addressed them to Auntie Bess."

Charles let out a bark of a laugh, so loud that two boys in front of him turned around for a moment. "Well, let's go see Auntie, then." They made their way down to the wharf.

Bradley and Bess seemed to be wrapping up some little conversation that amused the superintendent when the boys arrived. "Splendid!" said Bradley, turning to them. "I thought I would have to send one of the boys to find you, but here you are. Your charming aunt found she was able to rearrange her schedule at the last minute so that she could visit." Charles wondered if there were indeed appointments that were rearranged; if there were, he was sure that they were not of the sort Bradley was imagining.

Bess smiled an unfamiliar smile at the two boys. Charles was sure he had never seen this smile on her face before. It was an expression that seemed apart from the grim nature of the waterfront, perhaps unaware of its very existence. While her face was still too hard to be pretty, it had somehow shed the shell that was necessary to protect it from the life it saw back on the mainland.

The voice that came from Bess was also one Charles did not recognize. "The weather did threaten today, but it will only get worse as we head into winter. And I couldn't wait until spring to see you two." Bess stared into Charles's eyes, imploring him to play along, but he could also see that she was having great fun with all of this.

"Ma'am, I am a bit confused," said Bradley. "I don't recall seeing any relatives listed on the boys' applications."

"I am a distant aunt, one that had lost touch with their mother. I've only recently learned of their whereabouts. I was the sister of the brother-in-law of their father, God rest his soul."

"Well, that explains it," said Bradley, though he still looked slightly confused. Just then, another visitor asked Bradley a question, giving Bess the opportunity to whisk the boys away from the wharf, her sober skirts rustling.

"Well, hello, you sons of bitches," Bess said in her regular voice when they were away from the crowd.

"Bess, what the hell are you doing here?" asked Charles.

"Visiting my nephews, of course. I always wanted to see this place." She looked around from their vantage point on the lawn. "Lotta trees, not a lotta buildings. Where are all the saloons?" she wisecracked, almost giddy.

As she continued to scan the island, Charles looked her over carefully. If it weren't for her face, he would never have recognized her. Bess's most recognizable feature from a distance back in Boston, her cleavage, was now covered with a high-collared dress in a matronly shade of gray. He had never seen her in a hat, and she looked strangely pale without her rouge and lip paint.

"Ain't this takin' a risk, comin' here?" asked Aidan.

"Look who's talkin' about takin' risks—you, writing to your old Auntie Bess?" She tweaked his ear cheerfully. "Little pup, I take risks every day. Every time I take on a new john, could be he's got the clap." She took apparent pleasure in seeing Aidan blush at her comment.

"What's with all the high-falutin' talk there with Bradley?" Charles asked as they started to head up the hill with the rest of the crowd. "I didn't even know you could talk like that."

"There's a lot that you don't know about me, Nephew," she replied archly. Charles thought about the note she'd written to

Stryker and wondered if Bess wasn't just grandstanding. Maybe she was more than he had assumed her to be—but what that might be, he still couldn't figure.

All the boys and their visitors bunched up around the doors to Bulfinch as they filed in. Bess, Charles, and Aidan hung back a short distance, waiting for the crowd to thin. Bess smiled and took a big breath. "Air here is damn clear, I'll say. Nothing like that stink on North Street."

When most of the crowd was inside the building, they moved to join the last people entering. Bradley was standing by the door with friendly comments for the visitors. When Bess passed by him, he said, "Miss Matthews, I hope the band concert is to your liking."

"I've no doubt it will be delightful," she replied in her not-Bess voice, and Charles fought not to laugh.

In the afternoon, after the concert, the tours of the carpentry and print shops, and the midday meal—which was of decidedly higher quality and refinement than the typical Saturday dinner—several boys from each class went to their classrooms to prepare their readings from their written essays. Aidan's, entitled "Alexander Bell's Telephone: Will It Replace the Telegraph?" was one of three that The Coffin had selected from the Third Class. Bess and Charles stood in the yard with the other boys and visitors waiting to be called into the building.

"It's good I got you alone," said Bess. They strolled around the flower beds while they talked. "I got some news."

"The cops? We been found out?" said Charles anxiously.

"Nah, it ain't about that. It's about Aidan's ma."

Already Charles knew what she was going to say.

"I gave some urchin a nickel to run the first letter to Aidan's ma, and he never did come back. I figured he delivered it. But when the second letter came, I did the same with a different urchin, and this one shows up back on my doorstep, still with the letter. Seems this one was the nosy type, and when he didn't get no answer at the door, he started askin' around the building. Probably hoping I'd give him an extra tip for his detective work. He found out she passed two weeks prior."

Charles looked out at all the flower beds, way past their prime now that it was mid-autumn. Finally he said, "When are you gonna tell him?"

"I ain't. That's your job."

"Bess, can't you—"

"Forget it. I don't even know him. He's your friend. Tell him when you want to tell him."

"Christ." Charles rubbed his face. "Do we even know where she's buried?"

"You're lucky that urchin came back at all. He coulda kept walkin' like the first one." She paused. "I did give him a big tip."

"Well, that's just grand," said Charles wryly. "That will make all the difference to Sully."

The matron appeared from the building and called out to the visitors and boys that they should proceed to the classrooms. Bess and Charles made no move to leave the flower beds.

"Bess, is this why you came over to the island? To deliver this news?"

"Partly. But also I always wanted to see this place, ever since my nephew came here."

"You're really different when you're here."

"I feel different here. I could be anybody here." She looked up at the sky, where the sun was trying to break through the cloud cover.

That night, the dormitory was in its usual post–Visiting Day heightened activity. Many boys displayed on their beds the things they'd received from their families that day, and trading was in high gear. Merton Poole, seeing that Charles and Aidan had nothing, gave them each a gingersnap from the tin his mother had brought. "It's a bum deal, not having an older brother," Poole complained. "Older brothers know what you need here: a slingshot, a decent aggie, a penny dreadful. Lookit Davidson over there—his brother gave him a pair of dice he carved himself! Drop of India ink in the pips, the whole bit." The three of them looked over to Davidson's bed, where a half dozen boys were admiring the dice. "He ain't even got a bed box with a false bottom. Where's he gonna stash them things?"

"You got gingersnaps," Aidan pointed out as he ate his. "Can't eat dice."

"And I also got this picture from my little sister." Poole held it up. "She drew her dolly. Can't eat it *or* play a game with it." But he placed it carefully on the table beside his bed. "Maybe your aunt will bring you somethin' next time."

Charles thought about what Bess had brought—the news about Aidan's mother. He lay back on the bed and stared up at the ceiling as Aidan and Poole continued to chatter on. The more Charles thought about it, the more difficult the situation seemed. Aidan would naturally be upset when he found out, but there would be no way to explain to anyone here why he was upset. Their mother was supposed to have died months ago. Aidan might even want to go back to the mainland to try and find his sister or visit his mother's grave. Who knows what he might do? Or say? He could end up putting them both at risk.

On the other hand, if Charles didn't tell him, no one would. Bess was the only one who knew. If there was nothing Aidan could do about it, then why upset him unnecessarily? Charles looked over at Aidan, who had talked Poole out of another ginger snap. He looked happy, Charles thought. So did Poole, and so did most of the boys he could see in the dormitory. But they all had some misfortune to bring them here—parents dying or being too poor to keep them.

The happy ones weren't thinking about the past, though. They were living in the present, eating cookies and admiring dice. That's what he and Aidan had to do, Charles decided: They had to live in the present.

CHAPTER 32

N<small>EXT</small> S<small>ATURDAY, AS YOU SHOULD REMEMBER, THE BAND WILL PER-</small>form at our Autumn Festival at Faneuil Hall," the superintendent announced at chapel the next day. "As was the case this summer, we have contracted the large steamer to take the whole school in one trip. We will queue up Saturday morning at eight sharp by the bell and proceed to the wharf."

With all the business of Lucifer's trial and Bess coming for Visiting Day, Aidan had forgotten all about Dec's mention of the mainland concert.

Both Dec and Charles, who were sitting on either side of Aidan, leaned in at the same time to whisper in Aidan's respective ears.

"Big boat, Sully, it's gonna be a snap—" started Charles.

"A wee trip, over in a heartbeat—" began Dec.

Charles glared at Dec. "Why don't you leave off with them Irish words of comfort and mind your own—" he said a bit too loudly.

"Is there a problem, Master Weston?" Bradley's voice boomed out over the rows of boys.

"No. Sir," Charles said.

"Master Moore. A problem?"

"Not a one, sir. Me and the lads is just excited 'bout the trip," said Dec, managing to irritate Bradley with both his exaggerated brogue and bad grammar.

"Contain that enthusiasm, Master Moore, or you will find yourself demerited."

Dec said nothing, but out of the corner of his eye, Aidan could see him smiling. To his right, however, he could tell that Charles was not.

Later in the day, Aidan and Dec were practicing their clarinets in Starlight Cottage when a loud knock came at the door. Without waiting for a response, Charles walked in and threw himself into one of the chairs around the table.

"Moore." He ignored Aidan.

"Weston. What brings you here? Are you a music lover?"

"Since you ask, I could give a fart about music. I'm here to talk to you."

"I'm listening."

There was a pause. It looked to Aidan as if Charles were gathering his thoughts, or perhaps gathering strength. Aidan was fearful of what might come next.

"Listen, Moore, it ain't no secret I don't much like you. But seems like whether I like it or don't, we have this one in common." He jerked his thumb in Aidan's direction, but his gaze remained on Dec. "And it also ain't no secret that this boat trip, the first one since we come here, ain't gonna be a walk in the park for him. So I'm suggestin' that we . . . that we work together a bit on this."

Dec looked amused. "Still listening."

"We flank him. The whole time. Me on one side of him, you on the other. Just for the two boat rides, there and back."

Irritated, Aidan interjected, "I'm sitting right here, you know."

"'Tis true—your brother's being a mite rude, ignorin' ya," said Dec, though he also remained looking at Charles.

Charles took a big breath. "Fine." He turned to Aidan. "Do you want some help with this crossing or not?"

Aidan took a moment to think about this whole conversation. Putting aside Charles's usual and reliable lack of diplomacy, Aidan was surprised at this turn of events. He knew Charles had taken a swift dislike to Dec, both because Dec was Irish and because Dec had befriended Aidan. And Charles was averse to accepting help from anyone. But the reality was that Charles's suggestion was enormously appealing to Aidan. In fact, there might not be anything more distracting than observing these two attempting to get along through a common task.

"It's a grand idea, brother," he said. "First rate. I'd be in your debt. Both of you."

"Well, then, it's settled," said Dec as he picked his clarinet up off the table and played a little trill—to annoy Charles, or so it seemed to Aidan.

Charles grunted and left the cottage.

"Charming fellow, that," commented Dec as he flipped the pages of his sheet music.

"You know, it took a lot for him to do that," said Aidan.

"Mmmm." Dec played a quick scale. "Perhaps there's hope for him after all."

Aidan was not so sure that there was hope for Charles once the boat ride commenced.

Things started out in the spirit of cooperation. They proceeded down the wharf to the boat, Dec in front of Aidan and Charles behind. Involuntarily, Aidan halted when he saw how the boat bobbed next to the immobile wharf, but Charles nudged him forward, and Aidan complied, albeit with legs of rubber and a sheen of sweat on his brow. Dec convinced some boys to move back a row so that Aidan could be in the middle of their bench, as far from the sides of the boat as possible.

Aidan rooted himself to the bench. With Charles and Dec tight against him on either side, he willed his peripheral vision to narrow so that all he could see were the blue wool uniforms of boys. He was trying to slow his breathing when he was shoved from behind.

"Sorry there, Sully," said Caleb Hart, an innocent expression applied to his face. "Boat's kinda wobbly, know what I mean?" Beside Caleb, Warwick snickered and added, "Yeah, I'm feeling a mite queasy already."

"Why don't you two arseholes get lost?" said Charles.

Caleb lifted Aidan's cap off his head. "Sure thing, Weston, but I'm gonna need this to puke in when the waves start up." Charles stood to go after them as they shifted several benches back, but Dec stopped him. "You're just gonna get yourself in hot water, boyo. They're not worth it."

"Easy for you to say. They ain't pickin' on you."

"Weston, perhaps you haven't noticed, but I'm *Irish*. I know a thing or two about being picked on."

Aidan's cap came sailing over several rows of boys to hit him squarely in the back of the head. Charles picked it up from the floor behind him and handed it to Aidan.

"Well," Dec remarked, "you got to admit, their aim is brilliant."

After the boat got underway with a nauseating surge, Aidan tried to concentrate on the banter between his two benchmates as he perspired and trembled. To be fair, it did seem that Dec was adept at making innocent-sounding comments that were irritating to Charles. Or perhaps they were truly innocent comments and Charles was just irritable. Was Dec's accent a bit more pronounced than usual? Was he using just a little more Irish slang? It was hard to say. Aidan had seen him use these tactics in exaggerated form with the superintendent, but it was more subtle here, if he were doing it at all.

After what seemed like a long time indeed, Aidan heard the steam engine slow, but because he had his head down, he was surprised when the boat bumped up against the wharf at City Point, and his stomach gave a lurch. Charles gave him a slap on the back. "Made it here in one piece, Sully!" As soon as they climbed off the boat, however, Aidan's relief of standing on firm ground was tainted with the growing anxiety of being back in Boston. Charles must have been thinking along these lines, because he murmured to Aidan, "Keep your cap down low and stay with the group. Don't do nothin' to call attention to us."

The turnout for the concert was excellent, in part due to the weather. As can happen on the best October days in New England, the sun streamed down, unobstructed by clouds, from a background of deep and startling blue. Were it not for the seasonal wind gusting unexpectedly, Bostonians might have been tempted to head off to the beaches of Nantasket. It had been raining most of the week, making this Saturday weather seem like a gift not to be squandered on indoor activities.

Though Charles couldn't stop shifting in his seat—nervous? bored?—Aidan soon forgot him when the band began to play. Just as when he'd heard them play at Visiting Day, the fact that it was boys, just regular boys, who brought this all together was incredible to him. Before he had come to the island, he had never heard more than one instrument played at a time. He had heard of the phonographs with their wax cylinders that the well-to-do could afford for their parlors, but he had never even seen one. As the band launched into their finale, Sousa's "Gladiator March," Aidan felt a shiver run down his back. What must it be like to be on that stage, surrounded by the throaty buzz of the trombones, the teakettle song of the flutes? He resolved that when he got back to the school, he would redouble his efforts to improve his playing so he could join the band as soon as possible.

When the last of the applause for "Gladiator March" died down,

Aidan dragged Charles toward the stage. "Dec!" Aidan called out, waving.

"Fer Chrissakes, Sully, what happened to not calling attention to yourself?" said Charles. But Aidan ignored him, working his way through the crowd with Charles in tow.

"Dec, that was just grand," Aidan gushed when they reached him. "The last piece especially. You didn't play that for Visiting Day."

"'Tis a crowd-pleaser, that one, eh?" Dec took his clarinet apart and lovingly tucked each piece into its felt-lined crevice. "What about you, Weston? Which was your favorite?"

"Shut it, Moore." Charles looked over his shoulder, searching for a more important place to be.

"Oh, wait, I forgot that we are in the presence of one who is not a music lover. Hard to believe that the two of you are related."

Charles swiveled his head around to lock eyes with Dec. "And what is that supposed to mean?"

"Not a thing," said Dec, caught off guard. Aidan looked at him in panic. What was Dec doing? Was he trying to reveal to Charles that he knew they weren't brothers? Dec glanced over and gave a little shrug. "Just pullin' his chain," he said apologetically. A slip of the tongue, then. He could see that Dec regretted his choice of words.

Charles rotated his icy glare from Dec to Aidan, and Aidan felt everything falling apart. He knew, knew with great certainty, that he should just shrug this off, citing the chip that Charles carried around on his shoulder all the time, make a joke, slap his arm, move on. But Charles's gaze pinned Aidan like a nail to a wall, and the part of him that knew what he should do melted and puddled, leaving only the truth.

"He guessed. He knew I was Irish. He was like one of them mentalists—he was reading my mind!" Aidan could hear himself babbling, a runaway train, powerless to stop. "He swore he wouldn't tell no one, and he didn't. He's the only one who knows in the whole school. He won't tell. I trust him. I really do." When he stopped talking, there was a moment where he felt good—so good, as light as a sack of feathers. How sweet it felt to finally tell the truth about something, to put down the heavy box of lies he'd been carrying around and to stretch his aching muscles.

It was, as it turned out, a short-lived feeling—one that ended when Charles lunged for Aidan. Later on, when Aidan had ample time to reflect on this incident, he realized that, like Dec, he had chosen his words poorly. It was the last thing he said, about trusting Dec, that had pushed Charles over the edge. Aidan had meant to assure Charles that their secret was still safe, but Aidan figured out—too late, of course—that to Charles, those words were salt poured into the wound of betrayal.

And yet, even given all those words that had been uttered and regretted, Dec's and Aidan's both, it still might have just blown over if they were not standing precisely where they were. It so happened that this conversation occurred in front of the percussionists, who should have been packing up their instruments but were instead eyeing a group of three attractive young girls in the crowd. The table holding the smaller percussion instruments had been built for travel, made of lightweight wood with detachable legs, so it was no match for the body of an eleven-year-old boy being shoved into it by an angry twelve-year-old.

The sound of two large cymbals hitting granite cobblestones rang out and stopped all conversation within a surprisingly large radius. Every eye turned to the source of this sound and saw two startled boys trying to right themselves, one cap lost beneath the broken table. They stood stupidly, looking around, and in that heartbeat, the triangle, whose strap had been caught on one of the broken table legs, chose that moment to slide off and hit the ground with a comical *clink*.

The sound of the triangle had the effect of breaking the crowd's silence, and laughter and conversation swelled to fill the air. Before Charles and Aidan could say anything to each other, Bradley was on them.

"Your fraternal differences are not to be worked out during our public performances! You are disgraceful, the both of you. I shall spend the return trip contemplating what appropriate punishments will be levied upon you."

Aidan and Charles hung their heads and thought the worst of it was waiting for them back on the island.

CHAPTER 33

Bradley contemplated the Boston police officer sitting opposite his desk. To the superintendent, the officer looked comically big in his chair as compared to the countless young boys who had sat there, their skinny buttocks covering only half the seat. But there was nothing comical about what the officer had spent the last twenty minutes telling him.

Bradley had asked all the questions he could think of, requested clarification on every element that he considered unclear, and now the next move was his. But he was loath to make it. He wanted not just a few moments to gather his thoughts, but an hour or two to ruminate on all this new information. He wanted this officer to go away and come back tomorrow, when he had absorbed everything and made sense of it.

Without the luxury of that time, he did his best to review what he'd been told. A woman, obsessed with a crime that she'd witnessed perpetrated against her husband that summer, had been contacting the police department incessantly to determine their progress and had given them more than one lead that had amounted to nothing. She had attended the performance at Faneuil Hall the previous day and recognized one of the Farm School boys who caused the cacophony with the cymbals as the perpetrator. After lengthy conversations with several officers and the commissioner, she convinced them to apprehend this boy.

"The one that was fighting that lost his cap?" Bradley asked, although he had already asked this earlier.

"Yessir. That's how she could see his face." The officer's finger combed his sizable handlebar mustache with remarkable patience. Perhaps he was enjoying being away from Boston, thought Bradley. Perhaps the two of them could sit here indefinitely, each one content to put off the future. Mrs. Bradley could bring them tea, the afternoon shadows would grow long, they could chat about the prospects of the Beaneaters this year. Bradley could inquire after the officer's wife.

After a few moments, the officer cleared his throat. Like a bubble, Bradley's fantasy popped, and the reality of what he had to do now pressed down upon his shoulders, a python resting there that he would have to carry around on the island as they looked for the boy the police officer needed to arrest.

Charles threw his remaining two sausage links to Lucifer rather than breaking them into pieces for training rewards. He was too angry to concentrate on training today. He and Aidan had not spoken since they'd boarded the boat at City Point yesterday.

"I don't need either one of ya," Aidan had stated, pushing through the line to sit between Cantrell and Poole. Charles had shuffled among the other boys so that he'd ended up on the end of the bench, where he'd stared out at the water for the entire trip, wishing for rough waters that would rock the boat.

The barn was so cold that Charles couldn't feel his fingertips. He wiped his greasy fingers on his trousers and shoved his hands under his arms to warm them. Lucifer was busy twitching his head to the side, using his back molars to break the sausage apart. *Son of a bitch,* he thought to himself. Lucifer stopped chewing for a moment and looked at Charles. Perhaps he'd actually said that out loud.

Where the hell did Aidan get off not talking to *him?* Shouldn't it be him not talking to Aidan? Who couldn't keep his goddamn mouth shut for one minute once he got to nattering on with his Mick pal? A slipup, he could understand. But to tell that lousy bog-trotter and then to keep it a secret? For who knew how long? It went against everything he and Aidan had agreed on before they came to the island.

Charles rose abruptly, and Lucifer skittered to parts unknown in the barn. He was filled with a sudden resolve to confront Aidan, to make him admit that he had done a terrible thing. If that meant additional punishments from Bradley, so be it. Because it might take a bit of pounding to make Aidan see things clearly.

He stormed out of the barn and up the hill. Starlight, that's where he'd look first. Starlight, where Aidan didn't even belong, probably playing a duet of "Danny Boy." He would break that clarinet over Aidan's goddamn head.

So intent was he to get to Cottage Row that he was only yards away from the superintendent and the police officer when he finally saw them. Seconds before, he would have sworn that nothing could have deterred him from his purpose. But when he saw the brass buttons of Boston's Finest, buttons he had trained himself to spot from much farther distances, his plan evaporated like ether.

To run away seemed attractive, desirable, the best possible thing to do, but his legs didn't agree. And really, where could he go? *It's a goddamn ISLAND,* he thought to himself, and he almost laughed. They'd come to the one place where there wasn't any place they could run away to.

Bradley and the officer must have spotted him before he had seen them, because they were on an intercept course. Charles pondered the date. Mid-October. About three months they'd made it here. That was something, at least. He'd had his first kiss and became a lawyer. It was more than he had expected.

Bradley planted his feet in front of Charles, the officer by his side. "Master Weston," he stated, his face a portrait of displeasure.

"Sir," said Charles, straightening his spine. If this was going to happen, he would go out with some dignity. No pleading, pissing his pants, asking what was going to happen to him. He'd leave with his head up.

"Where," Bradley asked, "is your brother?"

Charles froze. Aidan. Not him. Aidan and not him. He stopped breathing for several seconds while his mind attempted to rearrange the old reality into the new.

"Charles?"

He had to warn Aidan. Aidan was likely to start babbling facts and truths that would damn them for eternity. He had to make sure Aidan shut it until they could figure this out.

"Not sure, sir. Haven't been keeping track of him. But I thought I saw him by the flower beds. He's always there."

"In late October? I sincerely doubt that." Bradley turned to the officer. "Let's check the cottages."

They left Charles as if he no longer existed and headed toward Cottage Row. Charles followed close behind, but they seemed oblivious to his presence. Without knocking, Bradley opened the door to Laurel. Charles calculated whether he could walk over to Starlight and slip inside without anyone noticing.

"Arthur Weston?" said the officer in a deep baritone, projecting his question into the cottage.

Charles moved in front of Bradley so he could see into Laurel. There, at the warped wooden table with Tink's folded-up geography exam jammed under one leg to stabilize it, sat Aidan, pen still dipped in his inkpot, mouth ajar, still as a statue. The wind whipped in through the open door, lifting the papers on the table and floating them to the floor, and Charles saw that he had been writing to Maeve.

PART III

Justice

Charles Street Jail, Boston

CHAPTER 34

Even before the guard's footsteps had died away, Aidan was overwhelmed by how awful his cell smelled, but it was a few minutes more before he realized that the worst of it was coming from him.

It seemed fitting that he should smell so foul, and he even took some grim satisfaction in knowing that the outside world would perceive a body that was as rank as his black soul. He had always imagined hell to be a place of putrid smells. Old Father Healy at St. Joseph's was never more animated than when describing the sights and sounds of hell to the younger parishioners, but Aidan's mind had always supplied the olfactory experience of decomposing bodies that eternally screamed for help.

He sat on a straw mattress that had been pressed so flat and hard over time that it was only marginally more pliant than the metal bed frame on which it rested. As he scratched at his bug bites, the number of which was mounting hourly, he played a grotesque version of a game he and Maeve had invented years ago, during the days of Dan Connolly. Back then, Aidan would try to guess all the foods his mother had cooked for dinner—even singular ingredients—based on scent alone. He became good enough to be able to tell rosemary from oregano, ginger from molasses, white potatoes from sweet. It was all about separating out the different smells for individual consideration.

The first smell he isolated now was his own vomit, which of course brought to mind the boat ride from the island to the mainland.

The policeman had grabbed him by the arm before he had even cleared the door of Laurel Cottage, and at that moment, he'd realized that he was going to be taken off the island forcibly, without any time to get used to the idea, without Charles or Dec. His heels made their own decision to dig into the ground, but they were no match for the biceps of the burly policeman. All he could do was look over his shoulder at Charles, who was restrained from following them by the superintendent. It was impossible to read the expression on Charles's face. Or maybe there were so many expressions there that they started canceling each other out, leaving a sort of neutral affect that was only belied by Charles's slightly open mouth.

It was clear to Aidan that there was no point in resistance, but at the end of the wharf, he froze anyway, unable to lower his foot into the boat. His pulse pounded in his ears, and his breath came in little short puffs. Sweat ran in rivulets from his armpits tickling down his sides. It was as if he had come to the edge of a cliff, where no sane person would take a step further. But with the policeman directly behind him, taking a step back was not possible.

This deadlock was resolved by the policeman giving Aidan a shove to the small of his back, causing him to fall into the boat on hands and knees.

"I've hauled in thems that was twice your size, lad," said the policeman as he lowered himself with a muffled grunt into the boat, causing it to bob in the water. "You'd do best to recognize that you're going where I'm taking you, no two ways about it." He dug in his jacket pocket and emerged with a set of handcuffs, which he snapped onto Aidan's wrists. "I'll not have you diving overboard and swimming to shore. You try that when you're double-cuffed, the city will be plantin' you in Potter's Field, and you'll be savin' them the expense of a trial—that is, if your body ever washes up. Your choice."

The thought of going overboard while handcuffed, sinking like a stone in the steel-colored water, had brought on a wave of nausea, which happened to coincide with the lurching of the boat as it left the wharf. Too terrified to lean over the side of the boat, Aidan had vomited between his shoes.

After that, he didn't remember much. He vaguely recalled being asked some questions at the police station, but it was as if the people asking the questions were far away and the words didn't all make sense. Responding had seemed irrelevant, like answering a man an hour after he had left the room.

But everything had snapped into focus when they brought him through the doors of the jail. As he walked into an atrium where the ceiling was as high as the dome in Faneuil Hall, it was as if he woke up. Tall and narrow windows, gracefully arched, broke up row upon row of cell doors like a cathedral in hell. The place reeked of wet stone and human bodies. As he progressed with his jailer through the atrium, a rising chorus of harsh voices began to fill up that space, echoing off the damp granite. The jailer, who had not spoken a word to Aidan thus far, commented, "They do like this when a new prisoner come through. They ain't always this loud." Aidan began to tremble.

One voice rose above the din. "That one looks a tasty treat! Five dollars to you, jailer, for a half hour of him in my cell!" Aidan looked over to see a filthy bearded man with his torso plastered against the bars of his cell. One yellow tooth hung beside his protruding tongue.

Urine spread down the front of Aidan's trousers.

"Fuck off, Haggarty, or I'll put you back in the hole," the jailer called out without breaking stride or looking over at the cell.

"Don't worry," the jailer addressed Aidan as they continued to walk, "you ain't gonna be near that nutter. They got you down the

Women's Aisle. Any little shavers we get is put with the females. Most of them ain't off their bean, least not yet."

As they walked, they left the atrium and proceeded down one of the four corridors that connected, cross-like, to the atrium. The voices calling out here were higher in pitch, less angry, more pleading. More desperate. Without the echo of the atrium, Aidan could make out whole sentences.

"Tell my son to bring more food!"

"Please get this note to my husband!"

"I'm in need of the infirmary!"

He covered his ears. The chain between his handcuffs dug into his chin.

They arrived at an empty cell. The jailer took off the handcuffs, and Aidan walked into the cell like a lamb, not an ounce of resistance in him. He turned and faced the jailer, who observed his wet trousers.

"Someone from the Charities will be by today. If you got anyone on the outside that can get you a change of clothes, you tell them." The jailer had shaken his head in pity before turning away and walking down the corridor.

Now, having exhausted his inventory of the offensive smells surrounding him—his own vomit and urine, the toilet bucket that had been emptied but not rinsed, the sour mold growing in the corners of the cell—Aidan lay down on the unforgiving mattress, feeling as tired as he ever had in his life. He pulled a straw from the mattress and held it lightly between his thumb and forefinger. He pushed it against the mattress and let his fingers slide down its length, then flipped the straw over and did it again. In this way, he passed an amount of time that may have been a half hour or may have been many hours. He may have fallen asleep and woken up, still pushing and flipping the straw. His mind was blank. It was time he would never get back and would never want back.

This went on until a plump man made his way down the

corridor. He carried a wooden chair and placed it outside Aidan's cell, then arranged his coat and hat on its back before sitting. Aidan saw him but couldn't muster the energy to rise from his prostrate position. He did, however, put down his straw.

"Arthur Weston, correct?"

Aidan said nothing. He felt another bite on his neck but made no move to scratch it.

"I'm Mr. Sutton from Boston Children's Aid. I'm here to talk with you about your case."

Aidan rolled onto his back and stared at the ceiling.

"It's not uncommon for boys to resist talking about what they've done. But I'm also here to collect information about your family and your circumstances. Let's start with your family. Do you have a living father or mother?"

Mother.

Aidan sat up so quickly he felt dizzy. "Can you contact my mother?"

"In fact, I must contact your mother and your father. Their demeanor and personal circumstances will be taken into consideration at your trial."

"Her name is—" Aidan stopped. Was this really what he wanted? How would he explain to her why he was here? Maybe it would be better if he claimed to be an orphan. He could spare her seeing him like this.

"So she has a name, but you're not inclined to reveal it. This is also not uncommon." Sutton wore spectacles and took this opportunity to take them off and polish them with a handkerchief. "You have done something of which you are not proud. In your case, this is of a very serious nature. Your mother does not yet know and is happy, comparatively speaking, in her ignorance, and you, having a heart, do not want her to know of your crime and see you in this place." He put his spectacles back on his face, where they balanced on a pink and bulbous nose. "But what you may not know is that those in this jail who do not have a supporter on the outside will suffer. The city will feed you enough food to survive, but they will do little else. And she will find out anyway. I am obligated to attempt to find her, so you might as well make my life easier by telling me her name."

He thought of his mother bringing him food here, and that was something he wanted, selfishly, on so many levels, despite the pain it would cause her. "Maeve Sullivan. 47 Chambers Street, in the West End. I need food and . . . clothes. How soon can she come?"

"Sullivan? She remarried?"

"No," said Aidan, and then he remembered. The false name, pretending to be an orphan, it was all unnecessary now. It could all be unwound. "My name is Aidan Sullivan." He felt a flush of pleasure in saying his name. The one thing he had not been able to say for so many months, a thing he could now say and not worry that he would be caught out in a lie. "Aidan Sullivan." His name was like an old friend he hadn't seen in a while.

Sutton looked down at the card in his lap. "But this is the right cell. You're the only boy your age in here tonight. I don't understand."

"Your card there, it says Arthur Weston, don't it?"

"Why, yes." The man frowned.

"Well, that was the name I went by at the school, but my real name's Aidan Sullivan."

Sutton leaned forward in his chair and peered over his spectacles through the bars of the cell door. "Son, are you Catholic?" he asked with a note of suspicion in his voice.

"Yes," said Aidan, confused. What did that have to do with anything?

"Well, that's a fine kettle of fish, I'll say." He gathered his papers and put them in his satchel. "It would be nice if they could sort this out properly at the police station, but they seem not to care if the Charities waste their time seeing the wrong juveniles."

"What's happening? Where are you going?" Aidan jumped off the bunk and grabbed the bars of the door.

"I see the Protestant boys. It's St. Vincent's that will be taking care of you." He put his coat on.

"When are they going to come? Are you going to go see my ma?"

He looked at Aidan and sighed. "You must understand that we are all volunteers. We do what we can. The man from St. Vincent's sees boys in the mornings. I will make sure you are on his list for tomorrow. I recommend you cooperate with him fully, as he will represent you in front of the judge. You should know that he will also be representing the Commonwealth, so he will have information about your crime from other sources. If he feels you are not being honest with him, you can be sure the judge will hear about it, and it will affect your placement."

"But what about my mother?" Aidan was on the verge of tears.

"St. Vincent's will help you tomorrow. I wouldn't have contacted her tonight anyway—far too late to go knocking on doors in the West End." He placed his hat firmly on his head. "Good evening to you, boy, and may God guide you on the path." He spun on his heel and walked with purpose down the corridor. Aidan craned his neck to watch him until he was swallowed up by the atrium.

Aidan lay down on the mattress and stared at the ceiling. Before the man had come, he'd thought he had nothing more they could take, but it seemed the man had taken his mother from him—had dangled the possibility of her food and presence and comfort in front of him and then walked away with it. Tears ran from the corners of his eyes and pooled in his ears. Later, when the guards called out the two-minute warning for lights-out, he didn't move, and when the gas was cut to the lamps in the corridor, the total darkness was a relief.

CHAPTER 35

Aidan and the policeman had not yet disappeared from view when the Bulfinch bell for dinner rang. "Off you go to lineup," said Bradley sternly, removing his hands from Charles's shoulders. "But I should like to see you in my office after supper to discuss this matter. I shall expect you at 1830 hours."

In the dining room, the news spread like a quick fog rolling in. The matron appeared and stayed throughout the meal, gliding from table to table. Conversations were squelched by her silent presence but bloomed again when she slid out of range.

At the Laurel table, Dec, Tink, and Salt persisted in asking questions despite a complete lack of response from Charles. Sumner ate in his usual silence, and Bill was uncharacteristically quiet but watched Charles between forkfuls of chipped beef and turnips.

"But what could they possibly think he's done?" asked Tink as he poured milk into his glass. "I know you know, Weston. You're gonna tell us eventually, might as well out with it."

"Maybe it's one of them cases of mistaken identity," offered Salt. "Some mug that done a crime that looks just like Sully. I bet they'll get it all straightened out and he'll be on the next boat back with quite a story to tell."

Dec banged his fork down on his plate. "Listen, Weston, I know you'd soon as spit in my eye, but this isn't about you or me. Can't you let us know what is going on? He's my mate, and now he gets hauled away by a copper with no warning and we don't know a bleddy thing. Just fecking *tell* us something." Dec was practically pleading.

Charles wiped his mouth on his sleeve and left the table. He fully expected the matron to call him back as he headed for the door, to let him know how many demerits he would be receiving for leaving the table before the bell. But she said nothing, and it was that, more than anything, that drove home just how bad the situation was.

~

Bill trailed Charles down to the barn. The wind had picked up since their farm work that morning, and Charles entered the barn just as the first fat raindrops began to fall, with Bill close behind.

They sat on adjoining hay bales. Charles hugged his knees and tucked his head down. Bill plucked three long pieces of hay from his bale and slowly began to braid them.

Lucifer slunk in and hopped up on Charles's bale, turning around once before lying down in a perfect oval, nose on tail. He made no physical contact with Charles but was only inches away.

"He likes you," observed Bill.

"No accounting for taste," said Charles, his voice muffled by his thighs.

"He ain't the only one who likes you here, you know." Bill tied off his braid. "But the question is, do you like any of us?"

"Why wouldn't I?"

"Oh, I couldn't agree with you more. Laurel's a winning bunch. There's no better on the island. But you see, how would we know that you appreciate us, what with you being such an arsehole?"

Charles raised his head off his arms. "If I'm such an arsehole, why are you here? Why don't you leave me alone? Oh, right, you're here to find out what happened to my brother so you can tell every mug on this rock and they can all be talking behind my back. Sure, why don't I just start spilling my guts?"

"First of all, I don't think you are an arsehole at heart. I think you act like an arsehole a lot of the time, and I ain't sure why. But I've known a few genuine arseholes in my life, and I can tell you ain't cut of that cloth. I went to bat for you to get you into Laurel, and I don't regret it. And secondly, I ain't here to get the news on Sully."

"Then why are you here?"

Bill twirled his hay braid between his fingers for a while before he spoke. "I figure it must be kinda rough to be separated from your brother like that. Not knowing when you're gonna see him again."

Charles remembered the story that Tink had told about Bill's younger brothers, how Bill thought they would be with him at the school here but he never saw them again. The silence and the hay dust settled around them.

"I'm supposed to see Bradley after supper," Charles said finally.

"Are you gonna ask him if you can go see Sully?"

Charles had not begun to think about what he would say to Bradley. "Yeah. I mean, you think he'd let me?"

"Dunno, but if I was you, I'd ask." After a moment, he added, "Maybe you can find out what happened to him after he left. You know, where they took him and all."

Charles thought back to his arrest for stealing the sandwich and everything that came after. "Oh, I already know that," he said miserably.

After an afternoon of class, during which he heard nothing, and a supper that tasted like nothing, Charles arrived at the superintendent's office. Beyond Bill's suggestion to ask Bradley if he could visit Aidan, Charles still had no idea what he would say. His mind had gone blank every time he'd thought about it throughout the afternoon.

"Master Weston," Bradley intoned once Charles was seated— but then he hesitated. Charles thought that perhaps Bradley was also at a loss as to what would be discussed in this meeting, but after a few mustache strokes, Bradley continued. "Last week was my two-year anniversary as superintendent of this school. So far, my experience has been quite satisfying. It has been what I had hoped and expected when I first arrived here. That is, until today." He paused. In prior conversations with Bradley, Charles had noticed that the superintendent liked to pause for effect, to let the weight of his words sink in, but it seemed now that he was pausing for a different reason, as if he didn't really want to go on. Or was he waiting for Charles to say something?

Bradley knitted his fingers together and propped them under his chin, elbows on his desk. He gazed out the window. "Instead of eating supper tonight, I went to the chapel to pray for guidance. I asked God to forgive Arthur for what he did. And I asked Him why He brought Arthur to this island, why He brought him to me. What is to be my role in all this." Bradley turned his gaze from the window to Charles. "But as we know, God helps those who help themselves. To that end, I need to know everything about what happened."

Charles went numb. His body was frozen, but now his brain was working. How obvious it was now. Of course Bradley would press him for all the details. What else would he want from Charles? This is what his mind had not let him think all afternoon. Now he was completely unprepared, had not thought at all what he should and should not tell Bradley. His mind raced.

"The two of you are as close as any brothers I've seen. I will not believe you if you insist that you have no idea why he was arrested."

The question is: How much does Bradley know?

"If you claim not to know, I will be so certain that you are lying that you will be punished for it."

The copper musta told him what Aidan was being arrested for. Bradley wouldn't have let anyone take one of his boys otherwise.

"I assure you that you will regret withholding information from me."

But they didn't arrest me, so they either think only one boy killed that swell or that the other one is still out there.

"Master Weston, I am waiting."

Stalling for time, Charles asked, "Can I go visit him?"

"I have asked you a question, and until I am satisfied with your answer, you can be assured that you will *not* see your brother."

"If I tell you what happened, will you agree to take me to him?"

Bradley's nostrils flared. "You are in no position to be negotiating, young man."

"Sir, I apologize." Charles saw his error but wasn't ready to back down on the issue of seeing Aidan. He shifted into the polite and well-spoken persona he used when he was approached by the police. "I'm just so worried about my brother, it's hard to think about anything else. I'll be happy to tell you whatever you want to know, but it would be a load off my mind to know there was a possibility of me getting to see him."

Partially placated, Bradley tugged at his vest. "Well, I can understand your concern. I am also concerned for Arthur. So let's hear what you have to say, and then we will discuss what will come next."

Charles figured that was as close as he would get to a promise. "I was there when it happened."

Bradley leaned forward. Charles knew that everything depended on what he said next.

"We both were. We were out late, like you are when you got no parents." He thought about his night-owl existence back in Boston.

"It was summer, too hot even at night to stay inside. We turned down an alley, trying to cut through to another street, when we saw these two street Arabs rolling a drunk."

"By that you mean two young men robbing an intemperate man who was unconscious."

"Yeah, that's it. But the intemperate man, he wasn't completely unconscious. He woke up, and one of the boys knifed him, and then they ran across the street to where we were. Some lady screamed and pointed to us, and we all scattered. She musta seen my brother and fingered him somehow, but he had nothing to do with that knifing." *And*, Charles thought, *he really did have nothing to do with the knifing—the knife going in, at least.* He thought of Aidan pulling the knife out and all the blood that followed. All of a sudden, Charles felt dizzy and slightly nauseous. "There was a lot of blood," he said, almost to himself. He loosened his collar.

"God in Heaven," said Bradley softly. "You poor boys."

Bradley's reaction could not have been more pleasing. The relief Charles felt hearing the superintendent's words wiped away his dizziness, wiped away all the worry that had been grinding away at him all afternoon. He had to pat himself on the back for thinking on his feet so successfully. He wished Aidan were there to have witnessed it—it was a fine lesson in how the best lies are close to the truth.

Now all he had to do was to get to Aidan and make sure he stuck to their orphan-Weston-brothers story, and then everything was going to work out fine.

CHAPTER 36

Two days later, the matron brought Charles down to the wharf after breakfast. Bradley arrived a few minutes later, and Fielding piloted them over to City Point. Beyond their initial greeting at the wharf, Charles and Bradley exchanged no words during the trip. Even Fielding, who had been known to chat with farm animals if no humans were available, had nothing to say.

A carriage met them at City Point, and for the first time since Aidan's arrest, Charles was able to completely, if briefly, forget about the mess they were in. For all the carriages he had seen every day of his life in Boston, he had never ridden in one. He stepped up into the cabin and was struck at how all the street sounds were pleasantly muffled, as if he and Bradley were eggs swaddled in a straw-lined crate. A moment after he sat down, he felt a pleasant warmth near his feet, and he bent down to see a small brazier half full of glowing coals underneath the bench. Carriages had heat? He thought of all the times he had trudged through snowy sidewalks with holes in his shoes, shivering uncontrollably, and he now realized the swells in the carriages that had passed him had been warming their fine leather boots. Had they ever looked out the window and seen him? And if they had, what had they thought?

Charles was still peering into the brazier when Bradley pounded twice on the ceiling of the carriage. They lurched forward, and

Charles nearly fell to the floor before he righted himself. He felt embarrassed until he realized that Bradley was so preoccupied that he seemed not to have even seen Charles fall.

Travel was slow going. Every street seemed to have an obstacle of some sort: a vendor's cart crossing, another carriage stopping to pick up a customer, a dead horse that protruded into the street. Charles would have been happy if it had taken all day. It was a revelation to see the city from this vantage point—slightly elevated, warm and safe in their quiet cocoon, without the need to navigate or even choose where to go, all to the heartbeat of their horse's hooves clopping on the cobblestones. He found himself seeing common things that seemed different and new: a woman lifting her long skirt to avoid a brush with a pile of manure, two men in bowlers buying oysters from a pushcart, a newsie his age hawking his last paper on the corner.

His sense of thrill and wonderment came to an abrupt end when they pulled up in front of the Charles Street Jail. Back on the island, Charles had stopped to contemplate the fact that he would be entering this place of incarceration—a place where he had briefly been a guest before being sent to Westboro—but he had told himself that it would be different knowing that he would be on the other side of the bars this time. Now that he was staring up at the gray granite building, however, that distinction seemed less compelling. Despite knowing that Aidan was inside, he wanted nothing more than to stay in the carriage and ride around the city. But already Bradley was propelling him, hand on shoulder, out of the carriage, and in less than a minute, they were through the main doors.

Through an archway, Charles could see the atrium, unforgettable in its scale and, as he now remembered, its cacophony of voices coming from cells in all directions whenever someone crossed the floor. But to his surprise, Bradley's hand guided his shoulder not toward the atrium and Aidan but down a narrow corridor and into an office, where several adults waited.

"Sir, aren't we going to see my brother?" he asked, trying not to reveal the panic that he was starting to feel.

"In time. First there are some people for you to meet." Bradley looked at him for the first time today, and Charles knew that the time had come for him to start thinking on his feet again. Like the nights when he'd felt someone following him down at the Waterfront, his senses went on heightened alert, and he began taking in as much information as possible and processing it as quickly as he could.

There were three men and a woman in the room. They had all been sitting but rose when he and Bradley entered. By the way they were dressed, one of the men likely worked at the prison, and one was clearly a police officer. The remaining man and woman were dressed well and stood together, the woman's hand on the man's forearm. Bradley shook everyone's hand, and they all sat down.

"This is Charles Weston," said Bradley to the group, "brother of the accused. Charles, this is Warden Lewis, Officer Dolan, and Mrs. Pemberton and her nephew, Mr. Hanley." Bradley stopped to clear his throat. "Mrs. Pemberton is the witness that saw the attack on her husband."

"She didn't," said Charles quickly. All eyes turned to him.

"I beg your pardon, young man," said Mrs. Pemberton, her hand digging into her nephew's arm as her brows formed an angry furrow. "I believe I will be the judge of what I did and did not see!"

"You seen him on the ground bleedin' right after, but you wasn't in the alley when it happened."

The police officer leaned forward in his chair. "And how exactly do you know this?"

"Because I was there. With my brother."

"And you saw your brother knife Mr. Pemberton?"

"No, he didn't do it, but we saw the mugs that did it. Two of them."

The officer leaned back in his chair and crossed his legs. "This is getting to be a pretty crowded alley now. We have Mr. Pemberton and then Mrs. Pemberton, and you and your brother, plus two others. Men?"

"No, young, like us."

"About your age, then?"

"Yes. Sir. Looked a lot like us, in fact," he added.

The officer started to say something, but Mrs. Pemberton cut him off. "No, that's not right."

A feeling of horror, like ice water dripping down his scalp, descended onto Charles. Now he could see the flaw in his story, but it was too late. Frantically, he tried to think of a way around this flaw, but he came up empty.

Mrs. Pemberton crossed her arms. "There were only two boys in the alley. They had run across the street but turned when I screamed. The one I identified, he was in front with the bloodstains on his shirt. The other one I couldn't see very well. I could only say that he was . . . well, he was blond."

Everyone, even Bradley, looked at Charles's hair. Charles wished he could put his cap on. Or, even better, sink through the floor.

After a moment, when it seemed that no one had any more to say about what happened in the alley, the Warden said to Bradley, "And then there is the issue of the accused's relationship to this boy, as I wrote to you about, Mr. Bradley." Turning to Charles, he said, "The boy we have locked up here says his name is Aidan Sullivan of the West End. This name was not familiar to your superintendent."

All Charles could think was, *Shit.*

Bradley rotated in his seat to face Charles. "Explain this," he said urgently, half angry, half pleading, in a way that made Charles feel like he and Bradley were the only people in the room. Charles's vision tunneled. He could see one of Bradley's eyebrow hairs angling up out of line with the others and a streak of brown in the hazel iris of his left eye. "Explain to me how Mrs. Pemberton could be wrong and why Arthur is lying about not being your brother. Convince me that everything you told me back at the school is true."

But Charles could not.

~

There were visitors every day on Aidan's corridor, but when each one had failed to be for him, he had given up hope and stopped even bothering to rouse himself when footsteps approached. So he was unprepared when Bradley arrived, and he didn't look up from his bed until the guard cleared his throat in annoyance.

"Mr. Bradley," Aidan said with some reverence as he stood.

Bradley's posture was ramrod straight as he considered Aidan through the bars. "They tell me you are not who I thought you were. I came to hear this from your mouth."

"Sir, I'm sorry, I didn't—"

"Spare me your excuses. I want to know your name."

"My name is Aidan Sullivan, sir."

"I see. And why should I believe this name when the previous name was untrue?"

"I have nothing to hide now."

"Really. Tell me. Did you knife that man?"

Aidan opened his mouth to speak but stopped himself before any sound came out. What should he say? He didn't plunge the knife into the man's belly, but he didn't want Bradley to think that he was protesting his innocence. Most of all, he was tired, so tired, of lying. He needed to say only true things if he wanted any chance of redemption.

"I am guilty, sir."

Aidan would wonder long into the night what Bradley would have said in response if they hadn't been interrupted by another guard bringing another visitor. At least, Aidan assumed Charles was his visitor, until the new guard opened the door and shoved Charles inside.

After the door clanked shut, the boys both stared across the divide at Bradley, who looked from one boy to the other. Had he seen Bradley's face out of context, Aidan would have said that the superintendent was trying to mask a physical pain. Finally Bradley turned away, and with the guards trailing him, he trudged down the corridor, abandoned by his straight posture, eyes cast downward.

Charles turned to Aidan and was able to say "Hey" before Aidan slammed him with his left hook.

Aidan remained in boxing stance, waiting for Charles to retaliate, but for once, Charles's temper didn't ignite. He rubbed the side of his face as he lay on the floor, then pulled himself to sitting and leaned his back against the wall with a groan.

Aidan stood over him. "Why the feck didn't you tell me about me ma?"

"Jesus, Sully, I'm kinda having a bad day here. Can't you just say hello like everyone else?" He looked up at Aidan. "Wait, how did you find out about your ma?"

"Well, it sure as hell wasn't from you back on the island, was it now?" Aidan's brogue was free of constraint now, and it bounced harshly off the granite walls of the cell.

"I couldn't! Think about it! I knew you'd be all broken up, and how could we explain it to anyone there? You would've had to pretend that you weren't grieving her, that everything was grand! How could you do that?"

Aidan sat on the bed and looked at his hands. He couldn't have pretended. He hadn't thought about it like that, and now he grudgingly admitted to himself that Charles was right. His vision swam as his eyes filled with tears, even though he thought he had cried every tear he had yesterday when he got the note.

Charles got up and sat on the bed next to him. "How did you find out?"

"Bess wrote me."

"Really? In here? How did she even know you were here?"

Aidan wiped the corner of his eyes with the heel of his hands. "I dunno. Guess she has her sources. Knew how to bribe the guard to bring the note pretty quick, too."

"I don't get it. Why would she write you about your ma?"

"That's not what she wrote me for, ya eedjit. Mainly she wanted to remind me that we agreed not to finger her for helping us get onto the island. But then at the end she mentioned that she was sorry about me ma and how she would have told me when she visited but she didn't want to wreck the day, so she hoped *you* broke it to me gentle."

"Can I see the note?"

"She told me to tear it up and eat it so nobody would see it."

"You ate it?"

"Better than some of the food they serve in here." Aidan allowed himself a little smile, despite everything.

They sat side by side for a while, listening to the sounds of the other inmates echoing off the corridor. Someone nearby had a hacking cough that was so constant Aidan hardly heard it anymore. Farther away, a woman cried. It sounded muffled, as if she were sobbing into her skirts. In the cell right next to them, someone started pissing into a pail.

"Jesus," said Charles, his voice shaky, "I swore I'd never get sent back here. Being locked up . . . Jesus. I don't think I can take this."

"Not much choice now, is there?" But Aidan regretted his words as soon as they were out of his mouth. He wasn't used to seeing Charles like this, without his defenses, without a plan. It reminded him of when Charles went all woozy after seeing the blood pouring out of that poor swell in the alley. "This is where you were before Westboro, right?"

Charles nodded.

"Did someone from the Charities come and see you in here?"

"Yeah, that's right, they did. Children's Aid. Did they come for you?"

"It's St. Vincent's for the Catholics, but yeah."

"How'd that go?"

"I dunno," said Aidan. The man who had shown up that morning, Mr. Flynn, had been friendly, but with every answer Aidan had given, the man had seemed to become more and more discouraged. Once Mr. Sutton had left the night before, Aidan had realized he would be asked about the crime in great detail, and he'd resolved that he would tell the truth about all of it. The only part that had given him pause was Charles's involvement. As far as he knew, Charles had not been implicated, and Aidan did not want to be the one to do it. Right before he fell asleep that night, he'd decided he would relay all the details truthfully but withhold the identity of his accomplice. But Flynn was not pleased to hear his description of the events. Aidan got the impression that the man thought he was lying, and he had clearly been disappointed to learn that Aidan had no relatives to be interviewed or to provide a character reference.

Charles covered his eyes with the palms of his hands as he spoke. "When I was in Westboro, I met plenty of mugs that was there for robbing people, some for hurting other people bad in a fight, but I never met anybody that killed somebody." He took a deep, shaky breath. "Did that St. Vincent's fellow say what was gonna happen to us?"

"They didn't tell you?" When Charles's confused face didn't clear, Aidan slapped Charles on the thigh. "Well, on this day when you thought there was no good news, I have some good news for ya. Turns out we didn't kill that swell after all. Old Pemberton's alive and well."

CHAPTER 37

Mired in his own thoughts, Bradley didn't hear the chapel door open. He sat with his eyes closed, his elbows on the pew in front of him, his hands in prayer position against his forehead. Only when the matron sat next to him was he aware of her presence in the room, her silk skirts rustling as she settled onto the bench. He sat back with a quiet sigh, grateful for the interruption. He had been getting nowhere with God.

Mary reached out for his hand. "You did not come to breakfast this morning."

"One of the houseboys brought me coffee in the office." But Bradley had not been able to remain there. None of the paperwork on his desk made any sense. He'd started to write a reply to a minister who wanted to donate hymnals to the school, but after the salutation, his fountain pen had halted and formed an inky blob on the page. He'd looked down to discover the ruined sheet of paper and wondered how long he had been frozen in that position. Frustrated and scattered, he'd torn the sheet in two and proceeded to the chapel, where he'd been for the past hour.

He knew he should talk with her. He had arrived back at the island yesterday much later than anticipated, and it was only to Mary that he had explained why Charles had not returned with him. But he hadn't discussed the situation in any detail, only telling her that Charles was also implicated in the crime and was now incarcerated along with his brother, who was in reality not his brother at all.

"I was asking God if I did the right thing by turning Charles in."

"When you went to the mainland, you were not sure he was involved. Had he not been, the two of you would have simply visited with Arthur. Or, I suppose I should say, Aidan." The matron's thin lips became even thinner as she pursed her mouth in disapproval.

"But had I not brought Charles along, he would not be in a jail cell right now."

"Is that not where he deserves to be?"

Bradley leaned back in the pew, which creaked loudly. "I seem to be getting more straightforward answers from you than from God." He smiled a sad smile that faded away almost as soon as it appeared.

"Those two boys have done nothing but lie since they arrived here, and they lied to get here in the first place. You said so yourself yesterday. God punishes the wicked."

"But it is man who will decide their placement. Yes, they robbed a man and knifed him, and he nearly died. We may safely assume this was not their first robbery. Wicked deeds, without a doubt." Bradley seemed poised to say more but stopped.

After a moment, Mary echoed, "Without a doubt." Bradley said nothing. She prompted, "So . . ."

"So they did wicked things—but are they wicked boys? They sat across from my desk. Arthur, Aidan, whatever he calls himself, he watered his flower garden ever day. Charles defended a dog that no one else would defend. I'm simply saying that a boy is not defined by just one thing that he has done."

"But they are criminals," Mary said with some confusion.

"No, Mary, they are boys who committed crimes. They are not even adults who have committed crimes. They have not yet become the persons they will be as adults for the rest of their lives."

Mary took several breaths before she spoke. "You have known these boys for three months, and you do not know the victim, Mr. Pemberton, at all. But Mr. Pemberton is someone's husband, and likely someone's father. What if it had been your own father who had been robbed and knifed by two boys you had never seen? What if you had sat by your father's bedside as he bled through his bandages, as his fever rose, as he lay unconscious, and you thought he would never wake and you would never get to say any final words to him before he went to meet God?"

"Mary, please, that is a most upsetting image."

"Yes, I'm sure it was quite upsetting for the Pemberton family." After a moment, she said, "I have prayed on this too, and I believe that God led these boys here so that they could be at Faneuil Hall that day, so that they would be discovered and arrested and justice would be served." She stood. "In any event, it is out of your hands now. The court will decide what is best for them. If you need me, I will be in the kitchen—Mrs. Culligan says there is a problem with the flour that came over on the last boat."

Bradley watched her leave the chapel with her excellent posture and unshakable convictions. He wished he could be more like her, so sure of the answers. In truth, everything she said made perfect sense. Pemberton was the victim, and he did deserve sympathy. The boys were guilty—Aidan had confirmed this right to his face. And it was out of Bradley's hands now; the die had been cast, for better or for worse. He should go back to his office, finish his paperwork, consult his meticulously penned list of things to do, and push this whole matter from his mind.

He leaned forward and put his elbows on the pew in front of him, his hands in prayer position against his forehead. He closed his eyes.

CHAPTER 38

THEY SLEPT HEAD TO FOOT ON THE NARROW PRISON BED, AND Charles's feet smelled like a ripe cheese. Still, Aidan didn't much mind, as it was one of the better smells in the cell. On nights when the guards didn't get around to emptying their toilet pail before lights-out, Aidan found himself turning toward Charles's feet to block out the stench of their own waste.

On this night, neither of them was sleeping much. The stew they'd served for supper had smelled off, but they were so hungry they'd eaten it anyway, and it had gone right through them. All night they alternated on the pail, and the cell smelled worse than it ever had before. Finally, as the sun began to rise, the cramps subsided, but neither of them could get back to sleep.

"Charles," said Aidan softly, pushing his big toe against Charles's ear.

"What."

"You're still a fecking bastard for not telling me about my ma."

"Yeah."

For the past two days, Aidan had tried and failed to get a rise out of Charles. Charles was clearly agitated about being locked up, and it seemed to transform his entire personality. He looked nervous all the time and refused to get angry about anything. This scared Aidan almost as much as their trial, which was scheduled for later that day.

"Charles," he said again. Charles didn't respond. "Tell me about when your mother died."

The silence was so long that Aidan concluded that Charles would not be telling him. But then Charles said, "It weren't no picnic."

After a few moments, he continued: "First ones in our building to get it were the Sheas, on the first floor. My ma says it figures, the Irish is a sickly race, dirty too. But then when the Torelli girl across the hall got it, Ma shut us up and told me I didn't have to go to school 'til it passed."

"She was protectin' you," observed Aidan.

"She was protectin' herself. She made me go out to get food. But in the end, it was her that got it. Smallpox. You ever seen anybody with it?"

Aidan shook his head.

"It don't happen so much anymore, but my ma said it used to happen left and right. I guess some of her people had it and all but one uncle made it through, but she had a horror of it. She said they didn't look human, their faces with bumps and scales like a monster. It gave her nightmares. I couldn't really picture it in my mind, but then when it happened to her, I saw that she was right. Like a monster. Like the monster that's chasing you in your dreams at night, only it's real and it's calling your name from the bed and asking you for water."

Aidan lay still, waiting for Charles to continue.

"Took two weeks. Gave me plenty of time to think, and it was then I decided that there weren't no God. God wouldn't have created people and then lay them low like that, so they don't look like a person no more, boiling their brains with fever and then letting them die in front of their sons who ain't got a clue on what to do next." Charles covered his face with his hands, but his voice didn't waver.

After a while, Aidan said, "What did you do next?"

"I ran." Charles brought his hands from his face and rested

them on his belly, eyes dry and voice monotone. "When it was real clear she was gone, I left so fast I fell down the last two steps in the stairway and gave myself a shiner on the newel post. I went down to the wharves and watched the boats go in and out of the harbor." After a couple of heartbeats, he continued. "All afternoon I was lookin' out at the water, and finally I come up with a plan. Well, not so much a plan, more like a decision. And that decision was, I ain't waiting to find out what they're gonna do with me. I'm takin' the reins. So I snuck back into my apartment like a criminal, makin' sure there weren't nobody from the Cruelty or any Temperance ladies sniffing around, and I took all the money we had and as much food as I could carry. Looked through the drawers to see if maybe she kept a wedding band or some sorta jewelry I could sell, but there was nothing. And I got the hell outta there."

Aidan thought about Charles's decision. "I don't think I would have the balls to do that. Go out on the street on my own."

"Then you and your balls woulda found yourselves locked up in some place where they tell you what to do every minute of the day."

"Like the Farm School?"

Charles paused. "That's different."

"It is different. Why aren't all them places, the House of Refuge and such, why aren't they all like the Farm School?"

The first light began to creep across the floor of their cell as Charles responded, "Question is, why ain't the Farm School like all them other places?"

When they arrived at the Suffolk County Courthouse later that morning, the smell of unwashed bodies was a welcome change from the human-waste smell of their cell. There were a dozen boys there, some attended by mothers and younger siblings. One held his younger brother's cap high in the air, beyond the reach of the boy's highest jump. There was a pretty girl sitting with her father and mother, looking as despondent as if this were the last day of her life. Up near the railing, a reporter tapped his pencil slowly against his pad, exuding boredom.

Charles and Aidan found a space on one of the benches in the front of the room. Although they were flanked by Sutton and Flynn, it was noisy enough in the high-ceilinged room that they could talk without their agents overhearing. "This where you were before?" asked Aidan.

"Yep," said Charles. "Judge is through there." He jerked his chin toward the door behind the clerks' desks. "Has his desk on a little platform, wants to make sure you know who's the big man in the room." He cracked his knuckles with a grimace. "No chairs. Don't want no one to get comfortable, even the agents."

"What did you say to the judge when you went in?"

"I told him I stole that sandwich because I was hungry. Then he sent me to Westboro." Charles looked down toward his lap and started picking at his cuticles.

Aidan could see, could almost feel, Charles losing his confidence, as if it were draining off of him and seeping through the scuffed floorboards below them. His cockiness, ever present on the island, in evidence just now when describing the judge and his chambers, was what Aidan had come to rely on when they were together in uncertain circumstances. And now the circumstances could not be more uncertain. Aidan needed the old Charles now. At least he had been through this process before, albeit with an undesirable outcome.

Aidan leaned in closer to Charles. "Listen to me," he hissed through gritted teeth. "We need a fecking plan."

Charles continued to decimate his cuticles. "I don't know—"

"*Look at me,*" Aidan said, more softly and more menacingly than before. Charles looked up. "I know you don't know. But I don't fecking know either, and we don't know how much time we have out here on this bench before they call our names. I say we just tell the truth."

"We can't finger Bess."

"We ain't gonna. We'll say . . ." Aidan thought for a moment. "We'll say we appealed to that minister Stryker directly with our story. Leave Bess out of it."

"So much for telling the truth," Charles said wryly. "If we're going to lie about the minister, why not make one up? Then we can have him conveniently disappear."

"But Bradley knows it was Stryker that got us on the island. I bet that's in our record, and Bradley mighta showed our records to the police."

"Yeah. All right."

"And I say we don't try snowin' the judge. I bet he can smell that a mile away. Plus, I mean, we don't have to fake being regretful and all." Aidan stopped. "You are sorry we done it, ain't you?"

"What kind of a question is that?" Charles was louder than he had intended, and Mr. Sutton looked over at him with an angry glare. Charles continued more quietly. "Am I sorry I stuck a knife in the belly of a swell when I only wanted his roll of bills? Yeah, Sully, I am. What kind of a mug do you think I am?"

"The kind who can't keep his temper in his pocket," said Aidan, but he couldn't help but be pleased to see Charles get his dander up, even if it might work against them. "Just try to keep from yelling at the judge. We done something wrong, it was an accident, we are mighty sorry."

Just then, the clerk called out their names. "Charles Wheeler and Aidan Sullivan!" he shouted above the din. As they rose from the bench, Aidan's cap, which he had placed beside him, fell off the back of the bench, and when he turned to retrieve it, he glanced at all the people behind them. He punched Charles on the arm as they started to file past others on the bench.

"You ain't gonna believe who's here. Look in the back row."

Charles looked back. "Bradley. Huh. I thought he washed his hands of us."

"Yeah, but look who he's talking to."

Bradley's conversation partner turned just enough to reveal, underneath the brim of her hat, a chignon of beautiful blond hair that could belong to only one woman.

Before they could fathom why in the world Bess would come to the courthouse, they were ushered into the judge's chambers. Judge Cook offered no greeting and did not rise from his seat. "Stand beside my desk here, boys," he said, pointing to the right of his desk without looking up, and he continued to peruse their paperwork. Charles's instinct told him this was for effect, to make sure they knew that the meeting started when the judge said it started. Charles pushed down his dislike for this man who years ago had sent him to the worst place he'd ever been to. Knowing that he could do it again made the man all the more loathsome.

"Well," said the judge as he removed his spectacles and placed them on the desk, "it is rare that I see two boys in my chambers at once. But the nature of your crime is most serious, and I must be sure that the three of us agree on the course of events that led you here." He leaned back in his chair. He was a tall man, and his height, combined with the desk platform, allowed him to look laterally into the boys' eyes as they stood. Charles imagined that had Judge Cook been a smaller man, he would have had the platform built higher, keeping him at eye level with the accused.

"I've had a nice long chat with the Pembertons at their home. Lovely people. Quite a close call Mr. Pemberton had this summer. The doctors said he'd lost a large quantity of blood, and the infection that set in almost killed him again." The judge picked up a pencil and balanced it between the pads of his index fingers. "So why don't we start with what happened that night. Aidan."

Charles had been ready to speak, having become used to being the voice of the two of them. Suddenly he was very glad that Aidan had forced him to discuss a strategy just minutes ago.

"Sir," Aidan began, "we were out to make some money that night, I won't deny it. We were hungry, and my ma was sick, and we didn't have jobs." Charles had heard Aidan perfectly suppress his brogue before, but he had not yet heard such an effort in good grammar. By the look on the judge's face, this was a smart move. "Mr. Pemberton came out of the side door of that saloon and was, er, vomiting his drinks onto the sidewalk, and then he passed out, or at least we thought—"

"Mr. Pemberton," Judge Cook interrupted, "had not imbibed in excess. He was suffering from oysters that had gone off. He told me himself."

To Charles, this looked like a test, and he hoped Aidan would say the right thing. Charles remembered the boozy stink that had wafted off Pemberton that night, and with Aidan's keen sense of smell, he knew Aidan had smelled it too.

"Yes, sir," Aidan continued after a moment, "I believe I had that wrong. He was vomiting the oysters, and he was feeling so poorly after that, he, uh, took a little rest there on the sidewalk. That's when we went to . . ." he trailed off.

"You went to . . ." the judge prompted.

"We went to take his cash," Charles jumped in. "I took his cash."

"Charles Wheeler," the judge said as if he had just realized Charles was in the room. He put down his pencil and picked up a paper from his desk. "It seems you and I have met before. Taking things that do not belong to you, this is somewhat of a habit, is it not?"

With all his heart, Charles wanted to tell the judge that being hungry was really the habit he could not seem to break, but he dug his nails into his palms and took a breath. "Sir, I have not always done the right thing. And I sure didn't do the right thing that night. But I never meant no harm to Mister Pemberton. The knife, it was an accident, plain and simple."

"Plain and simple? Please explain to me how a boy can accidentally knife a man."

"The knife, it was in his pocket next to his roll, and I took it out to show Aidan here, and Pemberton grabbed my ankle, and I fell on him."

"So *you* took the money, and *you* knifed—accidently as you say—Mr. Pemberton." The judge shifted in his seat to gaze directly at Aidan. "And what were *you* doing during all this time?"

All at once, Charles realized that this was something they should have discussed in the waiting room. Ever since Sutton had told him days ago that he and Aidan would be seeing the judge together, he hadn't given a thought to how their involvement in the crime differed. But now that the details were being laid before the judge like dominoes, one by one, he could see that they painted him in a different light than Aidan. And after all, wasn't that the truth? In all their nights together, all Aidan had done was look out for someone coming. He had never lifted a single dollar out of a drunk's pocket. If the judge knew this, it seemed certain that they would receive a different sentence. Which would mean being separated. But there was nothing that could be done now.

"Tell him," said Charles to Aidan. "Go on." He looked at Aidan with resignation.

"I was the lookout"—Aidan took a deep breath—"on that night. Other nights we switched off, and I did the stealing and Charles looked out."

Yes, Charles thought, not smiling but wanting to.

"Mr. Flynn," said the judge, "I've only just received your report this morning. Can you summarize your findings?"

Flynn was clearly pleased to finally have something to say. He ruffled his notes. "Your Honor, the tenement apartment at the given address was occupied by an unrelated family, but a canvassing of the neighbors turned up one that confirmed the Sullivans had indeed lived at that address. The neighbor, a Mrs. McGarrity, is currently caring for the younger sister."

"Ella," Aidan said. "Is she all right?"

Flynn ignored him. "Mrs. McGarrity and other neighbors portrayed the accused as a good boy who didn't court trouble and the family as occasional churchgoers. But there was no father, and the mother was intemperate and consumptive and thus unable to provide the appropriate structure and discipline for the children."

"Is there any more common story in this city?" Judge Cook mused, half to himself, as if Aidan were not in the room. Charles tamped down a little more hatred as the judge continued. "Mr. Sutton, I don't have your report at all."

"Your Honor, my apologies." Sutton produced a report from his folio and handed it to the judge. "It was more difficult to unearth information on my charge."

"I see that," said the judge after donning his spectacles. "There's very little here."

"There was no one at the tenement who recalled Mrs. Wheeler or her son—all had taken up residence after my charge says his mother died. We have only what the boy has provided us and, of course, his prior criminal record."

"There was the minister that wrote to the superintendent pleading their case," said Sutton. "Stryker. But I could not meet with him. The church secretary said he was ailing. I didn't press the matter, since we know Stryker didn't know the boys—not much light he could shed on their character."

"What about the church where they did worship?"

"No church for my charge," said Sutton with a face that telegraphed deep disappointment. "Even before the mother's death, they did not attend regularly, by the boy's account."

"Father Healy at St. Joseph's did vouch for my charge," said Flynn. "Attendance varied with the health of the mother. But he had no problems with the boy."

Charles looked at the judge to gauge how much this information might put Aidan and him in different categories for sentencing, but it was impossible to tell. Mostly the judge looked frustrated at the lack of information, and possibly dyspeptic.

"Is there anyone else to speak for them? Distant relatives, perhaps?"

"There is one who can speak for both, as it turns out," said Mr. Sutton, and he excused himself to the waiting room. A few moments later, he returned with Superintendent Bradley.

"Charles!" Judge Cook said warmly, and for one confusing moment, Charles thought that the judge was talking to him. But then he remembered that the superintendent had the same first name.

"Good to see you, Richard," said Bradley as they shook hands.

The judge poked his head out the door to the waiting room and asked a clerk to bring in a chair for Bradley. "Didn't know you'd be coming mainland for this hearing."

"I didn't know myself. Until yesterday, I thought I'd just let the law sort out this whole situation. At least, that's what Mary has been advising."

"She's well?"

"Well as ever." Bradley settled himself in the chair offered by the clerk. Charles wasn't surprised that the matron didn't want any further involvement in this mess, but he noted with interest that Bradley was going against her advice just by being here.

"We've a dearth of background on these two here," the judge said as he waved his hand in their direction without looking over. "And as you know, I've got decisions to make on their placement. They've confessed to robbing and knifing poor Pemberton, but they claim the knifing was an accident. Pemberton doesn't actually recall being knifed, if you can warrant that. So I put it to you: Do you think they are lying about the knifing being an accident? Are they liars?"

With a feeling of impending doom, Charles recalled in painful detail the last time he saw Bradley before his incarceration. *Convince me that everything you told me back at the school is true.*

"These two boys came to my school under false identities." Bradley looked only at the judge. "They somehow convinced a minister to submit their application and have it expedited. There is no doubt that they can lie and have lied."

"Quite disturbing," murmured the judge as he rubbed his chin.

"On the other hand," continued Bradley, "their conduct at the school gave me no reason for concern. Their school work was acceptable; they received no punishments, few demerits."

"Mmmm," said the judge, nodding. Charles thought he looked slightly bored.

"But, Richard"—and as Bradley tilted his head, Charles heard the superintendent's voice change—"what I think you really want to ask me is, are these the sort of boys who would knife a man? Is their modus operandi to rob a conscious man at knifepoint and plunge the dagger in if met with resistance? And I would have to say to that question: These are not those kind of boys."

"But can you be sure? They have only been at your school for a few months."

"Of course I cannot be sure. But neither can you be sure that they *are* that type. And of all the people in this room and all that these agents were able to locate, I have known them the longest."

There was a pause as the judge thought about this.

"Sir?" Charles addressed the judge. The judge looked surprised, almost as if he had forgotten that Charles was still there.

"Yes?"

"The knife, it was Mr. Pemberton's. Isn't that right?"

"Yes. Pemberton confirmed that."

"Well, then I certainly couldn't have come upon him intent on knifin' him if I didn't even know he had a knife, right? So it couldn't have been pre . . . uh . . ." Charles racked his brain. Judge Cook looked at him blankly and offered no help. But then the word came to him. "Premeditated."

The judge swiveled his head around with a quizzical look to Bradley, who noted, "Charles was quite the student of civics at our school."

"I see," said the judge with raised eyebrows.

Bradley and the judge went on to speak for some time about the boys' behavior on the island. Charles could sense Aidan shifting from foot to foot next to him. Finally, Judge Cook seemed satisfied.

"Well, I must thank you for your time. I realize it is quite an effort for you to be here today, and I don't wish to delay your return to the island."

"If it's all the same to you, I'd like to remain for sentencing," Bradley said casually. "If that's all right."

"Of course, of course." The judge flipped through the papers on his desk once more before laying the pencil down on top of the stack. "Based on the character reference from Superintendent Bradley," he said to no one in particular in the room, "and absent any other information, I will give these boys the benefit of the doubt in their claim that the knifing was an accident. It may even be that one or both of them have the potential to rise out of their life of petty crime and join good Christian society. No one would be happier than I if this were their fate. However." The judge leaned forward. "The places that would normally accommodate the boys I see for status offenses and minor crimes simply would not tolerate a pair of knife-wielding thieves, regardless of the explanation. An accidental knifing is still a knifing."

Trembling, Charles looked over at Aidan, who was breathing so heavily in short breaths that Charles could see the rise and fall of his chest through his thin coat.

"It's quite a pity," continued the judge, "because given their farm experience, there are families out west who could use boys. But I'm afraid once we disclosed the criminal history, there would be no takers."

Judge Cook turned to the men in the room. "Mr. Sutton, Mr. Flynn, I am open to placement suggestions. Mr. Flynn first."

"Your Honor, I don't see these two boys in the same light. My charge really had nothing to do with the knifing, nor even with the robbery that night. One could argue he was merely in the wrong place at the wrong time. His sin is one of poor judgment in associating with this street Arab. I feel that time in a reformatory environment would only do harm. A Catholic foster family would be the best place for him."

"You make a compelling argument, Mr. Flynn," said the judge, nodding. "Mr. Sutton, what of your street Arab?"

"Your Honor, I'm not sure that farming families in the west should be discounted so quickly. As you mentioned, my charge has already been introduced to the farming methods and lifestyle at Mr. Bradley's fine school, and the boy appears quite strong and robust. In addition, he was raised in the Protestant faith, so there will not be issues of religious assimilation as has happened with Catholic boys."

"The Orphan Train?" Charles interrupted. "That's what you're talking about?"

The judge responded to Mr. Sutton as if Charles had not spoken. "And what of his crimes? You propose to disclose this?"

"There is a town just across the Wisconsin border that we've had great success with of late. A strongly religious community, committed to hard work and daily prayer. Last year, one of the families even accepted a young Jew boy, and they have turned him into a happy Christian, by all accounts."

"And you think they might accept your charge?"

"I would propose that here is a soul in need of salvation. With a letter of introduction from Mr. Bradley, I believe they would accept him. If they will not take him, he will return on the train and can be sent to the reformatory."

"I have to disagree, Mr. Sutton. He has already spent time at Westboro for stealing, and upon his discharge, he committed a violent crime. There is a pattern of escalation. Sending him west is a waste of a seat on the train. No family would accept such a boy. I believe the reformatory is the only place for him."

There was nothing Charles could do to stop a tear from each eye from making slow progress down his freckled face. As much as it made him ill to hear "the reformatory is the only place for him," it was "no family would accept such a boy" that cut even deeper. They couldn't see that Aidan *was* his family. They only saw that Charles was a lapsed Protestant and a two-time criminal without a roof over his head, while Aidan was a Catholic boy who—until recently, at least—had a mother and a priest to vouch for him. He could see that they thought they were saving Aidan by making sure he wouldn't see Charles again.

He felt Aidan's hand creep into his. *Maybe they're right*, he thought. *Maybe I'll only bring Aidan down if we stay together.* Aidan was the type of boy that a family would accept. Unlike Charles.

He realized that Bradley was staring at him. Charles had almost forgotten that the superintendent was in the room.

"Son," Bradley addressed him, "what is the reformatory in Westboro like?"

Charles was tired all of a sudden—too tired to figure out what the right answer was to that question or why Bradley was asking it. He closed his eyes, which forced two more tears to stream down. *It doesn't really matter what I say now. Your fate is your fate.* "It's a hard place"—and here his voice broke a little, to his embarrassment—"but I guess it's where I belong."

"I beg to differ." Bradley stood and addressed the judge. "Richard, I would like to take custody of these boys."

Aidan squeezed Charles's hand so hard that it hurt, but Charles could only feel it distantly.

The judge looked dubious. "I'm quite surprised to hear you say that. Aren't these just the type of boys you strive to keep out of your school?"

"But that's just it. You see in front of you two boys who have committed a crime. But I see a boy who learned the clarinet on my island and brought a flower garden back to life, and a boy who became a lawyer in the school government and tamed a mean dog. These boys are more than the bad decisions they made on the mainland. And we both know that time spent in a 'reformatory' does little to reform."

"You would never have admitted them to your school if you knew their true past."

"You're right. But now I know more than their true past."

"How will you explain this to your board?"

"Leave that to me. Will you release them to my custody?"

"Why both of them? Only one would have gone to Westboro."

Bradley looked over at the boys, and Charles could see a little smile beneath his mustache. "How could I split up two brothers?"

"Certainly you realize they are not related?" asked the judge with a frown.

"I do," said Bradley. But he was looking at the boys.

In the carriage to City Point, the three of them rode in silence for a while. Charles had so many questions scurrying around in his head that he couldn't formulate a single one. Finally, Aidan spoke.

"Why did you come to take us back?"

Bradley looked at Aidan and then gazed out the window. "I didn't, actually." After a moment, he continued. "Well, to be truthful, I wasn't sure of all the reasons I came today. Certainly I felt an obligation to give a character reference to ensure the best placement for you. But of course, I knew what would likely happen, regardless of how well you tended your flower bed." He smiled. "Do you know where I worked before I became superintendent of the Farm School?"

Both boys shook their heads.

"I was an instructor at the State Primary School in western Massachusetts. So I know about reformatories. And I jumped at the chance to come to the island and run my own school, a school that would not be a reformatory, that would teach boys trades and place them in jobs."

Bradley looked out the window and was silent for so long that they assumed he was done making his point. But then he continued. "Last night, I prayed on this situation. I asked God to tell me why this happened, why he brought you to my island. The matron believes it was so that you could be brought to justice. But the more I prayed, the more I felt that God had brought you to the island so that you could change your lives. After all, is that not the business I am in? I take the lives of one hundred boys and make them so they are better when they leave than when they arrived. I've had many sleepless nights wondering if I have successfully screened out the bad element in accepting my one hundred boys. I've refused to see many boys based on their histories. But I think this was God's way of telling me to trust my instinct more."

The carriage had arrived at City Point. The *Pilgrim* was waiting for them at the end of the wharf, Fielding sitting there reading a seed catalog with his legs propped up.

"My instinct tells me you will give me no more trouble. Of course, as I'm sure you are aware, I can deposit you back with Judge Cook if trouble arises, and he will be happy to implement his original placement plan. But I don't believe it will come to that."

"No, sir," said Aidan.

Charles said nothing, but he realized there was something he needed to do when he got back to the island.

Bradley was finally settling in to concentrate on the mounting paperwork stacked in neat piles on his desk when a knock came at the door of his office. He sincerely hoped it was not Mary again. She had been none too pleased when he had arrived back at the island that morning with Charles and Aidan in tow, and their ensuing discussion had lasted well into dinnertime, but eventually she'd resigned herself to the fact that the boys were here and that they would not be leaving any time soon. Her arguments had the benefit of showing him what issues would come up in his monthly meeting with the board next week, and he had already begun to address these issues in his mind. But he did not have the energy to revisit the arguments right now, and so he was relieved to see that it was not her who sought to gain admittance.

"Master Wheeler, how can I help you? Please have a seat."

Charles walked over to the superintendent's desk, but instead of sitting, he deposited an object on his desk. Bradley picked it up and turned it over in his hands.

"You realize these are forbidden here at the school."

"Yes, sir."

"And for you to have this is especially troubling."

"Yes, sir."

They both looked down at the pocketknife in Bradley's hands.

"Sir, that's why I'm giving it to you. I had it here, hidden. The bed boxes, they got these hidden compartments in the bottom that no one knows about."

"I know about them, Charles."

"Oh." Charles looked confused but shook it off. "Anyway, I had that knife in there from the get-go. It had nothing to do with the, uh, you know, with Pemberton and all. But I ain't—I mean, *I'm not*—hiding anything anymore. 'Specially a knife." He looked embarrassed.

Bradley looked at Charles for a long time. After several heart-beats, he said, "I will keep this for you, Master Wheeler, and you may have it when you leave this island for your apprenticeship." He looked at the knife again, more closely this time. "With your initials, even. Mother of pearl, too."

"She's a beaut, sir, no doubt about it."

"I agree," said Bradley. "There really is no doubt about it."

EPILOGUE

Wharf, Thompson Island

EPILOGUE

February 2, 1922

THE *WINSLOW* CHUGGED THROUGH THE HARBOR, SPLITTING the steel water in front and churning it white like boiling laundry in the back. Fueled by gasoline, it had the power to cut through the thin sheet of ice that had formed on the harbor. The wind was wicked out on the open water, and all the passengers were hunched against it, so much so that when the boat bumped against the wharf, Charles could not tell one wool coat and hat from another. But only one passenger was peering out from his muffler, looking for Charles.

They shook hands, neither letting go right away. It had been years since they had seen each other.

Aidan spoke first. "Jaysus, we live in the same fecking city, and I've got to hop on a bleddy boat to see you."

Charles smiled a little but looked down, embarrassed. In truth, he didn't have much of an excuse for not staying in contact these past few years. When Aidan married Maggie, he had inherited her extensive Irish family in the West End, which kept them both busy with christenings, birthdays, holidays, and general visiting, and life had only gotten busier when Sean was born. Charles, on the other hand, had no such distractions. For the thirty years he had been in Boston, ever since he'd left the island for his apprenticeship at the Law Office of Hardricourt and Banfield, he had devoted most of his time to struggling his way through the legal profession. As one lawyer at the office had put it to Charles when he was twenty-three, "You've got plenty of passion for the law, son. Problem is, people don't like you much." Charles had left that conversation fuming, but he later admitted to himself that this analysis at least explained why other clerks in the office had been promoted while Charles was consistently overlooked.

"Hey." Aidan slapped Charles's shoulder. "I could have called too. We've both got telephones." Aidan's brogue washed over the both of them. Soon after they graduated from the Farm School, Aidan had given up trying to cover his accent, telling Charles that he was willing to risk some discrimination in favor of never having to keep straight in his head which voice to use with whom.

The two of them began walking up the curving road to Bulfinch. "Can't believe I'm back here," said Aidan. "The trees are so tall! They weren't this tall when we were here."

"You haven't been back since, right?"

"Nope. Not much could make me want to get in a boat for a wee harbor cruise."

"Looks like you did okay today," observed Charles.

"It's not as bad as back then." They rounded the bend, and the building came into view. "That wing in the back, that's new."

"New dormitories. They had a bit of trouble with the builder on that one. Used the wrong materials on the roof and the thing wouldn't stop leaking. Had to threaten to take him to court to get him to fix it. That was the last thing I helped out with. Before this last bit of business."

They fell silent. The only sound was the crunch of shells under their shoes and the shoes of other alumni as they walked along the path up the hill.

It was right after Christmas that Charles had gotten a call from the matron. "The day after Thanksgiving, he took to his bed. The pain is worse now. He wants to make sure his affairs are in order. He's asking for you."

"He's sure he wants me? This isn't even close to my area of expertise."

"His lawyer was here last week. But he says he wants your eye on it as well." The matron paused. "I think he just wants to see you. Before . . . while he still has time." Being the matron, her voice did not break, but Charles was disturbed to hear a slight quiver when she spoke—it was like seeing a crack in the Statue of Liberty.

Charles left the office a half hour later and took the next boat over to the island.

He had only been back a handful of times since he left at age fourteen, but Bradley had asked his legal advice over the phone on several other occasions. Of course, in the beginning, it was Charles asking Bradley about how to pursue his legal career. When he was finally, after years of dogged attempts, licensed in the Commonwealth of Massachusetts, he wrote to Bradley to tell him he would help the school out in any way he could, pro bono. But when he'd made the offer, he hadn't imagined this last scenario.

Aidan and Charles stopped in front of the building, and Aidan consulted his pocket watch. "We're a bit early for the service," Aidan said. "Do they still have that bench around the oak tree on the other side?"

It was cold, but less so once they got out of the wind. They sat facing each other on the bench.

"So." Aidan tucked his hands in his armpits to warm them. "Tell me about when you saw Bradley. This time."

"He was so sick, Sully." Charles sighed. "Plenty of old men just pass in their sleep, or their ticker gives out while they're turning the crank on their auto. He should have been able to go that way. But he'd been in that bed for almost two months. Cancer eating at him. He didn't deserve that."

"Was he lucid?"

"At times. Had a lot of morphine. Mary said he actually insisted on taking less that morning because he knew he wanted to meet with me. When he was talking about his will, he wasn't looking at me much, seemed to be in a bit of a haze. But he perked up when he started talking about all his boys over the years, how proud he was of them." Charles stopped for a moment. "How proud he was of me." He discreetly wiped one eye.

"I guess us Catholic boys don't get a mention, eh?" Aidan said, trying to lighten the moment.

"Actually, he talked about you too. He said he'd been less worried about you turning out well. Despite your being a Pope-loving Mick and all."

"He said that, did he?"

"Well, maybe not in so many words."

Smiling, Aidan said, "You know, there have been times, with Sean and all, when I wasn't sure what to do, how I should punish him, or whether I should trust him to go off on his own somewhere or what have you. And when I felt really stuck, sometimes I would think, what would Bradley have done?"

"He would have loved to know that." Neither mentioned but both thought about the fact that Bradley would never know that now.

"Speaking of fathers and sons, is Henry here?" asked Aidan.

"I think he's inside, greeting people or getting ready for the service. I guess he turned out all right. Mary told me he's in advertising, went to Harvard."

"I hear that's a pretty good school."

"That's what they say."

"You really call the matron 'Mary'? To her face?" Aidan asked, dubious.

"First time I came back to the island, she insisted I call her Mary."

"How long did it take for you to be able to call her that?"

"Only about five years." They both grinned.

After a while, Aidan said, "Any more of us old-timers gonna show up today?"

"Not sure. The family put a notice in the *Globe*, but I didn't call anyone except you." They both thought of their classmates. Until Sean was born, Aidan had kept up sporadically with the Laurel boys— organized a few saloon get-togethers, updated Charles with news of them whenever he had any. But ultimately, even Aidan had lost touch.

"Bradley did tell me something interesting, now that I think of it. Did you know that he had been in touch with Bess for a while, after the whole business with the judge?"

"No!" Aidan was incredulous. "Did he ever figure out what she really did for a living? He must not have had the full picture."

"He did. She told him."

"I don't believe it. Why in the world would he have stayed in contact with her?"

"Well, it turns out that Bess was not originally trained to be a whore. Remember that note that we brought to the minister?"

"I remember we brought a note. And we read it, but I don't remember what it said."

"Me neither, but remember how it was well written, with proper grammar and all? And we thought, how the hell does a whore write like this? Well, Bess was originally on track to be a teacher."

"A teacher! How do you get from being a teacher to being a prostitute?"

"She never made it to being a teacher. Some fellow took advantage of her when she was sixteen, got her up the pole, and when she started showing, she had to leave school. Then she lost the baby, but her family had kicked her out, didn't believe the man forced himself on her."

"You got all this from Bradley? Was the matron in the room while he was telling you this?"

"Are you kidding? Of course not. She had no idea about any of this, and Bradley made me swear I wouldn't tell her."

"But I still don't understand why they were corresponding."

"Bradley was trying to convince her to become a teacher."

"You're joking. Who would take her?"

"Bradley would. He wanted her to come teach on the island."

Aidan punched Charles in the arm. "Go on."

"Dead serious."

Aidan started laughing. "Now I've heard it all. Not only does he take two little criminals from the Waterfront into his island sanctuary, he wants a whore to teach them."

"Hey, I bet she would have been better than The Coffin."

"Faint praise, my friend."

"I'll give you that."

"But she never did come here to teach," said Aidan quietly.

"No, they talked about it on and off for a few years and Bess always had some excuse, but Bradley thought that the real problem was that Bess just didn't believe she was good enough. Not her ability to teach, but that she wasn't a good enough person."

"Really? Jaysus, that's sad."

"Bradley said if he'd had another year, he thought he could have convinced her. He thought she was getting tired of the life, thought the customers were getting rougher. But then, well, you know." Charles thought about what happened to Bess, how he'd met Aidan outside Aidan's apprenticeship office after work one day and told him how her body had washed up in the harbor. Charles hadn't been able to find her for a while, and finally the whores at the brothel on Bess's street had told him the story. He had thought he would spare Aidan the details—how her forehead was bashed in, how some said that could have happened in the water, but no one at the brothel believed her death was an accident—but he had ended up telling Aidan anyway.

"Did Bradley know how she died?"

"I don't know. We didn't talk about that."

After that, there didn't seem to be much to say.

Charles broke the silence between them. "He really just wanted to save everybody."

They heard the Bulfinch bell begin to sound—slowly and mournfully, at half the tempo with which it had announced every meal and class time for the last ninety years. Charles and Aidan rose from their bench and started to walk toward the sound.

"You taking the one o'clock boat back to the mainland?" asked Aidan.

"Planning on it."

"Maggie's holding dinner 'til I get back. Interested?"

Charles had only seen Maggie once since the wedding. She was such a happy person and a natural conversationalist that most people never noticed she wasn't especially pretty. In personality, she was the polar opposite of Charles. "Are you sure she'll be okay with a spare for dinner?"

"Maggie cooks for an army. C'mon, I know you don't have other plans."

Charles bristled a bit. "You feeling sorry for me?"

"Maybe. You coming?"

They walked a few steps more. Charles looked straight ahead. "I suppose that's a pretty good offer."

And they rounded the corner of the building.

AFTERWORD

IT WAS 1989, AND MY CONSULTING FIRM WAS BIG ON BOONDOGGLES. Our department went on a boat cruise around Boston Harbor for "team building," and as we sipped our Bloody Marys, our guide, home from college for the summer and casually steering the boat with his foot, gestured to Thompson Island as it came into view and mentioned that there used to be a "boys reform school" there.

As we disembarked on Thompson, where a pit of coals was already cooking our lobster (yes, stuff like this really did happen back then), I couldn't stop thinking about that school, mostly about how it would be a great setting for a novel. Was it like *Lord of the Flies*? Or more like the workhouse from *Oliver Twist*? Were there Alcatraz-like attempts at escape, swimming to the mainland?

When we returned to Boston, I took a pamphlet about the Harbor Islands from the boat office and stuffed it in the pocket of my denim jacket, with vague plans to write that novel. But in the weeks that followed, I became pessimistic. When would I ever have time to do all that research? And even if I could somehow manage it, what if no publisher wanted it? The thought of completing a novel only to have it languish in a drawer was heartbreaking.

A month later, the denim jacket was undeniably in need of washing, and when I emptied out the pockets, I found the pamphlet. And I threw it away.

Twenty years passed.

My friend threw a party for her mother who had just published a book through iUniverse. I stood off to the side as they cut a sheet cake with the image of the book cover printed on the frosting, and my friend's husband asked me, "Did you ever think about writing a book?" And I told him about the Thompson Island idea, and how it just seemed too hard to do at the time. Soon he wandered off to chat with someone else, but I stood there, tumblers clicking into place in my mind. The Internet. Nontraditional publishing options. Even though now I had a husband, a house, small children, and a job, I could do all this at odd hours from the comfort of my desk chair—and I could see it published come hell or high water.

I started my research that weekend.

It didn't take me long to figure out that the school wasn't a reform school, at least not in its first one hundred years. The Boston Farm School was a rare good place, due to two evolved and kindly superintendents who served long back-to-back terms (the latter being Charles Bradley), and also due to the fact that they were funded privately rather than publicly and thus could cherry-pick their students. Frightening options abounded for the unlucky and the poor. For example, *The New York Times* had this to say in 1860 about the State Reform School in Westboro:

> . . . *boys 17 or 18 years of age have been kept confined in dark, impure cells—"black holes" the Committee term them—from eight to sixteen weeks, a portion of the time with their hands manacled behind them and with no food but bread and water.*

The details about the Sweatbox at this school that Charles recounts to Aidan are, unfortunately, true.

There were also almshouses and workhouses, some on other islands in Boston Harbor, full of people who made a string of flawed decisions and people who had just one stroke of bad luck. So how wonderful that there was an option for young boys that wasn't abusive or dangerous. And yet . . . should I really believe what I was finding on the Internet? How can you know for sure what it was like there more than a century ago? What I really wanted was to talk to someone who went there.

Enter Dave Haeger. Hilary Lucier from Outward Bound on Thompson Island put me in touch with Dave, who attended the Boston Farm and Trade School (renamed in 1907) from 1938 to 1943. While it wasn't quite the era of my story, Dave was an incredible resource. And indeed, FTS (as Dave calls it) was a good place, a place he says "equipped me for life with skills and a work ethic that I most likely would never have developed elsewhere." For more about Dave's experiences at the school and photos (he happened to be the unofficial class photographer), go to www.conniemayo.com.

So my only challenge after that was: If the school was a good place, what's the narrative tension of the story? And thus Charles and Aidan were born, two kids who are good on the inside but would not be considered good enough for the Boston Farm School. The more I wrote about them and researched what their lives would have been like, the more it struck me that life at this time, right before the start of the Progressive Era and the establishment of a separate juvenile court, was perilous in a way that is hard to really understand today. However you feel about our social safety nets in the United States, it's hard to deny that life without them was a scarier and riskier proposition, especially for children. So I knew Charles and Aidan would be navigating some tough terrain, but in this story, what seems like very bad luck—accidently knifing a man—leads them on a journey that ends up saving their lives.

A note about the book cover: The photo used for the cover was dated 1890 and came from the school's archives, which are housed at the University of Massachusetts. As you can see, it shows a scowling blond boy and a slightly taller, gentler-looking dark-haired boy, which one could imagine represent Charles and Aidan. However, I wrote the characters of Charles and Aidan and all their physical characteristics before I ever saw this photograph in the archives. So maybe Charles and Aidan did attend the school after all.

344

ACKNOWLEDGEMENTS

I'D LIKE TO THANK HILARY LUCIER, DEVELOPMENT OFFICER AT Thompson Island Outward Bound Education Center, for showing me around the island and sharing historical information with me. Though the Bulfinch building burned down in 1971, it helped me to stand on the site of the old foundation and imagine Charles Bradley looking down the hill at the wharf. Hilary wisely pointed out that the mission of the Outward Bound program on Thompson today is not so different from the mission of the Boston Farm School—they are still empowering young people through hands-on experiences.

Thanks also to alumni Dave Haeger, class of 1942. In addition to giving me confidence about the worth of this story, he shared with me many interesting and useful details. For example, it was through Dave that I learned about the job of mail carrier, which inspired Webber, the only boy who gets to regularly go to the mainland. Dave also sent me the part of his brother Bruce's autobiography that covers Bruce's four years at the school, which was also a great asset to my effort.

All surviving documents from The Boston Farm School belong to the Joseph P. Healey Library Archives & Special Collections at University of Massachusetts Boston. And the man that was always happy to have me dig through those boxes was Dale Freeman, who at the time was the Digital Resources Archivist. Dale also hooked me up with *The Beacon*, the monthly newspaper written by Farm School students and printed in their print shop from 1897 to 1959. Someone patiently scanned all the newspapers and put them on the library's Web site, and these were probably the single most important source of information for my book.

Thanks to Wally Wood for his advice on how to be an author out there making it happen for yourself. Even though I didn't end up self-publishing, his help and kindness were a boost when I needed it.

Thanks to Grub Street, a wonderful and supportive writing community in Boston, and author Rosie Sultan, who gave me great feedback and encouragement.

Thanks to She Writes Press, for taking a chance on me.

Thanks to my beta readers Carolyn Blankenship, Pat Brinegar, and Karen Katz, and my proofreaders Linda Mayo and Carol Rothenstein.

And last but not least, thanks to my husband Dan for all his support and my children Sydney and Alex.

PHOTO CREDITS

Dedication: Courtesy of the University Archives & Special Collections Department, Joseph P. Healey Library, University of Massachusetts Boston: Thompson Island Collection

Part I: Courtesy of the Bostonian Society

Part II: Courtesy of the University Archives & Special Collections Department, Joseph P. Healey Library, University of Massachusetts Boston: Thompson Island Collection

Part III: Courtesy of the Bostonian Society

Epilogue: Courtesy of the Boston Public Library, Leslie Jones Collection

ABOUT THE AUTHOR

© Sivan Lahav Photography

Connie Hertzberg Mayo finally felt old enough in her forties that she thought she had something to say in a novel. During the years it took to find the time to write this book, her family made up the adjective "hoop-and-stick" (referencing the turn-of-the-century children's toy) to describe her penchant for simple things of the past, particularly that have no technology component (as in, "Mom likes chess because it's so hoop-and-stick"). She fully recognizes the irony of this, given that she wrote this novel on her laptop.

She lives in Massachusetts with her husband, two children, two cats, and her heirloom-tomato garden.

SELECTED TITLES FROM SHE WRITES PRESS

She Writes Press is an independent publishing company
founded to serve women writers everywhere.
Visit us at www.shewritespress.com.

Bittersweet Manor by Tory McCagg
$16.95, 978-1-938314-56-8
A chronicle of three generations of love, manipulation, entitlement, and
disappointed expectations in an upper-middle class New England family.

The Belief in Angels by J. Dylan Yates
$16.95, 978-1-938314-64-3
From the Majdonek death camp to a volatile hippie household on the East
Coast, this narrative of tragedy, survival, and hope spans more than fifty
years, from the 1920s to the 1970s.

The Rooms Are Filled by Jessica Null Vealitzek
$16.95, 978-1-938314-58-2
The coming-of-age story of two outcasts—a nine-year-old boy who just lost
his father, and a closeted young woman—brought together by circumstance.

Pieces by Maria Kostaki
$16.95, 978-1-63152-966-5
After five years of living with her grandparents in Cold War-era Moscow,
Sasha finds herself suddenly living in Athens, Greece—caught between
her psychologically abusive mother and violent stepfather.

All the Light There Was by Nancy Kricorian
$16.95, 978-1-63152-905-4
A lyrical, finely wrought tale of loyalty, love, and the many faces of resistance, told from the perspective of an Armenian girl living in Paris during
the Nazi occupation of the 1940s.

Beautiful Garbage by Jill DiDonato
$16.95, 978-1-938314-01-8
Talented but troubled young artist Jodi Plum leaves suburbia for the
excitement of the city—and is soon swept up in the sexual politics and
downtown art scene of 1980s New York.

The Vintner's Daughter by Kristen Harnisch
$16.95, 978-163152-929-0
Set against the sweeping canvas of French and California vineyard life
in the late 1890s, this is the compelling tale of one woman's struggle to
reclaim her family's Loire Valley vineyard—and her life.

CPSIA information can be obtained
at www.ICGtesting.com
Printed in the USA
BVHW031318190419
546008BV00002B/344/P

9 781631 520013